OMNIBUS EDITION

The Last Italian

A Saga in Three Parts

THE COMPLETE TRILOGY

Anthony Delstretto

THE LAST ITALIAN: A SAGA IN THREE PARTS

CONTENTS

For my grandsons

BOOK ONE
GOD'S TEETH

Fear not; our fate cannot be taken from us.
It is a gift.

—Dante Alighieri, Inferno, Canto VIII

Part I: The Rocks
1882

Chapter 1

June 1882: Castrubello, Kingdom of Italy

Flowing black water spangled bright silver as daylight awoke over the ancient canal. Another oven of a day, thought Carlo, eyeing the cloudless sky. The fisherman crab-walked sideways down the sloped bank of Naviglio Largo until he stood at the quay under the old stone bridge.

Ponte Spagnolo stood on pilings sunk three hundred years earlier by Filippo II of Spain. The Spaniards were long gone, replaced by Austrians, the French, then Austrians again. Wars of national independence had finally driven off such foreign powers; the fledgling Kingdom of Italy was but twenty years old.

The span protected a cluster of twenty-foot-long fishing dinghies beached on the slanted, slick embankment. The *battelli* were shallow-drafted and narrow-beamed, bows sharply pointed, their sterns flat across. The shape allowed efficient navigation on the nearby Pirino River's rills, sandbars, and half-sunk boulders. Carlo added the long-shafted pitchfork he carried to the gear already in his boat's gunwale, and with a heave, slid the craft into the water.

He knew his father, brother, and brother-in-law Vito would soon be out casting their nets for the whitefish and trout that flourished in the waters near the commune. And at some point today, he would be also. But right now, his prey were three rocks.

Carlo boarded his boat with a final push. The water was calm under the bridge's double arches. He fixed the single oar in the notch at the stern, then stood and sculled back and forth to line up the craft. As the battello caught the slight current, Carlo worked a figure-eight pattern with the oar. On an embankment nearby, he saw Castrubello washerwomen starting their day, like their mothers and foremothers had done. The women knelt on stone slabs and pulled shirts, sheets, and linens from deep wicker baskets and rubbed each with lye soap on flat rocks embedded at water's edge. After a hard scrub and rinse, they wrung and slapped the items on the stones with sharp—even bitter—ferocity.

The distinctive silhouette of Torrquadro loomed as the bridge fell behind. The wooden-soled clogs of hundreds of women and children clacked on the cobblestone walkways as they arrived for their shifts at the big silk mill. Food was scarce for local families; labor came cheap. The mill paid women one lira per thirteen-hour shift, children one sack of corn every week.

The Austrians originally built Torre Quadrate fortress to impose tolls on bridge and Naviglio traffic. The hulking square structure with its four brooding towers served as a landmark for miles. The crenellations along the thick stone ramparts stood out like stunted teeth above the canal's tree line.

In time, a Milanese count acquired the property; his most recent heir was gripped by a vision. Adding gas lighting, brick smokestacks, and three hundred imported machines, he converted the building into a smoke-belching, loom-clattering, steam-powered silk factory. The sputtering gas lamps and a dearth of natural light kept the work floor in gloom. Rows of great iron vats bubbled on hearths, boiling silkworm pupae to death. Workers unbound the softened cocoons then spun the twisted strands into silk thread.

Carlo turned his face from the stink. Inside the building the stench was far more appalling. The only ventilation was whatever squeezed through narrow gunslits designed for Austrian musketeers. The fetid air reeked of sweat, machine oil, mildew, dye vats, and worms-a-boil. In summer, the intense heat made workers regularly pass out.

Like he did every day, Carlo craned his neck as he passed, hoping to see Tonia arriving. This was about the time she began her long day. But he could not spot her among the shawled shadows hurrying through the doorway. He dismissed his disappointment with a hard push on his oar that sent the dinghy gliding into the center of the canal.

Trenched as an irrigation ditch seven centuries prior, widened and deepened as the decades progressed, the Naviglio extended from the great northern lakes all the way through Milan. Hundreds of barges used the waterway daily to transport produce, passengers, and increasingly, manufactured goods of all types.

The fisherman soon steered the battello's bow into a skinny side channel that connected to the parallel Pirino River farther west. Much wider than the Naviglio, the Pirino flowed south from alpine Lake Maggiore into the great Po Valley. Unnavigable in many places for larger craft, fishermen along the shore and in their small boats had been pulling trout, eel, whitefish, sturgeon, and pike from the rich river for millennia.

As the broad expanse of water caught the sun's sharp glare, Carlo tugged at the brim of his hat. He was childish to fret about not seeing her, he thought. Better to concentrate on what he was doing out here right now. After all, it was for his Tonia that he was doing it.

"My Tonia," he self-mocked. Not yet his.

He and Tonia had been aware of each other for some time; among the residents of Castrubello there were no strangers. She was slender and tall with startling gray-blue eyes and light hair. Her lithe gracefulness was apparent even when she walked to market with a basket on her head. Perhaps especially then, Carlo mused, remembering the sway of her hips.

Her parents served as domestics at the great villa of the Marchese d'Ambrosso. The estate rented out Tonia and her brother Ettore, the last of eight siblings still living at home, as laborers at the silk factory.

Tonia also at times helped in the villa's kitchens, and it was there that three weeks before, he'd last seen her. Occasionally the d'Ambrosso manor house ordered fresh fish from the Comos for the marchese's meal. Lorenzo, his father, had sent Carlo up to the estate with a delivery.

"What are those fish you bring, Carlo Como?" Tonia asked, drying her hands as she stood in the doorway.

"Today, fresh trout, a fine batch," he answered, holding up two pails. "Where do you want them?"

"There." She pointed to the butcher block.

"On the butcher block?" he asked, like a dumb one. She had nodded, stood aside. He set down the pails, looked up, cleared his throat, examined his boots, departed.

'On the butcher block?' He still cringed, recalling his slow-witted words. Not exactly inspired poetry, thought Carlo. But their eyes had stayed fixed on each other's the entire time, and a smile played on Tonia's lips as she'd spoken. He had felt his heart leap and a stirring in his loins and knew he was in love. So, I will marry Tonia, he decided then and there.

But Carlo knew he must offer her father more than self-confidence and a pail of fish. He needed two things. The *soldi*—the cash—to prove that Tonia would not merely be trading one version of threadbare poverty for another. And he needed to offer her a home within Casa Como.

A hundred years earlier, Ambrogio Como, born near the great northern lake of the same name, mustered out of the Hapsburg army and settled in Castrubello. He bought a small *casa* with his bonus pay, then set to work starting a family.

In fits and starts over the subsequent years, the Comos built extensions onto the original structure. The result was a quirky two-story rectangle surrounding an open courtyard. The building now housed Carlo, his parents, his brother Francesco and his family, and his sister Rina and hers. Carlo had two corner rooms with an attic to call his own. Not much, but Carlo was confident he could make the space worthy of a bride.

Tonia was a poor man's daughter. Her dowry would be modest at best. To Carlo her dowry was *non importa*, though naturally it must not be an insult to his parents. But it was up to Carlo to provide her security and a home.

And now, with yesterday's astounding discovery, perhaps the means was at hand.

Pirino fisherman instinctively kept their eyes out for rocks. But not only for rocks that might stove their hulls. They all knew that ceramic makers prized certain large, densely white river stones that tumbled downriver many leagues from the mountains. So white were these large stones, so smooth to the touch, and so fortuitous to find, that the locals called them *Denti di Dio*, 'God's Teeth.'

The *ceramisti* crushed the stones into powder and melted the dust to make a superb glaze for their wares. The rare stones brought a high price. They lay thinly strewn along the many miles of the Pirino's bed, resting among thousands of ordinary boulders and rocks. Though very white, they were difficult to spot even in shallow water. Finding even one was worth nearly a full month of fish catching, as much as forty lire or more. Such a sum was a windfall at a time when five hundred lire could support a family for a year.

All week the river had been a challenge for Carlo. He came home every night exhausted from fighting the surging waters caused by the spring melt-off farther north. The icy torrents gave the Pirino the raw strength to carve away large stretches of riverbank. The day before, an unexpected boulder forced Carlo to suddenly veer, and he'd slammed his boat's prow into what he thought was the shoreline. Instead he broke through a debris dam and into a calm pool. The surge had scoured the soft soil along the steep shore, freeing trapped rocks and creating a crescent the current didn't touch. As he used his oar to prod the battello away from a toppled tree trunk, he'd looked into the clear water and gasped. There, before his eyes, clustered three of the great white *denti*!

But daylight was fading, and he had no tools. After carefully noting landmarks, he had sculled the battello out from the pond and back into the current.

Today he would harvest his windfall. He skirted the east shore looking for the copse of four trees he had marked in his memory. After several false sightings he finally saw them, their long shadows casting over the water. Carlo oared his way again through the debris until he spotted his three prizes, waiting like giant eggs in a gravel-bottomed nest. He sculled the craft sideways and dropped his bow and stern anchors, flat heavy rocks with a crude iron ring forged directly through each. Squaring himself on both knees, Carlo knelt with the rake he brought with him today, the one he used to land the big sturgeon when they were running. Similar to pitchforks used by peasants to heft freshly sickled hay, the river version had a longer shaft that flexed with the weight of a catch. He leaned toward the water where the *denti* waited plucking.

The first rock lay angled in a declivity. Carlo reversed the fork and tried to snag its three long tines on top of the rock. After failing twice, he felt the prongs catch the rock's edge, and he pulled it free from the shallow hole. He scooped under the white stone, then lifted and swung the bending fork around and placed the bulging catch gently in the boat.

He knew he had rushed his first effort and determined to work more patiently going forward. Consequently, the second stone gave him less trouble. Using the age-old technique of the Pirino's 'fishers-of-rocks', he deftly pried the stone from the riverbed and, careful to stay balanced, painstakingly freed the sunken treasure and smoothly brought it aboard.

Carlo drank water from the wineskin in the bow. He looked at the sun, was surprised to see how high it had risen. Two down. Now to finish. Hefting the fork overhead and down, Carlo pursued the last remaining rock, the largest of the three.

He pushed the tines under his target and lifted. The big stone tipped a bit as one side lifted but then rolled farther away. Standing, Carlo oared the battello closer to where the stone now lay. This time he pushed the prongs fully underneath. As he slowly raised it to the surface he leaned forward too far. The white rock slid off the rake and back to the river bottom.

"Sangue dolce di Cristo!" he exclaimed. His back was stiffening and his forearms burnt from exertion. He shortened his grip and, leaning back, raised the fork again. Pivoting, he carefully, carefully brought his dripping prize up and around and gently lowered it next to the others.

He stared at his bonanza and raised both arms to the heavens. The *denti* were his!

* * *

A sudden hoof-stamping and a whinny sounded from the riverbank. "You, man, in the boat! What is that you have there?"

Intent on distributing the weight from the rocks along his boat's bottom boards—and distracted by his daydreams—Carlo had not heard anyone approach. He looked up to see two horsemen near the shoreline, peering down from their perches. The horses were fine and well-groomed, their noses in the scrub grass.

Carlo knew the rider of the smaller chestnut horse from his visits to Villa d'Ambrosso. Gaetano Baldassare, the estate manager, was in his forties, lean, with a hound's face. He wore a dark coat and gloves, tan breeches, tall boots. And the other? The sun was behind him, his mount now nervously cantering.

"Do you not see who is here, you ignorant clown?" Baldassare barked. "It is Marchese d'Ambrosso himself, show him respect!" Carlo lifted his hat to shade his eyes.

It was indeed the marchese. Known to everyone as a heavy gambler and spendthrift, Federico Benedetto Lucantonio d'Ambrosso was the latest rendition of a much diminished line. Carlo had seen him occasionally through the window of the villa's coach as it passed. He recognized the nobleman from his large gray mustache waxed up on its ends and the red, heavy-lidded eyes. The marchese wore a black silk top hat and grasped a telescope in one hand. His paunch protruded through his unbuttoned blue coat onto his saddle.

"What is your name, fisherman?" asked d'Ambrosso, with a tug on the reigns to stop his mount from fidgeting.

Carlo held his hat forward to provide further shade and spread his feet for balance. "I am Carlo Como, Marchese," he said. "Forgive me, signore, for not greeting you. The sun, you see."

"Ah." The aristocrat nodded knowingly. Resting the bronze-trimmed telescope across his saddle, he opened a small silver box from his wainscot, pinched snuff up his nose and convulsively sneezed. His big horse nickered at the shifted weight.

"I asked what you have there," called Baldassare. "It is certainly not fish."

Carlo looked down at the three stones sitting plain in their stark whiteness. "No, signore, you are exactly right. Not fish," Carlo responded. "They are rocks!"

Carlo heard a snort from the marchese. Baldassare frowned and dismounted, keeping hold of his reins.

"Your rudeness is appalling," the estate manager said. "Let me remind you. To fish on this river is a privilege, it is not a right!"

The fisherman drew in a breath. His smart mouth had put him in hot water before. Baldassare was known to be a prickly one, keen to assert his authority. The marchese leaned heavily on Baldassare's advice. It was a stupid gamble to cross him.

"Yes, I understand this, excuse me, Signor Baldassare."

"The fee that you people pay to do your business out here, the estate can refuse your annual payment, you know. Then where would you be?"

Nearby, the marchese raised his telescope again and stood in his stirrups as an elegant, black-crowned heron glided overhead.

Refuse my annual payment? Carlo inwardly scoffed. Certainly, a joke. Everyone knew the lord spent money like water. He steadied his boat with a push on his oar. "Believe me, signore, we fishermen know exactly how thoroughly you bless us."

Baldassare gave a sharp look. Carlo bit his evil tongue.

"Stand to the side, let me see better," said Baldassare. Carlo slid a step, slightly rocking the boat. The white rocks shone against the worn brown boards beneath them. Carlo saw a glitter of greed in the manager's eyes as he recognized their value. But the flash of avarice quickly returned to a blank stare. "Those belong to the marchese, not to you," he said officiously.

"Signore, surely you are mistaken," Carlo said, too quickly. "As you say, we pay for the right to support ourselves from this river. Why would there be any question about this?" He fought to keep quick anger from affecting his voice. His temper had never been his friend.

"You purchase from the estate the right to catch fish," replied Baldassare, dismounting. "Not to dredge the riverbed for whatever you want. Bring those to me."

"Marchese d'Ambrosso, good signore, I appeal to you," called out Carlo, looking past the manager. "My family and I, we use these stones to weigh down our nets in those parts of the river where the current is strongest."

The startled nobleman had barely been tending to the conversation. "What is this fuss, Baldassare?" he said, flustered at being caught off-guard. "We have wasted too much time with this meaningless matter. Let the man be."

The estate manager's color rose on his neck. "Don Federico, this man is a liar and a poacher," Baldassare insisted. "Of course, the stones in themselves are meaningless, you are right to care nothing for them. It is the principle, my lord. He has not the right to scavenge!"

Carlo viewed Baldassare with thin-lipped disdain. Obviously, the manager was angling to sell the stones for himself, to line his pockets with Carlo's hard-earned prizes. A corrupt man, thought Carlo.

D'Ambrosso squeezed his eyes closed and sneezed loudly from another snuff dose. "Poaching rocks, Baldassare? Tish, Tosh. Lying about fishnets? Enough of this nonsense. They are just stones, after all! Look around, we have plenty, everywhere! I want to get on with my morning ride." He suddenly stopped talking and again stood in his stirrups. "*Dio mio*, man! A red-throated diver!" With that, he spurred away.

Carlo suppressed his smirk by pursing his lips.

Baldassare's face was a mask as he turned back to Carlo. He leaned toward the boat, pointing at the fisherman's chest with a gloved finger. "Listen to me, Como. You may think you won here today but think again. I will not be made the fool." He remounted and followed Marchese d'Ambrosso, riding in hard pursuit of his bird.

Chapter 2

Carlo arrived home to find dinner nearly finished. He had unloaded the rocks at a storage shed the family kept on the Pirino and covered them with unused netting. With only half of a day to fish, his catch had been pathetic, though he remained on the water an extra futile hour.

His lateness was a rare occurrence, and, without words, the family awaited the explanation. He thanked his mother for the plate she brought him and finally said, "My apologies, Papà. I stayed out longer trying to make up for a poor day."

"A poor day?" Lorenzo responded, seated at the table finishing his fish stew and fried polenta. He scraped his chair back and folded his arms. His shrewd eyes pierced Carlo's. "Yet elsewhere today we found success. True, Vitorio?" he asked, looking at his son-in-law to his left. Vito Ameretti nodded, clearing his throat. "It was good, yes, Papà. Francesco and I both worked our usual places. The hook lines were only half-full, but our gillnets yielded plenty."

Francesco sopped a piece of polenta in the juice on his plate and teased his brother. "Our Carlino is smitten, this is the problem. Every day, he drifts past the silk mill with longing eyes and sighs like a poet. While he daydreams of love, the fish make a buffoon of him!"

"Oh, look at the pulpit this sermon comes from!" Carlo retorted, glad for the banter. "Tell me, Francesco, who wept with heartache before Gemella lost her wits and said she would marry you?" Francesco's wife, pregnant, laughed from the cucina where she and the other women of the house cleaned up from dinner, listening.

"Don't hide your shame by changing the subject, little Carlino," answered Francesco in a singsong voice, wagging a forefinger back and forth. He knew how his younger brother hated that childhood nickname!

"Tomorrow, the catch must be better," Lorenzo interrupted, ending the exchange. "A full stomach comes before love!"

The women in the cucina rolled their eyes.

The time was now, Carlo judged. "I have something to tell you," he said, and with that, he told of his discovery of the rocks, of his intentions for Tonia, and, briefly, of the encounter with Baldassare and the marchese.

After a momentary silence, during which the women emerged, wiping hands on aprons, Lorenzo spoke up.

"Baldassare is a thief, I have always thought so. You and I will sell the *Denti di Dio* in Guardetto, there is a man I know. And I will speak to Luigi Vacci about the dowry, then you shall go ask for his blessing."

His mother Lucrezia added, "She is a good choice, Carlo. Tonia Vacci will make you a fine wife. She is from a hardworking family, like our own. We share some relatives with the Vaccis, you know."

Francesco laughed and slapped his brother's shoulder. "I knew that love was your problem, Carlino. How can you hope to outwit the fish with your brains addled that way?" He smelled the sweat and the river on his brother. "At least now as a suitor maybe you will find a reason to bathe!"

Carlo smiled banally and flipped his right forefinger several times under his chin.

Lorenzo said, "Mauro La Porta is the ceramics man in Guardetto. He is fair in his dealings, as far as that goes," Lorenzo told Carlo. "But it will be good for me to be with you. Merchants are never not merchants."

Two days later they started out early on a barge heading south. Batta the Boatman was Lucrezia's distant cousin. As family, Lorenzo and Carlo and their freight naturally traveled gratis; to offer payment would have precipitated a loud, time-wasting melodrama with no change in the outcome. They floated south past mulberry groves and fields of maize to where the Largo linked with the smaller Guardetto Canale. The narrower channel continued south for seven miles until it dead-ended a mile short of their destination.

"In the ass of a whale!" shouted Batta cordially, as he left them onshore. Lorenzo answered the good-natured wish for good luck with its typical response. "Just pray it doesn't shit!"

Ashore, Carlo hefted the handles of the old barrow loaded with the three heavy *denti*. The creaky wooden carriola had certainly seen better days. The uneven roundness of its only wheel, fashioned from a single thick slice of hard tree stump, made for a balky push, forcing numerous pauses. A distant locomotive whistle echoed. Pavia, he thought.

The elder Como watched from behind as his son muscled the primitive barrow. The boy has resolve, I must give him that,

Lorenzo thought, perspiring in the sun. Ahead, the dusty road sloped down a slight incline revealing the first outlying buildings of Guardetto.

At age twenty-four it was time his son married, Lorenzo knew. Carlo's account of his attraction to the Vacci woman, of his determination to provide for her, and of his enterprise in securing the three white stones, all had impressed him. But his son's story of the exchange with Baldassare had interested him as much.

Lorenzo despised the greedy manager who continually pressed him for extra lire beyond the annual river license. To not pay the bribe meant several weeks' delay with tiresome, needless obstructions. Lorenzo had a family to feed. Consequently, like the others, he bitterly paid the blatant rake-off. It was not as if there was a magistrate he could turn to! This chance to give the manager a kick in the *culo* was too good to ignore.

The road took a turn, and with that, they were on the bustling main street of Guardetto. "I have not been here for some time. But I am certain that is the place, on the right," Lorenzo declared. They quickly arrived at the three-chimneyed brick building. A sign shaped like a miniature door hung above its entry with writing across it. *"La Porta,"* Carlo confirmed.

A long wagon sat in an open bay next to the shop's door. Two men loaded heavy wooden crates as a third provided slouched supervision. The wagoneer sat hunched over the reins of a sag-backed white nag that had obviously been there before.

Carlo set the barrow down on its square peg legs. The factory extended farther back than Carlo first thought. Heat quivered from three large kilns along a side wall. Closer to the door, workers shaped clay forms on turning, horizontal wheels. Elsewhere, artisans at workbenches painted elaborate designs on pottery pieces.

"How can I help you, signori?" asked a short, heavyset man from inside the showroom. He took off his spectacles as he approached and mopped the sweat from his bald head with a red handkerchief. "I am La Porta," he said.

"Lorenzo Como, signore, and here is my son, Carlo," said Lorenzo, giving La Porta's hand a vigorous shake. "We did business together a few years ago." La Porta listened, folding his arms. He wore his sleeves rolled up, his thick forearms bristled with black hair. "My Carlo here has something that you will want to buy." La Porta smiled and waited, having heard such claims before.

Carlo stepped to the side of the carriola and dramatically threw back the cloth covering the three rocks. "From the bed of the River Pirino, signore."

"Ah." La Porta drew in his breath as he recognized them for what they were. "Perhaps."

Before Carlo finished the story of fishing the rocks from the river, and why, La Porta raised his hand. "Stop there. You are a zealous young man in love, this is what I am hearing." He paused. "And so, these rocks, other than knowing they bring you closer to the young woman you desire, do you have any idea what they are? Or do you, signore?" he added, thrusting his face toward Lorenzo.

Lorenzo straightened his shoulders. "I am no mineral expert. I only know that these types of stones fetch money. It is why we are here. Are you interested? Have we come to the wrong place? I believe we saw another factory down the road."

La Porta snorted. "Rocco? He steals the food from the mouth of his dying mother." He gesticulated with both arms. "But by all means, go, go ahead, if you think he is your man."

Carlo broke in, "No. Tell us your price." Lorenzo scowled.

LaPorta smiled. The young one's impatience is to my advantage, he thought. "First, signori, I ask you both, please come with me."

They walked past artisans with fine-tipped paintbrushes beside shelves where their work slowly dried. At one table, a worker used tongs to dip a painted vase into a yellow emulsion. In less than a minute, she pulled out the dripping bowl.

"Now you see, this is a glaze," La Porta said. "When pigmented, as this type is, a function of the rock it came from, it changes the color of the vessel we are creating, altering the colors of the paint we use. The final product is as you see."

He gestured to a rack of finished vases and small statuary with intricately painted designs. "Quality work, you will agree, but because of the glaze, the colors are not exactly true. Now, compare." He opened the door of a wooden cabinet and carefully removed an elegant platter painted in vivid blues, yellows, and greens. With both hands, La Porta held it up to the light. Carlo's eyes widened as the lustrous colors jumped from the surface.

"Here you are seeing the actual paint colors, completely unclouded by its coating. Only certain rocks"—he glanced to where the carriola stood—"when crushed and heated, provide such a glaze of absolute purity. We dip three times, drying between each. The result is a glasslike surface that magnifies the brilliance of the colors beneath. The process makes the piece more durable, incidentally. As a result, its price is higher!"

Carlo spoke. "With all respect, what you say is spellbinding. But perhaps you can tell us, what will you pay?"

Thirty minutes later, when the haggling, remonstrations, feigned final offers and gesticulating entreaties finally concluded with warm handshakes all around, Carlo was beyond pleased. In his hand was a leather pouch containing one hundred thirty lire in gold coins. He counted forty of them out to Lorenzo. "Please accept these, Papà," he said. "Is it enough?"

Pride swelled within Lorenzo. While his son had much to learn about business transactions—he felt his boy's obvious impatience had cost them at least another ten lire—overall, Carlo had performed well in this matter of the stones, from the river to the purse. He knew boys who would have cheated their own families—Oh yes! Such was the corrupting power of gold.

"Sì, Carlo," he said, placing the coins in his coat pocket. He walked to the cabinet that held the plate of the woman, perused the other items within, took out a piece.

"This pendant, signore? Is it for sale?" He held up a red ceramic *cornicello* about an inch long, with a small metal loop on its top. Through the loop was a leather cord.

La Porta smiled. "Ah, yes, of course it is! Small, yet a true work of art. And far more! To wear such a talisman is to stay on *fortuna's* good side! Moreover, the *malocchio*, the Evil Eye, will never touch you, nor will you ever be made a cuckold—always a worry with a beautiful wife!" The merchant winked. "It is also said that this little curved horn guarantees that the prow of your 'boat' will always 'point upstream!'" He chortled. "Every fisherman's dream, eh, Signor Como?"

"As for that, La Porta, I don't know about you artisans, but no real fisherman's boat ever sinks!" The two men shared a brief guffaw. Lorenzo handed the talisman to his son. "For you."

Carlo was surprised and moved. His father proved his love for his family more by long hours on the river every day than with sentimental gestures. His love was no less for that, but it gave significance to this moment.

For his part, La Porta was well pleased with his purchase of the stones, certain to yield more than a thousand lire in finished products. In a burst of magnanimity, he came to a decision.

"It is true that I struck this deal today for a profit, as you have done yourselves. But I am an advocate of love, who is not? Therefore, I declare, no, Signor Como! No! The pendant is not for sale. Instead, accept it as my gift to your boy!"

A half-bottle of grappa appeared. With dainty ceramic cups, the three men shared a toast. "May this groom be the wise head of his family!" offered La Porta, eyes smiling at his guests. "And his bride, forever its kind, loving heart! *Evviva gli sposi!*"

Chapter 3

Villa d'Ambrosso sat on the former hunting grounds of the first Marchese di Castrubello Maggiore, Giampiero d'Ambrosso, an affluent wool merchant who had purchased the title from the Austrian court. With the family seat firmly established, the newly-minted nobleman spared no expense in constructing a neoclassical shrine to the aristocratic ideal of *dignitas*. He had succeeded and more.

The two-storied manor house stood resplendent with red tile roof, cream-toned walls, and granite porticoes. Two matching wings, slightly lower in height than the main building, extended toward the gate, facing each other. The one to the west provided for large scale social gatherings and included a two-hundred volume library, a chapel with a fine Caravaggio, and well-appointed offices for the villa's management. The east wing, with its matching facade, cunningly contained the estate's stables, tack rooms, agricultural equipment, and wood and metal fabrication shops. Another long building out of sight behind the main residence housed much of the staff and their families.

The combination of structures amounted to some forty-thousand square feet. Arriving carriages entered past a pair of stone statues of watchful, recumbent lions. The imposing compound surrounded a "Court of Honor" that featured a tiered fountain crowned by a plump cherub poised on one leg, perpetually gushing water from its hard granite lips.

Each subsequent occupant did his part to maintain the property's magnificence, intuitively understanding that the image of power enlarged its reality. When the Kingdom of Italy was declared, the current marchese did what he needed to do to see that his noble title, originally an imperial Hapsburg one, smoothly converted to the patronage of the Italian House of Savoia. With good legal assistance and a flurry of gold florins crossing the right palms, all documents related to renouncing past loyalties and swearing to new ones had been officially signed, stamped, and be-ribboned.

Marchese Federico d'Ambrosso was determined to outshine his ancestors in maintaining appearances even as he acted as if money sprung from thin air. He began by leveling an adjacent olive grove to create a remarkable walled garden, complete with faux Roman ruins and a large pond featuring lilies, tall grasses, and belligerent black geese. A stone obelisk stood on a rock in the center, emblazoned with the scrolled d'Ambrosso motto in Latin *Est Voluntatem Dei*: 'It is God's Will.'

* * *

Gaetano Baldassare impatiently thrummed his fingers on an oval table. He sat in the manor's oak-paneled library, its shelves lined with leatherbound classics and first editions, most never read. Before him lay the estate's black financial binder. Today was the day of each month he and the marchese reviewed the estate's finances. For Baldassare, it was an increasingly frustrating exercise. D'Ambrosso's prolificacy was enough in itself to challenge the finances. But a litany of disasters over recent years was crippling not only the estate and its peasant workers but all the country around.

Grapes grown on the estate had once produced profitable wines; one street in Castrubello bore the name *Via di Vino d'Ambrosso*. But a ravaging scourge of leaf aphids had descended twice within twenty years on the great vineyards of Lombardia. The blight irrevocably demolished the wine industry within decades. A subsequent drought drove starving peasants into withered fields grubbing for stunted roots to boil into thin soup. Many others turned to migrant work in the farm fields and orchards of France and Switzerland, sending back their meager earnings to their families. Rolling epidemics of bubonic plague, cholera, and the 'bad air' sickness called *mal'aria* continued to kill thousands every summer. And *la miseria* showed no signs of abating.

As estate manager, Baldassare's challenge was to keep the place functioning regardless. But really, how much can I do, he thought. Despite his advice, d'Ambrosso stubbornly pursued one bad investment after the next. Early in the marchese's tenure, he decided to breed *trottatori Italiani*, the steeds that pulled the sulkies in the popular sport of harness racing. His Florentine breeder promised that with enough money he would build the estate a stable of champions. The actual result was a string of nine finely-featured, narrow-chested trotters, eight of them too short-legged, short-winded, and short-tempered for competition. These Baldassare sold to Remi the butcher; the ninth horse, the chestnut, bigger and stronger, he kept as his own. The Florentine breeder was stripped of his belongings, thoroughly beaten, and sent packing. The failed investment was typical.

To cover the steady losses, the manager was quietly selling off other items of value. These included excellent Madrid saddles and lesser pieces of art from seldom-used rooms in the villa. The estate's ornate gilded sedan chair was the latest sacrifice for auction, this despite d'Ambrosso's petulant protestations that having two sweating, be-wigged servants lug him through town was exactly what peasants expected of their lords.

Deferred maintenance helped. The residence was overdue for new shutters, new paint, new plaster, and new carpets. Its main rooms remained presentable in a genteel, tired way, but the close observer might notice various small signs of decay, wallpaper beginning to curl with mold, or brown ceiling stains from leaks in the corners.

Distressing, certainly. But thus far, the manager was keeping the fief, on the surface, looking much as always—if one did not scratch that surface very deeply.

It hardly helped that the marchese had not grown wiser with time. Never serious enough about life to actually be cruel, he stayed indifferent to the slow decline of his fortune, leaving most details of the estate to Baldassare. His gambling habit had grown progressively worse. Baldassare was alarmed that this vice alone could well be the estate's ultimate undoing. It was not unusual for his lord to lose a thousand lire or more in a single night playing cards at his Milan club; the record was two thousand in one sitting. Add his wife's prolific buying splurges in Milan, the great balls hosted by the villa, and the money the couple tossed away to the Church, and the formula for eventual disaster was complete.

Periodically, the piper demanded payment. At those times Baldassare and his employer rode in the lord's elegant coach-and-four to Milan. With solicitor Aurelio Maggio, they petitioned the provincial senate to allow the sale of a parcel or two of estate land. The 'Petition Prior to Sale' gave local nobility the first option to buy, which kept the transfer of land mostly within the circle of the privileged class. Baldassare cared little who ended up with the property. He only knew that the sales, combined with the other economies he worked every day, were the only way the estate stayed afloat.

By the same token, the manager mused, on a personal level big expenses were good. The more complicated the numbers that flowed across the pages of his thick ledger, the better he could bury his own private dealings without his master's attention. His father had once told him, "Gaetano, listen now. Skimming is the timeless way of the world. Not to skim when you can is irresponsible! But," he added, "always with patience. A little at a time soon fills up your wallet!"

Baldassare agreed. Hidden in the wall of his bedroom, his two chests of gold and silver coins were in fact filling up.

Baldassare's greatest source of graft was the estate's exclusive rights to the Pirino River's resources. It took the form of private arrangements with the locals for preferential treatment by the manager or protection from his interference. Or both. That was why the matter with Como and the rocks stuck like a fishbone in Baldassare's throat. If he allowed a nobody like Como to do what he wanted, the thread of his control would unravel until no garment remained.

When the door of the library opened, Baldassare assumed it was d'Ambrosso finally arriving. Instead, a servant entered, limping. The tray he balanced clinked with two glasses and a full brandy decanter. "Excuse me, sir," he said. "Refreshments."

Baldassare shrugged, gestured to a side bar. He watched as the man hobbled over to settle the tray. "Tell me, Vacci," he said. "Remind me again how your freakish accident took place."

Without expression, Luigi Vacci turned unevenly to face the estate manager. He was of medium height, a bit bowlegged, slightly stooped. His thin hair was gray, his eyes watery brown.

"Yes, sir," he replied. "Some years ago, I and another porter were carrying the previous marchese, Don Franco, in his sedan chair to confession at San Giulio. Marco stumbled, my end tipped down, I fell to my knees on the stones, cracking my kneecap severely."

"Yes, I recall the story now," Baldassare grunted. "How uncomfortable for you. You are fortunate the marchese retained your services after such clumsiness."

"God smiled on us," Vacci said, without irony. "We did not drop the chair. Don Franco was frightened but unharmed and chose to forgive us. He was a gracious man. As is his son today," he added quickly.

Whatever the state of the old man's kneecaps, Vacci had retained the wherewithal to father eight whelps, Baldassare mused with begrudged admiration. One in particular interested him.

"And how is your daughter, Vacci? Tonia is it? We have rented her to the Torrquadro mill, as I recall."

Luigi stiffened slightly. "Thank you for inquiring, signore. Tonia is very well. She has no complaint." He waited awkwardly.

The daughter is a beauty, thought Baldassare. And from the looks of her, full of...what? Fire?

"Only she and your son remain living at home?" Baldassare inquired, his voice blandly nonchalant. "That apartment that your family occupies must seem positively vast. Perhaps it is time for me to assign you more suitably compact quarters."

Vacci blanched. He and his wife and two children shared two rooms as it was. The only smaller servants' quarters were common spaces in the basement partitioned by curtains.

Ah, the reaction I want, Baldassare observed. Leverage for an understanding, certainly. But not at this moment. "A matter for another day, I think."

Luigi bowed his head and proceeded to exit. But at the doorway, he turned again quickly and announced, "The Marchese d'Ambrosso."

As Baldassare came to his feet, the lord approached the table where the butler helped seat him. Don Federico flipped the tails of his powder blue coat past the back of the chair and dropped into it heavily. His bulk crushed the chair's puffy gold cushion with a sharp "*BRAP!*" of air—from the cushion or the marchese, Baldassare could not be certain.

D'Ambrosso signaled Baldassare to sit with a backhanded wave. "Manager," he said, by way of a greeting. Spotting the thick black ledger on the table, he emitted a long, melodramatic sigh. How he wished he were out riding. "I trust we will not be all day at this, Baldassare," he pouted.

Chapter 4

A fortnight later, Carlo faced the gateway to Villa d'Ambrosso.

From Carlo's fish deliveries to the villa, he knew his way around the large compound. Instead of going through the main entrance, he veered toward a gate that opened into the livestock corral. He walked across the paddock, careful where he stepped.

Ahead, the two-storied servants' quarters jutted out at an angle, attached to the villa but hidden from view from the main gates. The sounds of children and families came from open windows. Drying laundry fluttered at windowsills; as he watched, one wife leaned out to pull in a pair of trousers.

Next to Carlo, in front of the residence was the workers' latrine field with its collection of rough wooden privies. Carlo found its reek barely tolerable in the late afternoon heat.

He followed the stone walkway edging the field until it turned at right angles in front of the door of the servants' quarters, opened, as were all the apartment windows, to release the heat inside. In the middle of the small foyer, Luigi Vacci sat in a chair. He stood and hobbled forward.

"*Buona sera*, Carlo Como, *buona sera*." Vacci wore his black servant coat which, while sagged and a bit shiny at the elbows, was rather splendid for his present surroundings. "Welcome," he said.

"Thank you for seeing me, Signor Vacci," Carlo said. He shook the older man's hand.

"Your father said that you have something to ask me," Luigi replied. "As you know, he and I have had several discussions about the matter you bring. Francesco and I have been acquainted many years, and our relations have always been cordial. And your mother is a Vacci through the family of my great uncle, you know." He leaned forward slightly and clasped his hands. "So, Carlo, tell me what it is you have to say."

"I come to speak to you about your daughter, Tonia."

"Ah, to the point. Good. Come, please join me in my home." He motioned to a chair next to his.

Seeing the surprise on the face of his guest, Luigi explained. "Yes, I know. This is the foyer for the entire building." They could hear children running and laughing on the stairs. "But I have lived here so long that I feel as if the whole place is my house! Also, my wife Fiorenza is somewhat unwell. That time of the month, I am afraid." Luigi shrugged his face and shoulders then again gestured toward the chair. "Please, young man."

"Certainly, signore."

Carlo sat beside Luigi. A man came through the door, briskly bid the pair, "*Ciao, Ciao,*" and disappeared down the hall.

"Taddeo, one of the gardeners," said Luigi. Then he smiled and patted Carlo on the knee. "Now, young man, what is it you have come here to say?"

Carlo gathered his wits, plowed ahead. "Only this, Signor Luigi. I want to ask your daughter Tonia to marry me. I come to you this evening seeking your permission. I ask you humbly, signore, please allow me to approach her."

Vacci leaned back in his chair, folded his arms, and silently looked at Carlo, not unkindly.

Carlo took this to mean the older man needed further convincing

"Signor Vacci, I am a hardworking fisherman. I have my own battello. My own fishing nets, traps, lines. My income is reliable throughout all the months of the year. My vices are few. We will live at Casa Como with my family. There is an apartment with several rooms that we will have for our own."

Now for the surprise, Carlo thought. He pulled out his purse, fat with coins.

"I want you to know that I am prepared to care for her, signore." He poured some coins into his other hand so that Luigi could see. The gold was dull in the dimming light. "Through my own honest efforts, I have gained this sum," Carlo continued. "It is for our household, Tonia's and mine, for the care of our children, and to improve the rooms where we will live."

Luigi looked at the coins impassively, then up at Carlo. "All very good, Carlo," he said. "I admire your determination." He nodded at the money. "And your enterprise. You plead your case well." Luigi shifted, repositioning his legs to lessen the pain in his knee. "All very good, young man," he repeated. "But tell me this one thing, Carlo, fishing aside, apartment aside, and your impressive savings. Do you love my daughter?"

The question embarrassed Carlo. Love? Had he not already expressed his love by what he had just shown Luigi? But, no, he thought. Obviously, he had not made himself clear.

"Signore, yes, your daughter Tonia fills my mind and my heart at all times. I want us to be together always. I will love her, care for her, and provide for our children. I will not beat her. These are my true feelings, Signor Vacci. I swear on the blood of our Savior."

Luigi smiled. The young man is earnest, with good intentions, he thought. And acquiring such a sum for the marriage, a rare feat, a sign of true competency. He cleared his throat.

"Thank you, Carlo. Tonia is my treasure, you see. You have answered my questions. Young man, I am pleased with this match. Therefore, yes, I grant my consent."

Carlo wanted to leap in the air but refrained.

"I will speak to your father regarding the dowry. If he agrees, the marriage shall go forward." Vacci's eyes twinkled. "That is, assuming my Tonia tells you yes!"

* * *

Lucrezia plucked at her son's woolen black jacket and pushed at his hair where it curled on his forehead. "Carlo," she said, "you are going to ask a girl to marry you, not to help mend a net!" She straightened the white collar of his shirt and took a step back. "Wear your father's shoes, not those clodhoppers," she commanded.

"I am already wearing more of Papà's clothes than my own," Carlo complained. "Now his shoes? Tonia will not recognize me!"

But he eagerly slipped out of his work boots and laced up his father's shoes, with their black leather uppers and thick wooden soles. The only pair of real shoes in the house, the men shared them as needed.

"Be grateful my things fit you," said Lorenzo, smoking a long-stemmed pipe at the table.

Carlo donned his brimmed hat with its tapered crown and looked at his mother. "Well?"

"Go, go, you are as good as you will ever be!" Lucrezia kept her eyes on her son, smiling. Carlo leaned down and kissed her cheek. "Thank you, Mamma," he said.

"We will be there shortly," she said.

Each evening, when there was a respite from daily labor, the people of Castrubello congregated in the town's central Piazza San Giulio. The enduring tradition was an opportunity to see and to be seen. Old couples walked arm in arm or sat at the outdoor tables of one of the three cafés and watched and conversed and enjoyed the relief of the slowly lowering sun.

Eligible females walked two or three together or in a gaggle, smiling demurely at the men, then turning to each other to giggle and gossip. Young males feigned casual indifference while summoning the courage to approach one of the ladies. Couples walked together, officially courting. Entire families followed, children cavorting, new babies on display, the parents in leisurely conversation, stopping to greet acquaintances whom they saw every day. Dressed in their best, the townspeople promenaded leisurely, a few brief hours to set aside *la miseria* and refresh themselves with a sense of life's promise. Today being a Sunday, the *passeggiata* would draw nearly everyone in town.

Carlo immediately spotted her when he arrived at the piazza.

Tonia wore a long blue skirt and a white blouse with billowing sleeves. She had tied a blue ribbon in her uncovered hair, and her clogs had leather bows on their toes.

She strolled with a friend, arm in arm, young Annetta Pasqualli, with whom she worked at Torrquadro. Other longing eyes besides Carlo's followed their progress. Both girls, free from the looms and the drudgery of the silk mill, radiated vitality. Their eyes discreetly acknowledged the young men nearby, who raised their eyebrows, pursed their lips, spoke over-loudly, or otherwise mildly made fools of themselves for the women's attention. Tonia and Annetta chatted and smiled as they walked, seemingly oblivious to such antics, but sometimes raising their hands to their faces to mask their mirthful reactions.

Carlo knew two types of fishing. One was to string baited gillnets and hook lines and wait. It took patience and time but seldom failed. The other was to attack directly with a pitchfork and a net, the way they occasionally took the great sturgeons. Of course, if you missed, there was seldom a second chance. He had already decided which approach to use with this quarry.

"Tonia!" Carlo called from behind, quick-stepping to catch up to her and Annetta. "*Buona sera*, Tonia, *Buona sera*, Annetta."

The pair turned to stare at this hoped-for interruption, Tonia having seen Carlo approaching the piazza from a side street. Nonetheless, she blushed.

Annetta spoke first. "Ah, Carlo Como, where did you come from? And why are you shouting at us like this?"

It was Carlo's turn to go red, but he pushed ahead.

"I do not shout, my voice is naturally deep," he responded, hoping Tonia would draw the logical anatomical conclusion. "I am pleased to see you, Tonia."

Tonia's eyes met his again, and she smiled. Her glory stunned Carlo near-speechless.

Annetta worked in the silk mill as a common laborer, but she was not stupid. Seeing the pair mutually enraptured, she had the good grace to bow out of the scene. "Ah, there I see my father and mother," she said, her parents nowhere in the vicinity. "I promised I would spend time with them. Farewell."

Tonia embraced her friend. "I will see you tomorrow at the mill," she said. Annetta flashed a smile as she left. "I cannot wait!" she laughed. *"Ciao, ciao!"*

"Ciao, Annetta," they both responded, then resumed their stroll.

Carlo hesitated a moment before blurting, "Tonia Vacci, I find you very beautiful."

Tonia smiled with pleased surprise. "Thank you, Carlo. But how serious you are. What makes you always so serious?"

"I am serious when something is important," he replied. "Many things are important to me." This was his chance, strike now, he thought. "Of them all, you are the most important." He plunged ahead. "Tonia, I want us to marry."

Tonia stopped walking. "You want us to marry?" she said, but with a smile. "This matter is up to you alone? What about my opinion, Carlino?"

For once Carlo did not bristle at the sound of his childhood nickname. It was a sweetness when Tonia spoke it.

"In the old days, our fathers would decide the matter and neither of our opinions would be worth a dried fig," Carlo said. "We would talk for the first time in our wedding bed!" Tonia blushed again, and Carlo noticed. "Excuse me, Tonia, please, for my coarseness."

Tonia looked up at the young fisherman. "I do forgive you, Carlo Como. Because my opinion, if you are at all interested in it, is that I too want us to marry." Her eyes shone brightly. "So that we can 'talk' in bed," she added coyly, making Carlo ache. They stood face to face, eyes fixed on each other in their life-altering moment.

Luigi and Fiorenza Vacci and Carlo's parents, who together had watched the proceedings from a slight distance, quickly strolled up behind them, chatting loudly.

Chapter 5

Relentless knocking battered the rectory door of San Giulio church. The pastor hastened from his parish office in the back of the house. What is today's emergency, he wondered?

Padre Umberto had served the parish of San Giulio for over thirty years. He came from nearby Lodi, a town much like Castrubello. It had proven a good fit. Now in his early sixties, he held a central place in the life of the community: celebrant, confessor, comforter, teacher, arbiter of disputes. Almost all lines of Castrubello life, occasions joyful and sorrowful, celebratory and calamitous, flowed through his hands.

Padre Giancarlo, Umberto's assistant, answered the door first. Umberto heard voices as he entered the front room.

"A miracle, Padre, at the silk mill!" exclaimed young Alberto Figli, a boy who worked at Torrquadro. Flush-faced and panting, he had obviously run the entire way from the factory. "You must ring the bell! You must come to the factory!"

Umberto opened the door wider as Giancarlo stood to one side. "Take a breath, 'Berto," he said, as the boy stepped inside. "Tell me now, what happened?"

"A miracle, Padre Umberto!" exclaimed the young man again. "Less than a half-hour ago. I was shelving spools of thread in the storeroom. I heard a big noise out on the work floor, then everyone was shouting. Before I could see, Maria Rossa grabbed me and said, 'There has been a miracle, by the Virgin herself! Run to the church, tell Padre Umberto!' So here I am! Should I ring Great Gabriele, Padre?"

The campanile of San Giulio was the tallest structure in town and the deep *bong!* of its great bronze bell, nicknamed after the angelic herald, radiated for miles. When it clanged any time outside of its fixed weekday schedule of 6:00 am, noon, and 6:00 pm, it alerted the populace that something of import was at hand.

"No, my son, I think Gabriele will stay still for the moment," said Umberto. The other priest gave Alberto a cup of water from the bucket in the cucina. The boy drank greedily.

Umberto grasped his walking stick from its place by the door. He turned to his assistant. "I shall ride Agatha," referring to the old parish donkey they kept saddled and ready. He gathered his bag containing a vial of holy oil and the ornate silver *aspergillum* scepter used for sprinkling holy water on the faithful. "Stay here, Padre Giancarlo, prepare the church in case we do need it. Alberto, follow me when you are able."

By the time Umberto arrived at Torrquadro, a semblance of order had returned. Fidele, the mill's manager, had shut down one row of steam-powered looms; their operators waited for instructions. Several of the women sat on a bench to the side, one of them holding a blue cloth to her neck. Everyone else had been sent back to their stations. The loud sounds of production were returning to full volume. Miracle or no, time was money!

To Fidele's dismay, the sight of the priest entering the room brought the place to a complete standstill again. The women on the bench rose to greet their pastor, praising God, the angels, and all the saints, arms uplifted. Machines came to a stop as workers left their posts and crowded toward the cleric. Their spontaneous jabbering reached such a din that nothing was intelligible. Umberto raised his walking stick like Moses dividing the Red Sea. "*Silenzio*, everyone, *silenzio!*" When the noise subsided, he continued. "Please, let me hear what has taken place."

"A miracle!" cried someone in the back. Further exclamations rose. "The Virgin saved her!" "Our Lady pulled her from death!" To stop the noise from reaching a new frenzy, Umberto proclaimed loudly, "Let us pray," and took to his knees. Everyone copied his action. Calmly, Umberto led them through the *Pater Noster* and *Ave Maria*. The short, familiar ritual settled the crowd. The priest stood, beckoned the workers to do the same, and addressed them again. "Now, who was it that the Virgin saved?"

The woman with the blue cloth stood. "It is I, Padre, Magdalena Tonte." She was a middle-aged woman, slight, in a gray work apron. Umberto knew the Tontes, as he did all his parishioners.

"Please, Magdalena, tell me what took place." The priest leaned on his stick, smiled benignly, noted the red welt on the woman's neck. Foreman Fidele came up close, respectful of the cleric but hoping to move things along. The workers stood, leaned in.

"Padre, I was at my place at the loom. There," she pointed to the one at the end of the row. Umberto knew little of machinery, he noted a contraption with belts and a large pulley wheel. The woman paused, aware of her audience's rapt attention. Most had not heard the full story. "I leaned too far forward you see, and my scarf caught in the wheel! I could not reach to the brake! Padre, it pulled my face close, I felt the scarf tighten, tighten, tighten around my throat!" Those crowding to hear murmured sympathetic distress and made signs of the cross as they shared the drama.

Magdalena began sobbing softly and rapidly fanned herself with her hand. Umberto placed his hand gently upon her shoulder. "Go on, please, Magdalena."

The woman collected herself and continued. "But just then, I heard someone cry, 'Sacred Maria!' and Padre, I swear on my children, the Madonna was there beside me, right where you stand, as bright as the sun, with her hands helping my head go around with the wheel until, suddenly, I came free!"

This revelation elicited spontaneous exclamations of "Madonna, Our Queen!" and "Our Holy Virgin!" Some fell again to their knees.

"It was Tonia Vacci who cried out for the Madonna to come!" said a young woman in the back. "I heard her cry for the Virgin when she saw the machine reach out and grasp Magdalena!"

All attention shifted to Tonia. Those around her stepped away as if she herself was the Madonna. She stood near her workstation; steam from the bubbling vat of cocoons ribboned upward.

She was tall among her peers. The hair under her triangle scarf was a lighter brown compared to most of her co-workers. Embarrassed by the scrutiny, she kept her eyes modestly down, her hands folded at her waist. When she finally looked up, her piercing gray-blue eyes gazed directly at the priest.

She asked herself, do I tell him that I only blurted out the first words that jumped into my head when I saw Magdalena's predicament? No. So many faces around her held looks of wonder. Who was she to deny them their moment of faith reaffirmed? For all she knew, it was true that heaven had intervened here to avert certain tragedy. "I am glad you are safe, Magdalena," she said. "I only said what anyone would have, seeing your danger."

Padre Umberto was no stranger to miracles, but he knew God threw dumb luck into human affairs far more often. This appeared one such time.

"We thank God no harm was done to you today, Magdalena Tonte. Always cherish the holiness of Our Lady, and she will forever be with you, seen or unseen. Tonia Vacci, invoking Our

Lady was a virtuous act. God bless you, my daughter. Now, let us say a prayer of thanksgiving."

Everyone again went to their knees on the stone floor. "O Blessed Maria," he began, "Accept the gratitude we offer, though unequal to your glory, for your intervention in saving the life of your poor servant, Magdalena Tonte."

The priest raised his right hand, touched his thumb and first finger, and made the sign of the cross in the air. "*In nomine Patris, et Filii, et Spiritus Sancti.*" He waved the silver scepter and repeated the words, shaking God's blessing onto believers.

Not kneeling with the others and too distant for any holy waterdrops to strike, Gaetano Baldassare observed the scene. He had heard of the commotion at the factory and rode over to see for himself.

He watched from a side hallway as the pastor dispensed his final blessings then depart. What a business the old man does, he thought. While Baldassare went through the motions on Sundays—what choice was there for him?—he was far too cynical to be a Catholic zealot. Fantasy and illusion, piety and ritual, superstition and martyrdom. It amazed him the old formula still worked. The provinces and cities that the Vatican once directly possessed may now belong to the Kingdom of Italy, he thought, but that was mere politics. The actual power that the Church still wielded remained real and vast. And he knew that the beloved Padre Umberto, as kindly as he seemed, held enormous influence in and around Castrubello. This cheap passion play he had just witnessed was but the latest example.

But now that I am here, I should make the most of it, Baldassare thought, smoothing back his hair. He watched Vacci's daughter go back to work. She had been quite modest about her role as Heaven's handmaiden, he smirked to himself. In truth, the woman must have the self-respect of a toad to accept the task of stirring a hot tub of writhing silkworms all day. Regardless, Baldassare desired her mightily.

The manager sniffed. It was not as if he had no prospects of his own. He was currently courting the widow Di Muro from neighboring Montegallante. She was a bit older than he, a bit worn out, but comely enough in her own way even in black mourning silks. Moreover, she owned a small, busy inn that her dead husband had left her. Baldassare was confident that before long they would arrive at a marital arrangement that served them both well.

But that was not for right now, he thought. Right now, his pulse quickened when he saw Tonia speak to the foreman and then leave her vat to walk unwittingly in his direction. He drew himself back a single long step.

Tonia pushed hair from her forehead and under her kerchief. She set recent events to the back of her mind. All I need now, she thought, is a dipper of water.

She went to the barrel near a side entry, but it was empty. She would have to go down the dim hallway that led to the pump outside.

The deeper interior of the factory was a labyrinth of rooms and hallways, once used for storage, for billeting troops, for weapons, for eating, who knew? Various passageways led to staircases to the second floor; certain halls ended in sudden, bricked-up dead ends. Some of the rooms closest to the work floor contained active workbenches and machines, but those to the rear remained empty, many with their doors boarded up. The women and children in the Torrquadro workforce hated to leave the main floor to go deeper into the building. Tales of hauntings and other terrors abounded. One story told of the dreaded *strega*, the witch who stalked the halls and drank children's blood. Another described a headless specter in rusted armor standing in the shadows, brandishing a war-axe. Terrifying legends, of course. But for women workers the fear was far more real. Stories persisted of molestation and rape.

The Torrquadro mill employed scores of wagoneers and warehousemen. In fact, Tonia's brother Ettore was one of them, his labor leased to the mill by the villa. They worked in the castle's former granaries along the courtyard's north wall, for the most part all day. But the women instinctively knew that where men were involved, primal urges were never very distant. The social trinity of Church, *famiglia*, and long tradition usually held such impulses in check. But not always.

Tonia was grateful she had never faced such a threat. The townsmen knew her to be a virtuous woman, despite her flashing eyes. That did not mean she had no urges of her own. As she walked down the hallway, she thought of Carlo, his broad shoulders and strong chin, his hands. She knew he desired her equally as much. Their wedding day could not arrive soon enough.

With a fierce grab, Baldassare had her arm. He pulled her toward him from the light. "Oh, you smell sweet, Tonia," he rasped into her ear. She froze, then the shock of his sudden aggression triggered her impulse to survive. She instinctively slapped him in the face with all the force she could muster.

"Ah, ah, now," said Baldassare, clutching both of her wrists with one hand, putting his other behind her head. He planted his lips on hers and pressed, his thick hot tongue forcing itself between her clenched teeth. His breath smelled of garlic and tobacco. She felt his hardness grinding at her thighs.

Tonia wore clogs with thick, unyielding soles made of oak. She drove her right foot down on Baldassare's instep.

"You worthless whore bitch!" cried Baldassare, loosening his grip. She pulled to escape, but he caught her again by the arm, harder this time.

"Listen to me, *fica*. You forget who I am. We will finish this tonight. Be in the tack room at the villa stable, just after supper. Have your legs ready to spread, or you and your crippled father and the rest of your pathetic family will be out on the road with bundles on your back!"

Tonia's eyes glared contempt. But as she twisted from his grasp and ran back down the hall, she despaired.

* * *

Baldassare saw the stable door standing ajar as he strode up the path. Good, he thought, his excitement rising. She wants it as much as I do. Or she wants to get it over with. Either way, he was ready to give the *puttana* what she so badly needed. He belched low, tasted sausage from dinner, patted his chest.

A dim lantern burnt near a stall. Ettore Vacci stood in its light.

"You!" Baldassare cried. "Why in Christ's name are you here? Where is that teasing sister of yours?"

Ettore betrayed no emotion at the tirade. "I too was at Torrquadro this morning, signore. I arrived late and entered the opposite hallway as you. I saw my sister kick you and leave the hallway, distraught. She told me what you did. I tell you now, leave your hands off Tonia!"

Baldassare snorted disbelief. "You are telling me what? *Palle*, boy! You realize, don't you, that I can crush you with a snap of my fingers, yet you speak to me in this manner? Maybe I should bend you over that barrel and give you the same big treat I will be giving her!" He put his hand on the crotch of his trousers and leered. All a show. Baldassare disdained homosexuals but intended to make this boy squirm.

Instead, Ettore set his feet, raised his fists.

From the shadows came a new voice. "Enough, Baldassare. Your crudity tests even God's patience!"

First astonished, then recovering, the manager barked a harsh laugh. "*Mio Dio*, another great miracle, just like this morning!" He clapped his hands. "Two in one day! This time, a worn-out saddle has magically turned into a worn-out priest!"

"No, Gaetano Baldassare, no miracle here." From a corner where leather gear hung Padre Umberto came fully into the light. Over his cassock he wore a cloak, the cowl pulled back. "But I say to you plainly that if you persist with this lechery of yours, I will denounce you from the pulpit with Marchese d'Ambrosso in attendance. Then the miracle will be the speed of your disappearance from these parts!"

Baldassare's face froze; the priest saw and bore down. "I will also ride my mule to Montegallante and visit Signora Di Muro. I know you have an interest in her, perhaps even an understanding? What do you imagine she will say when I tell her that you roam the countryside like a mad stoat, eager to rut anything that crosses your path? Apparently, by your own words tonight, even young men!"

This demon-spawn of a cleric had the means to spread any lie he wanted, Baldassare knew. If he declared Baldassare humped poultry in their coops, it would be accepted by his doltish parishioners as true. Should the priest go to the marchese, Baldassare would be out of a job within hours.

As he realized how he had been entrapped, bitterness swelled within and he began to perspire. He drew a long breath, then fixed his gaze on Ettore.

"Whatever you think you heard earlier today, I tell you, you misheard. Whatever you think you saw, you did not. Telling this man of God lies condemns you to hell, Ettore Vacci. If I thought this was deliberate calumny..." he felt his heart pounding hard and had to begin again. "Were you a fully grown man, I would drag you to the piazza and thrash you in front of all of Castrubello!" he raged.

Neither listener reacted.

Baldassare knew his bluster rang hollow. Dropping his voice, he raised both hands, spoke to the priest. "Believe me, the signorina has no cause for fear. I freely admit, I am a man like any other, her beauty over-enthused me. Certainly, it was the work of the devil that caused me to misunderstand her sentiments. I will trouble her no further." He looked at

Umberto, saw the priest expected more, swallowed his bile. "I swear before God and on my own mother's soul, I will leave her alone."

Umberto's eyes bore into Baldassare's. "Our Savior, the Virgin, and holy Santo Giulio asleep in his crypt hear this oath of yours," he said. "Break it at your soul's peril, Gaetano. But, as *Gesu' Cristo* is The Great Forgiver, in his holy name I declare this matter *finito!*"

A silence enfolded the room.

Baldassare gazed a long moment at the two of them, stiffly nodded his head once, and turned away. He felt his neck and face flush hot with humiliation. Tonight's preposterous charade at least is over, he thought. But that family will pay.

"Thank you, Padre," Ettore said, as Baldassare disappeared into the night's rising mist.

"No, thank you, Ettore. There are many things in our village I cannot influence. But your desire to protect your sister has prompted some justice tonight." He looked at his sharp-minded pupil, who for more than three years had come to the rectory two nights a week, sometimes after thirteen or fourteen hours of work, to learn how to read and write and master his numbers. Yes, sharp-minded and disciplined, well ahead of his years, Umberto reflected. Instead of succumbing to raw temper, as many young men his age would have done, Ettore had instead carefully arranged the night's entire ambush. How clever of him to draw Umberto into the matter! What a formidable priest the lad would make! But in his heart, Umberto knew Ettore was not meant for the Church.

"Listen to me, Etto. Watch yourself, now more than ever. Gaetano Baldassare can be a vicious enemy. He will look to make you pay for his disappointment. Do not allow him to draw you into confrontation; nothing would suit him better. Warn Tonia and your parents to keep a wide berth. Do as he says, whatever it is, with no complaint, in all matters within his powers as manager. Do not argue with him. Do not gloat. Act as if tonight never happened—but in our prayers we must both thank the Virgin that it did!"

Ettore nodded. "I understand, Padre. I will do what I must. But the man is a pig."

Chapter 6

The biting flies were as bad as the stench, and the stench was eye-watering. Ettore pulled up the scarf covering his mouth and nose. The flies went for his eyes, which he could not cover. His sleeveless shirt was clammy with vile grit in the oppressive humidity. The buzzing swarm harassed his back, arms, brow, his neck, the sensitive edges of his ears, and crawled deep into the sweat rivulets under his armpits.

"Aaagh!" Ettore waved a hand to drive the cloud away. The tactic had not worked ten dozen times before; it failed again. Instead, inspired by Ettore's distress, the insects returned with increased vigor.

Two days earlier, he and his helper had harnessed an ox to pull the sagging, covered privy from over the cesspit. It housed a row of holes in a splintery bench. The exposed monstrosity beneath, over eight feet wide, brimmed with filth.

Waist-deep in excrement and rotting garbage, Ettore stood on a long ladder that was mostly submerged in the appalling muck. The circular mouth of the sump was even with the top of Ettore's head; above, he saw blue sky and the rope attached to an overhanging winch. He'd been working at this for two days, descending step by step as he slowly made progress. Beside him, afloat on the thick surface, was an open wooden barrel tied to the line stretching upward.

Ettore scooped a wood pail into the mire. The filth at this top level had the consistency of loose mud. He sank the bucket until it was full, then hoisted the abomination to the barrel and dumped in its contents. A gaseous reek hung in the heat.

The small field where they worked lay adjacent to the servants' quarters. Four privy sheds stood in a row next to the largest one they had started with, each set above its own pit. An uneven stone walkway connected the quarters to the latrine yard, aptly nicknamed *cacacampo*. It was used by the villa's workforce of laborers and servants; the chamber pots of the estate's guest rooms were emptied there as well. The family's own rooms in the manor house were equipped with indoor pipe plumbing powered by gravity and sluicing rainwater.

The two men wore leather overalls, tall boots, and kept their faces wrapped with coarse scarves. Every time it was Ettore's turn to descend into the hole, he became more alarmed by the condition of its decrepit walls. The original mortar work appeared badly done, the bricks poorly fired. The gaps between the bricks had widened over time, and mortar had rotted out in multiple places. The discolored clay bricks were black, gray, and brown, cracked from decades of absorbed urine and the moisture of stagnant waste. In some places they crumbled chalklike at Ettore's touch. The deeper the men worked, the more the stability of the cesspit's entire lining came into question. But when Ettore told Baldassare of his concern, the manager cut him off saying, "Stop your whining excuses, Vacci. Get back to the job."

Baldassare's deferred maintenance strategy unfortunately extended to the latrine yard. Besides increasing the likelihood of overflowing in rain, the odor relentlessly invaded the servants' quarters. Even the main villa did not escape the putrescence wafted by some evening breezes.

The layout of the estate's grounds provided for an irrigation canal with a steady current located a mere quarter-mile away from the buildings. Each loaded dump-wagon was taken to this wide ditch, run up a stone ramp, and its contents tipped directly into the canal. Workers raked at the chunky filth until the wagon was empty, then broke up the floating mess to start the detritus on its way. All such runoff from d'Ambrosso's property, and Castrubello itself, eventually emptied into the Naviglio. The waterway served the same useful purpose for every town and mill along its banks.

Usually the two Boschi brothers, Castrubello's regular night-soil men, cleaned the pits. But shortly after the confrontation at the stable, Baldassare canceled that arrangement. Instead, he had called in Ettore and told him, "You no longer work at Torrquadro. Come to the window."

Ettore looked in the direction the estate manager pointed.

"There, there is your new kingdom, famed Cacacampo! Start with the big one, *il pozzo nero*, long overdue, it has not been tended for years. Then the other four. Begin today and work until you have finished them all. You have four weeks."

Ettore understood what the manager was doing, of course.

"I alone?" he asked.

Baldassare smirked. "No, Vacci, you will work with il Muto."

"Il Muto" was the nickname of Carlo Ferrara, a sometimes-worker at the villa in his mid-forties. He had been born deaf and dumb, which accounted for his nickname and assumed stupidity. His short, bulky body, low forehead, and thick eyebrows reinforced the perception. When local mothers sought to motivate their offspring to behave, they occasionally threatened to invoke il Muto. "His hut in the woods is full of the bones of disobedient children," they told them.

To help manage their terror, the children sometimes sang a rhyme mocking the monster:

"È vero del tutto, il Muto è brutto!"

But never, though they knew he was deaf, did the children ever chant his ugliness within sight of the man.

As Baldassare waited to see his reaction to naming Muto his partner, Ettore remembered Umberto's advice. "Thank you, signore," Ettore told the manager. "Ferrara is a strong one."

Now Muto waited for him above.

With another wasted gesticulation to drive off the flies, Ettore bucketed a last load into the barrel then climbed the ladder. Muto grabbed Ettore's filthy gloved hand and with a deep grunt helped pull him up over the edge. He handed Ettore the jug of water they kept in the wagon's shade.

Ettore nodded his appreciation. He pulled off his scarf, stepped some yards away, took a deep breath. Once out of the confines of the pit, the sudden freedom to breathe felt amazing.

"There is a lesson here," Ettore said to Muto. "Never take sweet air for granted!" He drew in an exaggerated breath, smiling. Muto looked at him patiently, a hand on his hip, the other on the cart. This one is interesting, he thought. Accustomed to facing the mockery, pity, or sheer terror of others, he took Ettore's addressing him as if he was not deaf at all as a signal of friendly respect.

Ettore checked the ancient ox harnessed to the two-wheeled dump-wagon. The beast had been standing still for hours. Its tail methodically swished back and forth, futilely trying to alleviate the misery inflicted by the ceaseless insects. This is the gift that comes from being two thousand years old, thought Ettore. Hopeless persistence.

He motioned Muto to go to the opposite side of the wagon. Together they pulled back the tarp. A wave of nausea overtook Ettore as the smell filled his mouth, complete with a fat, eager fly. He retched into the ooze they had just now exposed.

Muto climbed up and heavily patted Ettore's back. His ghastly smile, an attempt at encouragement, exposed nubby brown teeth. He gave his partner's back a final strong thump.

"Thank you, Ferrara," Ettore said, turning his face from the mire.

He swished his mouth and spit out another slug of water. Over the pit, three twelve-foot poles formed a tripod supporting a block and tackle. Its rope stretched from a wooden cleat on the wagon to the barrel's handle in the pit. Ettore had pieced the arrangement together from parts he had found in the stable. It had held up so far.

He pulled on his stiff pigskin gloves, adjusted the scarf over his nose. When Ettore was ready, Muto untied the rope from the cleat. Yank by yank, the sloshing barrel slowly rose from the depths. The container cleared the top of the well. Raising the cask higher until it just cleared the wagon's slanted back end, Ettore gestured for Muto to hang onto the rope and get into the wagon.

Once Muto was in position, Ettore also climbed up, careful to not skid into the sopping pile that sucked at his knees. He used a pole with an iron hook to snag the lip of the barrel and swing it their way. At the same time, Muto slowly played out some rope until the container dropped upright next to their feet with a thick *flump!* Together they muscled it over until its contents had joined the rest of the ooze. Ettore used the hook-pole to roughly even out the new mound. Muto got down, pulled the barrel back into position, and tied off the rope.

He looked at his partner. Muto's turn. Ettore wanly smiled and made a mocking little bye-bye 'ciao, ciao' motion. Muto's eyes crinkled. He half-turned, puckered his lips, and gave his left ham a slap, inviting Ettore to kiss his rump, while making guttural "eh, eh, eh" noises that Ettore took for an outburst of mirth. Then Carlo Ferrara pulled his handkerchief over his nose and climbed down into hell.

Chapter 7

Gaetano Baldassare sat rigidly upright in the cushioned pew, sweat trickling down his neck into his stiff shirt collar. Marchese and Marchesa d'Ambrosso occupied the bench directly ahead of him in the first row. Generally, the d'Ambrosso family attended Sunday Mass in the villa's own chapel, Padre Umberto riding his mule to the estate in order to preside. But Don Federico and his wife made a point of attending the service at San Giulio once every month, traveling the short distance in the estate's elaborate coach-and-four. Often the estate manager and Aurelio Maggio, the family solicitor, also attended, clattering alongside the carriage on horseback.

Now the party sat in the family's two ornately carved wooden pews which otherwise remained empty, off-limits as they were to common worshipers. At the moment, Baldassare was resenting the fact that Padre Umberto had finished Mass but instead of departing to the sacristy on cue, now turned and stepped back up into the pulpit, forcing the congregation to continue to wilt in their seats. Returning to the pulpit after Mass had concluded was only done when a special announcement was called for, but Baldassare could not bring to mind any particular local news that warranted commentary from the Church. Perhaps yet another mention of the Virgin's miraculous intervention at the silk mill?

One thing Baldassare knew, Padre Umberto would stay silent about the entire insulting incident regarding Tonia and her brother. Baldassare had kept his end of the bargain, hadn't he? The memory of Tonia's hot mouth stirred him—such promise!— but in spite of his lust for the girl he had kept a wide berth. For the time being, it was better to allow the matter to slip into the past. Tonia's day will come. One way or another, I will make certain she pays for the way she flaunted herself at me, Baldassare told himself. In the meantime, it was enough to watch that brother of hers drag himself home every day caked in hardening *merda*, with Muto the idiot trudging like an ape-man alongside.

The only other news of the day was that a sickness was spreading in the north, panicked talk of a new outbreak of cholera. Epidemics of all types never disappeared entirely; like bad weather they cyclically inflicted themselves on Lombardia and the rest of Italia with savage fury. Less than two hundred years ago Castrubello had been ravaged by a resurgence of bubonic plague. Fifteen hundred townspeople, half the commune's population, were carried off within weeks, leaving no household untouched. Four generations later another pestilence had swept away a thousand more.

Cholera was more recent. The last great epidemic had struck Europe a half-century before and flared up every summer since. No one knew for certain what caused the disease. Hypotheses ranged from breathing fetid air to drinking water infested with tiny creatures that no one could see! One old assumption that was slow to disappear was that God sent the epidemics to punish mankind for its chronic unfaithfulness, or alternately, that Satan inflicted the disease when people were not warding off evil with enough ardent prayer. Medical or spiritual, no treatment thus far had met much success.

Padre Umberto ascended the pulpit, placed his hands on its surface, and began. "San Giulio humbly acknowledges the immense honor bestowed on his parish by the presence of the esteemed Marchese and Marchesa d'Ambrosso. *Grazie mille*, signore and signora. May God bless you both and keep you." The priest lowered his head and opened both hands in a symbolic embrace toward where the couple sat. Baldassare was reminded yet again how he despised the self-righteous charlatan.

D'Ambrosso acknowledged the priest's expression of gratitude with a nod and loud sniff-snort. The marchesa, who had been fanning herself with a large faux-palm leaf made of white lace, paused her flapping for a slow one-two count, then rapidly resumed. The priest continued.

"As well we all know, two weeks ago the Virgin Maria acted in compassion and kindness to save the life of Signora Magdalena Tonte." Those in the pews nodded as he spoke. Night after night, the story of the wondrous miracle had served as supper conversation for every household in the commune. "To honor this divine intervention, Famiglia d'Ambrosso has donated two magnificent silver candlesticks to this church, to be placed before the statue of Our Lady of Perpetual Help." He gestured to a side altar.

An eager acolyte, waiting for his cue, with a flourish unveiled the candlesticks already in place on each side of the Virgin's painted plaster statue. His fellow altar boy stepped forward and carefully lit the wicks with a long, brass, telescoping candlelighter. The two bowed to the Virgin and departed.

Another expensive inanity by his master, Baldassare thought. He had known nothing of this gift. What was the fool thinking? From the look of them, those candlesticks were worth more than the yearly earnings of anyone else in the building, including himself. Such impulsive largesse would be the undoing of the marchese. The old man loves to be loved. Why? Baldassare could not fathom it. Love and money both? And a play for eternal salvation to boot! So typical of the nobility's bottomless sense of entitlement.

"Thus, we have cause to thank our generous patron once more," Umberto continued. "Our dear benefactors," addressing their pew directly. "You will be forever remembered not only by the Sacred Heart of Christ for your love of his mother, but also with a year of weekly masses to be said for your undiminished health and wellbeing! In addition, in honor of these events, of the Virgin appearing amongst us and of the generous gift of the d'Ambrossi, the voice of Great Gabriele will sound from the belltower after our liturgy today!"

The cleric now looked, it seemed to Baldassare, in his own direction. "Another, equally joyous matter." Umberto put on his spectacles then made the sign of the cross, the congregation doing the same. "*In nomine Patris, et Filii, et Spiritus Sancti.*" Reading from the book he opened before him, he continued. "We hereby publicly pronounce the banns of holy matrimony between Carlo Como, son of Lorenzo and of Lucrezia, of the parish of San Giulio, and Tonia Vacci, daughter of Luigi and of Fiorenza, also of this parish. If anyone knows just impediment as to why these persons should not be joined in holy matrimony, you must now declare it." In response, the congregation buzzed happily among itself. So, the talk was true!

The pair of silver candlesticks had been an unpleasant surprise. But at the priest's latest words, Baldassare's face darkened. Arrogant Como? And the Vacci woman? He had not suspected the match, and his surprise turned to an even deeper resentment of them both. Padre Umberto left the pulpit, led by the altar servers, one carrying the processional cross, flanked by two others holding lit candles. The small procession swept past the left side of the altar and out through the sacristy door.

Once the priest disappeared from the scene, the congregation sat waiting until Castrubello's patrician families exited their front pews. Dressed in their Sunday finery, the landowning gentry followed the d'Ambrosso contingent down the center aisle and out the front doors. The hats and bonnets on the women displayed all the latest styles from Milan. The Countess Federici's in particular was noteworthy. Black, the smallish hat was set at a slant, one side of its brim turned up to reveal a cunning white underlining. White and gray flowers, made of the magnificent silk of Torrquadro, clustered across its crown. A waft of rich perfumes followed the aristocratic elite down the aisle, creating, as intended, a demarcation line of sorts between themselves and the less exceptional world around them. Then, prompted by ushers, the mass of laborers, tenants, craftsmen, farmers, and their families filed from their seats row by row.

Gleaming carriages and well-groomed mounts from the various estates awaited their riders, and typical of Sundays outside San Giulio, there was no particular hurry by the wealthy families to immediately leave. Instead, many gathered and conversed among themselves at the foot of the church's marble steps while those emerging behind them were forced to stream around each side. On this day, following their departure from San Giulio, a number of the elite were to attend a private business meeting at the nearby country house of Senator Testaforte of Milan, and these continued down to where their transportation stood waiting.

Baldassare was nearer the steps than his lord. He was speaking to Fidele Balossi, who managed the silk factory, and Gino Spezialo, estate manager for the absentee landlord Viscount Lapianta of Milan. Gaetano mouthed the right words to carry on his end of the conversation. But he still boiled hot from the news that the Vacci slut was to marry that insolent dog Como. He remembered the scene on the river with the white stones like it was yesterday.

"Congratulations young man!" Gino called out, looking past Baldassare. Gino knew the Comos from on the Pirino; the estate he served also paid d'Ambrosso for fishing rights. Carlo descended the steps slowly, talking to two of his close friends, Angelo and Romeo. Ahead was his family, Lorenzo and Lucrezia, Francesco and pregnant Gemella, Vito and Rina, the children. Carlo hoped to have a chance to speak to Tonia, but she was not in sight, around somewhere visiting with her own friends, he assumed.

When Carlo looked to the three men and saw who had called him, he responded, "*Si, si, grazie mille,* Gino," and returned

Fidele's gesture of greeting. He realized the third man with his back still turned was Gaetano Baldassare. His steps brought him closer. Several well-wishers paused, waiting a turn to congratulate the groom-to-be.

"She's a fine worker at Torrquadro," said Fidele, "and the one who so quickly invoked the Virgin's name." This prompted approving murmurs from those listening. "When is the wedding? I assume you cannot wait!" Carlo smiled. "Ah, you are right. We are to be married next month."

As Baldassare kept his back deliberately turned, Carlo became aware of the intended insult. "And I am a fortunate man, indeed," Carlo continued, louder, seized with an urge to rub Baldassare's nose in his good fortune. "Tonia is a rare treasure."

At this, Baldassare spoke up, as if to Gino, but for Carlo to hear. "I ask you, Gino. Who in the name of heaven would want a woman with worms in her hair? Every hair everywhere, no doubt." He loudly guffawed and turned to face Carlo.

Those hearing the remark gasped. To say such a thing about someone's betrothed! And on the steps of the church! Gino, already disturbed by Baldassare's rudeness, saw the pure malice on the man's face. What was this?

Carlo wanted to strike. His rage burnt white in his eyes. But the Vaccis were here. To create a scene in this place would embarrass them all. Especially Tonia. And if his own family became embroiled, he knew his father Lorenzo, Francesco, and Vito would respond in quick defense of Carlo's future bride. On God's holy day, on the steps of the church! And in front of all the strutting *pezzi grossi*! With difficulty, he fought his temper back into its cage. Yet his family's *onore* demanded a response.

"Bravely said, Baldassare, very brave," he responded, then raised his voice further. "Especially from someone cursed with such a tiny worm of his own!" Carlo raised his right hand so all could see and wiggled his pinky to mock the manager's tiny member.

The group of men nearby erupted in laughter. Romeo barked, "Ah-ha!" and Angelo slapped Carlo on the back. Other men on the steps who had heard the exchange shouted "Bravo, Carlo!" Those noble families still engaged in their niceties turned to the uproar. "Well, friend Gaetano, touché, I think," said Gino, privately enjoying Baldassare's public comeuppance.

Baldassare turned scarlet under the hail of laughter. Solicitor Maggio, who had witnessed it all, stepped up and grasped the manager's elbow. "Enough, Baldassare. This is unseemly. The marchese is impatient to get to the meeting. He has already departed." Baldassare, blind angry, turned sharply away, never looking at Como. To the sound of ongoing hilarity and the first toll of the great parish bell celebrating the Virgin's loving mercy, he descended to where his horse waited, mounted, and kicked hard into its flanks.

Carlo remained for some minutes receiving outstretched hands, keenly aware the matter was far from settled. For either man.

Chapter 8

"Thank you, Zio Giovanni. Yes, I am Dottore Ottavio Di Verde. I received my medical license from Collegio del Po al Lago di Garda. In the ten years since, I have established a thriving practice near Varese. Recently, I have become increasingly dedicated to the goal of discovering the medical means to eradicate the scourge of cholera!"

The seventeen men in the comfortable sitting room applauded politely. The three major local landowners in the Castrubello region, d'Ambrosso, Ruggero, and Sanfreddo, had joined the great absentee landlords Lapianta, and Alturo. Together with Senator Giovanni Testaforte, the six men controlled ninety percent of the arable land in southwest Lombardia. With each of the wealthy padrones was a manager and financial adviser or two to hear what this obscure physician from the north had to say. Testaforte had told them before they arrived, "Just listen, my nephew is no fool."

The audience grew by one as Gaetano Baldassare entered the room. Mumbling his apologies, he sat on a gilded chair next to the door. He used his handkerchief to dab at the sweat and dust on his face from his severe, angry ride from San Giulio.

The doctor smiled generously at the newcomer, referred back to his prepared notes, continued. "My dear signori, we live in an age of revolutionary medical advancements. As we throw back the curtain of superstition, pure science is revealing answers to maladies large and small. And it is in science's relentless, dispassionate experimentation that I place my absolute faith."

His listeners paid close attention. Modern medical research was just starting to yield results. The moneyed classes on the continent were keenly aware of the multiple dangers posed by masses of workers crowding into rapidly industrializing cities. As investors, they also sensed opportunity.

"But men like you already know that progress is made by the bold." Di Verde leaned forward, both fists on the table. He looked at his uncle who beamed encouragement. "Progress and money, both go hand in hand—benefits to mankind, profit to those who take the risks. All great enterprises contain risks. But, gentlemen, high risk but amplifies the reward!" The audience murmured; heads nodded.

Di Verde paused to sip from a glass of water. My uncle is right, he observed. The lure of self-interest never fails to concentrate a group's attention.

"Do you realize, signori, that in the past few years well over one hundred thousand of our countrymen have died from cholera alone? One hundred thousand men, women, and children stripped from fields and farms and estates and mills by the dreaded Blue Death. Even as we speak, thousands die by the month in Naples and the south. And with no end in sight! How can the labor force of enterprises like your own sustain such attrition without suffering crushing production loss?" He let the question hang.

"Upon earning my medical degree, I had the great good fortune to study further under the tutelage of a true pioneer, Doctor Rodolfo Rodolfi, chief physician at Brescia's Piety Hospital. Dr. Rodolfi has been courageous in his certainty that the answer to cholera is direct injection of a serum into the bloodstream. Yes, injection," he repeated, noting the arched brows throughout the room. He opened a polished wooden box on the table.

"You and your families may have received vaccinations to prevent smallpox. Usually, a physician cuts your skin, then smears on the serum for absorption into the blood. But perhaps some of you went to the hospital of Policlinico di Milan for inoculation. If so, you may well be familiar with a variation of this, the famed Pravaz hypodermic syringe."

Di Verde held up the device, an older model he had bought at a secondhand shop at Lago Garda. The tarnished silver cylinder and plunger together measured over four inches long. Its attached needle extended another three.

"As you see, the needle is a sharp, hollow tube with a fine point. We place the serum inside the cylinder, here. The 'plunger' of a Pravaz is actually a screw, that when turned, forces the serum through the needle. Punch the tip of the needle cleanly into a blood vessel, screw down the plunger to the proper thread mark, and the exact same dosage injects each time. Quite ingenious!

"Using the Pravaz syringe, Dr. Rodolfi began to tirelessly experiment on as many cholera victims as possible. Not limiting himself to the usual compromised subjects of insane asylums, he brought his inoculations to patients wherever he could find them. This allowed him to boldly vary his experimental formulas. Several successes occurred, along with others that were," he coughed, "excuse me, that were less conclusive. Nonetheless, Doctor Rodolfi's formula of strychnine and clear rainwater showed enormous promise.

"Alas, the good doctor's results were not yet conclusive before narrow-minded hospital authorities pressured him to halt his experiments. They told him, 'You cannot conduct tests like that on human beings! You must start with rabbits, then perhaps monkeys, only then on patients!'" The physician shook his head. "A feeble-hearted attitude, gentlemen. The great Cristoforo Colombo did not conquer the Atlantic with the *Santa Maria* tied to the dock! Like all great explorers, medical researchers must launch boldly into the unknown sea and sail beyond sight of land, proceeding with robust trial and error!"

A patrician voice boomed. "Dottore, a question!"

Di Verde recognized the speaker. "Signor Alturo," he answered smiling, hugely annoyed at the interruption of his momentum. "By all means, signore."

Giovanni Alturo stood, a slender man, borderline gaunt, with a white, pushbroom mustache and curly sideburns to his chin. "Dottore, did I hear you correctly? You are saying your cure for cholera is based on strychnine? Rat poison?"

"Thank you, signore," said Di Verde. He was expecting the question. "Yes, you are correct. Unadulterated strychnine effectively exterminates vermin, as you so astutely point out. But experiments in France and elsewhere indicate that, when properly diluted and dosed, strychnine can have salubrious effects. Much like good, strong coffee, strychnine can serve as a bracing tonic, keeping a man brisk and fit. Its convulsive effects, again, controlled by careful dosage, energize the body's natural defenses against fatigue. Using strychnine to fight off diseases makes perfect sense. That is the science of it, in any case."

Di Verde continued. "My respect for Rodolfi's work is boundless. But we differ on a crucial point. The esteemed doctor focused on treating patients already afflicted with cholera. In my view, the time for intervening with the serum is before the disease takes hold, not after! Therefore, I propose to use the serum on healthy subjects, as a preventative measure, not as a palliative for existing illness. With the dosage already injected, on guard like a sentry inside the body, the cholera will be stopped before it begins!

"From my observations and study, my belief is that pure strychnine, blended with lesser parts of quinine and hydrochloric acid and mixed with clear rainwater, shows

53

incredible promise. The combination is, in fact, the basis for the propriety formula I have developed as my serum.

"But what dosage will work for all? Here is how I will arrive at the answer. In my experiments, I will administer a different dose to each subject in increasingly stronger amounts—seven trial dosage levels in all, ranging from mild to intense. The subjects will all be perfectly healthy, providing a common starting point. When the cholera strikes, I will then observe which dosage succeeds in defeating the disease!"

A voice rose from the audience. "And if the cholera does not strike?"

"If the epidemic does not materialize, then I will simply inject the blood of cholera victims into each healthy subject, thereby guaranteeing the confrontation between cure and disease!" he replied.

The men in the room absorbed this information approvingly. Nothing would be worse than a cash outlay entirely dependent on chance infections.

Di Verde waited for the murmuring to fade. "Thus, signori, as I say, my work requires seven subjects." He scanned the room with a slight smile. "From among your laborers, of course, not one of you!" The witticism prompted a round of merry tut-tutting.

"I am proposing nothing less than the formation of a medical corporation to develop and market my cholera cure. To this end, I am offering two hundred and fifty shares at five hundred lire per share. My uncle has already purchased one hundred shares, the rest I make available, first come, first served, to you in this room. And, I might add, each healthy subject that an employer provides is worth two additional shares."

Time to put the bow on the package, he thought.

"Gentlemen, I invite you, become my partners in finding cholera's cure. What a day it will be when science makes that leap! How the hospitals, apothecaries, and physicians of the world will flock to our discovery! Of course, there are risks, financial and otherwise. And I want to be clear, there are no guarantees. A certain attrition is always the price of progress, and always shall be.

"But do you not risk more by doing nothing, watching cholera sweep lives away like chaff from the barn floor? What is your level of loss if that happens? As Christian men of means, you face both great responsibility and wonderful opportunity at this moment in time.

"God willing, let us create the answer that will keep labor numbers at a surplus! Let us save mankind and claim the reward! If this crusade appeals to your heart as well as your good sense, I have brought contracts for purchasing shares. Thank you so much, signori, for your kind attention."

His listeners responded with strong applause and much conversation. Before any others, Gaetano Baldassare hastened forward. "Marchese d'Ambrosso will purchase thirty shares, and myself, personally, three more." He handed over a note, leaned to Di Verde's ear, and in a low voice added, "We will also provide all the subjects you need. Here, I will give you their names."

* * *

Dottore Ottavio Di Verde sat in the seat of his high-sprung landaulet gratefully enclosed from the worsening weather. His driver was not as well-off, perched as he was on the exposed leather seat from where he guided the red and black carriage's pair of draft horses.

Next to the doctor was squeezed a bespectacled medical student who had volunteered for the day through certain connections at Sapienza University in Milan. The young man's forehead leaned against his window. He clutched to his chest his small wooden lap-desk as he fitfully dozed through the journey. Besides direct assistance with each patient, the doctor needed a careful record kept of the day's proceedings. Twenty-one-year-old Mario Binelli was by all reports competent enough for those limited tasks.

The conveyance skirted the farmlands of the great d'Ambrosso estate on its way to the villa. The fields rolling alongside them were covered with the green stalks of early summer maize.

Di Verde looked at his pocket watch. No problem with the time; they had certainly set out early enough. He felt a certain perturbation as across the green fields he spied the roofs of the villa in the distance. On the one hand, he had been gratified by the warm reception he'd received from the landowners at the Sunday meeting that his uncle, the Senator, had hosted just four days earlier. On the other hand, the rapidity with which the project had gone from theory to this, its actual application, was unexpectedly disconcerting.

Di Verde had been pleased and surprised when the manager from the d'Ambrosso estate had approached him to immediately offer all seven of the workers needed for his experimentation, a single collection of subjects all in one place. It was, in fact, a windfall of sorts. The doctor had expected to gain his subjects from two or three different locations, which would present him with the logistical challenges as to where to provide treatment, where to observe them, and the whole follow-up question. The fact that he could inoculate the entire group at one time, in one place, was highly advantageous.

But. The physician stroked his chin. Baldassare was not the manager of an important estate because he was slow-witted. The wily boss knew that Di Verde was flush with the investment cash that many in his audience had so eagerly put down. There was sufficient money on hand for rewarding the experiment subjects, a legal nicety which Zio Testaforte had suggested. Baldassare drove a hard bargain: thirty-five lire in gold that the manager promised to split among the seven subjects plus two hundred to himself for arranging the affair. A bit expensive, but Di Verde was happy to settle the matter of experimental subjects there and then.

So, arrangements were made, the investments set, his subjects were waiting for him at this very moment. All this was good, Di Verde thought.

But a bit more time before proceeding would have been welcome. The truth was, Di Verde had never actually done any real inoculations using a syringe before, his inferences at his presentation notwithstanding.

It was true that years ago, fresh from his studies, Di Verde had accompanied Dottore Rodolfi on two visits to a reeking asylum to watch him administer his solutions to raving, shackled patients. And while he had not personally mixed the strychnine and water serum, he had watched the proceedings with keen interest and made notes in his journal, copying as unobtrusively as he could Rodolfi's own formulas. He asked if he could try inoculating some of the subjects himself, but the stubborn doctor was adamant that the procedure took some practice and that only he would apply the experimental dosages. Rather unbecoming, Di Verde thought, for a man of Rodolfi's stature to greedily hoard all the fame and glory.

It is not as if Rodolfi is some sort of lone genius, Di Verde thought. Certainly, his own medical education and subsequent experience gave him a strong background in handling a wide range of cases. While the Collegio del Po al Lago di Garda, despite its elaborate name, was not exactly among Europe's finest—its five physician-owners operated the school as a side business—the curriculum did cover the basics. Whether it was inducing the sweats, applying robust enemas, or administering diuretics to restore the body's natural equilibrium, Di Verde felt quite skilled at them all. Moreover, he had learned how to examine a patient's eyes, tongue, urine, and feces to enable proper prescriptions of anti-inflammation creams, herbal pills, and other tradition-tested restoratives.

He also received high marks for his vesiculation technique employing Carlisle's innovation of a heated iron rod. The device was used to severely blister patches of a patient's skin, thereby draining off the various ferrous humours known to produce hysteria, gout, certain high fevers, and melancholia. The procedure was not for the timid-hearted, but he excelled at it. It was upon such ministrations that Di Verde had, up to now, been making a steady, albeit unspectacular, living.

Senator Giovanni Testaforte, who underwrote his nephew's medical education, had heard of Dottore Rodolfi's experiments from friends while dining at l'Athenceum, the senator's private club in Milan. Di Verde happened to arrive on a visit to his uncle soon after and, upon Testaforte's inquiries, had rather absently recounted his own observations of the physician's work from nearly a decade before.

Like a hound on a scent, Senator Testaforte showed a keen interest. Emboldened by his uncle's attention and a second, then a third, glass of claret, Di Verde had grandly expounded on his own embryonic theories—to the extent he could remember them from so long ago—as to how he could improve Rodolfi's approach if he ever was given the chance.

The senator had immediately seen the enormous windfall that discovering the cure for cholera would produce and set up the prior Sunday's meeting forthwith.

It had all happened so remarkably fast. Di Verde assumed he would have several months to ready himself, to review his old notes, those he could find, and perfect his rusty techniques. He did have the chance to practice with the Pravaz syringe on small, trussed, screaming laboratory animals but thought several more sessions would have been helpful. And as far as the formula itself went, well, he had developed some derivatives of Rodolfi's originals, but again, his notes were perfunctory. He told his uncle to give him but six short months, and he would be fully prepared to proceed.

The senator would have none of it, telling him, "Cannot you see, Ottavio? We are in hot competition. Whoever first develops the medical answer to cholera will reap all the spoils. It means a fortune for whomever has the nerve to proceed without delay! Now is the time to line up our investors, now is the time to get experiments underway. It is not, however, the time for timidity. I presume, nephew, you have the *palle* that greatness demands. Am I correct?"

Di Verde nodded decisively, his honor challenged.

"Well then, what is holding us back?" Giovanni Testaforte concluded. "Now is the time to act! Let the great contest begin!"

The carriage slowed as it approached a crossroads where the d'Ambrosso manor loomed to the left. The boxy compartment that carried the two passengers rocked at the adjustment in speed.

"Doctor, the villa!" Binelli said suddenly, prying himself out of his slumber. Still grasping the portable desk, the medical student used his free hand to rub his eyes. The rain remained steady. "Such a brief trip that was, sir. What a magnificent day for science!"

* * *

A half-mile from where the carriage started to turn, the estate manager impatiently waited astride his mount. He tipped his head from time to time, sluicing water from his hat's wide brim past his boots in their stirrups.

Baldassare wanted to finish this entire matter. Como, the Vacci girl, the brother, that wicked old priest—all of it boiled his blood past bearing. No longer would he appear impotent, he resolved. His position as manager depended on absolute authority, but that authority had eroded of late. Como cheating him of profit from those rocks, the woman rejecting his advances, her brother's brazen defiance, the exchange on the church steps, the meddling cleric and his machinations—all of it undermined him. When he gave a worker a command these days, he was not seeing the requisite fear. In fact, he suspected their blank faces masked a private joke at his expense.

Even the marchese seemed cooler to him these days. At the Testaforte meeting, when Baldassare returned to d'Ambrosso's table to recommend they provide all the inoculation subjects the doctor needed—having already made the deal with Di Verde—the nobleman had not immediately responded with his customary yes. This was unusual.

The hesitation caught Baldassare off-guard, and he became briefly concerned he may have to renege on the arrangements with the doctor. He took a different tack. "Don Federico, I certainly understand if you have misgivings about this venture. Not everyone can stomach such risk. To put money on the table for an enterprise of this magnitude," Baldassare shook his head, "is an enormous roll of the dice." He looked to where the physician was conversing with several landowners. "I do see that Count Ruggero seems up for the game."

D'Ambrosso, who prided himself as an ice-blooded predator at the gambling tables, stirred. He had gone up against the count before many times; it was to that smirking ass he had so recently lost two thousand lire.

"I know what you are doing, Baldassare," he said. The marchese sighed. "And it is working. Whatever Ruggero has staked to the doctor, surpass it." Baldassare stood and bowed his head in obedience. Thus, he gained permission for the deal already in place.

As for the doctor's grand plan, Baldassare did not know much medicine beyond the usual basic techniques for injuries he or his workers might sustain on the job. Most of the medicos he had encountered struck him as quacks—even this Di Verde, despite his silver tongue.

Would the experiments work? Who knew? The manager did know one thing. When he wanted vermin or wild dogs killed on the estate, his people baited their traps with meat laced with strychnine. Any notion that a substance so capable of killing was also capable of healing was, to Baldassare, patently absurd.

And he knew the doctor's mention of risks meant that the great march to medical glory Di Verde was pitching was more likely to be a random stab in the dark. One where *fortuna*, not science at all, might make all the difference.

Gaetano had seen the big hypodermic syringe the doctor had so ostentatiously flashed during his presentation, then later up close in its open box on the table. The device, with its long needle, cold metal cylinder, and threaded plunger, looked like an instrument of medieval torture to him. When the rest of the estate's laborers saw that he, Baldassare, had the power to inflict such terror upon these seven workers—and by extension them all—their dread of his wrath would become greater than ever.

Ultimately it was irrelevant to him whether the inoculations worked or not. What mattered was that they be as ghastly painful as possible, a clear demonstration of his control. If the experiments did produce protection from cholera, then good, the serum would make money for the estate. But if no cure resulted, it did not matter to Baldassare. And if, ideally, the injections brought illness, debility, or worse to the subjects, it would prove that crossing the estate manager came with a price.

Carlo Como, that *cazzo*, was beyond his direct reach. But by tomorrow the upstart fishmonger would know that Baldassare had violated his betrothed with that horrible needle just as foully as if he had slipped her his cock. And the meddlesome Padre Umberto? Baldassare scoffed. I will go to confession and pour out my sins afterward, he thought. And laugh in the old fraud's face through the confessional screen.

Baldassare had told the Vaccis to make themselves available after dinner. Tonia was to stay home from the silk factory entirely; Ettore was to report at the first sound of the signal bell. Achille and Gherardo, his laziest workers, would join them, along with white-haired Renata, the scullery maid, so much less efficient since her husband had died.

For their troubles, each of the subjects was to receive one lira. Baldassare chose not to mention the rest provided by the doctor. He would add that amount to his own two hundred as a well-deserved bonus.

The clopping of hooves and the grind of iron-edged wheels broke his concentration. Baldassare rode forward to confirm the doctor's arrival.

The bell on the servants' residence sounded, the signal for the subjects to gather. They knew to meet at the small stone farmhouse an adjacent field away.

Chapter 9

With a muffled *clunk!* Ettore's shovel struck the rubble under his boots, the brick bits the builders had broken to allow for faster drainage. A hanging lantern sputtered pale light from a stake driven into the side of the cistern. His and Muto's stretch of nine twelve-hour days had finally cleared the pit to its original dimensions. It was close to empty; where he stood, waste now only topped his calves. With any luck, tomorrow was their last day on the project.

Ettore did not like the walls, did not trust them. He especially did not like them now, as he stood at the bottom. The heavy rain slanted down from the hole above. He blinked as spatters of filth ricocheted onto the heavy cloth wrapped over his mouth and nose. The rainwater rapidly coursed down the sides of the cesspit, deepening the channels between the spaces and ridges of the uneven bricks.

Tomorrow it would be a matter of dragging the privy building back over the hole, and Ettore had already devised a scheme using logs as runners. He and Muto would slide them under the structure, then with the help of their ox they would pull it back into place.

As for now, Ettore must get to the old farmhouse, a bit of a hike. Baldassare had told him he was to be there when the bell began to ring. He already was late, for even at the bottom of the old cistern he heard the insistent clanging.

"Go up to the quarters," he said aloud to Muto, when he was back at the top. He pointed to Muto, and then to the servants' residence. He took off his gloves. "Eat." He pretended to scoop food in his mouth. The rain streaked caked filth down his clothes. "I need to go there." He pointed in the opposite direction, toward the isolated farmhouse on the edge of the maize field.

Muto looked up into the heavy rain, into the cesspit, then nodded at Ettore. He walked over to a pile of boards, dragged one out of the mud and laid it across the opening. Ettore saw what he meant and helped until they had loosely crisscrossed the black hole with slats. Then they pulled a canvas tarpaulin over the boards until it hung in a loose, saggy fashion. Good enough to prevent too much water from collecting, Ettore judged. They anchored the edges of the canvas to the ground with other random debris lying nearby.

There was more cleaning up to do, Ettore knew, tools to take back to their sheds, the ox and its wagon to get under cover. But he had to go. Muto saw his distress and slapped Ettore on his chest to tell him it was all right. He pantomimed that he would finish what needed doing, then pointed at the servants' quarters and himself.

Ettore nodded his thanks. He set out across the latrine field, past the residence. Through the murk, and still at a distance, he saw where a light shone, marking the fieldstone farmhouse. An unknown carriage stood outside.

* * *

Baldassare had ordered the abandoned farmhouse prepared for the doctor's use as an infirmary. The floor plan was simple: one large room with a dirt floor and a cold, blackened hearth built into one corner.

Yellowed curtains on metal pipe frames screened off the corner of the room opposite the hearth. Within the enclosure a cot waited for its first subject, and a table held Di Verde's equipment. This was where the inoculations would happen. In the rest of the room, seven more cots rousted from storage formed a row along the same wall. Next to each was a chair bearing a card with a different large letter on it, ranging from 'A' through 'G'. These were to be pinned on each patient.

A table and a chair were also there for use by Scotti, the coachman. He sat there now, arms akimbo. In front of him was a sheet of paper with the same seven letters written on it with corresponding names, a dip-pen, a pocket watch, and an inkstand. His job was to check off the letter identifying each patient after their inoculation and the time. Scotti was no scholar, but he knew the order of the alphabet. Then again, the former Piedmontese soldier was primarily there to assure the subjects' full cooperation. At that task he was an expert.

Di Verde measured two hundred milliliters of the fresh rainwater collected by Binelli into a large beaker. He carefully mixed in eight grains of strychnine, then added another four, a bolder blend than Rodolfi's formula by half. He added quinine and other amendments, including a half-dozen drops of hydrochloric acid. This last inspired ingredient was based on strychnine experiments a British army surgeon named Poole had conducted on native troops in India. Di Verde had read of the matter in a medical gazette, and despite Poole's inconsistent results, he considered the man's underlying logic to be sound.

Making the formula more robust than had ever been attempted before was the appropriate strategy, Di Verde was certain. Rodolfi's cholera patients had been too weak from the illness to employ the strychnine in their systems to their advantage. Healthy bodies ought to easily absorb a much stronger solution. Regarding negative effects, Di Verde did not anticipate a problem.

He swirled the combination until well-blended. Then, with Binelli's assistance, the doctor used a tin funnel to pour the concoction into the syringe.

The plan was for subjects to wait at their cots until called. Each would then go into the inoculation enclosure. Di Verde would insert the hypodermic needle into the subject's jugular—one of the body's major and easiest-accessed veins—and screw the dosage into their bloodstream via the threaded plunger. Binelli was to assist by strapping down the patients prior to injection and otherwise subduing any subsequent thrashing. Afterward, subjects would return to their own cots. Once Doctor Di Verde examined each again, they would be free to return to their tasks, barring complications.

Di Verde planned to inject each subject with the exact same formula, but in progressively larger doses. Thus, subject 'A' would receive a half-rotation of the screw, subject 'B' one full rotation and so forth. Subject 'G', Ettore, was due the largest dose, three-and-a-half turns of the plunger.

Inside the larger room, Tonia waited at the cot to the right of her father's. Manager Baldassare had the floor, explaining how privileged they were to have this medical treatment conducted by an expert.

The next cot over, last in the line, was empty. Ettore is late, she thought. She knew of her brother's confrontation with Baldassare in the stable. Though the manager had left her alone since then, she remained constantly apprehensive. And now they were in this place, the only entire family to have been so commanded. To take part in something unpleasant, she realized, hearing the estate manager speak.

"Thus," Baldassare concluded, "you have the honor of receiving the services of Dottore Ottavio di Verde. I insist you give him your full cooperation."

The doctor took center stage, "My friends," he said to the cowed group seated on the edges of their cots. "The inoculation I administer to you today will save you from the cholera, and God willing, save many others in the future."

A loud noise interrupted him as Ettore stamped his boots at the door. "I am sorry to be late," he said to the doctor. "The rain slowed my work."

The rain, however, had not fully washed away the foul effects of Ettore's day at his job. Everyone in the room recoiled from his sight and smell, including his family. Water streamed off his filth-spattered cloak, pantaloons, and hat, creating a brown puddle at his feet.

Di Verde, aghast, intervened. "Such uncleanliness is unacceptable. If you are here as a subject for these proceedings, your repugnant condition renders you unfit. You must exit immediately. Come back cleansed!"

"Return quickly or face problems," said Baldassare. Ettore headed past him to hike all the way back to the servants' quarters.

Baldassare watched Tonia's brother depart into the gloomy deluge. He remembered the drain ditches by the mulberry groves and the irrigation canal farther out. Sudden, destructive flooding was always an issue during hard storms like this one. It warranted a look.

Everything here is set in motion, best to not be too close to these events, he thought. As much as he wanted to savor the suffering of Tonia Vacci, and through her, Carlo Como's, it was smarter to attend to his other duties this dangerous evening.

Di Verde noted the manager leaving. No matter, we must start, he thought. He said to the six men and women waiting, "We begin with Subject 'A'."

Scotti gestured to Achille, who tentatively came forward into the inoculation partition. A good subject to begin with, the doctor thought. Not very intelligent-looking and, as a man, unlikely to allow himself displays of fear.

Binelli secured Achille with three restraints. One belt went across his chest, pinning down both arms, one did the same for the ankles. He tightened the third across the worker's forehead, saying, "For your safety only. It is important you are as still as possible during the procedure."

"Open wide," Di Verde directed, then put a final leather strap between Achille's teeth. "Bite down, should you feel any discomfort." Achille's eyes became slits. "Please relax now, signore," Di Verde directed. Binelli stood at the head of the cot, prepared to intervene as needed. The doctor found the jugular vein easily with one hand, then from under a towel brought the syringe forward and impaled his subject with its needle. Achille clamped his jaws on the strap and squirmed to escape. Binelli held his shoulders tight.

Di Verde screwed the plunger until he reached a half-revolution. He found the screw turned easily, almost too much so. He plucked the needle straight out. Binelli undid the belts and escorted the stunned patient, clutching a cloth pad at his bleeding neck, back to his cot. Di Verde wiped off the needle with a cotton pad. Enough serum remained in the hypodermic for several more injections before he would need to refill.

Di Verde and his assistant worked through the subjects one by one. As he proceeded, the doctor found that calibrating the dosage was trickier than he expected. The extended squirming of the subjects as the needle stayed in longer did not help matters. He tried proceeding slower, but that only increased the subject's struggles. He noted to Binelli with some exasperation, "Next time we must be able to control the dosages more exactly. The device, I think, is not working exactly as designed."

After three inoculations, he paused to refill the syringe. He took a moment to allow his assistant to record the doses of subjects they had finished with thus far. Both he and Binelli were sweating despite the stormy coolness outside. The doctor's hands were damp with perspiration, and he wiped his palms often on the front of his white medical coat.

In general, the subjects so far had kept docile. Certainly, they had twisted in pain and bit into their leather strap, but who wouldn't do that? The awe they held for the doctor and his medical trappings—he wore his needless stethoscope over his white apron for that very effect—deterred anyone from making a scene. They also feared Baldassare would dismiss them from the estate if they dared to balk.

Di Verde looked from behind the curtains to the larger room before he resumed. Already inoculated, subjects 'A', 'B', and 'C', the first woman, were lying on their cots, all in some state of restlessness. Nothing alarming.

Four remained. The wife and her husband, subjects 'D' and 'E' and their daughter, 'F'. The last one in the row, the cesspit man, thankfully cleaned up now, wore letter 'G'.

The old man and woman each took twenty minutes. Di Verde continued to have difficulty applying the intended dosage. The data he periodically told Binelli to transcribe became more estimated than precise. Close enough, he thought, after he finished the limping male servant. I can only do what I can do with this equipment! Exactness was not really that important in any event, the doctor reasoned, as long as he gave each patient a higher dose than the one prior. He could finesse the numbers in the notebook later, once things calmed down.

Di Verde became anxious to finish. The pain he inflicted on the patients was very unpleasant for him, even knowing the suffering subjects would receive ample compensation. Nonetheless, doing so many at one sitting was exhausting, and he longed for a break from the tension. He wiped the perspiration from his eyebrows. "Next, Binelli," he told his assistant.

Subject F: Healthy female, age early twenties, Binelli wrote in his notes, then helped Tonia onto the cot and strapped her arms, legs, and head. She complied without a word, anxious to get the ordeal done with.

"Now, young lady, please remain relaxed," Di Verde said. Binelli stood behind her and held her head. Tonia closed her eyes, breathing fast, fearful.

"I will do this very quickly, to mitigate your discomfort." Di Verde hastily advanced the syringe toward her neck, but the instrument slipped in his clammy grasp and missed the jugular. The needle skittered until striking the jawbone, then snapped off. Tonia gagged on the leather bit, twisted her head hard sideways beneath the strap across her forehead. The doctor, aghast, dropped the syringe onto the floor.

"Now, now. Now, now," Di Verde repeated. Her neck bled where the broken needle-end protruded. Tonia gagged and yanked at her arm straps. "Let me extract that, let me extract that," Di Verde said, fumbling for tweezers.

At the same moment, Scotti frantically drew back the curtains. "Doctor," he cried, "you are needed out here!"

"Can you not see, that is impossible!" Di Verde retorted in a falsetto shout. He looked through the curtains. What he saw made his hair stand on end.

All the inoculated patients were violently convulsing. The subjects were in various stages of seizures that rendered them helpless. Their increasingly loud, garbled screams created a hellish din. Both Vaccis, who had received the strongest solutions thus far, contorted grotesquely, chests heaving, backbones furiously arching, arms jerking spasmodically.

At the end of the row of beds, Ettore, though not yet inoculated, stood frozen, unable to act. The shock of suddenly seeing both parents in the grip of uncontrollable seizures had made his mind simply stop.

Ottavio Di Verde was close to the same mental state. He rushed into the larger room, back behind the curtain, back into the room, fluttering his hands at his sides as he moved. Then, grabbing his coat, he fled out the door. Scotti knocked over the inkstand as he immediately followed.

Binelli adjusted his spectacles. His steady voice helped calm Tonia somewhat. He could see the blood-slippery end of the needle, perhaps a half-inch, extending from under her jaw. The medical student knew his fingers would slip; Di Verde had carried the tweezers away.

"Please do not be alarmed, signorina." He leaned over the woman. He held her head as he pulled the forehead strap as tightly as he could. It bit into the skin, locking her head rigid, tilted back. He lowered his mouth to Tonia's neckline, clutched the needle with his teeth and in one swift movement snatched it out. Tonia lost consciousness.

Binelli spit out the shard of needle and rinsed blood from his mouth and face. After bandaging both the wound on Tonia's neck and the angry red strap-welts on her forehead and wrists, he carried her to her cot. The nightmarish chaos at the beds was reaching a crescendo. He looked out the door, the carriage was gone! Could Di Verde have left him to face this disaster alone? Time was essential. Ettore was the only other person in the room not a patient. Binelli slapped Vacci's face, grabbed both his arms. "Get help, now!" he commanded.

The sharp sting broke Ettore from his shock. "Yes," he said. "Yes!" He rushed into the wet evening. The lights of the servants' residence drew him. Thank God, he thought, as he saw

Muto still there, under an extending roof, his rucksack on his back, finishing a pipe of tobacco before his long hike home. Ettore ran to him, feet slipping in puddles, and grabbed the front of his jacket. "Help me, Muto, help me!" he shouted.

Muto read Ettore's desperation, looked to the farmhouse, small at the edge of the field, tore from the boy, and ran to it.

Ettore slogged in the opposite direction, around the back of the stables, and down the road to the church. He pounded at the rectory door.

"Padre, Padre, you must come to the villa," he cried when Umberto answered. "Something terrible is happening at the old farmhouse. My parents, Tonia, they are dying!"

The priest pulled on his cloak and black flat-brimmed hat, considered Agnes the mule for a moment. He would be faster on foot. "Where exactly is this?" he asked.

"That old stone farmhouse, you know it," Ettore said. "On the far side of the road near the great garden. Where the Zuccheros once lived. I cannot go with you, I must tell Carlo."

Umberto called to Padre Giancarlo. They hiked their cossacks above their ankles and hastened into the storm.

Chapter 10

"What do you mean, 'afflicted'?" Carlo asked, stepping from his boat. Despite the rainstorm, he had been on the river checking fish traps when he heard Ettore calling.

"Sick, Carlo, maybe dying, everyone," said Ettore. "They look possessed by the devil! It was after a doctor with a, a...device." He did not know the word. "A metal cylinder with a long needle. He stuck it into people. After he did, my father and mother both, and the others..." He swallowed his sob. No time to become unmanned. "Tonia was bleeding and screaming!"

Carlo had no idea what Ettore was saying. A doctor? A device? "How did this come about?" he asked, as he threw a canvas cover over the grounded battello.

"Baldassare commanded us there," said Ettore. "After I arrived, the others told me the doctor was providing free medicine. Only seven people, my family and three others."

"Baldassare did this?" Carlo was already up the slippery embankment. "I will go up there," he said. "You get my mother."

The priests arrived at the farmhouse sodden and out of breath. The victims remained gripped by spastic delirium. Beds shook and scraped with their savage gyrations. A doctor, Umberto surmised, and the man known as il Muto were tying patients into their shaking cots.

"Padre Giancarlo, please begin to administer last rights," Umberto told his assistant, who stood momentarily stunned by the terrible scene. He addressed the white-coated attendant. "What can be done?"

"I do not know," said Binelli, clearly at his wits' end. They moved aside, back into the inoculation area. "Padre, I am a first-year medical student with three months of schooling." He shook his head in distress. "These poor people!" He told Umberto all that had transpired.

"This Dottore Di Verde used strychnine in his solution? What unholy madness is that?"

"I do not know his dosage nor formula," Binelli answered. "He did not share such information; he kept it his secret. All I did here was collect rainwater in a beaker and keep the patients from panicking. It was all experimental, a possible cholera cure was all Dottore Di Verde told me. He talked like an expert, but even I could see how completely inept he was with his outdated syringe!"

Umberto looked to where Binelli pointed. The sight of the bloody syringe on the ground with its broken needle made him shudder.

"Where is this doctor?" asked Umberto, surveying the larger room. He noted the brick hearth built into the wall.

"He is gone!" Binelli cried bitterly. "He left as soon as the mayhem broke out! At first, I thought he had gone to the carriage for more supplies. Instead, the coward and his coachman drove off! Padre, I pray, help me. These people." He gestured despairingly at the suffering subjects in the throes of their torment. He wiped his forehead with his sleeve.

Umberto was silent for a moment. "I studied with a monk once, a Camillian, an order that tends to the sick. He was knowledgeable about medicinal herbs, and he understood poisons. If I recall, the only substance that may alleviate strychnine symptoms is carbon."

Binelli looked blank. "Carbon? Coal? How does that help us?"

Umberto pointed at the blackened rock hearth. "Find something to scrape with."

* * *

The farmhouse had quieted somewhat by the time Ettore arrived with Lucrezia Como.

Ettore saw immediately his parents were dead, frozen in grotesque arch-backed spasms. He went to their side and, weeping, tried to force their bodies into some sort of repose, but could not. Padre Umberto stood near, performing the sacramental ritual of Extreme Unction.

Gherardo lay sideways on his mattress, lifeless, fixed in a stiff-legged, stiff-armed parody of death. Old Renata the maid was yet alive, tiring in her convulsions as Binelli tried to suppress her most vehement spasms. Achille sat, a propped-up corpse. A rictus twist marred his stone-white face, the letter 'A' still pinned to his tunic.

Muto scraped char from the hearth's bricks onto a plate. Padre Giancarlo circulated from one bed to another, administering last rites.

Lucrezia tried to feed Tonia black brick-scrapings with a spoon. Ettore sat near, holding her hand. The young woman was exceedingly pale; her carbon-smudged lips provided stark contrast. She had a bandage around her neck.

"Tonia," Ettore said. Her eyes slightly opened. He could tell she saw him. At least she had not convulsed like the others.

Binelli approached. "Your sister will live. The needle broke off in her neck, which saved her. None of the serum got into her system, as far as I can ascertain. She showed no symptoms afterward, like the others. The wound on her neck is severe but will heal in time. I will observe her carefully, but I am hopeful."

Ettore swore Baldassare would pay. He knew another who felt the same. Together they must act. "I need Carlo," he told Umberto, to the side. "Where is he?"

The priest looked at Ettore, saw the rage, the murderous intent. He answered, "When Carlo arrived and saw Tonia and her parents, he asked where Baldassare was. No one knew. This young doctor," motioning at Binelli, "told him the manager departed when the injections started. Then, Carlo left." He saw Ettore register the news, lean toward the door. He put his hand on Ettore's chest.

"Ettore, events are in motion that heaven has put into play. Do not look for Carlo."

Chapter 11

Night fully arrived. The driving rain made the mud of the latrine yard even more slippery. Great ponds of water were building up at the bases of the privies that Ettore and Muto had not yet dug out.

Baldassare dismounted his steaming horse in the dark stables and lit a hanging oil lamp. He wore a hat with a drooping brim bent under his hood. His waterproofed slicker reached to his tall leather riding boots, his trousers tucked into their tops. His inspection along the irrigation canals had taken hours. The downpour was forcing overflowed banks in at least six locations. Tomorrow would be a day of supervising crews to dig and repair, assuming the storm let up at all. The estate manager greatly wanted to know how matters stood at the stone farmhouse but decided to keep his distance until morning. The die was cast. Whatever would be would be.

A voice called behind him. "Baldassare!"

He turned at his name without thinking. Carlo's shovel hit him between the eyes with a loud *pop!* that sent his hat flying. Blood sprayed from his flattened nose.

The manager staggered, fell to one knee, lifted his hand over his head. "Wait, wait," he said.

Carlo drove away the hand and the arm. He swung the shovel up and down. It struck Baldassare's head with a metallic *pong!* that reverberated up the shaft to Carlo's taut forearms. Baldassare went down on all fours, the top of his skull now oddly flatter than it had originally been, his heavily gushing nose bent sideways toward his cheekbone.

Carlo circled to get in front of the manager again with his back to the stable door and the storm. Baldassare coiled, then desperately launched himself into Carlo's knees, forcing him off balance. Caught by surprise, the attack drove Carlo down hard onto his back with a heavy, dust-and-straw-stirring *whump!* Baldassare took advantage of the reprieve to stagger to his feet and stumble half-blind out into the rain.

The ground was a morass and the mud sucked at Baldassare's boots. The cold rain cleared his head somewhat. Adrenaline blocked the pain for the moment. He threw a look over his shoulder. In the dark he could see the silhouette of Carlo in the frame of the stable door, closing the distance between them.

The panic-struck manager struggled forward. Blood streamed down his face from the gash on his skull, impairing his vision. In front of him was the dark bulk of some structure—one of the privies? He made for the refuge, not far to go. Perhaps inside he could take a stand. The tight space would hamper Carlo's swinging shovel. Baldassare dared another look behind.

As he did, his foot stepped on the tarpaulin over the loose boards covering the dug-out cesspit. His head hit the tripod still in place over the hole. Days of rain had soddened the half-rotted wood under his feet. Now, with the weight of a man wearing drenched clothing and boots caked in mud, the weak planks gave way with a single loud *crack!* The canvas tarpaulin enshrouded Baldassare as he plunged into the hole. The tripod, breaking up, followed.

One minute, Carlo could see the manager's dark shape. The next moment it simply disappeared. He stopped in his tracks, wiping his eyes. All he could make out was a large privy structure, perhaps twenty paces away.

"*Managgia*," he swore. Where did the bastard go? He hurried forward as best he could but skidded to a stop after a dozen feet. Was that a voice?

Carlo realized with a jolt that he stood within two feet of a gaping black hole. It must be the cesspit Ettore had told him about. From its depths, came a muffled voice, "Mercy, Como. Mercy, I beg."

Carlo got on all fours and peered into the pit. Its brickwork lip was flush with the mud. A wind was up, rain sheeted sideways. As he leaned forward with his hands on one of the bricks, he felt it sink under his pressure. He pulled back his weight quickly. The brick fell away. Another one dislodged and crashed below.

"Mercy!" The voice was louder this time, panicky. "Mercy!"

What to do? Carlo thought for a moment. He got back to his feet and picked up the shovel he had left on the ground. He cupped his hands and called into the abyss.

"Baldassare!" The cries below stopped. "My mercy is this, Baldassare! *Vaffanculo!*"

He walked the circle of the dark hole, using the shovel to dislodge more bricks at the edge. It took little to start the cascade. Already compromised, once debris began falling, momentum and gravity did the rest. Within moments, the cesspit's rotted masonry began to collapse, pulling with it the soil it had been restraining. Carlo had to quickly jump back to not get sucked in himself. He heard no further cries.

Carlo looked around. Who had seen? As far as he could tell nobody was out. The windows of the servants' quarters were shuttered against the storm.

He approached the pit again with caution. He staggered his feet for balance, left foot ahead of the right, and inclining his upper body, slowly bent his chest over his front knee. Where before the hole had been totally black, seemingly without bottom, now it was crowded halfway up with rubble and muck. Waterfalls of muddy runoff cascaded into the depression.

Carlo retreated to the barn, trying to think through a plan. His hands shook from the shock of his actions, but he willed himself under control. He was cold and on edge but felt no remorse. Now he needed to sort this all out in a way that allowed him to continue his life with Tonia. If she lived.

The cave-in at the cesspit could easily have been caused by the rains, he calculated. Spontaneous sinkholes and structural failures of tired, old edifices and wells were a regular occurrence both at the villa and in Castrubello. But the disappearance of the manager?

Nearby, Baldassare's saddled horse nickered. Carlo scooped up the manager's misshapen hat from the ground. He put the shovel back where he found it, first wiping it clean in the hay a few times. He kicked at the straw where he had struck Baldassare until the blood was no longer visible, then used a rag soaked in rainwater to mop up anywhere else that showed signs of the assault.

With a start, he spotted his red cornicello pendant and its broken cord lying atop the floorboards. He retrieved the talisman and with a kiss placed it in his pocket. *Fortuna* had taken his side this past violent hour, and he was grateful.

Carlo gave the scene a second thorough look. He walked over to the wall where blacksmith tools hung from pegs on the wall. He took down a heavy ball-peen hammer. Then, with Baldassare's hat pinned under his arm, he led the horse out the stable door and into the rain.

Chapter 12

September 1882: Castrubello

The long tables arrayed in Casa Como's small courtyard were filling with guests. Terracotta pots held riots of yellow wildflowers; garlands of ivy hung eve to eve from the casa's windowsills. Carlo, in a borrowed suit, stiff collar and shirt, and new black fedora, greeted the neighbors, accepting warm wishes of *"auguri, auguri."* His father Lorenzo, shaking hands and touching cheeks, was at his side. Carlo's brother Francesco managed the wine casks, while their sister and mother basted a small pig over an open fire pit, with children assisting.

The pig was the gift of the marchese. After the events at the farmhouse three months before, d'Ambrosso had acted with generosity. Besides today's feast, he had paid for the burials of the five poor victims—the maid Renata had succumbed the following morning—and provided for Tonia's immediate care.

Gaetano Baldassare's funeral had been more extravagant. The marchese was a man who appreciated courage in others. How tragically heroic that his manager died galloping to the aid of his suffering workers! The task of hauling the dead beast and Baldassare's remains out of the collapsed cesspit had taken two days. The funeral Mass quickly followed, given the unfortunate condition of the corpse. A work crew had since refilled the unstable cesspit with dirt and debris.

D'Ambrosso was truly shocked by the medical disaster that had happened on his property. He did not deserve it! All he had done was try to facilitate the advance of medical science! Upon learning of the tragedy's extent, the nobleman immediately sought to fix legal blame. Absolutely, justice demanded accountability, he declared. The marchese's friend, Senator Testaforte, appointed a tribunal of three prominent physicians, personally vouched for by the senator, to examine what exactly had gone wrong. Within a spectacularly brief time, the board reached its unanimous conclusion. The debacle was entirely due to the incompetence of the medical student, Mario Binelli.

Based on the testimony of Dottore Ottavio Di Verde, newly-named professor at the Collegio del Po al Lago di Garda, it was Binelli who had mixed the serum incorrectly, who had allowed patients to gyrate during the inoculations, and as the emergency unfolded, who had descended into hysterics. When Dottore Di Verde then departed to gather more medical supplies, only to be prevented from returning by the impossible storm, Binelli was too panic-stricken to follow the simple instructions the doctor had given him. A second witness, the coachman Scotti, corroborated these facts.

The medical student, denied legal representation, disputed every charge, to no avail. The notebook he tried to present was dismissed as an irrelevant distraction, then confiscated.

Despite Padre Umberto's persistent offers to testify, the tribunal called no further witnesses. Instead, it presented the culprit a choice. He could resist the decision and face prosecution for five counts of accidental murder but, he must understand, his conviction and lengthy incarceration—perhaps execution, even—was certain! Or, he could permanently remove himself to the flyblown port of Assab, in Eritrea, Italia's new colonial foothold on the Horn of Africa. Assab had a nascent hospital; perhaps Binelli could be of some use. If the student chose this option, the review board would be inclined to grant Binelli a provisional medical license—good for colonial service only—after a year. The tribunal would then quietly file its findings without publication, and the entire distressing affair at the farmhouse would be at an end. Binelli was aboard a supply ship to Assab four days later.

As for the looming cholera outbreak, it did not strike the region after all, praise be to God and the saints!

* * *

Carlo sat at the table alongside Tonia surveying the festivities. Deciding to marry so shortly after the death of her parents had been difficult. But Padre Umberto pronounced he would temporarily suspend the proscribed mourning period to allow for the ceremony. Carlo left the matter in Tonia's hands. She had told him, "I want us to marry now. Life is short, who can know what *fortuna* intends?"

Marchese d'Ambrosso, by tradition, had received an invitation to this 'coming out' reception of Carla and Tonia, held eight days after the actual wedding. But he instead visited his club in Milan for some much needed relaxation at the gaming tables. A windfall had come his way, after all. When a post-mortem inspection of Baldassare's rooms turned up two chests of coins behind a loose board in the wall, the marchese was duly amazed. How frugal his estate manager had been with his salary, how disciplined! And with no known heirs, the estate claimed the funds. One chest went to Milan with d'Ambrosso.

Carlo found himself distractedly remembering Baldassare's horse. He had intended laming the animal with a blow to the foreleg, then leaving it to limp near the pit, as if it had stumbled, throwing its rider. A shaky plan, he knew, all he could think to do at the moment. But when he swung the hammer to strike, the horse reared in alarm, pulling the reins free of Carlo's grasp. Its hind feet lost traction. As the unstable ground gave away, the chestnut pivoted in a terrified pirouette, front hooves flailing, rear legs twisting, its mane wildly whipping in the storm's wind. With a single, ungodly shriek, the beast tumbled backward. It fell with a sickening awkwardness across the mouth of the pit, the head and neck striking full force the far edge of the hole. Its bent spine snapped with the sound of a tree limb breaking off in the wind. The horse crumpled into the abyss, hoofs up. Mud and debris chased after. The earlier landside from Baldassare's fall had already partially filled the pit. The horse and rubble and sluicing rain did the rest.

Carlo felt worse about the death of the horse than he did about putting an end to Baldassare. Baldassare deserved to be killed. The *onore* of his family demanded it. If *fortuna* needed the horse as an added sacrifice, so be it. His hand touched the cornicello from his father.

He set his thoughts aside and turned to his new wife. "How are you liking all of this attention, *cara mia?*" he asked. Tonia sat next to him, her neck partially covered by a silk scarf. She had been enormously self-conscious as she had walked down the aisle to the altar the previous week. While the strychnine had never entered her veins, the ragged, deep impregnation of the needle had left a discolored scar on her throat. Damage had occurred to her voice as well.

"I am happy today," she said, despite her grief. Her voice sounded like a froggy croak to her ears.

Carlo kissed her on the lips. She was perfect. "Tonia, I am also happy. Tomorrow, we will go on the river. But not to fish!" He laughed, reading her thoughts. "We will drift downstream, and I will show you where I place the traps and the hooks. You can see what I do out there every day." He touched her near hand.

"Perhaps we can do that for a short while," she said, but he could tell she was pleased.

Music started to play. Four musicians gradually blended the sounds of their instruments—clarinet, tambourine, mandolin, flute—into a frisky *giga*. Guests gabbled in animated conversations, enjoying this rare opportunity to dine on the roasted meat Vito served up. The women in the cucina stepped away from their plates of polenta and vegetables and cheeses and took off their aprons. Lorenzo proudly showed some of the men his notable tomato and vegetable garden, describing each planting. Wisps of high clouds touched the afternoon sun as it journeyed across a sea-blue sky. The vino casks were open and flowing, laughter erupted in hearty bursts.

Ettore sat down with his sister and Carlo. He was gratified the bastard Baldassare was dead, and he suspected Carlo was why. His brother-in-law walked heavier these days. He seemed older, his quick, sarcastic comments more rare. Padre Umberto's absolute silence on the matter also said much. Ettore's respect for Carlo had risen further. And there is no doubting Carlo's commitment to my sister, he thought, which matters most.

Time to give them the news. "I have decided to leave," Ettore announced. "Our brother Gio wrote me, Tonia. He says that he has heard there are jobs digging roadbeds for new tramway lines in and around Milan. I may not know much," Ettore smiled as he looked at his calloused hands. "But I definitely know how to dig."

Tonia gasped at the news, grasped Ettore's hand. "You are leaving, Brother? Just like that? Why, Etto?" she exclaimed. The thought of losing her younger sibling so soon after the loss of their parents shook her. Carlo, also surprised, put his arm gently across her shoulders.

"Are you certain of this, Ettore?" he asked.

"It is time. I cannot go back to the d'Ambrosso estate. How do I spend the rest of my life there? God holds Mamma and Papà in his hands, now. You have a new husband, Tonia, and I hope many new mouths to soon feed!" Ettore laughed. "And, Carlo, I know you will provide for my sister and allow no harm to touch her." Their eyes met. Carlo looked away.

"As for myself, I intend to make my own life." Ettore twisted to view the music and his fellow Castrubellese, then turned back. "But, believe me, my heart remains here. Castrubello will always be past, present, and future for me!"

Part II: The Road
1886

Chapter 13

March 1886: Milan

The trolley's dray horse methodically clopped along the iron rails set flush with the pavement.

A decade earlier, the Belloli Company had built the tramway from Monza to Milan's Porta Venezia, just short of city center. It was the first trolley system Ettore had ever seen when he'd arrived in Milan. He quickly found work with Belladonna Costruttori, which was extending the line to the great Duomo's piazza. Since then, the cathedral's vast plaza had become the terminal for a number of tramlines, their iron rails now crisscrossing the square.

After four years in the city, Ettore had risen from doing the most menial tasks to crew chief. His latest work, a spur line from Monza to Loreto, had circled him back close to the project where he had first begun. The day the job ended, he decided to take the tramcar back into town. Ettore was not one for extravagances. Yet despite laying their roadbeds for years, he seldom used the trolleys, and never this first route where his roadbuilding career had started. With a few coins from his pay he bought himself a ticket.

His friends on the last project thought him crazy to spend money to sit placidly for ninety minutes traveling into the city. Much better their precious wages go for something more energetically happy, like a day of rambunctious drinking and chasing *le ragazze!* After failing to swing him their way, they bid him '*ciao!*' with good-natured teasing. Benito called, "Eh, Etto, you altar boy, maybe you'll meet a nice nun at the Duomo!" Which prompted Aldino to chime in. "Yes, just look for the convent of the Little Sisters of Pity!" Giving up on their friend, the comrades set out, hanging on each other's shoulders, laughing.

Ettore remembered the scene and smiled as he leaned against the metal railing on the tram's roof. He lit the end of his Toscano cheroot and drew in the harsh taste of fermented tobacco smoke. There were a few other passengers sitting on benches atop the coach. Below, inside, a stream of riders getting on and off rocked the vehicle with their shifting weight.

The side windows of the coach were open. A top-hatted driver handled the reins. His patient horse, though new to the route, kept up its steady pace. Private carriages and other trams on the track heading in the opposite direction clattered noisily.

Ettore enjoyed the novelty of watching the busy neighborhoods pass by from an elevated perspective. His day job involved looking down into the ground. This first project had entailed tearing up endless stretches of the existing pebble and granite slab roadway, then graveling a foundation for the new tracks. His shoulders had put on more muscle from hours of handling a pick and shovel; like the rest of the workers he was extraordinarily lean. But the strength he had developed over time belied appearances.

The workers rotated jobs every few days. One day they would be unloading hardwood crossties and lugging them onto the rail bed. The next, his crew would hump steel rails onto the ties to bind them with screw spikes. Other times, they pounded flat river pebbles into place to make walkable surfaces.

All of it hard labor, thought Ettore, but he found the work to his liking. He admired the engineers with their plotted angles and technical precision. He had also come to appreciate the difference that cohesive teamwork could make on such projects.

Until then, Ettore had never spent time with people from villages more than five miles from Castrubello. He found them strange in their expressions, beliefs, and gestures, but Ettore learned to accept their peculiarities. It helped greatly they were at least, thank God, all northern Italians!

The Italian kingdom tried breaking down regional prejudices through universal military conscription, deliberately combining men from alien parts of the country within its regiments. Ettore never served when his year had been called up. Marchese d'Ambrosso simply paid a hefty fee that exempted his estate's vital laborers.

But joining a diverse construction crew had given Ettore something of the same homogenizing experience, and he thrived. His steady demeanor caught the attention of his foreman, Primo Fusco. In time, they struck up a friendship. The veteran became a mentor to the eager country greenhorn. Older than Ettore by more than two decades, Fusco had become comfortable managing younger men, though more than he liked were headstrong and thoughtless. He told Ettore, "This job looks like it only takes muscle. But without brains, mistakes happen, and too many of those get you fired!"

Fusco shared other management insights. Most bosses at the time ruled by physical authoritarianism. But his view was that an effective chief achieved results, no matter how. His formula was to combine clear instructions, patience, and a willingness to crack heads if needed.

Ettore appreciated the advice. He had known workers in Castrubello who worked from before dawn to dark every day to provide for themselves and their families. His parents included, God rest their souls. And they were willing to take verbal harangues, physical abuse, and barbaric working conditions for the same reason.

It made Ettore wonder. If farmers and servants and washerwomen and mill workers endured so much when the only goal was surviving life's cycle of give and take, gain and loss, what could they achieve if they clearly saw a better future to work toward?

The trolley came upon the Basilica di San Babila on his right. The ancient church was set back from the thoroughfare, creating one of the busiest crossroads in Milan. Across the intersection began several long blocks of massive four-story buildings. Heavy stone balconies featured ornate balustrades with long canvas awnings draped over the railings. Slatted shutters, some open, some closed, bordered the windows of the upper apartments.

Zambetti Farmacia dominated the corner opposite the church. Thick classical columns fit for a palace supported its porticoes, creating deep shade for pedestrians. Advertisement broadsheets, political posters, and the front pages of local newspapers plastered the pillars.

Dozens of people bustled on the sidewalks and on the *strada* itself. Long-skirted women with bonnets and parasols, hard-faced men with places to go, vendors with pushcarts shouting their goods, horsepowered trolleys trundling on tracks, delivery wagons hauling bulging grain sacks, and carriages conveying nobility with scented handkerchiefs pressed to their noses all vied within the space between the rows of buildings.

The tram jolted as the driver suddenly levered the brake and pulled back on the reins. A woman in a maid's apron darted at the last minute across the tracks. Her skirt swirled up, showing black hosiery as she took long strides to safety. The men on the trolley whistled and called, but the young lady hastily disappeared into a hotel doorway.

As the dray horse resumed its plodding gait, the rose-tinged marble of the Duomo loomed ahead. A series of pinnacles with a stone saint atop each crowned its elegant roofline. Soaring above on the main central spire, the shining statue of *La Madonnina* stood triumphantly. Holding a lance, with a halo of stars, Our Lady of the Assumption marked the tallest point in the city.

The sight brought a pain to Ettore's chest. It was not that he was especially religious; the catcall of 'altar boy' had not hit any deep mark. The looming cathedral moved him deeply, nonetheless. His emotions sprang from realizing its grandeur was the product of human brains, labor, and persistence, motivated by shared faith. What great works were possible when people acted as one! Padre Umberto had inspired some of these thoughts years before. But what Ettore felt now was more than a shred of somebody else's observations. His was a visceral reaction that brought a glint to his eyes and told him something that he knew to be deeply true, but which he did not understand and struggled to articulate. Eh, Ettore, he told himself, you are a dreamer and altar boy both! Get back to earth!

The Duomo's piazza teemed with wheeled and pedestrian activity. The trolley halted in front of the magnificent Galleria Vittorio Emanuele II. Under its epic dome, assorted shops and restaurants did brisk business protected from the elements. The wondrous glass and iron structure gleamed with the optimism of a new nation determined to make its mark. Already a popular gathering place for both Italy's privileged class and its working citizens, the Galleria was known as the *Salotto di Milano*, Milan's Front Parlor.

As Ettore descended the metal stairs, he suddenly heard, "Vacci!" He looked around in consternation. Whoever could know his name here? An arm flashed up followed by the man to whom it belonged. It was the foreman, Fusco, at an outside table of a sidewalk café, not thirty feet away.

"Foreman Fusco," said Ettore, pulling off his cap. "*Buongiorno*, signore!"

"Ah, Etto, I cannot believe it! What a stroke of good fortune! Come here and meet someone." He waited as Ettore made his way to him.

"Put that hat back on, Etto, I am no *pezzo grosso*." Fusco slapped Ettore on the shoulder and propelled him closer. "And, please, your politeness is an embarrassment to both of us. I am not foreman here, and we are not on the job!"

Fusco gestured to his companion seated at their nearby table. "Etto, here is Maurizio Pezzoli, a junior engineer formerly of the Swiss firm, Ticino & Bellinzona. I have known his family for many years. Maurizio, permit me to present Ettore Vacci, one of my crew chiefs for several projects, including last year in Bruzzano."

The two men shook hands. Pezzoli stood six inches shorter than Ettore, with black hair above a narrow face. His drooped mustache covered the corners of his mouth. He was about Ettore's age, twenty-four or twenty-five, with eyes sharp and penetrating. "Pleased to meet you," each told the other, then seated themselves at the al fresco table.

"What will you have?" asked Fusco. "Espresso perhaps? Café Zucca serves the best in the city."

The café extended outward from a long-mirrored room, elegantly appointed with brass fixtures and white tablecloths. Slim waiters in white jackets with black slacks and bow ties wove deftly among the clientele. Stylish hats worn by the ladies bobbed among gentlemen in bespoke suits as they sipped dark house-brew from china demitasses.

In contrast, Ettore's jacket and trousers were clean but simple, his shirt buttoned to the neck without a collar, let alone a tie. He was mildly self-conscious about his appearance until he realized his two companions wore clothes like his own, and they were not alone. A shared passion for fine *caffè* seemed to have surmounted class barriers. Eh, Ettore thought, relax and enjoy it.

"Yes, espresso," he said. Fusco signaled a waiter, who after several slow minutes deigned to respond. Fusco ordered one for the newcomer and another for himself.

"Signor Pezzoli here—may I use Maurizio?" the foreman began. Maurizio nodded. "Maurizio has made me an interesting proposition, Etto," said Fusco, taking a biscotto from a stack of them on the table. "He's asked me to be lead foreman of an enterprise he is launching. I regretfully told him that I am unable to accept, committed as I am to another project. In suggesting others that he might approach, I included your name. And suddenly here you are, climbing down from a tramcar! But perhaps, Maurizio, you would care to explain the matter yourself."

Maurizio cleared his throat and looked directly at Ettore. "It is all very straightforward, signore," he said.

"Please, call me Ettore."

"Certainly. Ettore, I am forming my own construction company to build roads of the macadam design. The government is sinking enormous funds into transportation projects throughout all Italia. This creates numerous opportunities for anyone bold enough to seize them." He sipped his caffè. "Formerly private properties have come up for sale, which foreign investors are pouncing upon, and the government is appropriating land for access roads, railways, bridges, and the like. What we see here in Milan is but a chip of the teacup, as they say."

Ettore nodded. "Yes."

"Ticino & Bellinzona was too cumbersome for my taste. I told my superiors, more than once, to stop being cautious, to get going on new projects even before finishing current ones. It startled them witless to consider doing two things at once. Yet the competition kept snapping up lucrative contracts because we preferred to remain a ponderous elephant, plodding along, plodding along."

"You told your bosses this?" asked Ettore. He nodded to the waiter as he delivered his espresso. "You told your bosses to 'get going'?"

Pezzoli gestured abstractly with a biscotto. "Naturally, I did, why wouldn't I? If they took on more projects, they would need more chiefs, and I would not stay an assistant engineer forever! But those know-it-alls acted annoyed whenever I broached the subject. 'Focus on the job at hand!' they said." He took a bite of the biscotto, scattering crumbs. "But why should I stop saying what they needed to hear? So, when they told me to end my complaints, I told them, 'Go piss up a rope!'"

"Ah," said Ettore, looking at Fusco, whose gray eyebrows flicked up and down. "And now you are without a job."

"On the contrary, Ettore. I am now free to pursue my own contracts. I am forming my own company to do just that!"

Ettore considered what he had heard. Brash, cocky, ambitious. Greatly confident. He liked this Pezzoli. "What about funds?" he asked.

"Loans are everywhere. The Royal Bank of Milan has shown a strong interest in financing me. But first it requires I complete my organization. And find several additional backers," he added.

"One thing he must do is show them he has a crew and a foreman," interjected Fusco. "That is why he asked me here today, but, as I said, I cannot. I recommend you for the post."

"Only if I approve, Signor Fusco," Maurizio added starchily.

This conversation has taken an interesting turn, thought Ettore. Was he ready for such a change? Or was the idea of joining Pezzoli, who, although dynamic seemed a bit, what? Impulsive? Was throwing in with him a stupid idea? Yet how often did sudden destiny slap you in the face as you got off a trolley?

"I am honored to be considered," he answered without committing. "Tell me, Maurizio, how did you come to be an engineer?"

"My father owns a carriage factory in Turin. The business does well, but I have no interest in it. Besides, I have an older brother and would only end up in his employ. My father knew my feelings. When I showed an early aptitude for mathematics, he sent me to Turin's Technical School for Engineers. Where I thrived, incidentally.

"Papà supports my idea, has provided a modest loan to get things underway. I anticipate the Bank of Milan will provide the bulk of the financing if I can land a government contract in advance. Again, my father is of significant help. In fact, he has several additional investors in mind in Turin as soon as I have a project.

"He also does business with a widespread collection of government officials. Through him I already know who to approach for pending projects. And," his eyes narrowed, "those who may be open to persuasion." He rubbed his first two fingers with his thumb, knowingly.

"And what of you?" Pezzoli asked. "You ask a great many questions for the one who wants to be hired. Fusco respects your work. I have heard of the projects you have done, your reputation as a crew chief. What about that last point? What is your approach to managing your workers?"

"Most of what I know Foreman Fusco here taught me," Ettore responded. "The rest I learned the hard way, through trial and error. I believe, at times, a boss must of course be tough. Some workers are lazy or careless. Such louts take constant supervision. But most others are fully capable without somebody always looking over their shoulder. I have learned to begin by treating men with respect, as if they already are what they should be. I have seen many good men rise to high expectations following this approach. Those who do not, quickly stand out. I give them a brief chance to change; if they cannot, I fire them.

"And the other thing I would say is that they must share a common bond. That makes for the best crews and the best work."

"An interesting approach," said Maurizio. He leaned back in his chair, crossed his legs, and sized up Ettore. He saw a young, intense, confident man. Honest. Someone he could work with, he thought. "I'm encouraged by what I hear, Ettore. Perhaps you would consider the foreman position at Pezzoli Thoroughfare Contractors. I mean, on a trial basis, of course."

Ettore folded his arms and leaned forward, elbows on the table. If destiny was truly at play, now was the time to saddle and ride it. "Your offer is a great compliment, and I am honored. But I feel I must decline."

Maurizio sat stunned.

"On the other hand, Maurizio, I will agree to become your full partner!"

The table fell still. Fusco cleared his throat, took another biscotto.

Maurizio erupted. "But no!" His eyes widened. "By no means! What are you saying? You think I am inviting you to split all the profits? I bring all the money, I bring the expertise, and you want to be my partner? I do not even know you! What audacity! No, foreman only, that is what I offer!"

"Yes," said Ettore, prepared to engage, "you bring the money and the engineering, great contributions indeed. But I know how to run a crew of united, productive workers. And more importantly, I know exactly where to find them!"

Maurizio gawped in feigned awe. "Oh, he will find workers, he says!" He threw up both arms, looking at Fusco who blandly dunked his biscotto into his cup. "Unbelievable, Fusco! He promises to actually find me workers in a city where men line up and implore to be hired!" He laughed and looked at Ettore. "What a great magician you must be! What a master conjurer! For your next great trick, Signor Wizard, find me air to breathe or earth to stand on!"

"Do not be so hasty, Maurizio," Ettore said, "There are workers, and then there are workers."

Pezzoli snorted. "Enough of this! 'There are workers and there are workers,'" he mimicked, throwing his napkin onto the table. "Well, Signor Vacci, there are fools, and there are fools, and you obviously think me one!" He nodded to Fusco. "*Buona sera*, signore!" With a theatrical flourish, he began stalking off.

Fusco quickly scraped back his chair and followed a few steps. "But no, Maurizio, here now, come back, I beg you! You are judging matters too quickly! At least let Etto finish what he has to say!"

A few foreign patrons turned their heads at the drama. No locals reacted; such demonstrative conversations were common, mere social scenery.

Maurizio stopped and reluctantly turned, eyes at the sky. Fusco hastened to his side and, gently grasping his elbow, steered the engineer back to his chair.

"Maurizio, believe me, I meant no offense," Ettore said. "I know what I'm saying is not what you expected. But think. Yes, you provide the idea and the finances to begin. But, with all respect, do you know where to hire steady, hard workers, ones who will not be problems or quit after two weeks? I do."

Maurizio seemed calmer, though with folded arms and not making eye contact. Ettore went on.

"I can find such men in my own town, Castrubello." He moved his chair closer. "With them, I will build a cadre of workers who already know one another, know each other's families, who have shared hardships and good times alike since boyhood! Think of the advantages of such a workforce! The crews here that I have managed in Milan have come from all over, with peculiar habits and haughty attitudes. They spend half their time offending each other over trifles! Think what is possible when the only challenge each day is the job!"

Maurizio shrugged, waved a hand. "All right. Let us say I concede your point. But a full partnership, Vacci? You did not even know this job existed two hours ago. If you are this pushy now, not even hired, who says you will not try to take over everything if you are?"

Ettore shook his head. "Maurizio, you are the one with the technical education. I know the miracles that you engineers perform. You are the maestros whose blueprints guide an entire company's labor. I cannot do those things, just as you cannot match new men with the right jobs. The truth is, we need each other for your idea to work! You must agree, Maurizio. We will build great roads together!"

Maurizio sat silent. He needed a foreman and a solid crew. His instincts told him Ettore was trustworthy. It was a bitter pill to take on a partner. But, realistically, he was tired of the preliminaries, was ready to start work. A partner could be useful sharing the headaches. From Turin, his father was watching to see what, if anything, his youngest son could make happen.

"Agreed," Maurizio said. Seeing Ettore's pleased reaction, he added, "But this I insist. My name must come first!"

Both men clasped hands as *Pezzoli & Vacci Costruzioni* was born.

Chapter 14

May 1886: Naples, Campania

Cavaliere Raimondo Rimaccio, Royal Minister of Roads for the southern regions of the Kingdom of Italy, pressed the fingertips of both hands together, making of them a sort of tent. Normally he would still be enjoying his daily post-lunch *riposa* with the rest of the city, two or three hours free of business with his feet on his desk. Or, much better, in a room at the Hotel Decumani with Lena. At the thought of her rounded, naked flesh he felt his blood quicken.

But, no, no, that was not to be, at least not today. Instead, here he was in his stuffy third-floor office, considering yet another bid for a government road job. Such a true and loyal servant of His Majesty he was, for him to work like a dog this way!

That being said, he knew self-preservation motivated his sacrifice. His immediate superior, here in Naples on a surprise visit from Rome, had made it clear that he, Rimaccio, was under scrutiny. The king was impatient for the completion of his great new cross-peninsula roadway. Why the delay? Could Rimaccio furnish an end date? Perhaps the job was too much for the esteemed cavaliere to handle?

No stranger to bureaucratic pressure, Rimaccio understood that much was at stake. It was imperative that the government snoop saw him making decisive progress. But what a headache, he mused. While the various sections of the new royal road across Italy continued to progress well, the great delay was in the stretch across the dangerous mountains some sixty miles east of Naples. Dangerous because of the banditry rampant in those parts which, Rimaccio strongly suspected, had already caused one company to abandon the work. The firm had not said anything about bandits when they gave up; their various excuses were embarrassingly shabby. But the minister sensed the truth. He had never seen anybody so eager to pay their breach-of-contract penalty and depart the vicinity.

The minister knew that nobody liked to talk about the outlaw gangs in the hills, living off kidnapping, smuggling, and bold raids on villages. It was too obvious a failure for the local authorities, whose excuse was access; it was impossible to get at the brigands in sufficient force. Since the abdication of the job by the previous contractors, an intolerable two months before, no other company had come forth to take up the challenge.

Rimaccio did have a firm in mind that he knew would succeed, the well-known London outfit of Jay & Company. Not only did they have the best equipment, they also were accustomed to providing their own heavily armed security. Regrettably, the company was currently committed to doing great things in the north. But perhaps in four months, they had told him. Come back in four months when the Bergamo-Brescia tramline would be finished, they would certainly consider the southern job at that time. Rimaccio told them he would, and that they could name their price.

But, for the present, with that insufferable ferret from Rome nosing around, his very presence an implied threat, Rimaccio knew that he needed to come up with a stopgap.

"Please send the gentlemen in," he called to his secretary out in the waiting room. He patiently waited as two young men in perhaps their mid-twenties entered the office and introduced themselves.

"Welcome, signori," the minister said. He gestured to chairs.

The one called Pezzoli had a certain impertinent eye, Rimaccio thought. His father owned...Rimaccio checked...a Turin carriage factory.

Rimaccio liked to look down his nose at self-made 'new men' like the Pezzolis. But he had to admit, without carriages he would be out of a job. The past forty years had seen a proliferation of increasingly comfortable and efficient horse-drawn conveyances. The result was strong demand for all-weather macadam highways in place of the dilapidated, unpaved roads throughout the kingdom.

Now the other one, Rimaccio observed, this Vacci, he has a different look entirely. A self-certainty born of, well, not wealth, judging by his attire. No, it was the confidence of a thinker with ambition, a thinker perhaps possessing a spine.

"Well, gentlemen," the Cavaliere said. "You come recommended. But, of course, everyone who walks into my office comes recommended. All seek contracts from the king, and I do have several available. But how to choose Company A over Company B?" He paused, gazed at the pair over the top of his spectacles. "Or Z?" Rimaccio emphasized his dilemma with a shake of his head.

"Pezzoli & Vacci will do the work better, and faster, and for less than any other," said Maurizio. "I guarantee you."

Ettore stirred. They had talked about this. Maurizio must not act too eager, nor promise too much. But it was like trying to hold waves back from a beach. "Of course, we aspire to those goals," he interjected, casting his impetuous partner a sidelong glance. "But of the three, I believe it is the quality of the work with which you will be most pleased."

"Your workforce, who are they, what have they done?" asked Rimaccio.

"Sixty prime workers, seasoned with experience," Ettore lied. The hiring of any men depended first upon having a contract. But when it came time, he knew where he would find them all. "Our core men are northerners, signori, with the work ethic of northerners," he continued. "If we need more, we will hire the best of the locals."

"Impressive. Impressive sounding, I should say," said Rimaccio. A Genovese himself, he had always found Lombardia people far too cocky. But capable. "Yet, while you both have construction backgrounds—though, alas, none I see as owners— as a company you have so far actually built," he shrugged, made a half-circle gesture with one hand, "nothing. And so many better qualified firms want this work..." His words tailed off. A lie, the word had obviously gone out that because of the danger this contract was a sour lemon. He gambled these neophytes had no knowledge of that.

Ettore and Maurizio had strategized carefully for this moment.

"We understand your misgivings," Maurizio opened. "A royal minister such as yourself carries a great burden. We can only hope..." At this, Maurizio began coughing violently. He stood, in an apparent paroxysm, raised his hand in apology and moved toward the window, still hacking loudly.

The minister hurried from behind the desk, patting his guest's back, guiding him to a decanter of water. "My apologies, signore," Maurizio said, fighting to catch his breath. He took a small sip. "An irritation of dust perhaps." He coughed into his kerchief. "Forgive me. Very embarrassing. Please permit me to continue my remarks, I beg."

"Of course, young man, if you are fully recovered," said Rimaccio politely. Both men returned to where Ettore waited.

"Now, Signor Pezzoli, you were saying." At that moment, the official spied the plump leather purse on his desk. A golden glint shone past its loose drawstring. Rimaccio suppressed a smile. Such amateurs, these two. Still, their instincts were sound.

"Yes, as I was saying," Maurizio resumed. Royal Minister Rimaccio raised his hand to interrupt. He had already decided. These boys had no experience with such a project, their company was green. He had no expectations they could possibly succeed. But to get Rome's foot off his neck, they would serve well enough until the British company took over.

"No need," he said. "Your ardor has convinced me. Where would our country be if it could not recognize the right men to serve it? I believe the project I have in mind will perfectly suit. A good first challenge.

"You are aware, of course, of the king's new highway being constructed across the Apennines connecting Bari on the Adriatic, to Salerno, south of Naples?"

"Oh yes," said Ettore. The partners knew the project was open but lacked details.

"It is immensely important that this highway be built, as much for military purposes as commercial ones. Look here," said Rimaccio. He cleared flotsam from his desk and rolled out a map. "Here is the entire route. Two other companies are doing different segments. From Salerno eastward to Addolorata, here you see, then the other, starting at Bari on the Adriatic, extending west toward Bastiglione. They have been hard at it for some time.

"A third segment, however, the middle one, sits idle, hardly begun. It is these thirty-eight miles here, between Bastiglione on the east and Addolorata to the west. The construction is to follow an old trail through the Campania Apennines near Monte Terminio, as you see. It was along this route that our previous contractor started a road. But they gave up on the work, thwarted by labor issues, incompetence, and if I must say, *fortuna's* indifference. It is up to you to revive the effort without delay. I will give you the month of June to stage your company in Bastiglione, with work to begin mid-July. By the end of October, the road must connect to Addolorata." He was almost embarrassed by the unreasonable conditions he had just set.

"So, that is the project. Here is what the government proposes to pay." He scratched out a figure on a slip of paper and slid it across to the men. "Do you agree?"

Maurizio and Ettore looked at the figure, then to each other. Enough to help leverage the loan at the Bank of Milan as well as recruit the workforce. The partners conferred. The timetable was tight, but it took less than a minute for their answer. "Yes, Signor Minister. Agreed!"

Rimaccio looked from the map to the introductory letter the partners had submitted to remind himself of the company's name. "Then permit me to offer, signori, heartfelt congratulations to you both. In the name of His Majesty, I herewith award,"—a second glance downward—"'Pezzoli & Vacci Costruzioni' the government's contract to build segment two of *La Strada Re Umberto I di Savoia.*

"Payable, of course, upon full and timely completion," he added, smiling broadly, showing his teeth, extending his hand.

Chapter 15

Turin, Piedmont

"Why are you just telling me this now, Mamma?" asked Marietta Pezzoli. Annoyance edged her voice. "Dinner is only three hours from now. How can you expect me to be presentable by then?" She unhappily coiffed her hair with one hand while holding the gilded vanity mirror in the other.

"How you prattle, my dear," replied Signora Pezzoli, watching her daughter fuss from the bedroom doorway.

"Firstly, you are presentable right now. This is hardly a grand ball you must primp for. Secondly, your father's note only arrived an hour ago. Your brother now has a business partner, as you know, and both will be at the investors' meeting your papà arranged for today. It is only good manners to invite the gentlemen to share a late supper here with us afterward. The note said the meeting may go on for some time. I doubt they will arrive before nine o'clock; we will hold off on dinner until they do. Have something to eat now if you are hungry."

"Maurizio will be like a ravenous wolf," Marietta answered. "Most likely also the one he brings with him." She paused and looked at her mother. "And who is this friend of his, Mother? I know his new business partner, but who is he exactly? Or should I ask, is he anybody at all? Anybody of pedigree, I mean?"

Signora Pezzoli paused. Aspiring to marry well was every woman's dream and encouraged, of course. It was one reason why she and her husband had sent their daughter to the exclusive Brilliantmont School in Switzerland. But it would not do for Marietta to forget that she was, underneath her layer of education, a carriage-maker's daughter. Any beau of true pedigree will expect her to demonstrate a becoming modesty, she thought. Particularly if Marietta succeeded in marrying above her station. On the other hand, in these dynamic times, certain energetic men with simple backgrounds were creating their own pedigree. Such a husband might be entirely suitable for Marietta. And, possibly, one was near at hand.

"His name is Ettore Vacci. From a small town on the Pirino. Your brother thinks highly of him." She took the brush from her daughter and began stroking the back of her auburn hair. "Your father is pleased that Maurizio has seized the initiative regarding this venture, and he is eager to talk to them both. That is the reason for the meeting when they arrive, to introduce them to potential investors. Our duty, Marietta, is to welcome your brother home and put Signor Vacci at ease. They must have an evening to simply relax."

"Well, it seems to me that anyone willing to work with Maurizio must be a self-flagellant," said Marietta. "Or an eager pleaser. I can understand how a country boy would be overwhelmed by Maurizio's hardheadedness."

The signora sighed. "Why do we not wait before jumping to conclusions, dear? By taking on the risk of a new business with a partner he has only just met, Signor Vacci does not strike me as a weakling. You may even find him interesting, a change of pace, as it were, from your other young men."

Marietta rolled her eyes. It was no secret both her parents were anxious to see her married off. And she would decide soon. Her three most persistent suitors were polished and mannerly. One was even French! Yes, she thought, I will decide soon and put my parents out of their misery. This evening with the bumpkin will be a harmless, humorous diversion to later share with her friends.

In a better frame of mind, she replied, "Mother, I for one am expecting Signor Vacci to truly regale us tonight!"

* * *

The last thing Ettore wanted to do was to make this sudden side trip to Turin. After a final whirlwind month with solicitors signing partnership and incorporation papers in Milan, he was more than ready to return to Castrubello for a brief visit with Tonia and Carlo. But, for the time being, such personal matters must be set aside. The other side of owning a business, after all, was assuring it had the capital to operate and expand. That took meetings, selling, presentations. And Maurizio's father was more than willing to assist with that piece. Moreover, the senior Pezzoli was their first financial backer. Ettore knew he must show proper respect and appreciation for the man's efforts on their behalf. Maurizio was also eager for him to later meet his mother and his younger sister.

"I do not believe you when you say you have never, ever— never in all of your life—seen my city of Turin!" exclaimed

Maurizio for the dozenth time, as the two jogged on horseback near the outer environs of the Piedmontese city. "If I had known at the beginning you were so tragically backward, I am afraid you would have been immediately disqualified as a potential partner."

Ettore took the chiding in stride. "What do you want me to say to you, Maurizio? The difference between Turin and Milan is as a sparrow to an eagle, I am afraid."

Still, Turin was very impressive, Ettore had to admit. As they clopped down the thoroughfare, Maurizio pointed out the sites: the statue of Caesar Augustus gracing the front of Porta Palatina, then the vast Parco del Valentina, site of the 1884 *Esposizione Generale Italiana* that displayed the best of the Italian kingdom's science and industry, art and architecture. And before long, towering above the rest of the rooftops, there appeared the magnificent Mole Antonelliana. The men stopped their horses to crane their necks skyward.

"*Mio Dio*," Ettore exclaimed, in spite of himself, "it is taller than the Milan Duomo!"

"So much for your inane bird analogy, Etto," Maurizio said smugly. "Yes, five hundred feet and still growing. Begun as a synagogue, if you can believe that, now owned by the city and nearly complete. It will soon become the tallest building in the world. The plan is for a magnificent spire to crown it, a symbol of our nation's dynamic energy. A wonder of modernity!"

"You talk like you are running for election to the Chamber of Deputies, Maurizio," Ettore said drily.

"Not I," his partner said. "I am only about our business these days, this day in particular. And now, on this day, Etto, we stop. Here on our left are the offices where our meeting is to be!"

* * *

After a late dinner that evening at Casa Pezzoli, Ettore, Maurizio, and Signor Pezzoli retired to the study for brandy and cigars. Ettore was not accustomed to such sophistication. He politely accepted the offer of a slender Dutch Agio.

Talk soon centered on their meeting earlier that day. The consensus was that it had gone as well as could be expected. They had met with Gaudenzio Sella of the new banking operation Banca Sella and with wealthy Francesco Cirio, who by age twenty had discovered a way to preserve tomatoes in tin cans. A third attendee, Captain Giovanni Agnelli, arrived late, having just left his cavalry squadron at the municipal army barracks.

All were men of credible means, each with an eye for opportunities. Banca Stella was just starting to lend funds to promising companies that stood to benefit from the monarchy's attention to national infrastructure. Signor Cirio, whose preserved food operation was rapidly expanding, understood how a robust network of roadways would allow his canned goods to travel in bulk to Italy's major cities.

Ettore found Agnelli the most interesting. The officer possessed a keen conviction that a fundamental change in transportation was on its way.

"I plan to resign my commission within a year or so," he told the two partners. "As if struck by a vision, I saw the future of travel at the Great Exposition right here in Turin three years ago, and, gentlemen, though I am devoted to my cavalry mount, that future does not involve horses." He went on to describe an exhibit he had seen of a strange three-wheeled vehicle developed by a Piedmontese engineer named Enrico Bernardi.

"The contraption was powered by a 'petrol combustion engine' and could carry a man," said Agnelli. "There are similar experimental steam engine contraptions, I know, but this petrol machine was far cleaner, far lighter and less cumbersome. In short, it is practical. The vehicle is very primitive, little more than a tricycle with a motor, but, signori, I see its future as clearly as if I had a crystal ball. That simple tricycle is the precursor for an entirely new mode of transportation: full-size carriages powered by petrol engines, much faster than our carriages now. They will require solid, hard, long-lasting thoroughfares to travel upon. Macadam surfaces are fine for the present, but in coming years, signori, I predict new roads will be built of concrete!"

All three investors, as well as Maurizio's father, understood that putting money into fledgling Pezzoli & Vacci Costruzioni offered an opportunity for sizable profits. One day. The two partners were personally appealing with their honesty, competence, and utter willingness to challenge long odds. Still, they were unproven, the risk in backing them hardly inconsiderable.

"Here is what I suggest," Aleardo Pezzoli had told the three investors. "We each put a small amount of money forward now in combination with the larger loan from the Bank of Milan. Then, upon successful completion of *La Strada Re Umberto I di*

Savoia, we pledge a much greater amount to expand the business."

Agreement was general. By the end of two hours, initial sums had been finalized and conditional notes signed for the future, all but guaranteeing the investment capital that Pezzoli & Vacci would need to grow. With one stipulation. The partners must complete the project in the Apennines on budget and on time. The meeting had concluded with firm handshakes all around.

In all, a good day, thought Ettore, though complicated. But now, finishing his second brandy, Ettore suddenly had enough. He excused himself from the two Pezzolis, still in deep conversation, and sought a doorway to the outside air. It was late, after midnight.

He found a passage leading to the courtyard and stood under the distant, pinprick stars. For a moment, the immensity of what he and Maurizio were trying to accomplish rushed over him.

"Your long day continues," said a woman's voice. Ettore turned to see Maurizio's sister standing nearby, her shoulders covered with a shawl.

"I am surprised you are still awake," Marietta continued. She had noted the self-effacing humor of her brother's partner during dinner, had consequently adjusted her instinctive disdain of the newcomer to a more neutral 'wait and see'. The man's gray-blue eyes reflected an intelligent perception that she found unexpectedly compelling.

"Signorina, please excuse me. Too much business talk today for me. My head feels like a spinning top! I hope I have not disturbed you. I did not see you there."

Marietta adjusted her shawl. "This courtyard is intended for reflection. There is no need for apologies, Signor Vacci. Out here, under the sky, it is my favorite spot, even at a late hour such as this."

Ettore considered the woman. "At dinner I could tell you are well-educated. Your comments about the king's colonial dreams show you are an avid reader of newspapers. More women ought to be like you, I think, not afraid to form their own opinions." He shrugged. "But what can I say? Not everyone has the courage to think for themselves, man or woman."

Marietta searched Ettore's face. She was familiar with flattery, although not quite of this nature. What she saw before her appeared to be an authentic young man without a veiled sexual agenda. Unusual among the men in her circle. A bit nonplussed, she responded.

"And Signor Vacci, I must tell you that your story of how you and my brother first met was very entertaining. It seems you have done much with yourself despite your..." She almost said, "low birth" but chose, "lack of patronage. I know men who squander their advantages. You seem to be making your own." She blushed, fearful her praise sounded like fawning. But in spite of herself, she didn't care. Against all logic, she wanted this man to like her.

"First, my friends call me Ettore or Etto. And thank you for what you just said. But aren't we all trying to do the best that we can with the cards *fortuna* deals us? At least, that is what we ought to be doing, don't you think?"

He paused. "I would very much like to know you better, signorina, if you allow me to speak plainly. But, as you know, Maurizio and I and our company are tied to this project. If we succeed, the next several years are impossible to predict, except that building the company will be all-consuming. We will likely accept anything offered to us, anywhere. That is the simple reality of things. Hardly the perfect way for two people to become better acquainted, is it? What are your thoughts? Sometimes I am too presumptuous."

Marietta felt herself flush, but not in an embarrassed way. This Ettore Vacci, she thought. "I would like us to become friends as well. Let us agree to correspond," she said smiling. The edge of her shawl slowly brushed his hand as she started to turn. "And we will see where that leads. And Etto, like you, I too have a first name!"

* * *

Castrubello, Lombardia

"A beautiful child," said Padre Umberto. "Young Lorenzo was quite calm during the service. Such is not always the case." The priest chuckled. "The Carpa twins, mah, quite different, this is all I will say."

Carlo thanked the pastor, handed him a coin. "For the poor box, Padre."

Umberto smiled. "On behalf of the poor of San Giulio, thank you, Carlo." He turned to Carlo's brother-in-law. "And Etto," he said, "I will see you in two hours?"

Ettore nodded. "Certainly, Padre."

Tonia held three-month-old Lorenzo to her bosom. The morning breeze blew cool across the steps of San Giulio.

"*Grazie* for coming, Ettore, and for agreeing to become Renzo's godfather," she told her brother, speaking slowly.

Ettore put his arm around her shoulder. "Carlo and you deserve this baby after all you have gone through." He blinked away a sudden image of the chaotic stone farmhouse three years before. "And little Lorenzo here, so healthy. And since he is part Vacci, so handsome, naturally!" He peered at his small, sleeping nephew.

Tonia's mother-in-law Lucrezia joined them from the church, along with Rina and Gemella and their combined seven children. The women fussed with the baby, disrupting the blanket, gently touching his hands and hair with affection. "Now Nonna will carry her new boy," the grandmother announced. Three sets of hands helped manage the transfer of the precious bundle. They started back to Casa Como. Behind them, the men fell in alongside each other.

The leisurely stroll through the neighborhoods acted as a tonic for Ettore. He had finally freed himself from organizing the business and returned to Castrubello two days ago. It was only the third time he had been back since first leaving for Milan several years before. The first time was for the Epiphany, which he had shared with the Comos. The second was the summer of the same year, when he had a layoff of two weeks between tracklaying projects in Milan. He came to visit his sister and brother-in-law but sadly arrived just in time for a heartbreaking funeral.

Gemella, the wife of Carlo's brother Francesco, had given birth to the couple's third child, a daughter. But the newborn contracted the dreaded '*mal grup*', the 'knot in the throat', and died the same day Ettore arrived.

Instead of a joyful reunion, he had found the Como household in the throes of dark grief. Padre Umberto was there as the family kept candlelit vigil over the swaddled corpse. On the following day came the grim procession to the cemetery as the mourners loudly lamented the infant's cruel fate. Francesco's stoic suffering, Gemella's shaking sorrow, the tiny coffin lowered into the grave with a final dull *thump!*—such grievous images drifted through Ettore's dreams for weeks. They were the same dreams that many Castrubellese would know that terrible summer. A scourge of diphtheria killed half the town's newborns before stopping as abruptly as it had begun.

Yet, Ettore knew, the population here and throughout Italy was actually increasing. Genetic fertility and determined intercourse played their roles; the mortal sin of abortion was no option. Birthing and crib deaths did much of an abortionist's work, in any event. But against all odds, fecundity was winning out. Women would lose four babies but still see a half-dozen others survive to adulthood.

The increase in workers made the labor market flush, which allowed landowners to keep wages low. In response, local farm workers and merchants, with Padre Umberto's assistance, formed the Workers Collective of Castrubello. The organization offered its members mutual support, financial and otherwise. More importantly, by speaking with one voice, the collective intended to get the landowners' attention to address workers' grievances. Such ambitions were premature; the laws favored the men with land and money.

Before visiting, Ettore wrote his old mentor that he wanted to hire Castrubellese men for Pezzoli & Vacci projects. The priest arranged a meeting of the Collective the day of the baptism so he could speak.

Arriving at Casa Como, Ettore excused himself. "I will be back. I have something I must do." He hiked two miles to the edge of the town, an area called Luponotte. Built of concrete and rocks, a dwelling stood alone back from the road in the shade of a poplar grove.

Cupping his hands, he peered through a small square of smudged window glass next to the front door. As he did, the door flew open and a bearded figure emerged, arms extended.

"Muto!" cried Ettore, jumping back despite himself.

The deaf man seized Ettore in a grunting embrace. "Ugh!" said Ettore, as the breath left his body. Nothing like digging out a cesspit together to create a lifetime bond, he thought.

Breadcrumbs flecked Muto's ample beard, a smile creased his weathered face. He beckoned Ettore inside. It was a simple space with a few rooms. A table and chairs and a cot on the floor comprised most of the furnishings. Wall hooks held Muto's clothes; a box near the hearth served as his larder. Sausage ropes hung from the rafters alongside a brace of ducks and something furry, a ferret? A wooden plate with scraps of fish and crusts sat on the table.

Muto gestured for Ettore to sit and filled a tin cup with pale wine from a leather flask. He pulled a broken loaf of bread from the larder box and offered it to his guest. Ettore tore off a piece as Muto sat down.

Despite his deafness, Muto and Ettore had always been able to communicate. Ettore had the habit of speaking aloud to Muto as he used basic gestures his friend could follow. By this time, he had a handful of them they both knew.

"I'm happy to see you," he said, smiling, as he pointed to his own eyes, then to Muto. "I need your help." He clutched the front of his own shirt then opened his hands. Muto nodded.

"I am digging," Ettore said. He stood, acted like he was handling a shovel.

Muto leaned back in his chair, frowned, shook his head, held his nose.

"No, no," Ettore said shaking his head. "No cesspit. A road." He pointed to the floor, mimed digging again, then theatrically strolled over the space. "Road."

Muto squinted for a second, got up and opened the door. He pointed at the path from the road up to his place, shrugged.

"Yes," Ettore nodded. Muto pointed to the ground. *Here? Castrubello?*

"No." Ettore shook his head. He pointed past where the distant church bell tolled midday, then to the sky, the clouds. "Far," he said. "Very far."

Muto pondered this news. He took a step back, grinned broadly, and arced his index finger left to right, simulating the path of the sun in the sky. *When?*

* * *

That night after the meeting of the Collective, men ready to sign on with the roadbuilding project crowded around Ettore. With only enough money to hire sixty, he faced twice that many jobseekers.

Padre Umberto, who had introduced Ettore as a true son of Castrubello, helped as he made his choices. The cleric knew the circumstances of every family in the parish and steered Ettore toward the men with the most mouths to feed.

"I had no idea how difficult things are, Padre," Ettore told the priest after the last man filed out. "I see desperation here."

"Desperation, yes," said Umberto as he tied his cloak. "I am greatly afraid of what is happening to our commune, Ettore.

More men are leaving every week. And I do not mean just coming and going for seasonal work, like sparrows chasing the seasons. They are departing for distant lands. Hiring agents from Argentina and America keep offices right here in Castrubello. Our men believe the stories that American streets glitter with gold. These men go alone, their families stay, fatherless, husbandless, sometimes for years. Oh, they all say they will return when they are rich!" The priest sighed. "And I think they believe they actually will." He shrugged sadly. "But an ocean away? After years of separation? No, instead, they send for their wives and never do return, leaving the rest of Castrubello behind for good. But I believe *fortuna* has brought you here, Ettore, to offer your Castrubellese a different future!"

"*Fortuna*, Padre?" Ettore jokingly raised his eyebrows at the pagan reference.

"Eh," sighed the priest, catching his meaning. "I have become too old for illusions, Etto. Call it *fortuna* or heaven above, one way or another all of us caper to fate's mad flute. Our chief task in life, I sometimes think, is to keep from despairing as we flail away." He put a hand on Ettore's shoulder, "As for the Church, consider how pointless our struggles would seem without its incense and pageantry!" He dropped his hand. "Forgive me, Etto, the devil has possessed my tongue." He laughed wearily. "Perhaps I have capered too long!"

Chapter 16

July 1886: Southern Apennines, Campania

Since ancient times, travel over and across Italia's Apennine range had been essential for maintaining political and economic connections between the region's far-flung communities. Now the Italian kingdom was spending significant sums for a network of roads, railways, and tunnels to formally bind the new nation together. Not an easy task in a land where most small communes, many of them isolated for the sake of better self-defense, felt only a limited regional allegiance, at best. After so many centuries of fragmentation, it was *campanilismo*—allegiance only to those within the sound of one's church bell—that commonly prevailed.

As their people and equipment were assembling at Bastiglione under the organizing eye of Vito Ameretti, Etto and Maurizio rode ahead to look at the previous work done on the route. What they found was encouraging, at least in terms of good engineering. Since the *strada* would be handling carriages and wagons in both directions, its width stayed at a fifteen-foot minimum. In addition, wherever possible the builder had created wider cutouts for slow vehicles to let others pass, or to turn around if need be.

As to why the first work on the road had stopped, one possible answer presented itself to the partners. The plan seemed to have been to excavate and grade the entire thirty-eight miles of roadbed as stage one. Stage two would be to then return and macadamize the prepared surface. The merit in such a strategy was that, as long as the weather was good, the laying out of the road's foundation could advance expediently. The goal appeared to be for the contractor to be able to stand in Rimaccio's office and show the company's raw progress in terms of sheer distance—despite the fact that the actual paving stage remained to be done.

"A sort of a ruse, perhaps," Maurizio commented as the two trotted on horseback up the route. "Perhaps it had to do with receiving payment by the mile or something like that."

"Well, it turned out to be stupid," Ettore answered. "They let the weather catch them before they were even halfway completed with their excavation. The unpaved roadbed turned to mud, equipment could not move. They could not press ahead, the trail too much of a mess. Nor could they start paving, lakes of water covered the places where they had dug. The question is, what slowed them down to such an extent before the rains hit? Remember how Rimaccio hemmed and hawed when we pressed him for details. What *merda* did he offer up, 'labor issues'? 'incompetence'?"

"Yes, incompetence," scoffed Maurizio. "*Porcheria.* Look at the good work they did all along here. 'Incompetence' does not suddenly strike like some fever!"

Ettore glanced at Maurizio. "Let us hope not, anyway," he joked. "You look a bit warm!"

His partner made a sour face. "Oh, ha, ha, Vacci, you are forever hilarious." He arched his eyebrows to emphasize his mocking. "This must be the irresistible charm my sister sees in you, no?"

Stop talking, Maurizio, Ettore thought. He and Marietta had exchanged several letters over the previous weeks, each one warmer than the one before. Now though, there was a hiatus in their communication as the road work proceeded beyond the range of any postal riders. He missed hearing from her.

They ambled on in silence for a distance.

"Look at how they had to work to broaden the bed here. Fifteen feet is too wide, don't you think?" Maurizio eventually asked. "The only people out this way might be local lumbermen. And rich foreign artists with their easels and picnic baskets, maybe."

Ettore swatted at a persistent horsefly that kept landing on the back of his neck. "They want to run the royal mail on this highway, I expect, but as Rimaccio said, its main purpose is military. Remember, not only woodcutters operate in these parts. There are still gangs of *banditti* in these mountains. I expect mild English tourists make profitable hostages. Our road will allow the army and the *Guardia di Finanza* up here in large numbers, perhaps to clean out any last rats' nests."

Maurizio shrugged. "I thought all those bands were wiped out ten years ago."

The previous roadbed work finally ended at an ancient dirt trail formed by long decades of foot and hoof traffic. The partners climbed down from their saddles, leaving their mounts to forage on scrub grasses.

Breaking out water and food, Maurizio and Ettore stood facing west, stretching their legs. They gazed south down a heavily forested mountainside that rose again into a parallel ridge. The heavy green mat of beech, olive, oak, and chestnut trees swayed and rippled in the sunny breeze, emitting the verdant perfume of the high country. On the opposite side of the roadbed, a jagged wall of natural limestone extended sharply upward forty or fifty feet. The cliff had flanked the route ever since Bastiglione and according to Rimaccio continued the entire way.

"This ledge looked much wider on the map," said Maurizio, pacing the width where they stood.

"That was just the thick ink the mapmaker used drawing the line," joked Ettore. "Now that we are out here, I see we will be doing a lot of work with pickaxes to get the space we need."

"And explosives," said Maurizio. The engineer had learned blasting as an apprentice on the great Gottard Tunnel project at the Italo-Swiss border. He had noted two spots during their ride where the previous builders had used controlled detonations to widen the ledge. No doubt more would be needed. It would be something of a tricky business not to blow the ledge itself clean off the side of the mountain. But it was the sort of technical challenge Maurizio relished.

Perusing the abrupt end of construction, Ettore shook his head. "So, they reached this point and said, 'We are done.' He kicked at ruined trenches lining the road. "Look here, Maurizio. Why did they dig these drains then break them up?"

His partner shrugged. "Maybe we can see something past that bend," gesturing to where the rough trail curved left. They walked another hundred paces, rounded the turn, and stopped. "*Cristo,*" Maurizio muttered.

Immediately after the curve, a crevice split the face of the limestone wall. The fissure was a dozen feet wide at the trail and widened as it rose. Beyond the gap itself, the opening sloped steeply upwards and broadened into a vale. It formed a solid wedge of green, its tip at the road, leaning back into the side of the mountain. Crowded with trees and growth, the gorge ascended, as far as Ettore could tell, all the way to the top of the butte. Maybe not all the way, he thought, trying to gaze through the trees. He could not be certain.

Dense as it was with foliage, a hiker could nonetheless leave the trail and, with some difficulty, climb. "I am going up in there," Ettore said. As Maurizio protested, Ettore left the path and began to ascend. The ground angled so sharply that he was forced to grab at tree limbs and trunks to pull himself upward. The difficult passage was made even more so by heavy underbrush. Who knew what beasts lived inside that jungle? He still could not make out how high the gouge in the hillside went. Too many trees and outcropping boulders blocked the view.

After struggling intensely for ten minutes he looked back the way he came. Maurizio was hardly thirty yards below, hands on hips, an amused expression on his face.

"Enough of this," said Ettore. He rambled back down sideways, his feet cascading stones and dirt clods as he came. Watching his footing, he saw something metallic among the debris. He stopped for a moment and scooped the object up, then continued to where Pezzoli stood.

"That was pointless," said Maurizio as he grabbed Ettore's hand to help him regain his footing. "At the end of the day, who knows what made those others quit work? Maybe it was a labor dispute, after all, or a question of money, like the minister told us."

"Or something we should have anticipated better, partner." Ettore held up the brass shotgun casing he'd found. "I think Rimaccio left something out."

* * *

Five weeks from Bastiglione later, Ettore peered from his vantage point on a crag above the construction. His workers were stretched along four hundred feet where two dozen men spread crushed rock over the leveled roadbed. They used rakes with tines and ones that were simply boards at the end of long handles. An engineer checked that the surface was level and set at the proper angle from center to sides.

Other laborers stood, sat, and knelt on one side of the road among a dumped load of blasted limestone. A wagon-mounted, steam-powered rock breaker reduced large pieces to the smaller rough-edged gravel they needed. The workers used hammers to break the stones further, as needed. Crew chiefs walked around the site as the men tapped away, spot-measuring samples of the work with calipers. A third group was behind them on the roadway itself, rolling and tamping the mix of rocks that had been laid down.

Macadam-paved roads like the one they were building were a huge improvement on the muddy tracks that traversed most countrysides. Introduced sixty years earlier, the pavement consisted of layers of rock over a flat dirt roadbed. A thick crown down the middle allowed water to run off into drain ditches along either side. The bed was filled with compacted layers of specifically sized gravel. The stones for the base layer were to be three inches, no more. The stones of the second layer were much smaller, three-fourths of an inch. At each stage, the pavement was compacted with mule or man-pulled iron rollers.

The process had been worked out by the Scottish engineer John McAdam. Many installations over the decades had proven that when the gravel specifications were followed and the layers properly compressed, the rocks locked together into a hard, impermeable surface, perfect for the iron-ringed wheels of modern carriages. Ettore had learned how to build the roads from Pezzoli, and in turn trained his team of crew chiefs.

He gingerly descended and greeting men along the way walked a portion of the completed surface. It was solid and smooth. But the work went slowly.

After breakfast that morning, Maurizio set out from the company camp. He rode a mule and held the long reins of another packed with his surveying equipment and charts. Riding alongside was Muto with his hunting rifle, a sturdy twelve-round Swiss Vetterli, slung across his back. Ettore made him take it, making it clear there could be danger. He had done this by tracing his thumb, wide-eyed, across his own throat, then pointing at himself and Ferrara. Muto shrugged. So dramatic. He nodded, yes, understood.

Besides serving as bodyguard, Muto's job was to position the tall measuring rod at the spot where the surveyor gestured— back up, come forward, right side, other way. Then Pezzoli with his tripod and surveying level took the readings he needed, jotted them into the notebook, then moved to a new location.

The two coaxed their mounts out of the camp and along the latest finished portion of road. The surface was sound and felt hard as iron under their hooves. When they came to where the work was in progress, they transitioned to the ground on the right to stay out of the way.

They eventually arrived at the place Maurizio and Ettore had stopped some weeks before, where the previous work abruptly ended.

They dismounted and unpacked the gear. The two spent the day plotting out another three hundred yards of road along the ledge. As Maurizio established the borders of the road, Muto hammered wood stakes in the ground to mark where the drainage ditches were to be dug. Sometimes as Muto drove in the stakes, he stood among tall saplings that encroached on the ledge. These would have to be chopped down and uprooted.

At noon, Pezzoli waved to Muto to stop. He opened a box that the camp cook had prepared and took out a loaf of bread and some white cheese along with a water flask. He patted the ground close by. As Muto sat down, he unslung his carbine and placed it across his knees. He looked up into the brush of the large crevice in the rocks where a bird of some kind suddenly flapped upward.

Each man tore off a chunk of the bread and sliced a piece of cheese. Maurizio tapped Muto on the knee. "It is going to get very hot," he said to Muto. He pointed at the sun and pretended to wipe his brow with the back of his hand. Muto repeated the gesture and nodded. Yes, he thought, hot. Obviously.

The engineer stood up and pointed at his tripod with its sight fixed on top. Then he pointed at Muto's measuring rod on the ground. He gestured vaguely out toward where Muto had last been standing with it.

"Four more readings," he said. Muto just stared.

Maurizio tried again. He put his eye to the sextant, then pointed down the trail again. He lifted his hand. "One!" he said, holding up one finger, unconsciously raising his voice. He pulled his head back, taking his eye away, then resumed looking through the device and pulled back again. "Two," he said, showing two fingers.

He didn't need to go further. Muto nodded impatiently, held up four fingers, one at a time, pointing at the tripod as he did so.

"*Si, si*," said Maurizio, repeating the same gesture. "Four more, then we go!" At that, he pointed at the mules and made a wide-elbowed *giddy-up* gesture.

Muto, amused by the man's need to make small talk, smiled blandly, nodded three times, and finished his cheese.

Chapter 17

The bandit Seppe Generoso slung his shotgun and climbed down from the tree. He wiped his face with his soft cap, returned it to his head. He had just watched the strangers perform their ridiculous mime show. The bigger one was obviously a dummy, he thought. Strong though, somebody who could do some damage with those arms and fists. And the carbine on his back—a nice firearm, one worth collecting at some point. That other one, bespectacled, mustached, thin, flapping his hands around, looked like a city fop. Six weeks ago, he had watched as two riders—the fop had been one—stopped and poked around the ravine for a bit. His partner had even tried climbing up into the ravine. Generoso had simply kept still as the outsider blundered nearly to where he was hiding then gave up and blundered his way back down again. Such things occasionally happened and did not in themselves set off alarms. But Generoso knew surveying equipment meant trouble.

The lookout turned and carefully headed back up the vale. The crevice was the only access to Corsicano's stronghold from this side of the mountain. Generoso must leave no easy markings for intruders to track. He gave a low whistle. An answering trill told him his partner Benito understood he was returning to camp.

The bandit huffed his way uphill among tall, shady beeches that blanketed the incline. He avoided sloshing into the occasional small creeks that burbled alongside his path. Two great bearded vultures searching for carrion careened above the treetops. Somewhere an eagle screeched. As he passed near a dark thicket, Generoso jumped at the grunt of a boar rooting deep in the brush. *"Porco cane!"* he blurted and gave the place a wide berth.

After an hour of climbing, the brigand reached an open plateau. From where he emerged from the edge of the woods, tree stumps extended three hundred feet further to a blackened stone wall.

The ruined hilltop monastery served as the brigands' main base of operations. Not easy to find and centrally located, from here the band could strike in any direction, thus far with impunity. A perimeter wall, eyeball high and three feet thick, surrounded the compound. It, like the rest of the buildings, was built of large fieldstones and mortar. From the signs of numerous rough repairs, it was clear these bandits were no builders.

A large, rusted gate marked the entrance where an iron archway displayed a bent Latin cross. Generoso greeted the guard, who stuck his pipe in his teeth then tugged on the gate. It reluctantly squealed open.

Generoso entered a rock-paved courtyard punctuated with weeds. Mounds of rubble and rubbish sat piled in corners, shattered glass bottles and broken crockery crunched underfoot as he walked. A headless gray statue with praying hands and mossy stone wings stood alone in a garden overgrown with vines.

Two long buildings faced each other across the yard. Thick granite-block columns, pockmarked with age and violence, supported arched cloisters in front of both of them. One of the long buildings was largely uninhabitable, its tile roof broken by time and snowstorms. Grown trees stood within charred walls and projected themselves through missing ceilings. Nevertheless, there was one large room, a barracks of sorts, housing a dozen bandits.

The other building was in better condition. The brigands had repaired its roof with salvaged tiles and thatched tree branches. While no palace, the rooms were large and kept decently clean. A thin tendril of smoke rose from a clay chimney. This wing provided shelter for the rest of the band's other forty-odd outlaws and included the chambers of its leader.

The doorless remains of a church enclosed the courtyard opposite the gate. A belltower with no bell crowned a corner of the roof where a lookout slouched inside the belfry. A man led a horse up a ramp built over the church's front steps into what now served as the stable for the band's assorted livestock.

The first time Generoso had walked into the makeshift stable several years earlier, he was startled to see the skeleton in black rags in the rafters. It hung by its neck from a rope, empty black eye sockets fixed downward. "Who is that?" he had asked Bruno, the gang member first showing him the place.

"You really don't know about him?" Bruno asked, grinning. "He is the famous *Nostro Corvo*, Our Crow, our band's good luck charm. In life, he was some traveler in a public coach that we captured. He was shitting his pants as soon as we pulled him out. We made him our hostage here, put a loaded gun to his head and told him to write his own ransom letter. He dropped dead, face-first into the inkstand, I swear on my grandmother's memory, he actually dropped dead, look, look right here where I'm pointing." Generoso saw a deep black stain on a tabletop. "Corsicano said, 'Hang his damn corpse. If we cannot have his money, he can motivate others!" We strung him up in the rafters. Now Corsicano tells everyone we capture, 'Look what will happen if your people do not pay!' You should see how hard our guests work on those letters!"

Generoso, grinning at the memory, unslung his shotgun at a door near the end of the restored wing. The sentry outside, smoking a short, twisted cigar, propped the weapon against the wall. He pulled the acrid black stinker from between his lips and said, "Go ahead in."

Most of the time, once inside the casa's vestibule, Generoso would see well-armed Emilio sitting on a chair facing the door. Today the chair was empty. He sat down himself and waited.

"Stupid Emilio ate too much rabbit, if you are wondering," It was Fulvio Penna, right hand of their boss, standing on the mezzanine above. "Now he is hunched like a dog in the weeds grunting his guts out. Serves the pig right."

The lieutenant's heavy black beard obscured his face; his long-armed, thick frame gave him the look of a powerful troll. But Penna was no *troglodita*. Keen, ambitious, with ideas of his own, he held the full respect of the men. "So, Seppe," he said. "Come tell Corsicano what you have to say."

Mounting the stairs, Generoso followed Penna into the capo's salon. As always, his heart began beating faster. A few salvaged furnishings offered a modicum of comfort to the room. Nothing very elaborate for such a rich man. But this was a working camp for hard action, after all.

Corsicano sat cleaning his Swiss revolver, a Modèle '72. He was in his mid-sixties with gray, unkempt hair. Wiry black and gray whiskers flecked his grizzled muzzle above a neck that bore a vivid pink scar. A sun-darkened face portrayed a lifetime of scrabbling for shelter, from his boyhood in the dark slums of Naples to these last decades ruling the mountains.

His father had been an officer in the Royal Corsican Regiment first posted by Napoleon in Naples. Despite the Emperor's ultimate defeat in 1815, Capitano Paolo Vesco refused to surrender. He led other like-minded patriots from the regiment into the mountains to resist their new Bourbon overlords. After suffering several years of hit and run raids, the Bourbons finally ended Vesco's career with a firing squad.

Vesco's son and the boy's mother became beggars in Naples. When malaria left him an orphan, Fernando Vesco, age sixteen, was forced to fend for himself. Two years in prison sharpened his life skills. Upon release he returned to the mountains where a semi-starving remnant of his father's band had become reduced to stealing chickens from hardscrabble peasants.

Vesco soon showed his ability as a leader. Before long, the gang was raiding villages deep in the valleys. Later, kidnapping became their best moneymaker, with smuggling a close second. Ex-convicts and deserters fleshed out their ranks. The men knew the boss had blood roots in Corsica and began simply calling him *Corsicano*.

When the authorities mounted punitive expeditions, the murderous ambushes that Corsicano sprang became lyrics for folk songs. Corsicano was happy to grease the palms of bigshots in the city; between the violence, the payoffs, and the band's difficult, unknown location, attempts to apprehend the group had slowed. Despite the monarchy's ruthless campaigns against *brigantaggi* in the mountains, after four decades Corsicano's brigands were among the remaining renegades still defying the odds and thriving in the southern range.

But recently business had slowed. Small signs of discontent were cropping up within the band. Small signs they may be, but, Corsicano's gut warned him, do not underestimate the threat.

Corsicano recalled when, three years before, Fulvio Penna came straight from prison begging him for a chance. Penna had led his own smuggling band farther south. But, one night, drunk as a monkey, he had bragged of his exploits to his whore. The next day she turned him in for the reward. A man too full of himself, Corsicano judged. But that dangerous confidence was also his strength. His deft handling of men and cool head under fire earned him Corsicano's respect if not quite his complete trust. He promoted him to second-in-command.

But lately a tension had risen between the two, subtle but real. Corsicano had survived this long by catching every change of pitch in the people he dealt with. If Penna was considering a leadership coup, Corsicano knew he had to act first. That time would come. The capo's black eyes flashed under his wire-brush eyebrows. He motioned Generoso forward, watched Penna follow. "Tell me," he said.

"The builders are almost at the keyhole, signore," Generoso responded. "Today two of them were using that...that spyglass on three legs, for measuring distance, to drive stakes. One was armed."

Corsicano looked down his clean revolver barrel, spun the cylinder. "Get food, take some back to your partner. Stay unseen," he emphasized. "Penna, add a third man at the road. For now, no bullets." He brusquely motioned Generoso out.

Uninvited, Penna sat down in a chair with a heavy grunt. Corsicano noted the disrespect—increasingly common as of late—but chose not to speak.

"They have been poking along for weeks," the lieutenant said. "But that strada they are building is much better than the earlier ones. Fucinello in Bastiglione says the workers are mostly all *mangiapolenti* from the north, although they also hired a dozen or so Bastiglionese. I made certain some of our people were among them. So, they have about eighty men, a big number compared to the last crew up here. Fucinello says they brought tools and rollers made of metal drums, pulled by mules. We have also seen weapons."

Corsicano stroked his chin. "We will do exactly the same we did with the first ones. If those boys are smart, they will pull out before we spill blood."

Penna replied, "Ah, I told you, it is the army and that fucking *Guardia di Finanza*, pushing for these new roads into the mountains. The bastards want to gallop up that highway with a regiment to overwhelm us here!"

"To hell with the army!" Corsicano exclaimed. "We have stayed out of reach this long. We do as always, hit, dodge, hit again. Make fear and delay. Now get that extra man on watch. Put the word out, we will strike at the road tonight."

Penna grunted back to his feet. There was a bigger chance here, and his boss was not seeing it. As usual.

Chapter 18

"Santa merda!" Vito Ameretti declared. The workforce he had led from the base camp to yesterday's worksite milled behind him, equally stunned. Directly in front lay mayhem.

Five hundred feet of prepared roadbed was now just a long slag of torn ground. Overnight, vandals had dredged up the careful layers of crushed rocks and scattered them downhill, then tore out the drainage ditches on both roadsides. The mound of topcoat gravel delivered the previous day was gone, pitched further down the dirt trail or shoveled into the green forest below.

A felled tree lay across the entire mess, blocking the way. On its trunk were crude charcoal markings: a skull over crossed daggers, with the words, *Morte a Te!*

"And tools are missing," Vito told the two partners, just arrived. "The box of hammers we left, chisels. Gone. It looks like they also tried pushing the roller we left here down the hill but couldn't. Too heavy."

"We are lucky there," said Maurizio, alongside Vacci. "We lose one of those, it takes a month to replace."

"Lucky?" said Ettore. The disconcerted workers around him murmured to each other. In these parts, a message of *'Death to You!'* was accepted as literal. "I want to know who did this."

"Who did this?" repeated Maurizio, incredulously. "*Cristo*, Ettore, the goddam *banditti* did this."

"Do you think me slow-witted? I know it was brigands, of course. But who exactly? Who is their leader? The Bastiglionese workers just shrug when I ask. But this sort of sabotage takes planning."

"They did not attack our main camp. Instead, they chewed up the end of our work in the dead of night. *Terroni* cowards."

"No, Maurizio, not cowards. Smart. They see our numbers and that we have weapons. Likely that is something different than the first company up here. They cannot count on us to run just by firing a few blasts of birdshot over our heads. If it becomes a real battle and men die, the army arrives in force, finished road or not. That is the last thing they want. So, these bandits, they plan a war of attrition. They bleed us of money and time by making us rebuild the same five hundred feet every day. When the weather sets in, the delay becomes extreme. Eventually our costs become too much, and we fold. That is their attack." Vacci walked toward the nearby crevice in the granite wall. He stared up the gorge of thick woods leading into the mountain.

"We must make a deal."

"Make a deal?" Maurizio repeated. "Ettore, be careful or you'll make a deal with the barrel of a sawed-off *lupara*. These men are more than dangerous. They are unpredictably dangerous. To think you can sit and reason with them is…"

"So, the answer is what? Throw everything away? You know failure here destroys Pezzoli & Vacci before we even begin, yes? Maurizio, we have staked everything on this!"

"You say, 'Make a deal!' But with what?" Maurizio pulled both his pockets inside out. "With what money do we make a deal, Vacci? We are in debt to our eyebrows! What can we offer that isn't an insult?"

"Maurizio, think. If we do not complete this job, Pezzoli & Vacci Costruzioni is finished. If these *banditti* allow a road to get close to whatever's up there," Ettore said, pointing up the crevice, "*they* are finished. Both sides have something to lose." He looked again at the ominous breach in the limestone wall and the sloping forestation beyond. "I believe I know what offer we can make."

"What, do you actually think these cutthroats are going to accept a promissory note, Signor Negotiator, redeemable when we get to Addolorata?"

"No," said Ettore. "But I do think they will accept a hostage."

Exasperated, Maurizio threw up his arms. His partner raised a hand. "Listen to me."

When he stopped explaining, Maurizio stared, shook his head. "Ettore," was all he said.

* * *

He sat on a wooden chair set in the middle of the repaved road where work had stopped for the day. He faced the dark gash in the limestone cliff, his arms folded, a lantern glimmering at his feet. The sun had set an hour before, leaving the light of a near-full moon reflecting through thin clouds. Though the day's warmth lingered, Ettore wore a coat. If things went as planned, he would soon be somewhere colder.

Muto lay on his stomach on the sloped side of the road, peering from behind the reed blind he had built. As the best hunter among the workers, the partners tasked him with following Ettore tonight. He wore dark clothes and a heavy knit cap. Work gloves protected and obscured his hands. He felt the bulge of a company revolver in his coat pocket.

Oddly, Ettore felt calm. Whatever will happen will happen, he thought. His eyes adjusted to the darkening night. He knew Muto was in place, waiting with him. A night owl screamed. Tree limbs rustled in the light wind. The limestone wall was a moonlit gray, split by the V-shaped gouge.

A sudden clanking and scuffing broke the silence. It took a moment for Ettore to realize it came not from the hillside but from his right, further ahead along the road. As he peered into the gloom, the darkness thickened into a dense, bobbing shadow.

He rose from the chair and faced the noise. As soon as he did, other boots rapidly crunched nearby. Hands on both shoulders pushed him down. "Do not stir, signore," a low voice said, very near.

He tried to turn but the hands gripped and restrained him. "*Calma*, signore, *calma*," the voice insisted. "No alarm. You chose to meet us tonight this way. Here we are."

Muto had seen the figures emerge from the vale as soon as Ettore left the chair. His instincts told him to react, but his instructions, conveyed in painstaking simulation, were clear. Follow, watch, tie a cloth to a tree, return to camp. Barring violence from the outlaws, nothing more.

"Let us see who exactly it is that we have here." The brigand picked up the lantern next to the chair and held it close to Vacci's face. He barked out a laugh. "Of course! Perfect! I should have predicted this! A blue-eyed polenta-breath! And a blondie to boot!" His four companions joined his laughter. "Who are you anyway, Austrian?"

For all the supposed jocularity, Ettore knew stammering hesitation on his part could be his death. "I am Ettore Vacci. No Austrian. My company is building this road. I want to talk to the capo of your band."

"The capo of my band?" The man snorted through the thatch of nostril hair that seamlessly blended into his mustache and beard. "If you are referring to those donkeys with the shovels, they are not 'my band.' They are nothing but dirt farmers from Bastiglione, here repaying my boss a favor." The brigand looked at the motley peasants, their moonlit shapes growing as they approached. He snorted again with disdain. "The 'favor' being that we all keep our *piselli* out of their wives and daughters. For the time being, in any case."

The men on the trail emerged into the lantern's circle of light. Shadows played over their lined faces and the folds of their rough field clothes.

"You recognize a few of these fellows?" asked the bandit.

Ettore peered hard into the gloom. He tried to check his shock as familiar faces peered back. He spoke to one he'd seen spreading gravel the day before. "Faustino, isn't it? We gave you work. You come now to destroy?"

The villager returned Vacci's gaze evenly. "When you are long gone, signore," he said. "I and my family will still be here."

Ettore saw more locals he'd hired. So, these Bastiglionese built the road by day, then crept from camp, circled along the hillside and back up to the worksite. There they joined more men from the town and tore up the construction they had recently completed.

The brigand beside him guffawed. "Surprised? The ones from the camp even bring along your tools and show the others how to rip up the work! Are you wondering how these men could be so disloyal?" Another laugh. His mouth dropped to Ettore's ear, his voice a sour-breath whisper. "But surely you see. They think they are saving their women!"

He turned and spoke loudly. "You men from Bastiglione, you know what to do. Start at the far end and work your way up to the same chestnut tree as last night, the tall one there on the right. Make plenty of work for the outsiders tomorrow!"

The workers went to their task. A few had lanterns, but the natural light from the sky was mostly sufficient.

Ettore sat quietly, surveying his captor. He was short like the others, but stouter, compact, thick-chested. A hawk beak of a nose dominated his bearded face. He wore a long jacket made of thick canvas, with large square side pockets. His waistcoat had wood buttons down its center. The butt of a pistol protruded from his belt. A rope cord around his neck ran through a ring in the butt of the gun.

The brigand faced Ettore again. "So, you are who, then? Somebody Vacci? So, what? Why do we care who you are, or what you have to say?"

"I and my partner are the ones building this road so we can make a profit. You tear it up for your protection. I come with a proposal so we both get what we want."

"A proposal that we show you mercy, no doubt. But you do have balls sitting out here, Austrian. Maybe no salt in your melon, but definitely *palle* between your legs!" He barked a laugh at his wittiness and considered the northerner. Opportunity sits here. "Eh, when was listening ever a hardship? Who knows where it might lead? Besides, the tongue of a businessman can come in handy when ransom talks start. Whether begging in your mouth or rotting in a box sent to your banker, it has its uses!"

"As for me, I am Penna. My capo relies on me like a third arm, but I am not him. To meet Corsicano, for that is his name, we must take a small walk." He pointed up the crevice.

Penna commanded two men to stay with the peasants to assure they did proper damage. He posted another in the direction of the workers' camp, three-quarters of a mile down the finished road. The fourth man joined him.

He pulled out his revolver. He aimed the gun at Ettore, carefully cocking the hammer. His eyes flicked to the remaining brigand, Generoso, who walked over to Ettore and roughly pulled a burlap sack over his head, cinching it with twine. "Try taking this off, and your eyes go to your banker, along with your tongue," he said.

Penna pulled Ettore to his feet. "My friend Generoso here leads, you are in the middle, I follow." They looped a rope twice around Ettore's waist. Generoso slung his trusty, double-barreled *lupara* on his back, then tied his end of the rope around his own waist so he could tug Ettore along with him. Penna brought up the rear, wrapping his piece of rope around his left hand twice.

"*Andiamo*, Austrian!" he said.

Chapter 19

When someone finally snatched the foul sack off his head, Ettore gulped for fresh air. Instead, he inhaled heavy grease-smoke and the reek of fried onions.

It took a moment for his eyes to adjust. A short-haired woman stood before him holding the sack, hand on her hip. She wore a man's clothing, as did two other women tending a large camp kettle in the middle of the room.

She motioned to a jug of water on the floor. He drank thirstily.

"Stop staring at him, Concetta," said Generoso, at the room's single table. "We checked his prick, it is the size of an acorn. You would do better with Pepino."

From within his bedroll, Pepino acknowledged his name by ferociously breaking wind.

Ettore sat with his back against a wall. Did I fall asleep in here, he wondered? The night was a blur. Their trek to this place seemed endless. Climbing blind made it worse. His filthy hands bore deep scratches and nicks. He remembered grabbing at air, trying to grasp something, anything, as the incline increased. Many times, either Penna or Generoso forced his hands onto a branch or a rock for him to grip. He touched the painful welt on his forehead where he had blundered into a tree.

Two men came into the room, conferred with Generoso. The bandit told Ettore, "Corsicano wants you." Ettore pulled himself up, brushed straw off his clothes. His stomach growled. Despite his first reaction, the frying onions, smoking and hissing, now made his mouth water.

They walked outside under the portico next to the courtyard. Ettore noted the compound's walls, guards at the gate, ample sleeping quarters, the sentry in the ruined church belfry. No wonder Corsicano wants to protect the place, thought Ettore, as he shivered in the morning cold. A refuge like this is well worth securing. Returning inside into another part of the building, his guards escorted Ettore up a staircase and into a large room.

A white-haired man stood, the revolver in his belt attached to a lanyard like Penna's. His waistcoat flashed gilt buttons. "Eat," Corsicano said. He pointed at a plate with a boiled egg and a bread crust, alongside a tin cup of water. Ettore took but five minutes to finish.

"Before you talk, Vacci," said Corsicano, from across the plank table. "Your name, right? Vacci?" He lit a black cheroot and clamped the smoldering rope between his teeth. "I am not happy you are here. Penna was wrong to bring you." He blew rancid gray smoke out his nose. To Ettore, it smelled like a goat turd on fire.

"But you make me curious. Obviously, you want to bargain. You think you have something to offer me, but I hold all the cards!"

Ettore answered with as much calm as he could muster. "With all due respect, signore, you are blind if you think you can stop Rome from building that road. I have met some of the men running the show. Not middlemen like me, I am talking of true *pezzi grossi*. A road on this side of the mountain will make them too much money for them to ever give up. Moreover, the military wants it.

"This is what I see," he continued. "You raid the valleys on your east, where there are many towns within reach. To the west, there is only Bastiglione nearby, a poor commune. As a source of goods and money it is hardly important. But on that same side, you have the problem of the crack in the limestone cliff, and now my new road runs next to it, making the crevice obvious to all. Your back door will be open. The authorities will discover it and drive you out."

Corsicano grunted, blew a ragged smoke ring. "Now, I am becoming impatient," he said. "Tell me, how much money do you offer?"

"As for that, we offer no money."

Corsicano smirked in disgust. "You *are* money, Vacci. All I need to do is send some of your toes to Minister Rimaccio in Naples."

"You can shred me inch by inch and you will get no ransom from the government. I am not important enough," Ettore replied. "My company has no money, either; we finish this road or go broke. What I offer is better than money. You have heard us blasting the mountain as our construction came closer?"

Corsicano made a slight tilt of his head.

"This is my proposal. We will use dynamite to seal the gorge. The debris will block your camp from the west; it is the answer to your unlocked door. After that, the road will not matter, and we go on building without further interference."

The brigand stood, snapped his smoke to the floor, crushed it. "Too complicated. Too much trouble. No, despite your words, I say there are big money men behind you. You claim they will not pay to save you, but I do not believe it. They will pay out of guilt. The others always have." This argumentative northerner was starting to anger him.

Ettore shook his head. "Those men are aristocrats, I am not; they will easily throw me away. Those people only take care of their own." Was that a squint of acknowledgment in Corsicano's eyes? Now for the gamble, the threat. "And, I have another reason you cannot keep me here."

Corsicano reached Ettore in two steps, grabbed him at the throat. His pistol swung clear of his belt on its lanyard. "Who the hell are you to tell me what I cannot do? I will kill you myself, on a whim." Ettore grabbed at Corsicano's grip with one hand, flailed at the dangling pistol with the other. The bandit leaned back and squeezed Ettore's throat tighter. As Ettore started to black out, Corsicano released him, pushing him back.

"That was a mistake," Ettore gasped. The capo's dark eyes relit with anger at the words. Ettore held up both hands. "You kill me, these mountains will swarm with the *Guardia* and army *soldati*. Rome may pay nothing to save me in advance, but as a royal contractor, once I am murdered their retribution is mandatory." He hardly knew if that was true, but he had gained Corsicano's attention. "They will attack directly up that crevice. You may think, how will they know of my death, how will they find you? Last night you had your men cover my eyes to conceal the route. But I am telling you, one of my own workers followed us all the way here! If I do not return to my camp within two days, he will guide the authorities to this place. Everyone will know exactly where your band is."

"You are lying," said Corsicano, pacing, barely under control. "You lie to save yourself. Nobody followed you. Penna told me he was certain."

"Penna is wrong. I can prove it. Send someone back the way we came. You will see a red cloth tied to a tree near the top. My man placed it there last night before he returned. That will prove the truth of what I say."

Corsicano gave the table a kick. The egg plate bounced off and shattered. He leveled a glare at Ettore, as Penna, hearing the commotion, stepped in from outside the door.

The capo angrily watched his lieutenant enter. Damn the man! Penna acted too much on his own, as if he was the boss!

And so carelessly over-confident that he let himself be followed! A reckoning was due.

Corsicano sharply addressed Generoso. "You and two others, go down, wait for me at the gate." He turned to Penna. "This wretch Vacci claims he had a man follow you back here last night, that he has left a sign that our camp no longer is safe. Yet you claim you took precautions! I am going to make certain he is telling a craven lie to save his skin. For your sake, Penna, pray he is a liar. Stay with him until I come back. Do not go anywhere."

Penna nodded briskly, swallowed hard, collected his thoughts. He had kept his ear at the door for the past half-hour and overheard every word. If they had been followed, like Vacci claimed, today was likely Penna's last day on earth.

He was not surprised the old boss had rejected Vacci's proposal; money and blood were always the capo's preferred choices. But the smart move here, he thought, would be to accept Vacci's offer. Perhaps, just perhaps, a desperate gamble was presenting itself, he thought.

"Remember, keep him here, in this room," repeated Corsicano. He tucked the revolver back into his belt and slammed the door behind him.

Penna pondered, heart beating rapidly. An important moment, he thought. It reminded him of playing a risky round of high stakes *briscola*. In the camp, Penna's card skills were legendary. This, now? Just another version.

He leaned onto the table where Ettore sat, decided his move, grinned at the prisoner.

"So, Austrian. Tell me of this big explosion of yours!"

* * *

Corsicano was met at the gate by Generoso who had gathered Pepino and Concetta for the search. Corsicano barely noted the presence of the woman. Both genders were fully expected to pull their weight in the band.

They left the protective wall of the monastery compound and proceeded across the cleared field of fire and into the looming woods. Since Generoso had led last night's trio of himself, Vacci, and Penna, he led the search group now as he did his best to retrace his path.

As he left Corsicano's room, he had seen Penna arching his eyebrows at him. The two men were close; such signals were well-understood. Penna was going to put some plan into play. Consequently, Generoso wasn't startled when he noted two shadows circling ahead as he searched for the signal left by Vacci's spy. And it was no accident Generoso had chosen two others for his search party who also saw Penna as Corsicano's logical heir.

"Capo, here, up ahead," Generoso called out to the brigand leader, who came heavily up through the brush to join him. "There, ahead, do you see it? A flash of red on the branch?"

Corsicano swore under his breath. He lumbered the thirty steps to where a rag fluttered from the low branch of a scrub oak. He broke the branch off, turned around, and waved it toward Generoso. "So, it is true, you fools led them straight to our refuge last night! How could you be..."

The brigand's rant was interrupted by the crashing pain of a cudgel striking down on his left shoulder, separating his arm from its socket and driving the old outlaw to his knees. He fumbled for his pistol with his good hand but was kicked face-first into the forest soil, then pressed into the dirt, a boot on the back of his neck.

Penna leaned to his ear as Concetta quickly bound the capo's hands behind his back.

"Shush, shush, now, Corsicano," Penna said quietly. "We both know life is a cycle turned by the gods. Your time was a wonder, a comet, a story to be long recalled. But now, signore," he said, as he gagged his writhing captive with the red signal flag. "Your time on the great wheel has come to an end."

Chapter 20

Only the detonation itself remained undone. Two bundles of dynamite lay planted six hundred yards into the crevice. Farther up, another bundle rested under an outcropping of rock. At road level, a thick log dam spanned the gap in the limestone wall to jam the rockslide. The shattered boulders and debris behind the logs would seal the gorge.

That was the theory. Maurizio took an entire day to get the details correct. Too much dynamite and the entire side of the mountain, including three hundred feet of ledge impossible to restore, would disappear in an avalanche.

At the base of the crevice, Ettore sweated through the final moments. Pezzoli & Vacci's maiden project was a complete failure if this didn't work.

"Time to move," said Maurizio. With Muto assisting, he unreeled the dynamite detonation wires past the log wall and down the road a hundred paces. Maurizio connected the wires to the terminals at the base of a square, wooden blasting box. "Prepare yourselves, everyone," he shouted to Ettore, Vito, and the others lying on their stomachs on the opposite roadside.

"*Uno! Due! Tre!*" Maurizio plunged down the T-shaped handle.

The ground shook as a quick series of roars forced everyone's face into the dirt. Billows of smoke and dust blew out from the vale as cascading rocks tore through the thickets and bounded off each other. The blasts tossed uprooted trees in the air, broke others in half, mid-trunk. The echoing rumble took long minutes to subside.

Gradually, the dusty murk settled. A boulder the size of a horsecart lay in the middle of the road, surrounded by others of various sizes along with branches and forest debris. A massive pile of rocks and rubble was avalanched against the log wall. Pulverized detritus of every type continued to rumble downhill, adding to the barrier; rock dust and shreds of leaves hung in the air.

"We did it!" cried Maurizio. He grabbed at Muto, who shook him off. Unfazed, Pezzoli broke into an awkward *danza*, one hand in the air. Ettore embraced Maurizio, partly in celebration, partly to keep his gamboling partner from breaking an ankle. Around them, workers shouted ragged huzzahs and threw caps into the air.

When Maurizio had settled a bit, Ettore walked down the road to survey their handiwork. Random boulders had pounded craters into the macadam surface. He told his crew chiefs, "We start here today, clearing the mess and resurfacing all of it." He breathed relief at their reports that no workers were missing or injured.

Vacci's eyes went to the ravine. The once verdant vale was now a sharp-sloped, extraordinarily uninviting quarter-mile of slanted landslide. Even a mountain goat would struggle on that landscape, he judged.

He stared upward, waiting. Within several minutes, through the diminishing grime he saw movement. Two men above the rubble hoisted a rope-bound, struggling form from the ground. One man took the shoulders, the other the feet. They methodically swung their burden once, twice, and, on the third swing, let go. The writhing body flew out from where the rockslide had started, bounced hard, then disappeared into a pile of blasted trees.

Ettore climbed. It was a slow, difficult hike, no secret pathways now. It took him close to thirty minutes to work over to where he had seen the figure strike.

He found Corsicano staring up at the sky though the rest of his body, completely reversed, lay twisted chest-down in the debris.

From higher up, Fulvio Penna half-clambered, half-slid down to his victim. Setting his feet solidly, he leaned in and lifted the dead man's head by its white hair, dropped it hard on a rock, wiped his hand on the corpse's shoulder.

"Thoroughly killed. As promised." He cut the gag from the capo's mouth, the ropes off his hands and feet, then kicked at the limbs to make their positions appear more random.

"So, Austrian, our deal stands. This masterpiece you created..." he gestured at the rubble around him, shook his head. "You have stopped up the bottle very well, I must tell you. We will stay off your road, my word as a gentleman. You can now proceed to get rich. I held up my end, sent the old man flying to hell."

He stepped within four feet of Ettore. "But this arrangement of ours, it is permanent, you know. You have Corsicano's blood on your hands as much as I do. How can you deny it? Our beloved Corsicano, the lion of the mountains, slaughtered, here, at your feet." He held up his hands. "My angry men will want to place blame, but I will tell them, *calma*, our leader's death was a terrible accident. He died heroically, insisting on overseeing this dynamite plan you and he had both agreed to. We shouted out warnings, but, eh, *che peccato*, everyone knows Corsicano, he was old, he was slow, his hearing, *meh*, not what it once was. Our dear Corsicano, he gave his life so his band would live on— blah, blah, I will blather all that goose-gabble. No need at all for retribution on anybody. Not for an accident.

"But listen to me, Vacci, if we see any of those army sons of *minchioni* sticking their long noses around corners, then I tell my men, no, wait, I was wrong, there was a witness to this event! Generoso, he saw you capture and murder our capo, our *padrone*, our legend—and in a most cruel and barbaric way! You lured him here with a promise of payment, then exploded him to death!" He spread the fingers of his fists in the air. "Boom! The men are simple, they will easily believe me, don't think they won't! Everyone knows you northern slicksters are untrustworthy men. If I but say the word, you and that other one will wake up one morning in your fancy beds to find yourselves garroted to death! All your *famiglie* as well, to your third cousins! For I believe what my father once told me, Vacci: A century-long vendetta is one just begun!"

Ettore immediately came back at the outlaw. "Do not ever speak to me again of threats, Penna. I assured you this matter is between only us, and I do not renege on my word. And here is a new promise I make. Yesterday, I sent sealed envelopes with maps of your compound to my acquaintances in government, in business, in the Church. If anyone harms me or Pezzoli or those whom we love, they will send those envelopes to everyone from the police and the army to the pope and the king. Word will reach your criminal rivals out here in these mountains. With the reward my people will post, and your location made clear, your enemies will be murdering each other in their eagerness to murder you!"

Penna stared at Ettore for a long moment.

"Eh. A good conversation, Vacci! I knew we were like-minded. Live and let live, this is what I always say." He grasped Ettore's hand and shook it vigorously. "A deal is a deal. My honor is no less than yours, signore! Perhaps we meet again!"

Penna took a last look at the old capo's ruined body and made the sign of the cross. He gave Ettore a slight tip of his cap, then started to climb back to Generoso. Ettore watched until their shrinking figures disappeared past a copse of shattered beech trunks.

* * *

It took another nine weeks before the new road through the Apennines reached Addolorata. The Castrubellese workforce, shorn of all local laborers, was split into two crews that each worked twelve-hour shifts. The hammering of pickaxes, the grind of rollers, and abrupt dynamite blasts echoed across the nearby peaks. At night, those living in the valleys could chart the company's progress from the glow of lamplights and torches against the black bulk of the mountainside.

Ettore and Maurizio drove the men hard but there were few complaints. Behind them the new road gleamed, a great coiling ribbon of gray through the mountains. Now, each day at dawn the camp picked up and resettled itself at the end of the latest new work. The immensity of what they were accomplishing filled the men with pride, an emotion many had never known on a scale such as this. That and knowing the end was fast approaching deferred the bone-weary exhaustion that could have brought the enterprise to a jarring halt. Instead, at the sight of Addolorata silhouetted on a lower hillside, the pace of construction sped up on its own.

A ribbon-cutting ceremony marked the moment when the missing piece of *La Strada Re Umberto I di Savoia* linked the road segments across the Apennines. Dignitaries from the region converged on the little town. A brass band played the anthem of the Italian kingdom, as the children's choir of Naples' Cathedral of Santa Maria Assunta, transported to Addolorata in a line of horse-drawn wagons, sang its stirring lyrics:

The drums roll, the trumpets sound and sound again!
Canticles of glory we fervently raise!
Long Live Italy, Italy, Huzzah! Long Live the King!

The king himself was not in attendance, an attack of indigestion the culprit, but the dynasty was represented by the extraordinary presence on the dais of nineteen-year-old Crown Prince Victor Emmanuel Ferdinando Gennaro di Savoia, heir to the throne and already grown to his full adult height of five feet even.

"Quite the shrimp," muttered Maurizio under his breath, as he and Ettore backed away, bowing, after receiving the prince's congratulations on behalf of the king.

"Quiet, you'll get us beheaded," Ettore whispered. "Show proper respect; he will be our monarch one day! Besides, his goodwill means future contracts."

The prince had presented each with an envelope marked by the royal seal. The government, in an unusual burst of largesse, had added a modest bonus for the partners for meeting the harsh deadline. It had reached this decision, in part, following a visit from a delegation of villagers from Bastiglione. Led by their parish priest, they had traveled to Naples in three oxcarts and presented Minister Rimaccio a petition. In it, they expressed their undying gratitude to His Highness, Umberto I, for providing them, first, with better market access via the new road; secondly, months of construction employment for so many of their menfolk; thirdly, relief from other, unspecified, local difficulties. Their praise of Pezzoli & Vacci Costruzioni was particularly profuse.

The commune's message, echoed by the town council of Addolorata, which stood to gain mightily from the new thoroughfare, redounded heavily on Raimondo Rimaccio. So much so that Rome saw fit to promote the minister for his extraordinary acumen in discovering Pezzoli & Vacci, exactly the right firm at exactly the right time. In the future, Rimaccio was to be based in Milan, from there to administer all the kingdom's road projects from Rome to the northern provinces.

As the choir began their next offering, Francis of Assisi's heartfelt *Cantico del sole*, the minister smoothed his vivid, silk, tri-colored sash across his chest. It had arrived at his office the week prior with a personal note from the king. Rimaccio was pleased to take so much credit, though he had never for a moment believed that the two upstarts would succeed. The cocky newcomers and their Castrubellese work gang had proven him wrong. And at such a low price!

Interestingly, when he had spoken to the partners the day before the ribbon-cutting, they did not bring up the issue of mountain brigandage. In the previous months, Rimaccio had heard rumors of certain violent doings in the mountains, but he asked no questions. He hardly wanted to stifle the innovative spirit or to implicate, in any way, promising young men capable of even greater service to the regime. It was enough that Pezzoli

& Vacci had proved they could get a difficult project done, and as promised, produce a quality product in the bargain.

With the conclusion of the hymn and, with that, the day's ceremonies, Rimaccio crossed to where Maurizio and Ettore stood shaking hands with various officials. He interrupted with the excuse of a pressing matter and drew the two young men to the side.

"Signori, I want to say this," he told them. "You have clearly done right by me and in so doing have placed me firmly in your debt. As a man of honor, I, Raimondo Rimaccio, am one who always fulfills his obligations. Therefore, I personally assure you I will do my part to help make the coming years fruitful for you and your impressive new company."

The man was as good as his word; within two weeks he had already presented Pezzoli & Vacci a second project to repave the major thoroughfares of shattered San Remo, still repairing itself after the lethal earthquake that had roiled the Ligurian Sea earlier that year. Furthermore, there was talk of government roads to be built in the Italian colony on the Horn of Africa. And then? There seemed to be no lack of prospective projects for the foreseeable future.

Chapter 21

1890: Castrubello

The traffic on Naviglio Largo was busier than ever. Industry was growing, raw materials and finished products vied for space on every canal barge that floated. Milan had grown into a city of more than four hundred thousand souls as peasants left the fields to work at its forges and textile mills. Throughout the north, rural estates hauled foodstuffs by the ton to canal docks for water transport east.

The commune of Castrubello had become a regular stop along the way. Even now, Tonia Como watched one of the low-slung barges pole up to the new stone quay on the far bank, near Ponte Spagnolo. The quay was a loading point for bolts of silk cloth produced at Torrquadro and local produce earmarked for markets in Milan. The pavers on the old bridge rattled with wagons and carts laden with goods.

The canal barges carried passengers as well. As she knelt scrubbing her household laundry, she saw several disembark across the way. One caught her eye, his movements familiar. With an involuntary intake of breath, she recognized Ettore.

"Brother!" She hefted herself to her feet to see him better. He appeared the same but not entirely. Much darkened by the African sun, he sported both a white, wide-brimmed hat and a full mustache the color of wheat. He wore a brown coat and a green vest with what was it? A gold watch chain! And his trousers looked new, tucked into tall leather boots.

Her brother was now twenty-eight. He had been gone over three years since he stood as godfather to little Renzo. As he came closer, walking faster, waving, Tonia saw in her brother's demeanor that his essential good nature remained. But other small signs—the way he carried his shoulders, the set of his jaw—spoke of success and brisk resoluteness.

When he reached his sister, Ettore dropped his canvas bag and tried to sweep her up in a great hug. But he did not lift her much, her pregnant womb got in the way.

"Ettore! Put me down," she laughed from her toe tips. "Why didn't you send word you were coming? We were expecting you later next week!"

Ettore laughed. "Whew, you are a load of rocks, plump Tonia." His sister gave him a mock swat. "Our steamer from Abbas broke all records. And, not wanting to wait, I left Maurizio with the company so I could go on ahead," he added. "While I am here, I have a business proposal for your husband that he will want to hear."

"You also wrote of visiting Turin," she said lightly. She knew how to read between the lines of her brother's letters.

"Ah!" Ettore laughed. "Sister, that is to be a proposal of a far different sort! But later with all that, Tonia! You are so beautiful!" She beamed as he patted her belly. "Famiglia Como grows, I see!" he said happily, with another embrace.

He turned to three-year-old Renzo who was watching his uncle manhandle his mother, not certain to rush to her aid or run for his life.

"Renzo Como, come here, give your Zio Ettore a great manly *abbraccio!*" called Ettore. The boy hesitated, but waved forward by his smiling mother, acquiesced to the embrace.

"Growing up so soon, a little man already," said Ettore, tousling the boy's hair.

"And this is Pietro," Tonia said, taking the two-year-old by the hand and thanking the women who had been busy watching him. Ettore held open his arms, but the child burst into tears.

"No, no, Pietro, I am your Zio Ettore. Look, I bring a gift!" With that Ettore pulled from his bag two small carved wooden camels set on wheels, a pullcord through their muzzles. Pietro and Renzo rushed to the toys. Prompted by his mother, Renzo smiled and said shyly, "*Grazie,* Zio!" Pietro was already roughly dragging his camel, fallen onto its side, over the stone causeway.

Tonia locked her arm in her brother's. "I am so happy to see you; you must tell us of all your adventures. The money you send, it helps so much." She looked at her half-finished laundry. "I am finished with this for today," she announced. "What remains can wait for *domani.* Right now, we go home! How amazed they will all be!"

When she tried to balance the clothes basket on her head, Ettore took it under one arm. "Anybody wanting to ride the great stallion named 'Zio Magnifico', must climb up here on my back! Starting with you!" Ettore exclaimed, putting the basket down, sweeping Pietro onto his back, then lifting the basket again. "You wear my hat, Renzo," putting it on the boy's head.

"And scout ahead for *banditti!*" The boy picked up a stick but stayed close to his mother.

"Help me with my bag, Sister," he told Tonia. She held one strap, Ettore the other. The bag sagged between them. With his other arm, he carried the wash basket on his hip. Pietro hung onto his neck urging his mount to speed up.

Thus it was that Ettore Vacci, overladen, laughing, greeting the townsfolk whose many men he employed, came home.

* * *

The big field did not look like much. The rough rectangle of twenty acres sprouted thorny bushes and a smattering of scrubby, stunted trees. Along one long side of the property flowed Naviglio Largo. Local tradition held that it was near this place, in the antiquity that far predated the construction of the canal, Imperial Rome had garrisoned a legion and constructed a palisade fort. Over the many years since, enough random artifacts had been found in the area—coins, hardware bits, broken weapons, and the like—to suggest the story was true. Certainly, it was commonly assumed that the name "Castrubello" was a corruption of the Latin *castrum bellum*, 'War Fort.'

Located some two miles north of Ponte Spagnolo, the property had once belonged to the Society of Jesus. There was an old priory on the site originally intended as a rural retreat house. But in 1733 the *gesuiti* had fallen victim to cutthroat Vatican politics, and the pope suppressed the order throughout Europe. Its twenty acres reverted to the Vatican and were never returned, even after the Society was eventually restored. When the Italian crown absorbed the old Papal States into the realm, scraps of former church land like this one became surplus. Six months earlier, the parcel went on auction. Leaping at the rare chance to buy country real estate, Pezzoli & Vacci Costruzioni put up the winning bid.

"Desolation," Carlo said. "There is nothing here."

"Look at what is here, Carlo, not what isn't," Ettore answered. He scuffed the thin topsoil with his boot toe, kicking up sand and small rocks. "Over there, we have dug core samples," he said, pointing to several heaps of subsoil. "It is all rock and very fine sand as far as we have seen, a natural source of roadbed material."

Carlo kicked at the ground himself with his boot. "You say you want me as a partner in this. Ettore, I catch fish. What do I know about quarries? I could manage a shovel, no more than that."

Ettore responded. "Look, Carlo, I was there when your brother Francesco announced to your parents his intentions to emigrate to America." He knew this was a touchy subject but had a bearing on the issue before them. After Gemella lost a second child, Francesco had made the painful decision that a new start was needed, far away from the cycles of illness and sad memories that had permeated their life in Castrubello. They were due to leave soon, intending to travel to a city called Detroit in America where other Castrubellese had already settled.

"When he leaves, you know the Como fishing operation will be affected and not to the good. Your father Lorenzo, God preserve him, is becoming too old for the river—you know this, Carlo—leaving just you and Vito to provide for everyone. At the same time, more boats than ever are pulling out fish day after day. At what point will there no longer be enough fish to go around? Is it not time for something new? I am thinking of my sister Tonia, Carlo, not only of you. I tell you a quarry will yield you far more security than fishing ever has." Seeing that Como was listening, he pressed ahead.

"I do not need your technical expertise. Do not allow that thought to keep you from this chance. We have men who will teach you all you need to know. Getting a new quarry underway will mainly require common sense and good judgment. You have those things in abundance already, Carlo, not to mention our complete trust. You know the people of Castrubello. Moreover, you are well-respected throughout the commune." He looked at his brother-in-law. Since that dark night at the old farmhouse, many in town now treated his brother-in-law with a respectful deference. Carlo stared impassively past Ettore to the canal.

"Think ahead, man, hear what I am saying. In time, this new business will make your family's fortune. This is not charity I offer, Carlo, if that is what you are afraid of. I already own this ground and will establish this enterprise with or without you. To possess the *cava* that provides gravel and excellent Pirino sand for Pezzoli & Vacci projects, with no middlemen, this will mean faster work and, yes, more profit for my company. I want to build a large concrete factory on this same site one day. That too will open all sorts of new possibilities for my business, for our families. Become my managing partner in this quarry enterprise, Carlo, you must agree."

Carlo paced, looking up and around to the fluttering flags that delineated the property's borders. His eyes went again to the great flowing canal, then the treeline hiding the Pirino beyond. He thought of his sons.

"Thank you, Etto," he said, finally. "I cannot say no. I only hope to justify your faith in me."

Ettore came close, put an arm on his brother-in-law's shoulders, spoke ardently.

"Listen to me, Carlo. I will say this once, then never again. You already have my faith. You always will. Here is why. I am indebted beyond repayment to the man who avenged the deaths of my mother and father!"

BOOK TWO
FATE'S RESTLESS FEET

I thought I was learning to live;
I was only learning to die.

—Leonardo da Vinci, Codex Atlanticus

Part I: The Oasis

1911

Chapter 22

11 October 1911: Tripoli, Libya

The landing barge struck the concrete quay with a jolt, rocked back, struck again. More than a hundred elite Bersaglieri light infantrymen, the distinctive black capercaillie feathers on their helmets bobbing wildly, fought to gain their balance as they struggled to stand at their lieutenant's command, "UP!"

In the vast harbor, bustling with activity and loud with toots and louder horn blasts of dozens of boats of every size, lay the fast troop transports *Verona* and *Europa*. The ships were well into the process of disgorging the troops of the 11th Bersaglieri Regiment and the 40th Infantry, along with assorted support and supply units. Sent post-haste from Naples two days earlier, the vessels had arrived to supply and reinforce King Victor Emmanuel III's newest colonial crown jewel, Tripoli, capital of the great coastal province known as Tripolitania. The bulk of the Italian Expeditionary Army was soon to follow.

Private Gianni Como queued up with the other members of 4th Company aboard the box-like rectangular barge. Built by ships' carpenters and cumbersomely collapsible—complete with flip-up railings—the ungainly wooden raft, fitted with long benches, held one hundred and twenty men. The other half of his company, as well as 5th and 6th companies—the rest of 27th Battalion—were aboard a convoy of similar craft strung out behind them waiting to land. The noisy steam launches towing the ungainly craft from the *Verona* chuffed heavy black smoke from their funnels into the bright African sky. Seagulls banked and keened in the offshore wind.

Royal Navy sailors still wearing their summer whites handled the lines, tying Gianni's barge up to pitted pig-iron cleats embedded in the battered old jetty. The men, packed like anchovies in a tin, involuntarily jostled against each other as they stood in front of their seats. Thank God the sea is somewhat calm for the landing, Gianni thought, as the raft banged on the concrete seawall again. How would this ever work in a rough chop?

The men kept their excitement in check, although for those from country villages, ocean voyages, even brief ones, were hardly the norm. Gianni and the other new conscripts were the most fidgety, wide-eyed, eager but not knowing what to expect. The older veterans, called up from the reserves for the invasion, occupied themselves with keeping their footing.

The troops wore the Italian army's new gray-green uniforms issued for the campaign. "Hotter than hot *merda*," Gianni's fellow Castrubellese, Marzio Volpe, said when he first donned the heavy campaign jacket. "It is damn overcoat material for the Alps, not this furnace," he groused.

"You woman," Gianni chided.

Gianni wore everything the army issued to him without complaint. Keenly aware of the great national adventure underway, he was proud and possessive of his uniform. He kept his brown leather boots, belt, bayonet scabbard strap, and ammunition pouches carefully conditioned with olive oil. His wooden canteen, stenciled *11th Bersag. Reg. 4th Co.* with the *G. Como* he'd engraved on its metal band, was at its one-half liter capacity. Normally his bedroll stayed tightly wrapped atop his knapsack, but what with disembarking into the barge and constant jostling ever since, the roll had loosened and skewed to the left. He prayed hawkeyed Sergeant Cena did not notice.

In Turin during basic training, Gianni had his photograph taken at a studio just off base. He wore his green dress uniform for the occasion, the military cloak dramatically swept back. Although a simple private, embroidered gold stars adorned both the collar of his tunic and his cape. On his head was his black, stiff-brimmed *vaira*, the formal Bersaglieri hat, iconic symbol of the elite rifleman unit. He wore it tilted back and to one side in the bold Bersaglieri style. Its long capercaillie grouse plumes—longer than those that graced his battle helmet—draped to his right shoulder. Beneath the brim's jaunty angle, Gianni's flaxen hair, a mark of his mother's Vacci blood—traceable to Longobardi tribal ancestors, according to family lore—presented dramatic contrast, matched by a boyish, downy mustache. In the sepia tones of the original photograph, the soldier's eyes appeared light on a face darkened by hard training in the sun. In the final hand-tinted version, the eyes showed a striking gray-blue. Gianni had sent one sepia print to his young wife Bianca, pregnant with their first child. The colored portrait had gone straightaway to his parents, Carlo and Tonia. It hung in Casa Como's entry hall, kept festooned with fresh ivy.

As he waited, Gianni adjusted the strap of his bolt-action Carcano rifle up higher on his right shoulder. He made sure the chin strap of his khaki cloth-covered pith helmet was secure. What worse scene could he imagine than his headgear flying off into the harbor, proud plume and all, just as he stepped foot in Africa!

Gianni saw Lieutenant Morella, his company's second-in-command, watching the proceedings from a spot on the wharf. He was leaning down, one foot up on the stone curb, with a relaxed half-smile on his face. This reassured the men in the boat. Despite momentary lapses, the landing of the regiment was apparently proceeding well enough.

There was also a collection of cameras on tripods set up above him as the unit finally began to move forward, one at a time, to hoist themselves up from the barge gunnels onto solid ground. Newspapermen from Italy, France, Germany, Britain, and Austria-Hungary all jockeyed for space near the water, eager to record the landing of the Italian kingdom's first two army regiments at Tripoli. Regular reports of the Italo-Turco War would be on front pages worldwide.

The troops had been debarking all morning. The 27th Battalion, to which Gianni's company belonged, was among the last to get ashore. The 33rd and 15th battalions that comprised the rest of the Bersaglieri regiment were already standing in easy rows of four deep, bored by the long wait for the last of their comrades.

Along the waterfront southeast of the quay, the 40th Regiment, a standard army infantry unit, was also rapidly offloading. A small fleet of assorted Sicilian fishing craft, pressed into military service at the port of Siracusa and dispatched for the purpose, busily shuttled crates of foodstuffs and barrels of potable water for both regiments. The 40th would soon be done, Gianni judged, from the number of soldiers assembling under their vibrant blue and bright red regimental colors. Unlike the Bersaglieri, the 40th was mustering toward the city's center and aiming itself, it appeared, for a march toward the south. Who knows where the Bersaglieri positions are? Gianni thought. *Non importa.* Our destiny will be clear soon enough.

Nearby on the quay, a band of navy musicians in dress uniforms was playing brassy music to heighten morale, although most of the men, relieved to be on dry land again, already were in high spirits. The long-promised reconquering of

Tripolitania, which for five hundred years had been a possession of the kingdom's ancient predecessor—Imperial Rome!—was finally underway.

The war with Tripolitania's current occupier, Ottoman Turkey, seemed to have sprung from thin air. Everyone knew that the sultan's six-centuries-old empire was in the throes of irreversible decline. At the same time, the young Kingdom of Italy faced social unrest, disease, and growing emigration. What better timing for a crusade to gain overseas possessions, an opportunity to resettle its crowded population, and for the kingdom to take its rightful place among the world's great twentieth-century colonial powers!

With barely a pretext, events had been set in motion, and on September 29, less than two weeks earlier, Italy had declared war. The regime quickly unleashed the eager Royal Navy from its Mediterranean ports, and within days the fleet was cruising off Tripoli. On October 5, its great ships began bombarding the handful of coastal forts held by the Turks, which offered a token, desultory protest from obsolete, sometimes malfunctioning Krupp cannons. As the naval barrage lay waste to the undermanned, and in some cases, empty fortifications, the Turkish garrison of five thousand troops commandeered every pack camel in the city, loaded them up with three months provisions, and strategically withdrew south into the desert hills, out of range.

Fifteen hundred Italian marines stormed ashore and took possession of the city. But the Turks had only retreated, not disappeared. Under the capable leadership of Colonel Nesciat Bey, they used the early days of the Italian occupation to regroup. Reinforced by mounted fighters recruited from desert tribes that hated these invading infidels, Ottoman officers led sharp, sporadic, reconnaissance raids against Italian lines. With the marines forced to defend an arc of seven miles covering the land approaches to the city, the streets of Tripoli went unpoliced. Civic disarray followed as some of the locals began looting empty buildings and abandoned barracks even before the dust of the Ottoman retreat had settled.

These developments shocked and unsettled Tripoli's newest liberators, and an urgent call went out to Italy's gathering expeditionary force: *Accelerate your arrival or risk losing Tripoli!* Now, within weeks, the 11th Bersaglieri and the 40th had departed Naples and landed in support. With the newly arrived regiments preparing to take over the front lines, the original marine units were back in the city to assure civic order.

Things were certainly calm enough here, Gianni observed. In fact, a fair number of locals were watching the landing with apparent goodwill, just as the Italian government had predicted, confident that the population was eager to shake off oppressive Ottoman rule.

Spectators observing the proceedings at the quay animatedly talked among themselves and even engaged some of the officers and Italian interpreters without tones of rancor. These watching the army arrive will be merchants and some of the municipal officials, Gianni thought, the ones already comfortable with interacting with the one thousand Italian citizens who called Tripoli home.

Sergeant Cena, a swarthy, thickset, army lifer, loomed out of nowhere. "Get in line, Como! Despite what you think, we are not on a fucking sightseeing outing! And square yourself away, soldier, your kit is a disgrace!" Like the other noncoms, Cena spoke a rudimentary common tongue that all the men, mostly illiterate and jabbering a gaggle of provincial dialects, could generally follow. Cena's severe facial expressions and amplified, insistent, highly expressive tone filled in any communication gaps.

The battalion was to form up at the far left of the other Bersaglieri battalions, the harbor at their backs. Gianni's 4th Company scrambled into position, verbally lashed by its sergeants and corporal-majors. Gianni found a place directly in front of his friend Marzio.

"Marzio, help me here with my pack," he said as he turned. Marzio reached forward and pulled Gianni's sagging bedroll back into place and cinched it tight. "You're set," he said.

"*Grazie, amico,*" Gianni replied. He resettled the sling of his rifle onto his right shoulder.

"Quiet, boys, quiet," said Lieutenant Morella, striding past. "We will be here a bit, alright? So, settle down and wait. Without all the chatter." Despite Morella's Abruzzi accent, talking in the lines briefly subsided. Once he moved on, it started up again, albeit a few decibels lower.

"When the hell do we eat?" whispered Emilio, the trooper on the right side of Gianni. He was a runt from Arcona, near Lake Maggiore. "I tell you, I am shaking with hunger!"

"Balls," said Marzio from behind him, mocking. "That is not hunger you feel, my tiny friend. You have seen your first *cammello* up close today. It is fear of being devoured alive that makes you quake in your boots!"

"Mah, no!" Emilio indignantly cried. "I will wring your chicken neck for that, just see me do it!" The threesome guffawed, joined by Patrizio, to Gianni's left. "I thought the *fannulloni* from the Mezzogiorno were black-skinned," he said, inclining his head toward a pair of Calabrians in the ranks to their right. "Now I see that those boys are snow-white doves compared to these *Musulmani*." He indicated three male civilians on the opposite sidewalk. Two were in plain robes and wore headdresses bound with woven bands; the other was in a wrinkled white suit, a red tasseled fez on his head. The threesome returned the glances of the soldiers with pleasant nods and smiles.

"Friendly enough, neh?" said Gianni.

"Smart enough to be friendly enough, you mean," replied Marzio. He turned to a sudden distraction. "*Porca merda*! What is this monster?"

The regiment rippled as troopers craned their necks. An alarming new noise blared from the sky as the roar of a single propeller made conversation impossible. The wood-framed monoplane, its pilot plainly visible in the open cockpit, flew hardly four hundred feet above their heads. Oversized, bicycle-like wheels hung on a boxy frame underneath the aircraft's fuselage. Two white canvas-covered wings, gigantic to the awed troops, threw a broad shadow over the ground as it passed.

The men in the assembling units erupted into a spontaneous, gasping cry of amazement at the magnificent sight. It was one of the nine aircraft, a collection of Austrian Taubes and French-built Blériots, comprising the embryonic Royal Army Specialist Battalion being deployed to the Libyan theatre. For most of the new men, simply riding a train for the first time had threatened their grip on the reality they knew. But what they were now seeing—a fast-moving machine suspended in midair? It was inexplicable, a defiance of truth, even as they gaped upward, slack-jawed.

Many had heard of flying machines, of course. But it was a fairy tale, certainly, like the story of the man-eating viper, the ancient *biscione*, said to slither through Milan's sewers. But this? Who could deny their very eyes? As the apparition approached, soldiers uttered *Madonn'*, crossed themselves, clutched at the blessed medallions beneath their tunics. Some did all three.

The begoggled pilot waved amiably at his rapt audience. Gradually rising another few hundred feet, the airplane resumed its short shakedown loop, tilting west back to where a fresh-scraped dirt runway waited.

"How can we lose? The *Musulmani* must be pissing themselves!' Marzio cried, even as company NCOs converged on their men to restore order. "Better check your own pantaloons first, hero," joked Gianni.

They stood in ranks for another half-hour. As the men became hotter under the frypan sky, banter diminished and finally stopped. Gianni was grateful for his cork pith helmet but sweat still streamed down his face into his collar.

Finally, the last barges emptied themselves and returned under tow back to their mother ships. Along the waterfront, bawling noncoms redoubled their efforts to goad their men to attention. To his right, Gianni heard marching boots arrive and crunch to a halt. It must be 6th Company, he thought. The falsetto pitch of their sergeant-major, Tombi, secretly nicknamed *l'eunuco,* the eunuch, was unmistakable. 27th Battalion's final company, the 5th, filled in the last gap.

4th Company's commander, Captain Marcuccio, emerged from a cluster of brother officers, sharp in their bespoke, slate-gray tunics and breeches with shiny leather boots and snug leggings to their knees. Marcuccio moved to the fore of the company as his companions proceeded to their own units.

Colonel Gustavo Fara, regimental CO, strode purposefully along the entire front line in a brisk assertion of authority. His executive officer, Major Bossi, accompanied him with three mustachioed staff lieutenants. A non-Bersaglieri officer completed the entourage. Fara reached the end man of the line in short order.

Recognizing this as their cue, two dozen buglers left their battalions and scrambled to form up to the left of 4th Company.

"*Dio mio,*" whispered Marzio. "Will they make us run in this sun?"

"Shut up," Emilio retorted under his breath. "What a soft muffin you are! Where is your pride, Marzio? Do you wear the Black Plume just to get laid?" Gianni, hearing the exchange, sniggered.

"What do you know of getting laid, Emilio? Do you even know what it means?" More sniggering all around.

Colonel Fara nodded to Major Bossi, who returned a snappy salute. He called, out, "Attention!" then "Left face!" The battalions pivoted forty-five degrees eastward on the road that clung to the seawall. The maneuver transformed the regiment into a single long column, four men across. To their left lay the harbor where fishing boats with lateen sails skirted anchored battlewagons and troopships. Ahead stretched Tripoli's coastal road that linked the capital to the great eastern oasis.

Fara and his staff positioned themselves at the head of the buglers and the regiment. The colonel turned to the troops with his sword raised and declared, "11th Regiment! Ready!" The men instinctively tensed. The three company captains raised their swords.

"*Avanti!*" cried the colonel in a clear voice. The column began an immediate double-time run-march, thighs rising parallel to the ground. The sudden tramping of their boots brought all nearby traffic to a fascinated halt.

Within three high-stepping strides, the lead buglers put their horns to their lips to begin their *fanfara*, Boccalari's *The Italian Rifleman*, one of 11th's favorites. The horns began blaring even as the regiment's riflemen ramped up their speed to the Bersaglieri's famous hundred and eighty paces per minute gait, a pace unmatched by any other unit, and one that prompted some to call them the kingdom's "Cavalry on Feet."

* * *

The 11th Bersaglieri Regiment consisted of nine rifle companies of two hundred-plus men each, designated sequentially as companies 1 through 9. These formed a trio of battalions of three companies apiece, with 1st, 2nd, and 3rd companies in 15th Battalion, the 4th, 5th, and 6th in 27th Battalion, and 33rd Battalion composed of 7th, 8th, and 9th companies. Together with its HQ company, machine gun batteries, support units, and supply company—which was still dockside gathering provisions—the regiment numbered well over two thousand men in all.

The Bersaglieri column left the coast road after clearing the suburb of Dahra where the edge of the sprawling oasis touched the city. The march changed to a slower but still hard-driving pace of one-hundred forty steps per minute. The buglers were silent and marched with the rest, instruments tucked under left arms. After another half mile, the column came to a crossroads. Fara called for a halt.

Gianni was close enough to see the officers conversing. They studied a map held by the adjutant and conferred with one of their local guides. Their nodding heads signaled a decision. The staff lieutenants hurried to relay the news to the battalion commanders and company captains.

27th Battalion's Major Negroni stepped to the side of the column. "Soldiers of 4th, 5th, and 6th companies. We proceed on this road to our assigned position near a village called 'Sciara Sciatt.' The other two battalions will proceed toward their own positions, southeast."

The soldiers listened with some surprise. This sort of information outburst was atypical. Usually, it took at least an hour for a regimental rumor to spread until every soldier knew some version of what was in the wind. For once, they were getting information directly, the major apparently feeling a need to explain why soon they would be marching alone.

"Interesting," whispered Gianni.

"Weak," judged Marzio. "Officers ought not to be songbirds. There are ears everywhere." He tilted his head toward several workers observing them from an adjacent olive grove.

"You are twitchy in the head," said Gianni. "Those people hardly know our tongue!"

As buglers returned to their original units, the colonel and his staff moved up to the fork in the road angling right. From there they would lead the remaining 33rd and 15th battalions to their deployments along the line southward.

With the road ahead cleared of brass, Major Negroni announced, "27th Battalion, forward! And on our lips, men, 'The March!'"

The column set out and with loud voices burst out singing, "The Bersaglieri March." This was nothing new for the men in the ranks. Bersaglieri doctrine had it that forcing the lungs to work overtime while marching was a prime way to condition. With gusto, they sang:

When the spirited Bersaglieri pass by,
I feel affection and admiration
for such military champions.
They move fast and light
when they march all as one,
when the wind on their hats
make the proud feathers flutter!

As the column advanced into the oasis, the sandy road narrowed. The city soon fell behind, and they found themselves increasingly surrounded by an intricate maze of gardens and dusty cross trails. The unit's pace slowed to a standard infantry march. Fig orchards, olive groves, and thousands of date palms merged into a series of thickets, divided by trails, large and small.

The column wound past tall hedges of prickly-pear cactus, their unforgiving, finger-long spines as thin, stiff, and sharp as steel needles. Zig-zagging clay walls marked the boundaries between mud-wattle huts. Occasionally, a few structures clustered around wells, forming random hamlets of low, single-floor dwellings and impoverished, open-air shops within the trees. Cooking smells from charcoal braziers made the soldiers' stomachs rumble.

In time, they marched through a larger village with more than one street. Locals cautiously emerged to watch. The children relished the spectacle of the battalion's rhythmic tramping boots, the uniforms and weapons, and especially the rakish black feathers displayed on the helmets. Their mothers in burkas shooed the littlest ones to safety toward the edges of the street or drew them close to themselves.

"Why do the women cover their faces like that?" Gianni asked out of the side of his mouth.

"I hear they are such great beauties they drive men wild. That is the reason all the men here have ten wives," Marzio replied, grinning toothily at a demure young woman and lasciviously winking.

"That means there are nine bored ones every night in each house. Good for us, I would say," Emilio chimed in.

"They will stay bored if you visit," Marzio teased. "Besides, what man with a harem would only do one at a time? Not me!" The friends snorted at the ribald fantasy.

"Ooh-hoo, such a braggart, Marzio," Gianni said. "But as usual you're all smoke and no meat, I think." The chortling hilarity built to barely stifled guffaws, and then, suddenly, Sergeant Cena was striding hard alongside.

"Once we hit camp, you three are with me," Cena told them. "You bigmouths are making fools of yourselves!"

They were not the only ones. Other soldiers up and down the column, especially those nearest the spectators, were trying to make eye contact with the surprised females on the route, who dropped their own eyes, turned away, and fled indoors. The Italians counted such reactions as proof of their charm.

The Arab men silently stared hard at the strangers ogling their women. In some cases, fathers angrily grabbed their daughters by the arm and forced them from windows. Such scenes went unnoticed by the troops.

"It is a truly great thing to be a conqueror," Emilio whispered with Cena out of earshot. "To us, the spoils!"

"*Idioto!*" Gianni whispered hoarsely, watching for the noncom.

The afternoon wore on. Now there was no breeze, and sweat soaked the chests, backs, and the armpits of the soldiers' uniforms. Only once did the battalion stop to draw drinks from their belted canteens. They stayed on their feet in ranks as they drank while the sergeants harried them to finish up.

In less than ten minutes they were back on their way. Aside from the hamlets, they passed occasional other freestanding houses and outbuildings, all made of clay and mud bricks, nestled in shadows among the trees. Gianni saw movement at windows and doorways but seldom a face. At a nearby, nameless crossroads, 6th Company separated from its two brother companies and redirected itself to a position behind the front lines. Its role was to stand in support as needed. Gianni felt a strange twinge as he saw the backs of its men tramping away into the dark shadows.

4th and 5th companies continued ahead in the clammy, insect-buzzing heat. The rest of the army, and Tripoli itself, felt a world away, far behind the dense labyrinth they moved through. Gianni stopped wondering when the march would end. They passed what looked like an ancient, disused cemetery, faded Arabic lettering over its entry arch. A wall surrounding the graveyard protected the tombs from feral dogs and flash floods.

The endless maze had become too complicated to remember direction any longer. Gianni, like the others, suspended all thought as they tramped within a pall of boot-stomped dust.

The units reached yet another forlorn, dun-colored village. From the head of the column came the sudden order, "Battalion, halt!" echoed by the sergeants.

They had arrived at Sciara Sciatt, consisting of three streets of adobe buildings organized around several communal wells. The boundaries of the hamlet were loose. Besides what passed as the town core, houses and structures of one kind or another sprinkled westward and southward out into the groves.

"We are home, boys," uttered a weary Emilio, after the order came to fall out. He dropped his knapsack to the ground where he stood.

"Yes, you are right, our own *paradiso!*" Gianni answered blearily. He swatted aggressive black flies from his face and head.

* * *

The dark-bearded man carefully watched as the crusader infidels marched through Tripoli's neighborhoods and beyond, closely observing how the residents reacted to these unholy Christians flooding the streets. A mixed response, he noted.

Ömer Uzun was a major in the Ottoman army. His unit, the 8th Nizam Infantry Regiment, and the rest of Tripoli's Ottoman garrison, including several light artillery batteries, had re-established themselves at the village of Gharian in the desert hills. There, tribal fighters were daily joining them, True Believers, determined to drive the papist Romans out.

The major's covert mission was to infiltrate Tripoli to observe the Italians and to harden internal resistance in preparation for a counterattack. He wore the dress of an Arab townsman: the white, flat-topped round cap known as a *tagiyah*, loose trousers, and his *holi*, a toga-like cloak tied at the shoulder. He had eschewed typical sandals, however, for sturdier leather boots, not as common but by no means out of place on the streets. For all the walking involved in his mission, he needed good footwear.

Uzun's physical appearance, religious faith, and familiarity with the culture, not to mention his fluency in the language, made it simple for him to blend into his surroundings. It was true that his own adherence to the Prophet's teachings was not exactly strict. The major had discovered much to enjoy from decadent western ways; he kept a silver hipflask filled with French cognac carefully tucked in his belt beneath his robes. But when he was among the ardent Muslims he recruited, his face became that of an intense zealot, the agent of Mehmed V, Sultan of the Ottoman Empire, Commander of the Faithful and Successor of the Prophet.

Major Uzun was only one of a handpicked contingent of Ottoman officers infiltrating the Italians' porous lines daily.

They came and went barely challenged since the day the Italian marines had first landed a week before. With a deferential smile, a slight bow of the head, a sincere gesture of the hand flat on the heart, a mumble of anything in the tone of a supplicant—these barbarians knew nothing of Arabic or its tribal derivations—and one could pass freely through the naive enemy's lines. This was particularly true within the jumble of paths and lanes spider-webbed throughout the groves of the eastern oasis.

Once amongst the civilian population, the officers contacted groups of Tripoli men enraged by the arrival of the Europeans. Uzun could not believe the arrogance of the Italian authorities, acting as if they were doing the native population the enormous favor of stealing their land! And fully believing that they deserved the Libyans' love for doing it! What incredible folly. Whatever intelligence the infidels were relying on to produce such false confidence, Uzun had no idea. But he was grateful for the All-Holy's gift of Italian obtuseness.

Having already recruited reliable ringleaders before they pulled out, the Ottomans worked to help them organize for the day—soon to come, they promised—for the population to rise up against the heathens. Before their retreat, the sultan's troops had armed the rebels in the city with good Mauser rifles, who carefully kept them from the eyes of the Italians. Now, as others joined the cause, even more weapons and rounds emerged from the scores of munition crates previously secured in Tripoli's cellars.

Uzun had liked very much what he observed of the Italian disembarkation and their haughty marches through the streets. The boorish entry of the unsuspecting battalions boded well. Many local Arabs were in fact pleased to see the Turks flee, Uzun had to admit, and had no intention of resisting. But, still, a large number were noncommittal, ready to blow with whatever wind prevailed. At the minimum, these and others were likely to join in the looting once the rebellion began, such was the state of their poverty. Their presence would add such energy to the chaos! It was up to Uzun and his fellow agents to coordinate the uprising with the counterattack the Ottoman troops planned to launch soon. The restless-eyed, naive Italians were already making that job easier.

His information gathering completed for the day, the Turkish officer adjusted his cloak, took a long drink from his waterskin, and began the circuitous trek back to his lines.

While 4th and 5th companies recovered from their march with rations and water, the battalion's commanders pored over maps indicating specific deployment. The two companies had been assigned to the far left flank of the regiment's long line facing east.

5th Company's own left flank was to anchor itself north at the harbor, linking to the south with 4th Company just past Sciara Sciatt. The 5th's two hundred and twenty men would set up their encampment a quarter-mile southeast of Fort Hamidieh, which overlooked the bay. The makeshift 'fort' was no more than a large earthen square with heaped-up dirt for walls. The former Ottoman position had been well worked over by the Royal Navy's initial bombardment of Tripoli. An Italian artillery team currently occupied the fort, sent there to repair the Ottomans' fixed Krupp artillery pieces knocked off their carriages in the Italian shelling. The work would take some time.

Starting at 5th Company's right flank, Gianni's 4th was to stretch southward another three-quarter mile. Beginning with 9th Company, the rest of the regiment was digging itself in from near the village of Henni to Fort Messri, the southernmost point of its lines. The gap between the 4th's trenches and those of the 9th belonged to 6th Company, though deployed nearly a mile to the rear.

Eastward, Gianni and his comrades faced a dense front of trees, random dwellings, and small gardens with walls. Mounds of prickly cactus, some twice taller than a man's height, reared up amongst the growth. Stands of tall date palms waved their green fronds in the slight afternoon breeze. Behind, to the west, the landscape was the same, broken only by the structures of Sciara Sciatt, and southwest, by Maqba, the old cemetery they had marched past coming in.

The troopers positioned themselves along a long, sandy track that provided a natural break of sorts through the foliage. It looked like a roadbed that had simply started and ended in the middle of nowhere. In fact, the swale had resulted from torrents of rainwater that roared through the oasis during the wet winter months. Dry irrigation ditches and sandy footpaths crisscrossed behind and in front.

The swath of open ground was useful for getting organized. The company began entrenching itself. In front of them, thickets of palm trees and masses of lower growth encroached within a few dozen feet of their lines. From no spot along their positions could the soldiers see the open desert. There were two miles thick with palm, olive, and fig groves before the oasis finally petered out and the Sahara appeared.

As the individual squads began pitching their tent lines among the trees, Sergeant Cena loudly called, "The following troopers report to me now!"

He bawled the names of any soldiers he had previously confronted for lack of discipline during the long march. Within minutes, Gianni, Marzio, and Emilio stood at sweating attention alongside eight others. Overlooked, Patrizio smirked a short distance away, secretly watching while pretending to unpack.

Cena called the delinquents to attention. He knew all about high spirits and big-mouthed swagger from his own early days in the army. Better to nip it now, he thought, than to let these boys go and stupidify themselves into real trouble.

The sergeant fixed his eyes into a hard squint, pulled in a breath, and for a full two minutes, unleashed a profane volcano of verbal abuse.

The noncom's insults included everything from his men's apish ancestry to the certitude of them returning home as drooling, pox-bloated imbeciles. He compared the size of their brains to the size of their balls, which themselves were smaller than dwarf parakeet eggs. Their behavior had been the worst display of wanton, self-serving juvenility that any Italian ever born had ever displayed! Did they not realize that King Victor Emmanuel himself would be told of their actions?

The sergeant touched noses with several quaking privates as he expounded on his spittle-flecked diatribe. Flushed by his effort, Cena finally paused to let the echoes of his displeasure sink in. The sergeant then moved to the practical.

"In a minute you are to take out your bayonets. Try not to fucking stab yourselves in your fucking foreheads with the pointy fucking end. Then, you will proceed into that jungle in front of our position and carve a big X on every fucking tree outward for a hundred paces. Should you find any buildings, like that shed-thing out there, tell whoever is inside to get the goddam hell out because we are knocking it down!

"The point of these orders, you doilies, is to create what actual soldiers call a clear field of fire. Once Supply arrives with our equipment, we will take out our saws and cut down the trees and then drag them out of the way. Am I understood?!"

From much past practice, and happy to say anything at the moment that might please their master, the eleven in unison shouted, "Yes, Sergeant!"

"No, I am afraid not, Sergeant," said a voice behind Cena. Those privates who had kept their eyes open during the verbal storm had watched the two officers come up behind the noncom.

The one who spoke was not a Bersagliere, but the liaison major posted to regimental headquarters. The other man was Lieutenant Morella. Cena kept his composure. He hated officer interference in front of the men but immediately came to attention along with the privates. On his cue, they saluted.

The sergeant recognized the major although he had never dealt directly with him. He was one of the political officers assigned to each regiment. No doubt the relative of a government big shot or the return of somebody's favor.

"I beg your pardon, sir?" he asked, arching his eyebrows.

The officer stood with his weight on his left leg, his right knee slightly bent. The pose of an aristocrat, Gianni thought, watching intently as he stood in his own frozen posture.

Morella intervened. "Sergeant, this is Major Orvietti from HQ. We are walking the lines, reminding..."

Orvietti interrupted. "I said, 'No, I am afraid not'. By that, I mean neither you nor your men are to touch those trees or any buildings. Not under any circumstance. What are you possibly thinking?"

Cena looked at him blankly. What a flaming *stronzo*, he thought. "I am thinking nothing, sir."

"Exactly my point, Sergeant. Let me remind you. Our mission here is to liberate these natives, and to embrace them into the Empire." His hand made an expansive circle referring, apparently, to all Tripolitania. "Liberate. Not drive them from us. Therefore, we do not destroy their date palms, their olive groves, their gardens, nor their houses, nor outbuildings. This is rudimentary logic, I presume. Do you agree?"

"Yes, sir," said Cena. "But if I may, sir?"

"Sergeant?"

"Our position here has no sightlines, sir. The enemy can infiltrate that forest and be on top of us before we can react. Clearing it even for a short distance will make a great difference."

A brief silence fell.

"It is not your place to question Major Orvietti, Cena," said Morella dutifully. He doubted the wisdom of the new orders himself. But he was a career officer.

Orvietti was not pleased. This was not a debate. And he did not need a lieutenant speaking for him.

"The 'enemy'? Where is that 'enemy', exactly? Our ostensible enemy, the Ottoman garrison, took one look at our gallant colors flying at the head of our troops and fled into the wasteland. In Tripoli, the people welcome us with open joy. Our soldiers give treats to the children, our doctors help heal their sick. We buy goods from their merchants without quibbling at their exorbitant prices. Were your eyes closed when we landed? The people lined the streets in joyful relief. There is no 'enemy', within our lines, sergeant, nor shall we create one. To that end, we shall do nothing to jeopardize the goodwill we enjoy. Understood?"

Cena answered, stone-faced, "Yes, sir, understood, sir!"

Had he put this upstart in his place? thought Orvietti. Would his father, the Count, think so? It was best to be certain. He fixed a stern eye on the sergeant. "You are to keep one other thing in mind, Sergeant. 'Commissioned' and 'non-commissioned' are important words. It is best you remember the distinction. The day you are yourself 'commissioned' an officer, by all means, feel free to share with me your tactical misgivings. Until then, your one task is to obey."

Cena's face, eyes fixed on a point in the middle distance, was stone. "Of course, sir."

The major waited expectantly. Cena met Orvietti's eyes, again saluted.

The officer turned on his heels. Morella hurriedly followed. He knew the sergeant's worth and had not liked seeing him humbled this way. He kept his eyes off Cena as he strode past.

Cena whirled back to the men to catch any glances, but even the slowest-witted private knew better than to register anything other than blank-faced banality. Besides, the sergeant, for all his coarseness, was one of their own. Major Orvietti, well, the gold braid alone told them he must be an expert at something. But in their gut, the troopers trusted their sergeant far more.

"Get out your shovels, you gaping butterflies!" Cena commanded. "Forget the trees. I suddenly feel a need to shit, but where is my fucking latrine?!"

Chapter 23

12 October 1911: Tripoli

A brisk desert breeze spun dust devils from the streets out into the harbor, alive with the further arrival of Italy's invasion army. Three more regular infantry regiments, the 6th, 84th, and 82nd had arrived just that morning. By mid-afternoon, they began deploying themselves alongside the 40th Infantry Regiment on the southern line facing the bleak Sahara front. Scouts reported that the craven enemy was lurking somewhere out in the windblown, distant, monotonous hills.

Artillery batteries, cavalry squadrons, and a brigade of mounted Carabinieri were still debarking. When the two dozen transports in the harbor eventually departed empty, over thirty-seven thousand troops would have deployed.

As for Tripoli's eastern flank, by all reports the line was well-secured. Given the fearsome reputation of the 11th Bersaglieri and the obvious docility of the oasis population, not to mention the nearness of the fleet's big guns, the Italian left flank was not the prime concern.

The Kingdom of Italy's tricolored banner snapped proudly from the roof of the port's red brick customhouse. In the flag's center, His Majesty's crest, emblazoned with the House of Savoia's white cross, surmounted by a crown, contrasted brightly with the sand-hued structures and slender minarets of the city.

Below the flag, in the piazza fronting the customhouse, Sergeant Renzo Como watched another of the fresh regiments marching southward. He leaned on one of his wagons, smoking. He was thinking of Gianni. The day before, he had watched as his brother's battalion quick-marched off into the oasis. I expect I will hear exactly where they ended up in a day or two, he thought.

Around him, the Bersaglieri supply company had assembled its vehicles, wagons, and mule teams in Tripoli's main square. The uproar of teamsters cursing and manhandling recalcitrant animals had subsided into the background. A few Carabinieri sentries guarded metal petrol drums stockpiled inside a makeshift enclosure. Enlisted fools with cigarettes approaching the area had their smokes slapped out of their faces. Officers received polite reminders.

Renzo was in charge of a convoy consisting of a half-dozen supply transports. All the vehicles were typical army wagons, pulled by teams of four mules. All, that is, except one. The pride of the unit was its single Fiat Tipo-2, essentially a motorized carriage powered not by animals but petrol.

A year earlier, Renzo's uncle, Ettore Vacci, had purchased a similar model to take him to his construction company's far-flung worksites. It was the only such wonder in Castrubello. Renzo learned how to handle the rig and even chauffeured for his uncle several times. When the army asked for volunteers to jockey their daunting conveyances, he had boldly spoken up. Now this marvel sat before him: a ton and a half of shining black metal, over thirteen feet long, boasting a four-cylinder gasoline engine with the power of twenty-four dray horses!

Scores of the vehicles had been unloading at Tripoli over the past two days, modified for use as ambulances and staff cars for generals. Open-bed truck versions like Renzo's went to the army's supply units. Even better models were being planned, according to the rumors, armor-plated ones, sporting Maxim machine guns in swiveling turrets!

Under the command of Primo-Lieutenant Bertoni, the regiment's supply company served all three of 11th Bersaglieri's battalions. For now, their only orders were to wait until all units were fully dug in. With nothing to do, several teamsters slept in the shade of their wagons. Others stood or squatted in small groups chatting idly. Or they stretched and strolled, gawping at their surroundings. The army never changes, Renzo thought. Bust your *culo* to get somewhere, then waste the rest of your time sitting on it once you arrived.

After each company deployed fully, supply convoys like Renzo's were to bring up provisions not carried on the march. The gathered wagons already bulged with extra clothing, foodstuffs, tents, tools, and barrels of potable water. Others contained armaments: Maxim guns and tripods, additional Carcano rifles, short, rectangular crates of ammunition. Renzo hoped he would draw 4th Company's position first; it was important that he maintain contact with Gianni.

When the army conscripted his brother, Renzo had immediately changed his status from army reserve to active duty. He did it to allay his mother's fears for her youngest son, promising her he would serve alongside Gianni if he could. As it turned out, he would have gone active in any event. The government, wanting veterans to season its raw recruits headed for combat, called up all its reservists for the Tripolitanian campaign. Still, by volunteering on his own initiative, Renzo gained his sergeant's chevrons. His brother was to serve as a rifleman in the 11th Bersaglieri; through his Zio Ettore's political influence, Renzo went to the same regiment as one of its supply sergeants.

Despite his supply posting, Renzo was confident he could get to his brother's side if heavy fighting broke out. Hopefully, he would not need to. From the start of the war, Italy's politicians and newspapers said the people of Tripoli yearned to shake off the Ottoman yoke, that the Ottomans were cowardly weaklings, and that once occupied, Istanbul would readily abandon Tripoli as too much of a headache to dispute. The Italian top brass repeated the same line of logic to its commanders, who filtered it to their men. Renzo wanted to believe all of it but was ready to be disappointed. He suspected most ranking officers simply parroted what their superiors expected them to say.

Renzo had to admit Colonel Fara, the 11th's regimental commander, was an exception. There were other good ones, of course. It was mainly the officers drawn from old nobility who spewed the hot *gasato*.

Renzo's musings ended with the arrival of a nervous private who saluted, then spoke with a thick Sicilian accent. "Sir, I bring word from Lieutenant Bertoni, sir!"

Renzo snapped his cigarette to the stones and spoke. "Private, listen to me. 'Sir' is for officers. See my chevrons here? Those make me a sergeant, address me as such. No salute for me, either. It is only the officers whom you salute. Is that clear? Now, who are you?"

"Novello, sir. I mean, Sergeant. I mean, I am Private Novello, Sergeant."

"Relax then, Novello. Take a breath. So, tell me, what is the word from the lieutenant?"

"All non-commissioned officers are to report to the command post immediately, he says. Sergeant."

Good, it's about time we got going, Renzo thought. "Fine. Thank you. Now go tell Corporal Sciavo over there the same thing."

Renzo straightened his tunic and adjusted his helmet strap more firmly under his chin. He strode across the piazza toward company HQ. He smiled thinly and shook his head, seeing the private snap to attention and salute Sciavo.

* * *

Our Sons,
I write for your mother and myself. We greet you with
kisses. Newspapers say the fleet has sailed and that Italy
has won a great victory. We pray you are both well.
Zio Ettore was ill but has recovered. It was more of the
mal'aria from his project last year through those
marshes near Naples. Zio says it is a small price to pay
for the king's letter of gratitude and gift of a ring.
Nanna Lucrezia stays in her bed most days. She
implores you both to come back to us soon.
Maurizio Pezzoli is offering to sell your uncle his half of
Pezzoli-Vacci. Sig. Agnelli wants Maurizio to help
manage his automobile factory in Turin. Ettore tells
Pezzoli what do you know of machines like that? Pezzoli
says he is bored with gravel. It goes back and forth.
The work at the quarry and concrete plant never ends.
The government orders have increased, we have hired
more men.
Renzo, Angelina sends her heart. She is ready for your
wedding day when you return. Gianni, Bianca is well.
God grant you are here for the birth of your first child.
Bianca is grateful that Renzo is there keeping you safe.
We are proud that you march for Italia. But I am proud
too of your brother Pietro. He never tires of the tasks I
give him and always asks to do more.
Old Carlo Ferrara died from the pellagra. Muto had
seventy-three years. A long life for a deaf one. Zio Ettore
paid for the funeral.
A letter came from my brother Francesco in Detroit
USA. His grocery market does well. Now he also builds
houses for other Castrubellese to rent. Your cousins
Paolo and Luca work with him. His daughter Claudia
married a man from Cremona! Still, they say he is not a
bad fellow.
I and your mother are in good health. She prays San
Michele the Archangel guides and protects you.
Embraces, Papà

Gianni folded the letter back into its envelope. He and Renzo sat outside Gianni's tent, pitched alongside the rest of his platoon. Today being a Sunday, 4th Company was enjoying long breaks and light duty.

"I feel so much better since he tells us we have already won! Oh, and thank you for keeping me so safe!" Gianni laughed, playfully tossing Renzo the letter.

"You are right to thank me, *piccolino*," Renzo responded. "But you must admit, it is not easy for them, not knowing where we are, what dangers confront us. How do they not worry? Let us both agree. We will take the time to at least send back a postcard."

Because so many of its soldiers were illiterate, the army supplied preprinted postcards with messages like, *'All is well! Viva Italia!'* and *'Best wishes to all. Viva La Patria!'* The tone was optimistic enough to reassure any recipient. The face of the cards featured color-tinted patriotic drawings. Gianni's favorite was that of *Italia Turrita*. It showed the image of a buxom, white-robed young maiden flying above the Mediterranean Sea, bearing Italia's tricolored banner to Tripolitanian shores.

He pointed at the letter. "It sounds like they are doing big business at the quarry. What do you make of Papà's talk of Pietro?"

"Mah, you know Pietro, always wanting to be Papà's favorite. Still, he knows how to work. I am certain Papà can use the help. It was *fortuna* at work when he drew duty at home with the provincial militia."

Mule-drawn wagons stood in a line behind the tents, where soldiers unloaded supplies and humped them into the encampment. Renzo had wanted to surprise Gianni by arriving with his gas-powered lorry. But this deep in the oasis no roads were wide or firm enough for the vehicle. Besides spoiling the dramatic entrance he had hoped for, it was clear to Renzo that supplying the lines near Sciara Sciatt would take more time than first assumed.

"More bread ovens," I see," Gianni remarked, shading his eyes with his hands. "That's good. The local stuff here, that smashed *pito* or whatever they call it, well, not my favorite, to say the least."

His brother laughed. "Always complaining, aren't you, Gianni? All I can say is that we eat very well at regimental HQ."

"Why wouldn't you?" Gianni responded. "Licking leftovers from staff officer plates. What is it like at headquarters, anyway? I have never even seen it."

"We call it 'The Castle' and it sits on a flat-topped hill at a poor little village called Henni. The place was originally the villa of an Ottoman lord. The building is a natural fort, quite large, surrounded by wild grounds within an iron fence around it.

"My supply company is bivouacked outside in tents near the vehicles and the livestock. Inside, it is what you would expect. 8th Company of 33rd Battalion mans the place. They have cut rifle slits in the window shutters and used axes to punch other firing slots through the brick walls. Outside, heavy machine gun batteries guard the front and rear. A sniper platoon is in position on the roof."

"It sounds like a castle, all right. What is Colonel Fara like? You must see him every day."

"Good, steady, reminds me of Papà," said Renzo. "All business, doesn't put on airs."

"Not many officers like that. Some arrogant major made our sergeant look bad a few days ago."

"Probably Orvietti, from HQ. Nobody likes him, not even Fara, I don't think. Always strutting like a peacock. But what do you expect, this is the army! There's no lack of assholes prancing about in fancy braid."

He noted the wagons were finally empty. His men milled around, smoking, waiting. "I need to get going," he told Gianni.

His brother got to his feet. "Let me show you our lines."

They stood and strolled to a spot where they could see the shallow trench extending north and south. Renzo shielded his eyes from the sand swirling through the oasis. "Not very deep and no sandbags, but decent enough, I suppose. Still, the boys facing the Sahara use plenty of them and have strung barbed wire." He looked to his right. "They also have dug in much deeper than you boys. So, you link with 9th Company to the south?"

"Not quite," replied Gianni, airily. "Our own 6th Company is down there somewhere, only further back enjoying the shade! Believe me, Renzo, there's nothing out here."

Renzo hoped that was true. On his map he'd noted no other units stationed in support of the thin lines of 4th and 5th companies. Elsewhere, he knew, Bersaglieri defenses were more stout. Deeper trenches and sandbagged ramparts stretched from the HQ's 'Castle' to southernmost Fort Messri, the corner position that linked up with 82nd Infantry, facing the Sahara. Moreover, the entire 15th Bersaglieri Battalion was in that same sector as a ready reserve for both positions.

"You're so damned close to the trees," he said, nodding forward. "Not easy to see what's going on in there. I expect you have patrols out all the time."

"Not from 4th Company," Gianni shrugged. "Maybe from the 5th." He felt he had to defend his unit's loose deployment from Renzo's criticisms. "Brother, things are so calm it doesn't even feel like we have a war. Where is the action we came for? A couple of petty thefts now and then, that is all. Have you seen these people? They are poor to the bone, in rags. It is clear to me our guns are aimed at nothing except goats and dogs and a handful of beggars in tumbledown shacks."

"Oh, *grazie*, my comandante, thank God for your expertise," Renzo scoffed. "But here is my advice, Gianni, listen, I am serious now. Do not assume anything. Keep your eyes open and your weapon clean. And remember, no matter where I am, I will come to your side if something starts up."

Gianni cocked his head. "Who's playing comandante now, Sergeant Como? Eh," he said, embracing his brother. "Stop worrying about me, you sound like Mamma. Take care of your own self, Renzo." He dramatically plumped the sides of his brother's trim stomach. "And for God's sake, stop overeating!"

The two men shared the laugh as they walked. "I will see you next week," Renzo said. Gianni gave a last wave as his brother mounted the lead wagon, watched as the mule-drawn convoy pulled out.

Returning to his tent, Gianni dismissed Renzo's worries. What did it matter if 4th and 5th companies' defenses were not the same deep trenches and barbed wire facing the open Sahara? The nearby mud walls and cactus hedges would provide plenty of cover in the unlikely event of an attack. The Bersaglieri were a rapid deployment force of crack sharpshooters, not stodgy emplacement infantry for whom no ditch was ever deep enough! Still, he looked at his rifle, then took out a bore brush from the Carcano's cleaning kit.

With the additional tents, ovens, and crates of supplies provided by Renzo's supply run, 4th Company was well settled in by their fourth day. Rations were boring but satisfactory; the fresh bread from the company ovens was the highlight of each meal. Packages sent from home were beginning to appear, and tentmates readily shared or bartered any edible windfalls with each other.

The young conscripts, suddenly unfettered by the daily taboos of Church, family, and village, found the new environment exhilarating. With no tolling belltower to remind men of their sins three times a day, army chaplains worked to fill the dangerous moral void. Their liturgies and confessional services were well-attended. Sergeants diligently meted out accountability for ill-considered foolishness, but their recriminations were no substitute for Mamma's silent disapproval or Papà's harsh leather belt. And an unbreakable code of silence among comrades-in-arms had replaced village gossips poised to spread the news of any youth's false step.

This level of freedom was heady stuff for twenty-year-olds in a faraway land. By ten days after debarkation, they were starting to feel a familiarity with their surroundings. Of course, some were homesick and many gripped by the fear of dying. But soldiers suppressed such womanish emotions, denied their existence. Bold bravado was the order of the day, and at least superficially, it fed on itself.

When 4th Company troopers received time off, they at first stayed close to the camp, playing cards, or singing village songs, accompanied by northern squeezeboxes or twangy, southern jaw harps.

Or they played what was fast becoming Italia's national game, *calcio*.

While room for a true football field was out of the question, there was a little open ground at the end of the line of pitched tents. Not enough space by any means, far too narrow and short. But it was mostly free of cactus, scrub growth, and rocks, and teams of five or six players could squeeze in to play.

The company's recruits from Piedmont knew football well, having followed the 'Turin Nobles' most of their lives. An apt name for a soccer team. Like polo and cricket, the ball-kicking game began as a sport for noblemen and the rich. Who else could afford the time? But the game's basic simplicity and small outlay—one ball—quickly drew the interest of all classes. The Piedmontese men in camp demonstrated the basics to the rest, and soon the company's leather ball was careening off tent lines, scattering stacked gear, and occasionally—to angry curses and threats of violence—blasting evening campfires to smithereens.

But such camp life charms had their limits. It was not long before off-duty soldiers were visiting nearby Sciara Sciatt. The sounds and smells of simple village life reminded them of their own. Shops offered fresh vegetables and local food; craftsmen spread their wares outside. Most of the merchants were familiar with soldiers; Ottoman troops had occasionally frequented their small bazaar. Street bartering led to animated, good-natured dramas that enlivened everyone's day.

And while the soldiers perused gourds, woven reed baskets, leather goods, and the like, they continually eyed the females whenever they could.

The Arab women in their burkas were a delectable mystery to the soldiers and one they longed to unlock. The *passeggiate* of their hometowns had made the young men confident masters of social intercourse. Neither at home nor here was mere social intercourse what they had in mind, naturally. Within their own villages' restraints, the primary means to that end was marriage. But here in this alien, far different world, where even the air had an exotic, earthy scent, who knew what was possible? Such was the gist of camp talk. But for every man eager to pursue his urges, others held back, afraid both of hell and the foreign women themselves, who, in their robes, reminded some disturbingly of nuns.

Already several minor incidents had occurred. Hardly matters of overt aggression, but for the jealous males of the oasis, perhaps harbingers of worse to come. Reports included several cases of soldiers flirtatiously bantering with cornered women on walkways, even playfully teasing to lift their veils. In one incident, three frustrated privates harangued a startled Arab tailor, loudly demanding, "*Postribolo? Bordello?* Tell us, where is your nearest damn whorehouse!" And, more darkly, claims of forbidden liaisons circulated as well.

It was not exactly that Italian authorities ignored civic complaints. The new provincial governor and commander-in-chief of the expeditionary force, General Carlo Caneva, was determined to establish a rapport with his monarch's new subjects. Still, some manly lustiness was natural, even desirable, among conquerors. It always had been thus, and always would be, would it not? What fool dared smothering an army's spirit of conquest?

The Ottoman occupiers, no strangers themselves to temptations of the flesh, had ruled Tripolitania with a heavy hand. But while Tripoli's Arabs may have suffered as the beleaguered vassals of an indifferent Istanbul, they remained related by religion. To the zealots among the Arab populace, these current Latin invaders were but the latest version of the same infidels against whom Islam had been contending, off and on, for the past thousand years.

Shortly after their arrival, Gianni and his tentmates had made a perfunctory foray into Sciara Sciatt, looking for something to eat besides rations. It hardly lasted thirty minutes. Now Gianni, Marzio, and Emilio intended a longer excursion. They had been steadily manning the trenches since Renzo's visit four days earlier, staring into the oasis, dully watching Arab boys herd bleating flocks through the groves. The excitement of picket duty had ended after the first hour of the first day. The challenge now was less mastering their eagerness to engage the enemy and more simply keeping awake. Sergeant Cena finally took mercy on their platoon and gave them a full six hours of their own.

When they arrived at the village, which took all of three minutes, other 4th Company men were already there. The street scene bustled with friendly interactions between villagers and strolling soldiers. Once the company had established itself in the area, initial shyness on both sides had worn off quickly. A mutual acceptance had established itself. The people of the oasis were extremely poor; some came to the soldiers begging for scraps of anything. Many of the young, conscripted soldiers, especially those from the smaller communes, understood poverty full well. The Italians freely shared rations and small treats with the local children.

"Let's start at this end," said Emilio. "We can try that place where they serve that whatever-it-was we had last week."

They had shared an egg dish the proprietor had called *shakshouka* that included lamb jerky, sautéed garlic, onions, and peppers. Emilio declared it *"fantastico!"* Marzio commented, "better than hardtack." Gianni had said nothing but retched his guts out later that night.

"*No grazie,*" he said to Emilio's suggestion. "You two go ahead. Enjoy. I will meet you both," he looked at his pocket watch, a gift from Zio Ettore, "in an hour, by the belt maker's, just over there."

He set out with an airy wave. Deciding to explore the next street over, he walked down a narrow alleyway between buildings. Gianni emerged onto a small piazza with a communal well. Mudbrick buildings crowded the street, more residential than commercial, although a few open doorways under cloth awnings seemed to invite passersby to enter.

Village women were coming and going at the well, filling tall earthen jars with water. They studiously ignored him as they went about their task. After filling their jugs, they set them on their heads. One hand balanced the water jar, the other was free. Somehow, they made the process effortlessly graceful.

Gianni found himself walking behind one such young woman. Her free hand clutched that of a small girl. The pace was slow, but Gianni did not want to try to squeeze past the girl in the narrow avenue. He shortened his steps, staying about ten paces behind. He was the only soldier on the street. He caught himself fixated on the rhythmic swish of the woman's rustling robes. Stop it, Gianni, he told himself. You have a wife! You will soon be a father! All that talk of women back in camp, it has crazed you! He looked for a side street to get back to his friends. I will join them after all, he thought. That place must serve some sort of normal bread.

The woman ahead suddenly stumbled and fell. The clay jar bounced once on the dirt street, then shattered. The child fell as the woman's grip held firm. The little girl began wailing loudly.

Gianni ran forward in an instant, as a few nearby doors opened. He turned the woman over, exposing her face and head. She was young, dark-haired, eyes closed, bathed in perspiration.

A few residents of nearby dwellings began to emerge, crying in Arabic, "What is this foreigner doing?" Emboldened by their numbers and the aloneness of the stranger, they began to surround where he knelt. Gianni only heard rapid, incomprehensible jabber. He looked around; the circle was growing. Why was no one stepping forward to assist?

"She took ill and fell," he said, looking into the uncomprehending, veiled faces. "She is not well." He unclipped his canteen from his belt and tilted back the young woman's head. At first, the water dribbled down her chin, then her eyes fluttered open, into his. She shut them quickly but sipped.

Gianni lifted the woman in his arms, her robes gathered akimbo. "Where is her house?" he asked loudly. Blank stares replied as the chattering increased. He freed a hand and pointed at various doors. "Door?" he asked.

One intent woman nodded. "Ah, *sakan!*" She lifted the sobbing child from the street and beckoned Gianni to follow. The rest of the group, heads bobbing as they prattled, surrounded Gianni and the woman in his arms, forming a burka-covered escort down the street.

They stopped before a door with unmatched iron knockers. Gianni and the first half-dozen of the group squeezed inside into a small anteroom. The woman with the child in hand gestured directly to the floor, but Gianni, despite her protestations, pushed past a wooden screen to lay the feverish mother on a pallet. The sick woman opened her eyes again as Gianni set her down. Her lips moved briefly. He pressed his canteen into her hands as the others fussingly converged around.

Gianni heard rapid steps and the women go silent as three men entered the room. The oldest, likely the father, Gianni thought, wore a striped blue and green scarf and gray robes. He and the two younger men neither smiled nor spoke. The black-bearded father stared at his daughter, then sharply back at the Italian intruder under his roof.

Gianni did not try to explain himself. To what purpose? He was not looking for gratitude. He had only done what any decent person would have.

"Please keep the canteen, signorina," he said to the girl, then, "*mi scusi.*" The men between him and the door briefly hesitated, considering, but stepped aside. Despite their hostile stares, Gianni respectfully touched his helmet and departed, ducking beneath the low doorway as the women outside parted to let him get by.

Chapter 24

23 October 1911: The Castle

Despite his exhaustion, Renzo could not sleep. His convoy had returned late to regimental HQ after fetching ammunition and food supplies to the Castle from Tripoli's quartermaster warehouse. In the morning, he planned to set out north with 27th Battalion's portion.

The scattered village of Henni sat amid thick clusters of fruit trees and cactus. A single hill sloped above the flat landscape, crowned by the heavily fortified white villa. A silver dome dominated one end of its flat roof; a crenelated rampart edged the rest. Extensive, unkempt gardens surrounded the building within an iron spiked fence.

Heavy machine gun emplacements protected the front and rear. The guns could easily rake any approach, rendered easier by an ample field of fire. On their first day at the location, on the colonel's orders, soldiers hacked back the greenery thirty yards in all directions.

Riflemen cradled their weapons at sandbagged windows. Others had knocked rough-edged firing embrasures through the villa's walls where windows did not extend. The sentries on the villa's roof held a commanding view of the surrounding terrain.

Renzo went to join them. The fresh air will settle me down, he thought. He emerged into a fading night; the thin, waning crescent of a new moon was barely visible to the eye.

As he stood peering into the gloom, he heard the metallic drone of one of the Italians' aircraft. Maybe his ears were playing tricks—the expanse out here sometimes made that happen—but Renzo could swear the sound came from the south, near the desert. It was the first time he had known one of the machines to venture beyond Italian lines. What was out there for the pilot to see?

A second monoplane suddenly rattled overhead, and for thirty minutes, Renzo followed the sound of both without spotting either. Gradually both engines faded toward their aerodrome west of the city.

The entire incident left him with a foreboding of... what exactly? As if in answer, deep booms of distant cannon fire commenced.

The cannonade came from the harbor warships and seemed directed far to the southwest. The enemy's cavalry is probing again, Renzo surmised. This was not the first time the navy lobbed its munitions at mounted Arabs boldly harassing Italian lines.

But now the staccato crackle of other sustained gunfire began to erupt. The villa was not under attack; the noise came from due south. There, Renzo knew from his deliveries, 7th Company held Fort Messri at the corner where the trenches turned west.

More naval shells exploded in the desert. Rifle and machine gun fire intensified as Italian units awakened to the threat.

Renzo hurried down the stairs. He hadn't heard a thing to the east, along the Bersaglieri front. But if something big was happening, he needed to get to his brother. On the ground floor, headquarters began bustling as a trumpeter sounded a shrill, rapid reveille.

"Stop there, sergeant," a voice commanded, as Renzo reached the doorway.

"Sir," Renzo replied, coming to attention. Before him stood the regiment's executive officer, Major Bossi.

"All movement is restricted until we ascertain what exactly is occurring," said the major. "Only by special command are any troops permitted to venture forth."

"But, sir," Renzo responded. "We have ammunition and water for the 27th. They are low in both. My orders are explicit, if enemy action begins, I must..."

"Countermanded," Bossi said. "No supplies move until we know the tactical situation. In the meantime, make yourself useful. Gather your drivers, proceed to the roof, report to Lieutenant Torricelli." He saw Renzo's distress. "Do your duty, Sergeant. Your brothers-in-arms need you here."

* * *

Sergeant Cena sat bolt upright. The barking of dogs had burst through his dream of a busty prostitute he'd once bedded in Rome. He pulled on his boots and, buttoning his tunic, stepped into the chilly morning air. He strode to the low berm that bordered their position.

Something was certainly disturbing the local dogs out to the east. In a growing crescendo, they incessantly voiced alarm. The cacophony spread toward 4th Company's lines, joined by sympathetically baying hounds in Sciara Sciatt.

Cena felt no breeze, yet the dark mass of the oasis seemed in motion. Palm fronds shook their silhouettes against the pale skyline; their trunks still blended obscurely within thick shadows.

Sentries posted along the berm all, like Cena, leaned hard toward the ruckus. Barking dogs in the morning were no novelty, but this racket was unnerving. The tent line moved with awakening men. A few of the troopers had already pulled on their tunics and began deploying along the berm.

From within the inky darkness came the sudden, startling swoosh of a great mass of men surging through dense undergrowth. As bugles blared, a thousand Arab fighters and Ottoman regulars burst from the gloom in front of the Italian positions. These tribesmen were no Ottoman conscripts running to danger because their officers would shoot them from behind if they turned back. They were Instruments of Heaven, determined to exterminate infidel devils, and they now charged with the fierce abandon of men with no fear whatsoever of death.

Gianni stumbled to the line coatless, pulling his braces up with one hand while clutching his rifle with the other. His tentmate Marzio was at his side. Both had their ammunition cases over their shoulders. They hit the ground with the others along the shallow ditch.

Gianni rapidly loaded a clip and aimed at the enemy closing fast. He fired and ejected as rapidly as he could, hoping his bullets hit something. Every six shots meant a pause to reload. He tried not to fumble the clips amid the frenzied storm of gunfire.

He kept pulling his trigger at the wall of attackers. More tribesmen joined the battle. Their turbans and flowing robes, flashing scimitars, fierce ululations, and blazing weapons—everything from fine bolt-action Mausers to antique muzzleloaders—created a daunting, deafening roar for the desperate men at the berm. The company's commander, Captain Marcuccio, and the other officers stood behind the line and shouted encouragement, brandishing swords. Heavy gunpowder smoke swirled over the action.

A turbaned head kicked back as Gianni pulled his trigger, but he barely registered the sight. He ejected the shell and pulled the trigger again. Next to him, Marzio suddenly clutched his throat, blood blurting through his fingers in dark spurts. He fell face-first onto the berm. Gianni heard somebody—Sergeant Cena?—shout *"cazzo!"* behind him. He had no time to look. Dirt and dust kicked up all around where he lay. A bullet whizzed so close he felt the vibrating heat of it on his ear.

The action was too intense for him to take a breath. The line seemed to be holding, though the attackers also stood their ground. For the moment it was a battle of murderous attrition at thundering, point-blank range. Help must surely come, thought Gianni, surely.

And then there actually was a sudden new sound from behind them, of cries, gunfire, rushing feet! Lieutenant Morella, his cheek bleeding from where a bullet had taken a bite, saw men in Arab dress emerging from the buildings of Sciara Sciatt with rifles, knives, swords. Behind them came some of the village's women, men, some children.

"My God, men," Morella cried, "Our friends rise to aid us!" At that moment the officer, with a suddenly final gurgle of astonishment, fell dead on his back, stiff-legged, staring, a bullet hole above his left eye.

It took Captain Marcuccio a moment to realize that the force behind them was no contingent of civilian reinforcements. They were coming to join in 4th Company's annihilation.

Hastily he and his officers issued orders. "Every second man, reverse direction to repulse the attack on our rear!" cried Marcuccio. Cena and other noncoms began to pull men by the back of their collars to face the opposite way, then yelled to start firing. Gianni was one of these, yanked from his spot on the berm and turned toward Sciara Sciatt.

For a moment, he was completely confused. What was happening here? But then he saw an officer firing his pistol past their tent line at what looked like local villagers. The townspeople were attacking? Why would they? He thought these things even as he began unloading his rifle's magazine into the crowd rushing toward them.

Semiconsciously, he heard hoofbeats rising above the battle-roar. He turned back again to the eastern jungle to see Bedouin horsemen charging from among the trees. They wielded rifles and glinting blades, slashing at defenders as their mounts clambered over the berm and the shallow trenches. One rider stopped, stood in his stirrups, and swept back and forth an immense green flag emblazoned with a crescent moon.

Its position assailed from both directions, with a mounted enemy firing down into them from horseback, 4th Company began to splinter. There were too many gaps, both flanks gave way. Contact broke with 5th Company, in similar straits north. Southward, 9th Company slid away toward the security of the Castle even as the entire 15th Battalion committed itself to the defenses of both Henni and Fort Messri.

With no reserves to its rear, 4th Company lay nakedly isolated.

Fighting turned hand-to-hand. Men drew their bayonets and used them as swords. Rifles became clubs. From the village, screaming attackers with flashing curved knives overran the tent line.

More by instinct than command, the troops abandoned the untenable trench. In a great burst westward, soldiers scrambled to find cover and reload. As the company moved, the enemy broke through, some rushing clear past the fighting and down the road toward Tripoli itself.

The battle devolved into packs of men rushing for respite from flashing blades and an endless storm of lead, returning fire wherever they could from behind wells, cactus mounds, random outbuildings. Troopers fought back to back until finally brought down. Men found temporary cover behind camp ovens and food crates. Some ran like deer for their lives, others started a fighting withdrawal toward Maqba cemetery. Dozens threw down their empty rifles and fell to their knees, arms raised in surrender. Scimitars hacked without pause, vengeful scythes reaping a red harvest.

Cena fought hand-to-hand with his back to a date palm until a cowled rider in a long white robe impaled him with a lance. The rider kicked the flanks of his steed, cantering it forward until the tip of the lance passed through the infidel and lodged into the palm trunk. He relinquished the weapon and rode on, the detested crusader left fixed in place, flapping his limbs in a ludicrous, wailing death-dance.

In the dust and smoke of the melee, Gianni spotted his captain leading two dozen men on the run toward a small nearby house. Gianni sprinted to join him. Taking fire from all directions, they protected their heads with their arms as if chased by swarms of wasps. They kicked in the door of the dwelling. Four small children cried in a corner. The soldiers tried returning fire from the two windows and doorway. Bullets from outside poured through the thin walls, shattering bones and brains. Men screamed, dropped in their blood, writhed on the ground. Gianni could not bring his rifle to bear, the room was too small, too packed. Marcuccio addressed the soldiers.

"Bersaglieri, my comrades. Fix bayonets!" The surviving ten men pulled their long bayonets from their scabbards and affixed them to their rifle muzzles. Gianni crossed himself. He touched the cornicello pendant around his neck that his father had given him the day he had departed Castrubello. He thought of his bride, Bianca, and his unborn child. He prayed to Christ and the Virgin that he would still, somehow, one day, see his family.

"Ready!" cried Marcuccio, sword upraised. "For honor! For Savoia!" He threw open the door. He and his troopers flung themselves forward. A thunderous fusillade from a hundred waiting guns met the charge. Riddled bodies contorted, knocked into each other. Helmets flew off, rifle stocks shattered. The entire contingent went down in a single blast.

On his back, the corpse of a comrade across him, Gianni opened his eyes. Wondrously, miraculously, he felt no wounds. Merciful God had answered his plea!

An Arab in gray robes and a striped blue and green scarf pressed his musket against Gianni's forehead, cocked the hammer. The black-bearded man gazed hard at his prisoner, paused, then motioned with his weapon for the Italian to rise.

* * *

23 October: The Castle, 4:00 pm

The afternoon sun broiled the combatants through a thin pall of gun smoke. Carnage littered the open ground near the Castle, proving the futility of charging emplaced Maxims. One of the guns was now useless, its warped barrel having melted from so many hours of nonstop use.

Furious fusillades starting at dawn riddled the villa and shredded its dense gardens. The initial attack breached the iron entry gates, the enemy spreading quickly across the grounds. But the HQ's defenders stopped the assault when it reached the villa's open field of fire.

With the late arrival of a regular Ottoman army regiment, obvious in their blue uniform tunics and pantaloons, enemy tactics changed. Now, volleys of rifle fire covered the attackers crawling forward foot by foot, using every stump, rock, or blasted bush as cover. They still made good targets for those on the roof where Renzo and the others kept up a deadly peppering. Despite this, Ottoman reinforcements continued to penetrate the compound, clawing their way toward the Castle's barricaded entries.

To the south, another three companies fought off waves of attackers at Fort Messri. In all, two-thirds of the 11th Bersaglieri Regiment was engaged at the lower third of the eastern line. 27th Battalion's 6th Company had arrived near the Castle as well. 4th and 5th companies presumedly held the rest although HQ had heard nothing from them since the attack first started.

Renzo huddled behind the parapet, reloading. He rose to a half-crouch, took aim at a shaking cluster of bushes, and shot. He ducked behind the short wall again.

Like every man around him, he had been engaged in the action since the start of the long day. But now, despite himself, as he sat with his back to the parapet wall, his mind went to his brother.

At Casa Como the last evening of his pre-invasion furlough, Renzo's mother had led him out to the terrace, where others could not hear.

"Renzo, you are my firstborn," Tonia said. "Firstborns always carry the greatest burden. Gianni is my youngest, a sweet one, not meant for the army or war." Her eyes pleaded with his. "Renzo, bring your brother home to me. Promise you will." She lowered her forehead to Renzo's hands. "This is a terrible thing to place on you."

He answered, "No, Mamma, not terrible at all. This war will be short, a few months. Pray to the Madonna and think of us until we return. Do not cry, do not worry. Gianni is no helpless babe. He will come back. We both will. I give you my word."

When he and Gianni hiked away the next morning, each with a loaf of warm bread under an arm, Tonia stood desolate on the doorstep, their father Carlo's hand on her shoulder.

A ricochet above his head brought Renzo back to earth. If he had only pulled out sooner with the supplies, he thought, at this moment he would be with Gianni. All he could bring his brother now was himself. Once under attack, the Castle had appropriated the ammunition meant for 4th and 5th companies for its own desperate defense.

Renzo's throat raged with thirst. He had drained his canteen hours before. Within the villa, an ornamental fountain still bubbled away, but he had not taken time for a refill. He slung his Carcano across his back and scuttled across the roof on all fours. He reached the back wall, next to a corporal methodically taking aim and squeezing his way through another clip. Gunfire was heavy, punctuated by sharp cries of men. Incoming bullets battered *chunk-chunk* against the villa's masonry like a horizontal hailstorm. Shell bursts from a Turkish field battery thankfully remained, for the moment, badly over-ranged.

A bullet blasted the wall at Renzo's left; debris stung his face. He ducked and clutched his eyes, full of burning stone dust. Finally, eyes watering profusely, blinking rapidly, he focused again. *"Cristo!"* he exclaimed.

"Don't complain," said the soldier next to him. "Look at my good friend Piero here." He leaned back from the parapet to reveal a corpse hunched over a rifle, a bullet through the bridge of its nose.

Renzo's heart ached sharply as he again remembered Gianni. Panic jumped his chest. *Dio sopra,* I need to get out of here. He peered down over the parapet. Two belt-fed Maxim machine guns hammered away, flinging casings into the air.

Como looked to his supply vehicles below. Every draft animal lay dead or dying in red lakes extending to beneath the wagons' wheels. The Fiat Tipo-2 was closer to the villa, largely protected. It still looks intact, Renzo thought.

He ducked again behind the parapet, crouched his way across the roof, and hurried down the stairs to the villa's main floor. Casualties were heavy. Medicos moved among the wounded applying what little remained of their supplies. Colonel Fara was at a window firing his revolver. At his feet, a dead major in braid lay face to the floor.

Renzo refilled his canteen at the fountain, occasionally stopping to take long slurps. With surprise, Renzo recognized a man from Gianni's battalion. It was that falsetto-voiced sergeant nicknamed *l'eunuco*. Tombi was it? The bandage around his head half-covered one ear.

"Sergeant, has the 27th Battalion moved here to the Castle?" he asked, crossing the littered floor. He suppressed budding hope.

"My 6th Company, that's all I know," Tombi answered.

Renzo did not follow. "The 6th was supposed to reinforce at Sciara Sciatt, was it not? Why would your company—"

"We tried," Tombi wearily interrupted. "We tried. When the commotion started, we advanced in support of the 4th and 5th. But the villagers, they rose like devils from the ground itself! Ottoman soldiers too, disguised in ragged robes, their trousers rolled up underneath. They shot at us from every ditch, wall, every cactus alleyway. The bastards were in the trees and on every roof we passed. I tell you, we started for Sciara Sciatt, but could not move that way. We fought our way here instead, doing it took all day. Many of my boys didn't make it. Look, a Mauser slug killed my arm. It is dead, no sensation at all. See here, my hand? It has curled up into a claw."

"What of 4th Company?"

"I tell you, we never got close enough to find them. We saw only those demons from the villages, those and the Ottomans, and they were everywhere."

"The Navy guns?"

"No help at all. Their fire was going far south, over our heads. Somebody said they had orders not to fire into the oasis. Too densely populated, according to Command." He snorted disgustedly, shook his head. "How stupid. Is this war or a novena?"

Renzo burnt with alarm. If what he heard was true, both his brother's company and the 5th were fighting alone.

He left Tombi without another word. He went to a corner where a half-dozen ammunition crates lay open and scooped up several boxes of rounds into the bullet case on his belt. He hastened to the rear of the villa facing his wrecked convoy and, ducking, jumped into the firing trench feet-first.

Italian riflemen leaned into the sloping sandbagged rampart. Firing independently, the line of Carcanos produced a steady, crackling staccato. Ejected brass cartridges covered the bottom of the trench. Puffs of sand exploded near eyes and heads as incoming rounds punctured the breastworks.

Renzo spotted one of his wagoneers and grabbed the man's shoulder. "Corporal Molise! he shouted above the din. "Follow me!"

Molise took his eye from his rifle sight. "Sergeant. What?"

"Help me get our truck started. I must get north."

The trooper looked at Renzo, at the motorized rig behind the wagons, out at the shattered garden with its distant entry gate, finally at Renzo again. "Somebody else, Sergeant. I'm not leaving this hole."

Renzo grabbed the man by his collar. But the corporal resisted with a mighty twist, pulling free. He brought his face close to Renzo's, bared his teeth and hissed, "I stay here!"

No time for this, Renzo thought. He pulled himself out of the trench, ran past the splintered wagons to the motorized lorry. He flipped on the ignition, ran to the front of the engine, grabbed the attached crank handle, and gave it a great turn. The motor fired to life on his second try. The crankshaft flipped the handle hard and fast; Renzo was lucky to avoid a broken wrist.

Once in the cab, he gunned the engine and lifted his foot from the clutch pedal. Gears stripping, the truck jolted forward, came close to stalling, sputtered back to full power. Grasping the wheel hard with both hands, Renzo floored the gas pedal, shifted again. Hemmed in by wrecked wagons, he plowed ahead, careened side to side, bounced over the forelegs of a white dead mule still in its traces. He avoided the trench by a single yard. Rounding the villa's corner, a few bullets peppered the chassis. They came from defenders caught unawares, with no chance to pause as the truck roared by.

The enemy quickly recovered from their surprise. As he made a left turn down the gravel driveway, every firearm in range opened up. The windshield shattered. Renzo slid himself low behind the wheel and relied on the sound of tires on gravel to keep on course. He kept his foot on the gas as the vehicle rattled fast toward the gate. Shots raked the truck, shredding the frame. Rubber sprayed from the tires, bullets thunked into the engine hood. Renzo fought the wheel as it yanked right and left. The machine veered sharply, jumped the road, smashed into the wrought iron fence beside the gate with a brutal *clang!* and stopped. Musket balls and Mauser rounds flayed the wreckage. The gas tank spewed fuel.

The explosion's shockwaves rocked walls at the Castle.

Renzo jumped an instant before the eruption. Flames from the fireball caught his right sleeve, threatening to incinerate his arm until he smothered the fire out on the ground. A ten-spoke wheel bounded, hit the earth, bounded high again. Shards of hot metal rained from the sky. He shook uncontrollably, nearly senseless from noise, the searing pain. His rifle was nowhere.

He lay on his hands to crush out their trembling; his smoking, burnt arm forced a gasping sob. Nearby, the enemy broke into joyful cries at the sight of their spectacular kill. Despite heavy fire from the villa, some stood, began approaching the twisted wreckage pillaring rich, oily smoke.

Renzo bit the inside of his cheeks to force himself still. His life depended on feigning death. Through the slit of his one eye not pressed into the earth, he made out scuffed, hobnailed Ottoman boots approaching. He clenched his face and stopped breathing altogether.

Fresh gunfire from outside the fence line sounded a different pitch. He opened his one eye again. Scuffed-Boots moved back a tentative step then quickly retreated. Renzo heard the firing of coordinated volleys followed by Italian shouts and commands.

He hazarded a fuller look, pushed himself up to a deep squat. The Fiat's solid smoke was blowing sideways across his line of vision. Shapes appeared through the entry gates. Italian uniforms, in force.

One man came up to Renzo as he started stirring, slung his Vertelli rifle, extended his hand. The trooper saw Renzo eyeing his helmet badge. In a Florentine accent he offered, "82nd Infantry. We are fighting our way to Sciara Sciatt."

Chapter 25

Two companies of 82nd Regiment's 1st Battalion pressed along the confusing paths of trampled sand that led northward behind the original Italian positions. Two Arab scouts assisted the units' advance.

The lines were a shambled wreck everywhere from the Castle north. At every bend, every crossing, every twist of trails that crisscrossed the oasis, a smattering of gunshots met the advancing troops. While it looked as if many combatants had withdrawn, deadly resistance remained from snipers. More startling were the sudden rushes from the brush by robed men with flashing curved knives.

It was obvious that some of the oasis civilians had risen against their occupiers. How many, to what extent, was not yet clear. But ragged Italian survivors were coming forward with accounts of stories they'd heard that made one's blood curl, tales of isolated soldiers rooted out of hiding places then gutted with knives, a stretcher bearer strangled by the wounded man he was trying to save, a well at Henni brimful of mutilated corpses, creeping crones with kitchen blades slitting throats from behind, of battlefield scavengers with ghoulish sacks of human limbs! The smallest rumor repeated in the ranks grew in horror with each retelling. The blanket assumption soon became that most, if not all, of the populace had risen in betrayal against Italia's kindly presence—a betrayal that demanded stern recompense.

Renzo had rewrapped his burnt right arm, but the pain was intense and getting worse. He carried a rifle taken from a dead man. He followed as an extra man in one of the infantry platoons of the 82nd. He did not care that he had left his remaining convoy drivers without saying a word. They weren't going anywhere anyway with all their animals shot. Things are so confused that procedures do not matter in any case, he thought. I must get to Gianni.

The platoon followed carefully down the isolated pathways. In the last thirty minutes the surrounding jungle of palm trees and cactus had quieted substantially. A random shot or bloodcurdling shriek sometimes rang out, where from was difficult to tell. The sudden falloff in gunfire created an eerie sense of solitude in the growing shadows of late afternoon.

We have been fighting since the sun came up, Renzo realized. Headquarters had held out for eight hours before the relief troops arrived. But out here, so far beyond the Castle, could there be any hope?

The platoon leader, a tall lieutenant, called for a halt. The men fell out in a loose line, grabbed a bite of rations, water. The platoon's two local scouts disappeared into the murk of the groves. They were employed by an Italian shipping company in the city before the war, from what Renzo understood, and had been steadily picking up news of the 4th and 5th from a mash of random civilian sources.

"The original trenches are farther ahead," the officer said to his troop, after consulting his map. "There, at a distance." They had stopped on a small rise with a slight view through the trees. Renzo stood, stepped some paces in that direction. A portion of the eastern line of the 11th was visible to the northeast. All that Como could make out was a shamble of tents, equipment strewn at random, nothing moving.

The scouts soon returned. They began to speak animatedly to the lieutenant, a short space away. With several others, Renzo moved from his position to where he could hear.

"According to those who saw them, the 5th retreated back toward Tripoli," one of the scouts was saying. "But they were waylaid at every crossroads with heavy losses. There were already Turkish soldiers wearing native robes between them and the city, joined by armed fighters from among the villagers. From the east, the Libyan warriors overran the lines and caught them from behind. Some men of the company still fought their way through, others surrendered."

"What of the 4th?" Renzo interjected.

The lieutenant, a slender young man with a fledgling mustache, raised his hand. "I will ask the questions here, if you don't mind."

"4th Company was overrun, many died, the survivors withdrew to the cemetery at Maqba, very close to here," said the second scout. "At the cemetery, they tried to fight but their guns ran dry, they finally waved the white flag. At least that is what the people say. The *saraceni* took their other prisoners to Maqba as well. Several hundred in all. What happened after that..." His eyes darted. "What happened is unclear. But all agree that no line of prisoners was marched out of there."

The lieutenant considered for a moment, wiped his brow with his sleeve, made his decision. "Take us to Maqba."

* * *

The walls of the cemetery stood bone white amid the surrounding groves. A bullet-pocked archway marked the entrance. From within came the harsh complaint of crows.

A line of stone tombs greeted the platoon as it entered, old marble markers streaked with grime. Weeds and scrub grass filled gaps in between. Late afternoon heat shimmered above the path. The entry trail dead-ended within five feet then forked right and left. The closely spaced tombs blocked any clear view of what lay beyond.

Half of the unit, rifles at the ready, went to the right with a sergeant. The rest, Renzo included, turned left. "Stay aware," the lieutenant compulsively advised.

They moved cautiously down the path until it cornered right. Opposite the turn, an ancient olive tree loomed. At first, Renzo did not recognize the form against the gnarled trunk. He took it for a massive burl of bark. With a start, he realized the grotesquerie was a human.

The man was naked, his limbs splayed in bent, unnatural ways to conform with the twisted trunk. Iron spikes fixed the arms and legs in place. Black blood from the terrible wounds spider-veined down the tree bark until it pooled in the dirt. The victim's face tilted upward toward green branches, his stiff mouth frozen open as if in appeal. The figure had no eyes or genitalia. A bent, empty scabbard hung in playful mockery around his waist.

He is not Gianni was the only thought that went through Renzo's head. Next to him, a soldier vomited into a shrub.

The patrol continued. On its left now was the cemetery wall, to the right more overgrown tombs in crooked rows. And now, between the tombs, along the walkway, against and on the trees, in a heap at a waterless fountain tipped on its side, in every open space, were Italian dead.

Bodies lay stripped of weapons and clothing, hands bound and tethered, one to the next. A line sat with their backs against the walls where killing volleys had blasted them, others were on their knees, their severed heads scattered.

There were other crucifixions, sometimes two to a tree.

The men of the platoon, spreading throughout the grounds, broke into cries of rage.

"Those bastards did this thing, the traitors!" some began shouting. "Ottomans, tribesmen, villagers, all the same, all animals!" The lieutenant fired his Bodeo '89 pistol skyward for order. "Enough!" he shouted. "Stay soldiers. Keep looking."

"Someone is here!" cried a trooper below an elevated strip of tombs at the rear wall. Soldiers joined Renzo in a scramble to see who may have survived. They found the man who had shouted. He tended to a survivor at his feet.

Not Gianni. The survivor writhed on the ground. Hundreds of cactus thorns protruded from his neck, arms, legs. Renzo could see where the man had escaped discovery by burrowing himself into a prickly-pear hedge. The delirious soldier bled heavily from countless punctures and slashes, repeatedly muttering something not Italian, "*alrahma, alrahma.*" Renzo knew the Arabic term. "Show mercy".

He turned away and scanned the elevated portion of the cemetery. A rock retaining wall supported a shelf of ground a few feet high. Long steps met the trail that edged its center, at their top was the ruin of a second stone archway.

Below the arch, in a row, were three large black stones, evenly spaced.

No, Renzo instantly realized, not large stones at all but men's heads, abuzz with flies. Their elongated necks craned stiff up from the earth, revealing hints of shoulders. He stared at the line of white, bugged eyes, at the tips of swollen, projecting tongues. The battered faces, cruelly scarred by rocks and boot kicks, caked with blood, had fried to crisp crimson-black in the sun.

Renzo now saw the one and fell to all fours as if struck by a hammer. Fly-clouds swarmed skyward at his approach. In gasping panic, he crawled to the buried dead man, began to dog-dig to drive the dirt out, tugged in futile rage at the gray-green tunic collar, scooped sand away, wailing in a voice not his, *no, no, o god no god no god no*, digging, pulling, weeping, his bitter tears of sorrow and of guilt falling onto the matted, flaxen hair.

* * *

The night was dead black. The coldness of the oasis that night felt as if it emanated from his own pulsing despair. Around him, within him, the ageless wind that blew out of the vast Sahara added its own low-moaning lament. Impossibly fine sand, though filtered by the jungly maze of surrounding shadowed thickets, stung his face and blinking eyes in a relentless, punishing rasp.

He had dug Gianni out of the imprisoning earth using only his hands. They were raw with torn skin, his burnt left arm, bandage-less now, seeped blood and pus. Dirt packed his cracked and broken fingernails.

The army burial details began their work as soon as the rest of the infantry battalion caught up with its lead platoon. Horse-drawn ambulances arrived, intending to save lives. Instead, they served as corpse-collectors. There were so many bodies found—at the cemetery, throughout the groves, and along the front trenches that the gravediggers buried them close to where they fell.

At Maqba alone were the remains of two hundred ninety Bersaglieri. Most were from 4th Company, along with dozens from the 5th. According to the three survivors found at the cemetery, there had been a brief defensive fight but, trapped and low on ammunition, the Italian force finally surrendered. Weapons were confiscated, the prisoners stripped of their gear and bunched into groups. Other captives from elsewhere along the Sciara Sciatt lines joined them. Then the executions began.

Renzo stayed with his brother's body until an ambulance crew arrived. They wrapped twenty-five corpses, Gianni included, in cloaks and canvas tarps salvaged from the shattered camp and carted them west into the groves. A waiting burial detail hoisted each body into a long ditch, one beside the other, tightly packed. Renzo tried to keep his eyes on Gianni's wrapped form, but by the time all twenty-five had been put in the ground, he had lost track of exactly which bundle he was.

The regimental chaplain then had stepped forward. He wore the uniform of a captain and a purple surplice over his shoulders. Reading from a black-bound breviary, he intoned:

Hear, O Lord, my prayer.
Let my cry come to Thee.
My days are vanished like smoke,
my bones have grown dry, like fuel for the fire.
I am smitten, and my heart is withered.

The cleric continued, using his right hand to bless the mass grave with a loose gesture in the shape of a cross.

Eternal rest grant upon these servants of thy will.
Let thy perpetual light shine upon them.
May the souls of all who depart this life in faith,
through thy divine mercy, our God,
rest in your everlasting peace.

No, Renzo thought. Too long had he sought to smooth his brother's contorted face, close those accusing eyes, force that swollen tongue past cracked corpse-lips back into the awful, gaping mouth. The vivid, torturous memory gave lie to any hope his brother's soul would ever know peace, nor would he.

Time had ended for Renzo then, replaced by a cascade of despairing self-shame for his failure. He crushed all excuses even as they formed in his defense. He had not been there to protect his brother despite vowing to do just that. Instead, Gianni had died in a way too horrific for him to ever explain or describe. Not even his brother's tortured body would return to Castrubello, to be cleansed and caressed by his parents one final time. It would lay instead in African dirt until the End of Days.

Other burials continued though night had fallen. At some point, Renzo, sitting with legs folded by the hasty trench-grave, realized activity around him had stopped. They could not have buried every corpse, Renzo knew. The two companies had lost too many. The others must lie in place until digging began again in the morning. In the meantime, pickets walked the area and chased off snarling, resentful dogs.

He rose heavily to his feet, gathered his rifle. His guilt was an anvil on his neck. He staggered ahead with his eyes on the ground, senses numb, enormous weariness overtaking him.

Past midnight, he thought. Far too late to return to the Castle. The platoon he came in with had left. Renzo began trudging toward the swale where 4th Company had first pitched its camp. But he soon became lost, surrounded by palm trees and cacti. He stumbled, in a stupor, step after step after step without end.

"Halt where you stand, what unit are you with?" a voice suddenly demanded. Someone was holding a lantern, posted at the end of a long row of tents. In the slight illumination, Renzo could make out the uniform of the Royal Marines.

"11th Bersaglieri," he responded automatically in a dull voice. "Como."

The marine advanced, holding up the light toward Renzo's tattered and filthy uniform, his streaked, exhausted face.

"*Merda*, man," the sentry said. "Tino, I need some help!" His partner came up. Together they grabbed Renzo's arms and guided him to a stool set next to their campfire.

Renzo gulped sloppily from the tin cup they gave him and that they refilled twice before he stopped.

"Where is this?"

"The devil's anus itself, that's where," answered the man Tino. His accent was Genoan. "We are in this wilderness between Maqba and Sciara Sciatt. Our unit is covering everything from Fort Hamidieh to here. Your 11th has consolidated to the south. There are some other outfits, I think, sent out from Tripoli to fill in the gaps.

"You are marines," Renzo said stupidly, nodding to their white sailor uniforms, tall boots, flat round caps.

"Certainly, the *Fanteria Real Marina*, none other," proudly replied the first sentry. "I am Di Silvio, here is Tino. We are from the dreadnought *Sicilia*. We are part of two marine battalions organized late yesterday to aid in the battle, units from the *Sicilia*, *Sardinia*, and *King Umberto*.

"We were ordered to land when we finally got word the Bersaglieri faced trouble. But it took some time. *Sicilia* was on the west side of the harbor, bombarding the desert. When we finally got here—" He fell silent a moment. "All I can say is that you Bersaglieri fought a battle for survival today. A terrible struggle. We saw many dead."

"Yes."

Tino broke in. "Do not be dejected, Sergeant, we know how proud you marksmen with the feathers are. Believe me, we found plenty of enemy dead as well. But tomorrow you will, all of us will, exact true revenge, yes?"

Renzo waited for some explanation.

"You have not heard?" asked Di Silvio. "General Caneva has issued an order. He praises the brilliance of today's fighting. A great victory, he says, for at day's end the enemy withdrew! He has ordered that tomorrow at dawn we counterattack!"

Renzo sat, uncomprehending. "Counterattack? Tomorrow? We attack into the desert?"

"No, no," said Tino. "Not out there. Those cowards have run back out into the sand somewhere beyond our reach. No, tomorrow, Sergeant, we attack right where we are. We strike the *traditori!*"

"The who?" Renzo found his mind was barely working.

"The traitors, I mean! The devils, the witches!" Tino saw Renzo's blank look. "We counterattack the civilians, of course!"

* * *

The morning burnt hot. The sentries let Renzo keep sleeping where he'd dropped into exhausted oblivion near their fire, now no more than blowing ash. The camp bugles never woke him; there had been no relief from the hours of plaguing nightmares. Several times he dreamt he was waking, only to descend ever more deeply into unrelenting, shadowy horror...

He opened his eyes to the sharp rattle of distant small arms fire.

"Get up now or you will miss your chance." It was Di Silvio. "It sounds as if we've already started west of the cemetery."

Renzo forced himself into a half-sit, pushing himself from shade into daylight.

"I envy you, Como. We learned this morning we marines are stuck manning this line, sending out pickets to search the oasis farther east." He spat. "Just our luck, what a genius the man must be who decided that! Everyone knows those monkeys are not out there, they are all behind us, from here to the city. But our officer is a good man. I expect he will turn his eye if some of us do a little hunting of our own. And, with any luck, some of the traitors may try to flee our way." He patted his rifle stock. "If so, too bad for them."

A wagon stood not far from the camp, men offloading fresh empty caskets. There had been no casket for Gianni, Renzo remembered. His face burned in shame. He remembered he had lost track of the body among the jumble of bundles in the mass grave.

The sergeant pointed his weapon toward men forming up a hundred yards north. "Those boys came in earlier. They marched right by here, you were like a dead man to the noise they made. You should jump in; I am certain they will welcome a sergeant. Not many officers over there, at least that I could see." He hefted his firearm to his shoulder again. "Anyway." He started to leave, turned back again. "Good hunting!" he said.

Renzo dragged himself from the ground. Half a bucket of water sat nearby, grayish, filled with floating whiskers and soap scum. Renzo dumped it over his head, slicked back his long brown hair, rubbed a hand over his face, his eyes, over his stubble, threw down the pail. It struck against a tent stake, banged loudly, and bounced. He walked to the latrine trench and relieved himself.

A few yards further was an open water barrel stamped *Prodotto di Sicilia*. He drank greedily, using the long-handled tin cup attached by a cord.

He peered past the cup to the armed force forming. Judging from the mix of uniforms, the contingent consisted of an infantry rifle platoon plus an equal number of random soldiers separated from their units. The grim-faced troops numbered around eighty. A captain and a sub-lieutenant stood conferring, their heads inclined to each other's. Renzo spat out his last swig and walked over.

Short of stature, with bushy sideburns and a thin beard, though no mustache, the captain stood on an empty ammunition crate so that all could see him. Holding a document in his left hand, he raised his right to gain the men's attention.

'You men have heard of the orders from General Caneva. I won't bother reading through them. Here is my version." The men slowly stiffened to attention though no formal command had been given.

"Despite our kindness to the population, despite us driving their Ottoman oppressors away, yesterday the native civilians here betrayed us most grievously. Though they acted as friends when we arrived, they secretly plotted all along to rebel. Behind their smiles and salutations, their hands out in supplication, they knew exactly where they'd hidden the weapons given them by the Ottomans as well as their own caches of sharp daggers and swords.

"As we know too well, when their masters commanded, they ran out of their shadows and struck those same daggers in our soldiers' backs. It was clear, there's no denial of this fact. We all have seen their cruel work, their evil acts."

The men in the ranks shifted, murmured, the straps of their guns, leather packs creaking. Unsettled feet stirred the dust.

"These traitors," the captain continued, "then faded back into their holes. Today, when we question them, I guarantee you, no one will have seen anything, done anything, heard anything of yesterday's events.

"Nonetheless, today we punish this contemptible scum. How do we know who they were? Simple. The possession of firearms was banned last week, before the attack. Here are your orders. If you find a man with a rifle, execute him. If a boy has a rifle, execute him. If there is a weapon of any kind in a dwelling, arrest everyone in the house, men, women, children. Bind their hands and march them to the harbor. If someone runs from arrest, execute them. There are innocent civilians as well, but don't be soft-hearted. Assume everyone is guilty until they convince you otherwise.

"Look for Ottoman officers dressed as Arabs. If they surrender, bring them to the harbor. They will be interrogated, and then face the justice of a firing squad.

"We know what a jungle this oasis is. We cannot march everywhere in a single body such as we are here. Instead, we will divide into four squads of twenty. Keep your wits about you. Those who killed your friends and comrades yesterday would like nothing more than to kill you today. We are short of officers, so listen to the commands of your sergeants and corporals. And if none of them are with you, I trust you will not fail your duty to Italia, and especially the duty we have to our sacred dead!"

Nobody cheered. The men checked their firearms. Few spoke.

Renzo fell in with the nearest group of men. A sergeant walked the ranks handing out magazine clips, five clips to a man. He was gaunt, his eyes red. He stopped when he got to Renzo. His hand holding the cartridges stayed poised in the air. "Who the hell are you?" he demanded.

"Como. I need some of those." Renzo nodded at the magazines.

The sergeant made no move for a moment. He eyed the filthy figure before him, noted the chevrons on his cuffs. He grunted and dropped the clips in Renzo's pair of cupped hands. "That fucker is cooked pretty good," he said, gesturing at Renzo's raw, blistered left arm. "I'd cover it if I were you or it will become a feast for the flies. I am Sergeant Alberosso."

Renzo said nothing. He dropped the rounds into the pouch on his belt.

"I could use your help," the sergeant told him. "Take some of these men. This search will be door to door all the way through Sciara Sciatt. We will be starting with these scattered dumps you see around here. There is a lot of oasis to cover before we arrive at the town."

Renzo said, "Yes."

The sergeant waited, as if wanting to hear something more. Then he shrugged. "Good. I'll get our orders."

Renzo waited in the ranks while the two officers briefly conferred with several of the NCOs. Alberosso returned to Como's side. "We are assigned the right flank," he said.

Men gathered their gear. The chance to make up for yesterday's murderous events sharpened everyone's concentration.

"Troop, advance!" the captain commanded.

* * *

Signs of the previous day's fight were everywhere. Gunshot holes pocked garden walls. Renzo saw spent cartridges of mixed caliber at the foot of a massive fig tree. Further along the trail, a corpse dressed in rags lay sprawled over a bush.

Distant rifle shots and the boom of cannon to the south disturbed the eerie silence as the patrol pushed ahead. A sickly smell like rotted fruit permeated the stillness. The sudden heavy drone of insects distracted Renzo. A young Bersagliere in a red-drenched tunic, throat cut, sat staring, tied with his back against a tree, trussed legs extended into a dead fire. A soldier from behind Renzo approached the body, his long-sleeved left arm across his nose. He covered the figure with three large palm fronds from among those lying nearby, then set the man's helmet atop a branch he stuck in the ground.

"With luck, our gravediggers will find him," the soldier told Renzo. From under the fronds, the dead man's bound legs protruded, his bootless, skinless, charred feet still caked with cold ash.

Renzo shut his eyes, saw Gianni's cemetery face, opened them quickly again. A low moan escaped his lips, but he quickly covered it with a false cough.

"Keep moving," he told the two or three men who had also stopped at the grisly scene. They hastened to catch up with Sergeant Alberosso and the others.

A thunderous shot rang out, echoing through the treetops, sending blackbirds cawing skyward. The ground around them began bursting into clouds of dirt. Renzo could see puffs of smoke from atop a dwelling to their right.

A hand pulled him down. It was Alberosso. "Have you lost your senses, man, standing in the open like that?"

"The firing is from that building there," Renzo motioned.

"Good," Alberosso said, then declared loudly, "That way!" The patrol had scattered behind trees and into dusty irrigation ditches. "There, where I am pointing. We move that way!"

Renzo ran ahead toward the sporadic gunfire. A rustling from behind and general cursing told him the others were following his lead through the tangle of trees and brush.

They arrived at a flat-roofed, gray-plastered dwelling. Except for an open gate, a short wall surrounded most of it, cactus enclosed the rest. Three clucking chickens stalked around in the courtyard ignoring the crash of the gunshots from above. A rooster crowed in full-throated competition with the blasts.

The soldiers scrambled to the wall and crouched, spreading out, as bullets clipped at the masonry. On the rooftop, it looked like half a dozen figures had weapons. Their firing thinned as, reloading, they repositioned to face the patrol.

Alberosso called out above the din. "On my command! Fire!"

Every rifle trained on the parapet erupted. The 6.5-millimeter rounds peppered the mudbrick upper walls. One of the figures on the rooftop fell sharply backward.

"We go in," said the sergeant, gesturing at Renzo and two others. "Bayonets!" He called to the others, "Keep firing! Do not stop!"

The four soldiers burst through the open gateway scattering the chickens in agitation. A panicky small figure ran into another room as they kicked in the door. The first trooper inside gave short chase, fired twice.

A ladder led to the roof. A rifle pointed downward at them from the opening. Renzo and Alberosso shot at the same time. A man fell headfirst, his body slithering heavily down the rungs. Beneath his robes, Renzo saw blue Ottoman army trousers.

He stepped on the dead man's back as he took the lead up the ladder. His bayonet made things awkward climbing the narrow steps. As Renzo burst on the rooftop with a savage shout, the survivors threw their weapons down and thrust their hands in the air. With an effort, Renzo resisted pulling his trigger. Alberosso was next up the ladder, then the other two.

One defender lay lifeless on his back, shot through the sternum. Four other men stood, hands raised. A gray-bearded oldster used both arms to hold back a wailing woman trying to reach the ladder.

"What hysteria," said the man who had done the shooting on the first floor. "The boy ran from capture."

Renzo approached each of the male captives and pulled back their robes to see if any were Turks. One said in Italian, "I am Major Ömer Uzun of the Ottoman 8th Regiment. I am in command of these freedom fighters. We surrender as prisoners of war."

"Huh," said Alberosso. "Is that a fact?" He shouted below. "The rest of you, stay down there. Spread out, protect the walls!" He turned back to the prisoners. "All I see here is a band of rebels with rifles. The family of this house is complicit in the treachery. Line them up over there."

Ömer Uzun refused to move. "I protest this action," he began, but a trooper clubbed him across his back and led him staggering to the rest. Others propelled the old man and the woman into place among them. A moment later, the men on the ground heard the crash of a volley from the roof.

The unit reunited down below. Several now carried an extra Mauser rifle strapped across their backs.

Alberosso announced, "Spread out again, let's get going. Keep your eyes up." Renzo reloaded his weapon.

Chapter 26

Sciara Sciatt stood a derelict town. Debris from the previous day's mayhem littered its streets, empty of life. Papers, bits of clothing, an overturned cart, gave dire testimony to the frenzied fight and panic that had engulfed the place. A dead local man and his dying dog lay near one of the doorways.

Of the two rows of buildings that Renzo faced, few windows overlooked the rutted dirt road. Occasional doors were all that interrupted the blank mudbrick walls along the street. The buildings, a mix of single and double stories, all had flat roofs. On several, small wood-railed balconies overlooked the road. At the end of the street stood a mosque, its tall minaret parapet empty.

The patrol had arrived after a perilous hike. For the entire distance, they encountered steady sniping from treetops and from behind low earthen walls. Along their tangled route they rousted out civilians from where they hid from the violence of both forces. Several possessed loot from the dead, mainly rations, boots, pieces of clothing.

"Fleabags and scum, to rob the dead like that," said Alberosso. "As guilty as if they had pulled triggers themselves."

Renzo noted the starved features of the various men and women who were guilty of robbery. Castrubello had plenty of poor. But no one he knew from his hometown looked as beleaguered as these wretches.

They had twenty-two of the unfortunates in tow. They ranged all ages, the oldest an ancient woman they had to beat to keep moving, the youngest a newborn, clutched to her mother's breast.

They arrived at Sciara Sciatt the same time as another patrol dragging along its own string of prisoners. Its leader was the thin-bearded captain in command of the retribution force.

"I do not see any point waiting," the officer said. "If the enemy is here, they know we have arrived. Waiting just gives them more time to prepare. You two," he said, pointing at Alberosso and Renzo. "Take your men down the next street, we will take this one. Put a couple of soldiers in charge of the prisoners, I will do the same. We will hold them in those pens over there, men in one, women in the other." He pointed to a pair of goat corrals at the edge of the village. "Go."

The squads adjusted themselves according to the officer's directions. They pushed their prisoners past a well into the corrals, made from interwoven tree branches. Five men in all guarded the groups. Some soldiers took out cigarettes, pipes. Easy duty.

Renzo was numb from the day's ordeal but grateful for the numbness. The trek had been laborious and dangerous, ugly without respite. But it had forced him to concentrate on the moment. His mind snapped back to the reality of Gianni dead.

"Sergeant!" Alberosso's harsh call delivered Renzo from the relentless trap of his conscience. "I say again, are you ready?"

Renzo looked at his four men behind him along the wall. He knew none of their names. They each looked back from their crouches, nodding their eagerness. He raised a fist. Alberosso set out with his squad. Renzo gestured his group forward.

They hugged the wall, Renzo leading. The first arched door was firmly barred from within. Renzo stepped out into the street, fired into the latch, then the hinges. His second man, on his own, ran forward, put his shoulder to the door. It caved in with a flopping thud.

There were shouts and gunfire from the next street over where the commander's unit had also started to move. Renzo heard running footsteps above them on the roofs. Heads appeared at the parapets, then rifle barrels. Bullets began pocking the dirt at their feet.

The squad took refuge in the dwelling they had burst into. At the same time, another patrol emerged from the oasis. It came down the center of the street, a dozen strong. Spurning cover, they kept walking forward shooting at the roofline. Their hot rate of fire drove the enemy heads back. One man plunged over the edge, robes flapping, and hit the street in a dusty *wumph!*

Inside, Renzo's men pushed through an anteroom, past a wooden screen, and found a stairway to the roof. They clambered up. Shouts and gunshots, more running steps. Renzo was the last one to the stairs. He put one foot on a step, took a final glance around.

His eyes settled on an object on a sleeping pallet with jumbled bedclothes. He moved to where it lay and picked up a Bersaglieri canteen stenciled *11th Bersag. Reg. 4th Co.* On its metal band was roughly etched: *G. Como.*

With a jolt, he realized what it was that he held. Someone had thieved it before murdering his brother. A blinding rage seized him.

The dark curtain that blocked entry to an adjacent room suddenly stirred.

Renzo advanced, fired through the cloth, ejected the shell, fired, ejected, pushed the tattered curtain aside, saw robed forms scrabbling corner to corner, a woman screaming, her protective hand upraised as if it could deflect lethal metal; he fired again, now screaming himself, ejected, a child cried out, he fired, ejected, fired, ejected; his weapon was empty now. He used it as a club.

He found himself out in the street, moving toward the mosque where people were still fleeing in terror. An old man in a turban wielding a saber rushed from an alley. Renzo pivoted, brought up his rifle stock in defense. The deflected flat of the sword struck his injured right arm, exploded open the infected wound. He dropped to his knees and blacked out from the pain. The old man cried out as bullets riddled his back, and he pitched directly into Renzo. They went down together in the swirling dust, face touching face, like fallen dance partners still locked in an embrace.

* * *

26 October 1911

The harbor wind flapped the flags of the medical encampment consisting of fifteen large tents grouped in two facing rows. Originally white, the sun-faded canvas featured large red crosses stitched above each entry.

The camp bustled with activity as it received more casualties from the front. A line of ambulance wagons was steadily arriving, unloading, and going. Shells blasted from the nearby dreadnoughts, striving to hit targets along the southeastern corner near Fort Messri. The projectiles tore through the sky, the shells at times visible from the ground, a steady bombardment of massed enemy targets. After three days to regroup, the Ottomans and their allies were energetically renewing their attack.

The doctor passed the surgery tent, its entry all but blocked by stretcher cases waiting their turn. He knew that within, three surgeons were hard at work. The rasp of their saws, the cries of their patients, the emergence of staff gasping for a bit of air, were commonplace sounds and sights whenever fighting was underway. His eyes avoided the barrels outside full of severed limbs.

He hurried to the one oversized tent in the camp that had two interior poles. They created separate twin peaks for the capacious structure, filled with cots bearing wounded. Nurses circulated among the injured, applying aid and succor. Here was where the already-treated recovered or died.

The trooper at the entryway came to attention and presented arms as the doctor passed. The soldier was of the Royal Ascari battalion, recruited from the local population of Eritrea, Italy's East-African colony. Barefoot, uniformed in loose white pantaloons and tunics, the Ascari were renowned as fierce, hardened, and reliable warriors. A detachment had arrived at Tripoli along with an army medical unit. They wore tall red fezzes sporting blue tufts of short feathers and blue waist sashes. Their assignment was to defend the field hospital on the edge of Tripoli's harbor.

The doctor was not a military man by trade but had received a commission at the start of the war because the army lacked medical staffing. His work in Eritrea had been at the hospital in Abbas, the capital city. There he was engaged in treating various diseases along with run-of-the-mill accidents. He had treated many native Eritreans since he first arrived in the fledgling Italian colony nearly thirty years before. He'd hated it at first, so different than his Lombardia. But now, at age fifty, the African land and its people had a deep hold on him. And as much as he welcomed more Italian colonists and the civic improvements they brought to Abbas, what he valued most was the peace he had found in a life of simplicity.

A life I cannot return to soon enough, thought the medical man. He had been here less than a month, and he already knew this Tripoli adventure was something he wanted out of. He could not leave, of course, he had a two-year officer's commission. And although his past, pre-Eritrea record was ancient history, he knew that it allowed no missteps on his part. No, this war was hateful, but he would hate it in silence. Other than that, he had his duty to the damaged soldiers surrounding him each day; that would suffice.

"Doctor, may I speak to you?" A young nurse stood before him, a volunteer.

"What is it, nurse?" he asked. As a unit administrator, the doctor was accustomed to continual questions by such volunteers. Patience was a natural virtue of his, but he was anxious to begin his rounds.

"The sergeant with the burnt arm and the headaches, with the night terrors, do you know the one?"

"Yes. What about him?"

"Last night he had to be restrained again. He awoke raving, disturbing the others. It took two orderlies to tie him to the bed. He is quiet now but awake. We must redress his arm, and he needs to eat. But we are afraid to undo the straps."

"I will start with him. Tell me his name again?"

"His name is unknown. He came in unconscious, as you know, with no identification.

The doctor was already moving toward the sergeant's cot. "I will manage this, nurse. Thank you."

He looked down at the patient who stared straight back. Four leather belts secured him firmly to the bed. The bedraggled bandage covering his right arm, stained red and yellow, had loosened overnight. The doctor removed the belts.

"I am Doctor Binelli," he said, tending the arm. The physician took the bandage off, unrolled a clean one, and applied it. The saber cut and angry, underlying burn were healing, albeit slowly. The infection was still causing a fever. "I would like to address you by your name, sergeant, but I do not know it."

Wincing, the soldier muttered something that Binelli couldn't make out. He arched his eyebrow, put his ear down closer to the soldier's mouth.

"Como," repeated the man in the bed.

The doctor paused.

"Como? From where, might I ask?"

"Lombardia," Renzo wanted this white-jacket to leave him alone. Maybe a few answers would satisfy the sawbones.

"Ah, the north. My country too. Who are your people?"

"Carlo," said Renzo. He shut his eyes to his splitting headache. "Mother, Tonia Vacci."

Binelli sat stone still. Vacci. The sound of the half-forgotten name stunned him. The night of those flawed inoculations at the stone farmhouse had visited his dreams for years. The woman with the broken needle in her neck, this was her son? Her son, here?

He drew a deep breath. I should not be surprised, he thought. His grandmother had often told him, "Fate has restless feet."

Renzo kept his eyes closed. Now that he was conscious, so too was his memory and with it, black anguish. His slaughter of the innocents in Sciara Sciatt, the face of his tortured brother, these visions made him groan loudly despite himself. He half-sat up, his hands grasping his head.

"Easy, easy," said the doctor, but there was nothing easy about the sudden desperate grasp of Renzo's arms tight around him as the soldier buried his sunburnt face into Binelli's chest.

Immediately Renzo pulled himself back, created separation, looked away. "My head hurts," he said.

"Yes, not unusual with an infection," answered the doctor. "This will help."

Binelli used a spoon to administer a dose of laudanum from the bottle in his bag. Tincture of opium was a standard medical sedative. Based on sound science, the doctor thought, not a hopeful guess like that inane strychnine theory, by now thoroughly debunked. Renzo lay back down, hands folded on his chest. Like a dead man in a coffin, thought Binelli.

He continued his rounds. But his thoughts stayed with the sergeant. His interaction with Como had strangely shaken him. In young Como's moment of distress, Binelli had seen a reflection of his own.

It had taken him months to overcome thoughts of suicide when the verdict came down that he, a lowly young intern, was entirely to blame for the tragedy at Villa d'Ambrosso. No matter how contrived the charges against him or how he had tried that night to mitigate the suffering, the fact remained he had directly participated in causing patients' deaths.

Run out of Italy, a disgrace to his family, Binelli's passage to Eritrea by steamer had taken only a week, yet a lifetime. His misery had brought him to within an inch of his life. He remembered standing at the stern rail of the freighter, watching its soft, phosphorescent wake, inviting his surrender.

He could not say what kept him from taking the leap. He liked to think it was rational thought that brought him around, his innate optimism, his youth, the lingering fragments of a tattered but not extinguished hope. He was Catholic, there was that. Suicide would mean the eternal forfeiture of his soul. In reality, he suspected it was sheer cowardice he could thank. Standing there looking down, he had imagined the shock of striking the corpse-cold water, the darkness of its weedy depths, the fierce tug-tug-tugging on his limbs by a lurking, ponderous sea beast.

For whatever force had stayed him, and it may well have been the blast of the ship's horn at that tenuous moment, Binelli was grateful. It allowed him to realize he had a lifeline, namely the practice of medicine. One sop that the corrupt authorities threw in when they assigned their scapegoat to oblivion was to sign off on his license in the medical arts, despite his lack of full accreditation. The kingdom's colony on the Horn of Africa desperately needed doctors, Binelli did have some training, and in any case, the authorities agreed, as his patients would mostly be black Africans, what was the harm?

Binelli took advantage of the situation and in such a vacuum of medical expertise eventually rose to respectability. He read medical journals assiduously and continually added volumes to his bookshelves which now his interns. some of them Eritreans, relied upon. He had helped *L'Ospedale Coloniale Africano* become the best in the city.

In his patient Como, the doctor saw another tortured soul, someone who, if left to his own devices, might decide life was not worth living. For the sake of the young soldier, and out of his own lingering guilt, Binelli resolved to provide the man with whatever help he could.

"I do not know your circumstances, soldier," he told Renzo the next day. "Why it is you suffer as you do from headaches and nightmares. But here is my sincere advice. You have two choices. Face the consequences openly, accept the repercussions. Pay whatever debt you owe. Do those things, defuse the guilt, so to speak, then go forward."

Renzo was sitting up in bed, his infection having abated, spooning himself thin soup from a bowl. "No," he said listlessly, having dismissed such a course of action long before. "Impossible."

Binelli waited for something further. When Renzo stayed silent, he continued.

"The second way, then, is to set forth on a different journey from where you are now. Leave the past, do not look back, become somebody new. I make no claim this is a heroic act, nor simple. But it can work."

At this, Renzo's eyes went to the doctor's. He felt the glimmer of possibility. But he gestured toward the other cots, the Ascari at the entry, pointed to his own helmet on his bedstead. "How, doctor?"

The question sounded like an answer to Binelli. Not the best answer in his view, but a choice other than surrender. He patted Renzo on the shoulder.

"Leave the how to me. Now rest."

For the next several days, as Renzo healed, he saw little of Binelli, and that at a distance. He lay flat on his cot all the time except for those periods when his nurse insisted that she must change his sheets. At those times he wandered into the tent-village and observed whatever business was taking place. The outside air and sights and sounds helped revive him.

Once, when Renzo walked to where he overlooked the harbor, he saw troopers herding long lines of prisoners along the quay.

"Headed for the prison islands, and good riddance, I say," a fellow observer mentioned to him. "It is another way of telling them, 'Die, you bastards!' Those prison isles are already full, and full of cholera, too. I heard they are dumping so many bodies in their waters the fishermen say it is ruining their catch! The fish eat them, you see, disease and all."

"That many guilty?" Renzo said.

The soldier, a private on a crutch with one leg missing above the knee, scoffed. "Sergeant, everyone here knows this. If they are not guilty today, they are certain to be guilty tomorrow. Why wait?"

Since Renzo had arrived at the field hospital, more attacks from the desert had nearly succeeded in breaking the Italian lines. The army pulled back toward the city by a full mile and reset its defensive perimeter, ceding Sciara Sciatt and all the original lines to the foe. While nobody admitted the fact, it seemed clear that this shortening of the perimeter, the lack of any offensive operations, and General Caneva's call for massive reinforcements from the homeland suggested that the great liberation of Tripolitania had stalled.

But Renzo remained indifferent to it all. Nothing interrupted his personal hell for long. He thought of simply getting up from his cot and walking out into the desert toward the Ottoman lines. He would take his rifle, make a one-man attack, let fate take its course. Foolish, he knew, he would never make it. The carabinieri would stop him and bundle him off to some asylum.

As time passed, his wounds slowly healed. He would always bear the old Arab's deep saber scar across his arm; beneath it, welted, raw-red, hairless new skin was replacing the burnt tissue. Flexing was painful. Still very stiff, but he had full movement. His sleep was fitful, but the restraining straps were gone. If he became too agitated at night a nurse sedated him with a laudanum dose. Seldom did he get a full night of rest, but sometimes in the early hours of predawn his roving mind finally succumbed, and he fell into a bottomless pit.

After one of those times, he awoke to find the doctor sitting beside him.

"Ah, it is about time," Binelli said, with a tight smile. "I was almost ready to give up and come back later." He watched Renzo blink, rub his face, come back to life.

"Here, I bear a gift," the doctor said. He handed Renzo an envelope with the seal of the Royal Italian Army printed in the left corner.

Renzo rubbed more at his eyes, coughed, sat farther up. He opened the envelope, pulled out a letter, read its contents. He got to the signatures at the bottom, scanned the names: *Caneva... Fara... Binelli.*

"A medical discharge?" he said, in disbelief. "This is a medical discharge."

"Yes," Binelli. "Effective immediately."

"For this wound?" He held up his mended arm and for some reason thought of the one-legged trooper. "How?"

"Originally, I had difficulty finding you on your regiment's roles. They had you down as missing in action. Once I cleared that up, I submitted my diagnosis that your arm will never properly heal, that your marksmanship is irrevocably compromised. In short, that you are useless as a soldier to His Majesty."

Renzo looked at the doctor's face. Calm, kind. Something in the eyes, though. "Why are you doing this for me?" he asked.

Binelli did not reply, shifted as if he would stand and leave. He paused instead and said, "Remember this, Sergeant Como, here is what I know. Life is a series of debts. Debts owed and debts paid. We must always be clearing the ledger if we hope to die in peace."

* * *

The corporal behind the counter at the army postal exchange drummed his fingers as Renzo secured the lid of the metal box. Because Renzo had one heavily bandaged arm in a sling, the corporal bound the box with twine while Renzo wrote, "Como, Carlo, Castrubello, Lombardia," on a piece of paper with a stubby pencil and slid it over to the clerk.

The corporal took the box and laid it on a stack of items behind the counter. He said, "It should get there in a few weeks." Renzo nodded, paid the postage. Then, one-armed, he hefted his haversack on his back and went out the door.

Immediately after his discharge, Renzo went to the area of the quartermaster's warehouse where the possessions of the dead were available for claiming. Not much had been salvaged from the debris that had been 4th Company's camp, but he had found one small parcel marked with his brother's name. In it were a pocketknife Gianni had prized since boyhood and a coin purse. Besides two lire, it contained a folded letter that Bianca had given her young husband when he had first set off for training camp. And Gianni's straight-edged razor and badger-hair lathering brush were there, as well as a small pocket mirror. Aside from his uniform cape, that was all.

There had been no possessions on Gianni's battered body when the search platoon finally pulled it out of the ground. No gold wedding ring, no pocket watch, those would have been taken first at Gianni's capture, Renzo presumed. His brother had not suffered castration like some others. The loss of blood would have killed him too soon, Renzo reflected bitterly.

He had found an empty metal ammunition box, put in Gianni's few belongings, and, today, without a note, posted it to his father in Castrubello.

He had discovered one other object that Renzo kept for himself. As he had feverishly clawed at the soil trapping Gianni's body, a leather strap had strangely become wrapped around his hand. On it was the red ceramic cornicello their father Carlo had given Gianni, whose own father Lorenzo had first presented to him. It must have fallen into the dirt as he had been buried, or perhaps Gianni somehow did it himself to save it from theft, Renzo thought. The small crimson horn had proved itself a failed protector. What better reminder of his own failures that day?

Renzo stepped outside the army postal tent pitched near Tripoli's newly repaired Spanish Quay. The overcast day was appallingly humid. The big harbor was active with troopships. The additional sixty-five thousand troops General Caneva had demanded of Rome were arriving daily. Several freighters and a large passenger steamship were also in harbor, anchored on the west shoreline of the city.

Binelli had staked him a loan of fifty lire. Renzo had simply found the coins on his cot the last day before leaving the hospital. There was a note with the money. "You will return the favor one day, and it need not be to me," was all it said. Renzo looked to thank him, but the doctor had gone to the civilian hospital in Tripoli for the day. A fiercely deadly outbreak of cholera was spreading within the city as it became more crowded with soldiers and civilians, its sewerage clogged and freshwater sources compromised. Renzo never saw him again.

With Binelli's money, the sergeant's pay he had been saving, and a modest sum doled out by the army for medical discharges, Renzo had a total of one hundred and forty lire. He used a portion of it to buy steerage passage on a transatlantic steamship.

He could not say when he decided he would live out his life in a self-imposed exile. Once he excluded self-destruction from his choices, the decision seemed to make itself. Emptiness consumed him. He understood full well who and what he was leaving.

His betrothed, Angelina, weighed on his heart. They had shared a love since they were children together in Castrubello. She wore a medal of the Virgin he had given her, his promise he would return, that they would marry. Another failed promise of his but breaking this one was for her sake. Renzo had seen the man who he was not, and the stranger he was. Angelina deserved a life with someone whole. Not him. He had thought of sending her a farewell note but could find no words to say.

He tried to block all thoughts of his parents. To go back would be futile torture for everyone. They would try to forgive him, would act as if they had, but how could they ever? Each day would be an ordeal of their masked recrimination and sorrow on the one side, his craven guilt and remorse on the other. No, Pietro would have to manage as the only son they had left. Again, he decided, no contact.

Binelli had said the military had originally declared Renzo missing in action. Perhaps it would now correct the mistake. Or not. In any event, that first army telegram home would serve as his only, fitting last message.

A blast from a troopship klaxon brought his attention back to the here and now. A noisy tender billowing cinders and smoke towed a barge full of soldiers toward shore. The wind was up, dotting the harbor with rolling whitecaps.

Holding both his ticket and the strap of the haversack with his free hand, Renzo headed toward where a local steam-powered lighter rocked at the quay.

"What vessel then, civilian?" shouted the Italian on its deck, as Renzo walked down the gangplank. "We do 'em all, we do them quick. We do them for twenty centissimi." The wizened sailor with a cigar held out his hand, blocking Renzo's last step from the ramp. "In advance."

Renzo paid the man, read from his ticket. "*Princess Irene*," he said.

"Ah, the *Irene*, that old rust-bucket whore," laughed the sailor. He grinned widely as he pocketed Renzo's coins. One of every three teeth was black to the root. "Out of Palermo, bound for *l'America!*" He sized up his new passenger, making his guesses. "A big leap from what you know to what you do not, eh?"

Renzo ignored him, brushed past, went aboard.

Part II: The Hall

1912

Chapter 27

June 1912: Piedmont

She sat in the back of the big hayrick with two dozen women and children from Castrubello and surrounding hamlets. The age of the youngest passenger was six, the oldest near sixty. Most wore the broad straw hats they used every day in the rice fields. Each had a small parcel or suitcase of things they had needed for their stay in the farm barracks near the Piedmont commune of Fara Varese.

Angelina Scrivatti, twenty-three years old, was not wearing a straw hat. She had given hers to Olivia the week before. A gust had blown her friend's own hat into the flooded rice paddies as they worked. Barefoot in sucking mud, with hiked-up skirts in water to their knees, bent-backed as they weeded the endless rows of rice plants, neither had time to react when the wind snatched it away.

"No matter, take mine," Angelina said over Olivia's protest. "No, I want you to have it, I have this cloth I can tie as a headscarf, while you have nothing."

"Silence!" yelled the foreman. He stood a short way behind them, legs planted wide, feet clad in tall rubber boots. "You know there is no talking allowed. While you yap away you fall behind! Speed up!"

Angelina made a face that only Olivia could see. Her friend stifled a laugh and furtively stuck out her tongue in solidarity. The overseers, all men, liked to hear themselves bellow, and the workers, almost all women, mocked them mercilessly. But not to their faces. As odious as the rice fields were, the women needed the money for their families.

Angelina passed her hat to her friend, tied up her scarf, and the two quickly caught up to the rest of their line. Count Orlandio's rice farm was vast, hundreds of acres. The women worked in long rows, eight hours a day, six and a half days a week. They toiled under the sun, backs straining, feet and hands seldom leaving the warmish brown murk.

In April, their job had been to plant the strands of seedling rice plants. A child on a raft pulled by a plodding mule dropped bunches of them in the water. The women would gather the seedling clusters, then plant them evenly spaced as they advanced across the flooded field. When they moved forward a row, the raft would again pass behind. Once the women planted the seedlings, they spent every day afterward keeping the fields weed free.

Their headgear was critical because the Po Valley simmered humid-hot in the summer. Sunstroke was always a danger; once started, the workers stopped only for an hour-long lunch. The women spent the rest of the day face-to-muck. When searing back pain forced a momentary stretch, it invariably triggered a foreman's harsh tongue-lashing. But the rice-women were resilient and shook off their aching discomfort and the verbal abuse as just the way things were.

Angelina and the other *mondine* lived at the rice fields from April through June. They slept in a barracks close to the flooded fields, a converted brick barn putrid with dung-stench. Scores of salvaged military cots sat on what was once the threshing floor. Laundry hung from wall-to-wall clotheslines. Persistent mosquitoes and horseflies were a buzzing torment in the barracks at night. The straw mattresses crawled with bedbugs and fleas. Latrines were an open ditch. A well, a handpump, a long wooden trough, and two oak tubs for quick, cold bathing completed the women's toilet arrangements. Malaria thrived in the region, though sickness seldom kept a woman from working.

The job did include three meals a day. Each consisted of boiled rice in a wooden bowl, although occasionally thin bean soup made an appearance. The bread was of cheap millet flour, ground from a cereal that doubled as animal fodder.

The wage was two lire a day. From spring to early summer, planting demanded many hands, and in September and August came the harvest. During those two seasons, over a hundred thousand *contadini* found work in the great rice fields of Lombardia and Piedmont. Those from nearby villages bitterly resented the opportunistic "birds of passage" who flocked from distant mountain towns, or worse, from the south, to compete for jobs. The estates were well-pleased; the huge labor pool kept costs down.

Hunger drove the migrants to desperate measures. Despite high death rates, the Italian population continued to boom. With the gentry in rigid control of most property, and the harvests of the estates carted to the cities for top prices, the peasants had little of their own. "The stomach is the true head of every household," claimed the proverb, and the old adage was proving to be true. Hungry families went on the road during parts of the year looking for work, near and far. And many thousands all through the country, north and south, were making the decision to abandon all they ever had known to seek salvation in the Americas.

"My cousin Elmo is leaving the day I arrive home," Olivia said. She sat next to Angelina on the wagon bed, their backs against the side slats. "He has found work on a rubber plantation in Argentina."

"How could he find work that far away? Who does he know?"

"The plantations send hiring agents to Castrubello. They know our men are good workers. My cousin saw an agent one day outside San Giulio Church. He says they are even paying for his ticket to Buenos Aires. Elmo's friend Giorgio Diamonte is going with him. There are other Castrubellese who went to another town near Buenos Aires. La Plata. You know Gio Batista, yes? Well, he is in La Plata and has sent for his wife and children now."

This is a conversation I do not want to have, Angelina thought. Talk of America, south or north, made her ache for Renzo. She remembered their own unresolved conversations about themselves taking such a chance. They were to be married when he returned from the war in Tripoli. Her hand found the medallion of the Virgin at her throat. His token of that promise. And then, the man had disappeared.

When the army telegram reporting Gianni Como's death arrived, followed weeks later by a dented metal box containing a few remnants of his possessions, it shocked Angelina to see how his mother Tonia aged overnight. Dressed in black mourning clothes, she hiked to the church every day since to say rosaries for the soul of her baby. Obsessive religion became the answer to her grief. She had become one of those women known in the village as a bizzocca, a 'house-nun'. In contrast, her husband Carlo now turned his face completely from God, spending fifteen-hour days, or more, engrossed at the quarry. His son Pietro was constantly at his side.

Eight days after the first one, a second telegram arrived, regretting to inform them that Sergeant Lorenzo Como was missing in action. The news threw the Comos into new torment.

The birth of Donatello Como in January of 1912 brought a measure of relief. Bianca, Gianni's widow, found in her newborn an outlet for her pain. For Tonia too, the new grandchild partially distracted her from her despair. Named for his maternal grandfather, Donato, so nicknamed, thrived under the stifling ministrations of sorrowing women.

The terrible uncertainty of her Renzo's fate tore at Angelina's heart. If only she knew. If he were captured or wounded, there was hope she would hold him close again one day. But what if he was dead, or lost somewhere in those godless sands? Until she knew for certain, she could only suffer.

The wagon slowed its steady pace on the west bank of the Pirino. The river rippled serenely over its rocks, swirled wherever the bed deepened. Small sand islands rose above the water in places. From this spot, Castrubello lay less than six miles to the east. The wooden bridge they faced was old and much repaired; the road swung south until crossing Ponte Spagnolo and passing into town. Thick poplars and beeches growing on the banks screened the shoreline in both directions.

The wagoneer snapped his reins and called out to his two plow horses, *"Vai, Stella! Vai, Luna!"* Upon hearing their names, the two swaybacked nags clopped ahead marginally faster. Burying their muzzles in the fresh water that they could smell would be well worth the extra effort! The wagon swung left off the bridge ramp, rumbled down toward the trees.

"Ah, finally!" said Olivia. "I thought we never would get here." The women chattered with excitement. Even Angelina, who was in no mood for frivolity, caught herself smiling. The women had found the wagon driver to be readily amenable to a bribe of one lira, and he had agreed to stop at this secluded shoreline near the bridge. The wagon bounced into the shade until, with a final lurch, it groaned to a stop. Powdery churned trail dust lingered in the air.

"Everybody out!" cried the teamster. He was a skinny, bald man, with a white, curly beard. His passengers, eager for their first full body scrubbing in six weeks, scrambled to the ground, flinging off garments as they moved. "Thirty minutes, my dears! And have no worries about me watching you," he added, face deadpanned, eyes laughing. "I appreciate feminine beauty, that is no lie. But I am far too old to do anything about it!"

* * *

Naviglio Quarry roared with activity, its products shipping out daily to dozens of construction sites. The Pirino's golden river sand, assiduously processed at the quarry, was prized as an additive for concrete projects throughout the north.

Ettore Vacci stood in the guest office of the renovated priory that served as the quarry's headquarters. At fifty-two, his sandy hair was going gray along with his impressive handlebar mustache. But his eyes shone as always with an intuitive intelligence tempered by iron. He wore a three-piece linen suit handmade in Milan; his shoes were of fine Spanish leather. On his left hand, he wore a wide gold wedding band, his happy marriage to Marietta Pezzoli providing the stable anchor he needed for a life of work and travel. On his other hand was the signet ring from Victor Emmanuel III, presented in recognition of Vacci's supreme effort in pushing a new road through the marshlands near Naples, five years earlier.

The room was a guest office both in name and practice, a place for the senior partner to keep a few things, have a desk. Ettore rarely made it out here these days. He found little need to maintain much of a presence, and it was good that there was no need. His brother-in-law and quarry partner Carlo Como had proven more than capable of managing the operation. With a last swallow, Ettore finished his cup of espresso, a rare indulgence for him on a working afternoon.

Carlo was his only partner now. The firm of Pezzoli & Vacci Costruzioni was no more. Ettore missed his fellow founder Maurizio Pezzoli tremendously. They had clawed their way up the ladder together—such a team they had made! But Maurizio was so frenetic, true to the nature God gave him, Ettore thought. An engineer by training, Pezzoli found the challenge of roadbuilding, despite the new surfaces, a creative dead end. Even before Giovanni Agnelli and his booming *Fabbrica Italiana Automobili Torino,* commonly known as FIAT, offered him his current position, Maurizio had been complaining of boredom.

Ettore knew Signor Agnelli well. He was one of the early investors in his and Maurizio's original roadbuilding enterprise. Once out of the army and on his own, the energetic entrepreneur had made good on his conviction that the future of transportation lay with the internal combustion engine. With a collection of partners, he had launched the great auto works rising in Turin, a brilliant success. After the Fiat Corporation subsumed many carriage manufacturers, including the Pezzolis', Ettore had anticipated that losing his partner to the great new industry was but a matter of time. He and Maurizio settled the dissolution of their partnership amicably. Their personal relationship as close friends and brothers-in-law remained as solid as ever. Ettore's wife Marietta, Maurizio's sister, made certain of it.

Rechristened *Vacci Costruzioni d'Italia*, otherwise VCI, the original company continued to prosper under Ettore's sole ownership. But he still made time to drop by the separate enterprise of Naviglio Quarry & Concrete here in Castrubello.

From his second-floor view, Ettore scanned the impressive operation. Over four hundred men were hard at work on any given day; knowing that nearly all were fellow Castrubellese was a source of great pride.

The concrete plant, with its tight row of four squatty silos for storage and mixing, dominated a third of the property at one end. Covered conveyer belts hauled rock and sand upward for crushing and blending; the silos were crowned by a long low-roofed structure where workers moved the mixed aggregate on to the adjacent square-shaped processing mill.

At the other side of the quarry, two steam shovels scraped great piles of raw stone from a pit and heaved them into mounds. Shovelers and yard boys fed the chunks into a massive stone crusher attached to a conveyer belt that carried the material upward to large metal hoppers. Extended over the canal, the crushed stone awaited barges for loading.

Ettore saw a low-slung *barcuu* maneuvering from the Naviglio Largo into the wide moat surrounding the quarry. Entering empty, the barges left full and headed back out onto the great canal to their destinations.

Among the sand and gravel pits, Ettore watched young Pietro Como, now twenty-three, directing a worker, pointing as he talked. Carlo's last son, Ettore thought regretfully. My brother-in-law has many hopes pinned on that one, he mused, but Pietro is no Renzo.

Where was Carlo anyway? On every previous visit, Tonia's husband had met him at the door. But not today. Today a nervous clerk in black sleeve garters and visor had apologized profusely for his boss's absence. Ettore finally told him, "*Calma, calma*, young man, it is not the end of the world."

After making caffe' for the esteemed signore, the young man, smartly dressed, punctilious, eager to please—one of the Collina boys, Ettore seemed to recall—had hastily mounted a bicycle and pedaled toward Castrubello in search of his master.

Ettore sat back down in a chair, returned to his musings. So, yes, the quarry was operating at its peak. But all was not well, Ettore knew. Carlo was by no means his usual self these dark days. The news of Gianni's tragic death and Renzo's disappearance had shaken them all. The emotional decline of Ettore's sister Tonia was most distressing. A light had also gone out in Carlo. As a young man, he had been cocky, smart-tongued. That quality had disappeared long ago with those terrible events at d'Ambrosso's. At first, dogged determination replaced it, which accounted for so much of the quarry's success. But since Tripoli and the loss of two sons, his brother-in-law had become a humorless, taciturn man.

Ettore did not hear footsteps on the stairs prior to a sudden, perfunctory rap on the door. Before he could respond, the clerk, flushed with perspiration, stepped in and announced, "Signore, I met Signor Como on his way. He has now arrived."

The men greeted each other warmly, embracing and touching cheeks.

Carlo told the clerk, "In twenty minutes, go out to the yard and tell my son to join us." He turned to Ettore. "Very good to see you, Etto. I am sorry to be late, a matter at the house."

Carlo's drawn, ashen appearance shocked Ettore. "I am in no hurry. I and Marietta came to see how our new villa goes. She is at the site now, aggravating the workers. Myself, I came here first to visit our quarry and learn how things are with you and my sister."

Carlo shrugged his shoulders and face, motioned to his guest to please sit, then took a chair himself. Ettore pressed on. "My sister, Carlo?"

"She is at the church until at least midafternoon."

Ettore noted the exasperation. "And yourself, Carlo, how do you fare?"

Carlo reached into his vest pocket and extracted an envelope. "This is why I was late, the post arrived when I was coming out the door. From my brother Francesco."

Ettore took the opened envelope and retrieved his wire-rimmed spectacles from a vest pocket. The postage stamps were American. He unfolded the single page with writing on both sides and slowly read the cramped handwriting. Carlo sat, hands on his knees. Ettore raised his eyebrows. "I am at a loss," he finally said when he had finished.

"Francesco only thinks it is him," said Carlo.

"'Lorenzo Como'? How many can there be?" Ettore shook his head. "And alive in America. How does he go from missing in action to working on a freight ship in the North American Great Lakes? But that is *non importa*, no? The news is good, Carlo, good! The army report was wrong—Renzo is alive, after all! But for him to be so close to Detroit City yet not visit Francesco and the family? What can it mean?"

Carlo took back the letter. "It means the army lost track of their damned paperwork!"

"This town that your brother named, Terrouge. I have heard of it," Ettore said. "There are men from Castrubello who have gone there, at least for a time. They mine copper ore. That area is full of Italian workers, including many northerners."

Carlo stood, paced, waved his hand. "I tell you, Etto, I do not care. All this time with not a word, allowing his mother, his family to despair? What loving son does that to his mother? I cannot believe it is my Renzo! If it is, he has turned his back on all of us!"

The office door opened, and Pietro Como entered. Not much Vacci or Como evident in this one, thought Ettore. Somewhat shorter and leaner than either of his brothers, he most resembled his grandmother Fiorenza's side of the family. Her father, Corrado Lualda, had stood a bantam 5'5". Pietro was taller than that by a few inches. Like all the Lualdas, his longish nose had a slight bump on its bridge.

"Zio Ettore!" Pietro cried, extending his arms. "You were here at the quarry but did not come out to see me?" His brown eyes shone with bright hardness, then softened. "But why would you go out there, of course; the sandpit, so dusty. Just look at those fine shoes you are wearing!" The young man beamed at his wealthy uncle.

Ettore smiled. "My nephew Pietro, always so polite. You know, Pietro, I am no stranger to dust. But, yes, you are right, I chose to be a stranger to it today. I watched you from here with the worker—a foreman was he, perhaps?"

Pietro thought for a moment. "You must mean Gio. Hardly a foreman. The man works hard, but he is such a dullard. 'One task at a time', that is what I would say is his motto. He requires constant watching and telling." Pietro looked to his father, handed over a sheet of paper. "Here is that invoice from the Dorios. I marked the so-called 'mistakes', Papà." He sighed at Ettore. "You know those pirates."

Carlo looked at the paperwork. "Yes. Good." He paused. Ettore sensed his brother-in-law suppressing a spasm of grief, admired his struggle to prevail. "Your Zio Francesco. He sent me a letter," said Carlo. "There is news of your brother, Renzo."

Pietro forced an involuntary frown to smooth itself flat, dropped his eyes, brought a hand to his brow. "*Dio mio!* Renzo? After these months? What is the news?"

Carlo gave the letter to Pietro. The room went quiet while he read it through.

"Mining in America?" Pietro exclaimed. "He has been gone so long. Now we hear this? What does Mamma say of this?"

"She doesn't know. Nor shall she."

Startled, Pietro and Ettore both stared at Carlo.

Reading his father's mood, Pietro took a calculated risk. "Papà, I will go to America and find Renzo. You and Mamma need him back!"

"Spoken like a loyal brother, Pietro, but no. What we needed was for Gianni to return from the war. We charged Renzo with a single duty. Bring Gianni home. Alive if he could, but at the least, if Death must be fed, then his body! For burial in hallowed ground, here close to us, not in that pagan wasteland." He gestured at Ettore. "This is why Tonia spends every day on her knees. Rosaries for Gianni's wandering soul, for it to find its way to heaven!" He gathered himself. "And Renzo lives, only to run away from us all? No, he does not live. Renzo is as dead as Gianni. Let him wander forever." He looked at Pietro. "I have one son left. You." Pietro deferentially bowed his head, secretly exhilarated that his bluff had held up.

Ettore recognized his nephew's feigned humility, suppressed his repulsion. "Tonia needs to know," he told Carlo.

"She does not. Tell me, why should she know, Ettore? Nothing will change if she does. Renzo will never return, or he would have by now. If she knows he is alive, her despair only deepens. And listen to me. I refuse to ever see Renzo again!"

Ettore's heart cried for his sister. What mother would not want to know where her lost child was? With no children of his own, he grieved for the rending of Tonia's family. But, reluctantly, he withdrew. He knew his place in this drama.

"I understand, Carlo. I will, of course, say nothing, even to Marietta. Renzo is at least alive and working. Alive and working means hope."

Carlo crumpled the letter, threw it in the waste can.

Pietro dropped his eyes as if in grief but rejoiced. He had always resented his brothers, Renzo for being the heir, and Gianni, the baby, for the fuss and attention he constantly received. Meanwhile, he, Pietro, languished between them, always overlooked. No longer. His father's raging grief was useful; it made him dependent. Elated by the change in circumstances for himself, he broke the silence.

"I must get back to the sand shipment. Not only does Genoa want its supplies on time, but they also demand a meeting to negotiate more gravel for the new Milan-to-Belluno road. You remember Giulio Bembo of the trucks, Papà? His son Secondo and I have something of a rapport. That could make a difference in the final numbers."

Quite the fast talker, quite the ambitious one, thought Ettore. And such an energetic pivot from the topic of his brothers. With Pietro, assume nothing, he told himself. "Carlo," he said, "Walk me around the quarry, do you have time? I would like to visit the men." He stood, looked at his nephew. "At the end of the day, Pietro, they are only shoes."

* * *

Andrea Collina valued his job. So, when he examined the waste bin in Signor Vacci's office, he did so carefully. He did not consider himself a spy. Spies and informers were the scum of the earth. But with his desk immediately outside the guest office, despite the closed door, he had heard the entirety of Signor Como's anguished talk of his son. And anyway, it was his job to tidy the office, to empty the trash baskets, wasn't it? By reading the discarded letter he soon clarified the full news.

For a moment he wondered, why am I doing this? Why take this risk? He knew the answer, of course. Because of the bewitching Angelina. How he loved her! After telling her that Renzo was gone forever—by Renzo's choice, the ungrateful lout!—perhaps his heart's dream would start responding to him.

He read the letter twice, memorized the scant details, then carefully returned the recrumpled paper to the trash bin. The office clock chimed eight p.m.

As he bicycled to his family's house in town, Andrea fantasized about Angelina's reaction. Surprise naturally, sadness. But also eternal gratitude because he would tell her what had become of her faithless Renzo. She may even swoon, her head on his chest. Her full, soft lips. He crossed himself. "Forgive me," he muttered.

Still, show that you share her sadness, he told himself, do not appear in any way pleased. Just be a warm friend with hard news, there to comfort. Then, in a few days, when he returned to see how she was, present her with a small gift, a hint of his warm esteem, a glimpse of his respectful aspirations.

The risk was worth it. Only he and Angelina would know how he arrived at his information. And why would she expose her future husband? Well, not as of yet future husband. Do not put the cart before the ox, Andrea, you fool, he told himself.

It was too late to visit her tonight. But the first thing in the morning, he would call on the woman he longed for.

* * *

"Above the main hall, Marietta, the mezzanine overlooks the floor. Wide enough here," Ettore said, with a jab at the blueprints, "to place musicians when we entertain." He stood with his wife and the project foreman, surrounded by the robust sounds and smells of construction. Although the interior walls were not yet finished, a roof supported by framing and tall stone columns covered their heads. Masons fit the fine, pinkish Candoglia marble slabs to the fireplace façade as carpenters with flashing hammers nailed down wide oak planks onto the floor's sub-base.

"*Sì*, Don Vacci, the mezzanine," said the foreman. "We build it once the walls go up."

"We have seen the sketches, we both have confidence in you," Marietta Vacci said. "It will truly be a thing of beauty. We look forward to the day we arrive to make this wonderful building our home." She took a deep breath, made a face at Ettore. "Oh, that dairy."

Ettore breathed in, instantly agreed. The odor came from what once had been the d'Ambrosso estate. Dead fifteen years, the dissolute marchese had left his property to his wife. Within two months, the widow sold the villa and all its acreage to settle the marchese's outstanding debts, which were numerous. The new owner, an enterprising cattleman from Lazio, surprised everyone by converting the place into, of all things, a dairy. His workers rebuilt the stables to house his milk cows and turned the fields over for grazing. From all accounts, the gamble was working. That is what Ettore had heard, in any event. He had not set foot on the property since the day he'd left Castrubello for Milan thirty years before.

"Ah, my dear, breathe deep the rich smell of life," Ettore told his wife, with a puckish smile.

Marietta made a face. "The smell of *merda*, you mean, Ettore."

Ettore laughed. "How cynical you have become, 'Etta. Yet you're right, life and *merda*, often the same, I agree!" The listening foreman snorted along convivially.

A distressed voice interrupted the moment of levity.

"Signor and Signora Vacci, forgive me! I have no right to intrude this way, but please, may we speak?"

A young woman in simple clothes stood outside the columns, wiping her eyes with her palms. She was Angelina Scrivatti, Ettore recognized, Renzo's intended. His once-intended, that is. What could this be?

Marietta nodded at her husband's glance. As they moved from the tall blueprint table, Ettore told the foreman, "Barto, excellent work. We will speak again soon." Arm in arm, he and Marietta approached Angelina.

"Signor Vacci, Signora, I am Angelina Scrivatti," she began, but Ettore said, "Yes, Angelina. But first, let us move out of earshot of these workers."

He guided her to a shady tree near the site. Just past here is where my grapevines will go, he thought absently. They stood on thin grass beneath the branches of the tall elm.

"Please, tell us now, signorina, what is it that upsets you so?"

She recounted everything she had learned from Andrea an hour before.

"But how is it you know of this?" Ettore asked sharply, angry at the breach of confidentiality. He immediately thought of Pietro.

She only paused a moment. "It was Andrea, the clerk, signore. He read the letter from America, and he knows how I worry about Renzo." Her neck flushed. "Please do not punish him, I ask you. He was right to tell me. Renzo and I promised ourselves to each other. Padre Robustelli read our bans in church before he left for the war! I must know where Renzo is!"

This one has a backbone, Ettore thought. And that Andrea Collina. Would a mere friend risk his job that way? No. More likely a suitor-in-hoping.

Marietta spoke. "Angelina, my husband has not even told me this news." She flashed Ettore a look. "But I know he would not keep secrets for secrets' sake. He was thinking of Tonia and of yourself. What purpose is served by reopening this wound? It is better that you forget Renzo. From what you say, he chose to abandon his family. And everyone."

"Signora Vacci, Renzo is not thinking clearly, can you not see? His father has expected much of him, in business, in protecting his brothers. Renzo never faltered in these duties until Tripoli. Why? Something made him seek to escape!"

"We all grieve for Gianni," Ettore said. "Whatever it is we feel, Renzo must feel tenfold. After all, he was there. Who knows what he has seen? But permit me to be straightforward, signorina. When you learned of the letter, why did you come to us and not Renzo's father?"

"I cannot go to Signor Como. I fear his anger. Everyone knows you, Signor Vacci, as the padrone of Castrubello." Ettore shook his head. "No, no," she continued, "it is not flattery. I come to you as our padrone, and as my future husband's uncle, to tell you this. I am going to America to marry Renzo!"

The Vaccis stood dumbstruck. Marietta recovered first. "How can you say this? Your heart is talking, not your mind. Voyage to America, alone? To find a man, if he even is there, in a village you never heard of, among strangers who speak a different language? You risk becoming a lamb among wolves, my dear!" She clasped her hands. "I am afraid your family will never allow it!"

Angelina's eyes became dark sparks, her fists went to her hips.

"Signora, I am going. My family has no say in this. Renzo Como promised me a marriage. The word you said before, 'abandoned'. I do not accept 'abandoned'. I will marry Renzo. Renzo is in *l'America*. That is where I will go!"

Ettore looked at his wife, then at the intent young woman. Decades earlier, before he departed for three years of roadbuilding in San Remo, then in Africa, he'd asked Marietta to marry him when he returned. She had waited, like Angelina for Renzo, because she trusted his word. And on that mutual trust, they had since built their happy and satisfying life together. How was this now any different? If Renzo, for whatever reason, could not come to Angelina, why shouldn't she go to him?

He gently touched his wife on her arm.

Raising his hand, he said. "What is it you need of me, signorina?" he asked. "Of us," he said, smiling, looking again at

Marietta, who confirmed her understanding of his intent with a nod.

"I ask only your blessings, signore, signora."

Marietta took Angelina's arm in her own. Ettore smiled kindly. "I am no cardinal, Angelina, no bishop. I am a worker like you. Just one who's worked longer." His eyes crinkled. "What I do give you, young woman, from us both, is our respect and our help. Renzo is my godson and our nephew. I will speak with his father about your plans. You are right, he will raise the roof. But his anger will pass. Of all people, Carlo Como knows the power of the heart!"

Chapter 28

Carlo Como did raise the roof, but Ettore helped him past that moment. Together the two sat with Tonia and told her of the letter regarding her son and of Angelina's plans.

"I know Renzo is alive," she told them, weeping. "I have always known this."

They were in Casa Como, renovated over the years and comfortable. Carlo had expanded their original home into adjacent structures. The residence now occupied the entire short block.

"He will come back to us, Carlo," Tonia continued. "Now that we know where he is, we can send letters."

Carlo gave no response. Tonia can tell herself all the stories she wants, he thought. His opinion of Renzo was no different than before. And if the Scrivatti girl wanted to go chasing across half the world, what was that to him?

"Regarding Andrea Collina," Ettore said later, speaking to Carlo alone. "I will handle him."

"Regarding Andrea Collina, he has no job," replied Carlo. "He will have no *coglioni* either if I ever see that snoopy bastard again."

"You won't, trust me."

Carlo grunted. He knew Ettore would cause no physical harm to befall the stupid young man. More's the pity, he thought. Yet he had seen Ettore break balls when he wanted. He only hoped the clerk suffered enough for his betrayal of trust.

Ettore wrote to Maurizio at the Fiat factory in Turin. Pezzoli promised to find something appropriately distasteful for the fastidious office clerk. Something involving grease up to his elbows, he told Ettore in a short note. But a job, a fresh start. The rest would be up to the boy.

Ettore also approached Romano Scrivatti, Angelina's father, a shoemaker with a small shop. To help allay his concerns for his daughter's departure to America, he ordered forty pairs of sturdy work boots from the merchant for his VCI foremen.

"I know this is difficult," Ettore told Scrivatti, "and a boot order is no daughter. But my opinion, if you care to know it? You must allow her to do this."

The men shook hands, eyes meeting, everything settled.

Through inquiries, Marietta Vacci learned that in October five Sisters of Charity from San Giulio would embark to New York City to teach at a new parish school. Signora Vacci arranged for Angelina to join them as their traveling companion. A generous contribution to the order's motherhouse in Milan smoothed the process. Angelina was grateful for the intervention. The stories she had heard of hardships during Atlantic crossings were daunting. Traveling with nuns could only help

In September, Angelina, armed with her new passport, joined the sisters at a meeting with the steamship ticket agent in Castrubello. Mother Bonifacia, in her robust fifties, was to be the new superior for the fledgling school. The other nuns were in their twenties.

"*Buongiorno,* Reverend Mother, everyone," said the agent, in greeting. He was a goateed, middle-aged man with large ears. "Please sit, please sit. I am Signor Cantante. I am incredibly pleased to meet you. Thank you so much for your visit this morning.

"I have been looking into your need for berths to America, and here is what I have found." Cantante moved to a large map on the wall. "It is the route and the service I most often recommend."

The agent used a wooden pointer to direct their attention. "Here, of course, is Turin, from where you will start." His pointer slapped the paper with a snap. "From Turin, by train to Macon, in France. Here." *Snap!*

"In Macon, a change of trains, then on to Le Havre." He tap-tapped at a circle of lines on the French west coast.

"The ship is *S.S. Auvergne* of Compagnie Generale Transatlantique. Very reputable, we do much business with this company. The vessel itself is a dependable workhorse of the seas, fast for its size. *Auvergne* has room for a thousand passengers in steerage alone. Coal-powered of course, thoroughly modern. This company is one that has adopted many recent recommendations for passenger accommodation reform."

The agent covered his mouth with a closed fist, cleared his throat. The word he had regarding the aging tub was that the conditions in steerage were barbaric. "All in all, Mother Superior, a good ship, a quick, comfortable cruise."

"The price, signore?" said Mother Bonificia.

"And a good price, Mother Superior, a particularly good price as well! For the entire trip, including the carriage to Turin, the train to LeHavre, and the voyage itself, merely three hundred lire."

Angelina found herself grateful yet again to the Vaccis. She had her savings from several years' work in the rice fields. But an envelope left with her father by Don Ettore made up the difference she needed both for the fare and all expected expenses.

"We are women of God," said Mother Superior. "Not wealthy bankers."

The agent's salesman's ingratiating smile froze on his face. These religious, he thought, trained like archers to pierce one's sense of guilt. "Exactly, Mother," he responded. "You anticipate my next sentence, which is to say that in your case, a ten percent discount applies. Leaving," he checked figures. "Two hundred seventy lire,"

"Agreed, Signor Cantante," said the nun. At least I reduced the man's sinful gouging, she thought.

"*Grazie*, Mother Superior!" The agent remained pleased with the sale. His 'discount' had brought the exaggerated price back to its norm. "The *Auvergne*," he said, flipping a page in his schedule book, "sails in one month!"

* * *

22 October 1912: *S.S. Auvergne*, Atlantic Ocean

Angelina pushed her way to the first open space she spied. The section of deck fenced off for steerage passengers was small and awkwardly obstructed by ship machinery. Overhead, black smoke from the ship's massive two funnels occasionally dropped hot cinders onto the crowd. She wedged herself next to a round ventilator shaft bolted to the deck. The choppy sea bucked the ship, but Angelina welcomed the occasional cold salt mist. Anything was better than the fetid air below decks.

Three days out of Le Havre, *S.S. Auvergne* bore slight resemblance to the picture painted by travel agent Cantante, largely due to what he'd deliberately omitted.

Steerage lay buried three decks below, just above the steamship's clamorous propeller churn. Angelina and her companions claimed six corner berths in the sleeping compartment reserved for unaccompanied women, many of them brides for men who had already started new lives. Another compartment, portside, was for families, a third, accommodating unattached male passengers, was located amidships.

The long, low-ceilinged dormitories slept upwards of three hundred persons apiece. Berths were either wooden shelves bolted to the bulwarks or bunks fixed to the deck. Each assigned space measured six feet long and two feet wide; headroom was two and a half feet. Mattresses were lumpy sacks stuffed with straw or dried seaweed, covered by coarse, white canvas slips. Another scratchy slip covered the pillow, which in fact was their stiff life jacket. Every berth came with one thin blanket.

There were no closets or hooks for clothing. Within her berth's thirty cubic feet, Angelina kept her few extra clothes and belongings, the tin plate and utensils she had purchased for her meals, and a bundle of simple toiletries. The ship provided no towels.

The bunks were two-tiered. Angelina slept on a lower one and used the bottom of the mattress frame over her head to hang the clothes she wasn't wearing. These drooped within inches of her face when she lay prone in her narrow nest. Pressed on three sides by cloth walls, Angelina felt like a corpse in a heavily upholstered coffin.

According to the steward's stern directions, passengers were to store nothing beneath their berths. As if she would want to! Black with ingrained filth, the boards reeked of soaked-in vomit, and worse, from previous travelers. The ship provided no sick-buckets or even waste cans; stomach-spew stayed where it was until the steward resentfully dragged his rancid mop over it. Two narrow ceiling shafts failed miserably in their hopeless task of ventilating the windowless compartment. The vivid stench from the head, where a row of ten stark toilets served three hundred, was hair-curling. Five washbasins with faucets provided cold saltwater. The single warmwater sink was in constant use.

Admittedly, Angelina thought, the food was ample though tasteless. Mixed with scraped leftovers from second-class compartment plates, it was invariably overcooked and flavor-free.

There was no dining space for steerage passengers on the ship. Once galley stewards thwacked the meal portion onto their plates with wooden spoons, the women returned to their compartment to sit on their mattresses and eat. Either that or they stood shoulder to shoulder in the passageways, scooping food into their mouths, or, if they could, went up on deck. Afterward, they washed their utensils in the compartment's latrine sinks. The lines at the basins were always long and slow; many just wiped their utensils with any handy cloth and hid them away.

Personal privacy consisted of whatever clothing one could twine onto her bedframe as curtains. The nuns' corner berths had the advantage of being away from the walkthrough used by sailors to get from one part of the ship to another. Most other berths were not as lucky.

Apparently a multitude of duties required the crew to repeatedly walk among the women, especially in the evening when the ladies were often in a state of semi-undress. Angelina noticed the sailors slowed at those times while their eyes kept leeringly active, and on many occasions, their impulsive hands quickly groped nearby flesh as they passed.

The Sisters of Charity carefully stayed out of the way. In their plain black bonnets and simple religious habits, hung with looped rosaries bearing crucifixes, they and Angelina, who took care to also dress in funereal simplicity, so far had escaped the crewmen's attention.

Another sharply cold spray doused the fantail deck. The clouds were heavy with pending rain, and the ship's motion changed to a nauseous series of rolling lurches. A horn blared from the ship's bridge, then twice again. By this time, the passengers knew the signal: *Exterior decks are now closed; all passengers proceed inside.* For first-class and second-class passengers this meant private cabins, dining halls, smoking lounges, libraries. For the lower classes in steerage, the horn signaled a return to the grim, airless chambers above the ballast hold.

For three days and nights, the seas ran high. Seasickness was rife; the nuns, when they weren't retching themselves, sopped the vomit from the floor with their spare habits, rinsed them in the seawater sinks, then returned to their hands and knees. Or they sat with the sick, offering what comfort they could. Throughout the ordeal, Angelina worked alongside her companions.

On the fourth day, the storm worsened. When the ship heeled hard to portside, throwing passengers from their bunks along with their possessions, Mother Bonifacia told her tiny group, "We have shown our charity. Now it is time to demonstrate our faith."

Bonifacia led the nuns and Angelina to the middle row of the compartment where others could see them. The six women in their unwashed black habits, stained with filth, knelt and bowed their heads over clasped hands.

"A litany to Maria our Mother," said Bonifacia above the furious wail of the rising storm. "For delivery from this tempest." She opened a well-worn book of prayers.

"In the name of the Father, and the Son, and the Holy Spirit." As she spoke, there was a rustle of attention from nearby berths. Women sat up, some rolled on their sides to see. A few went to their knees.

Oh Lord, have mercy on us! prayed Reverend Mother.

The nuns led the response: *Christ, have mercy!*

The familiar, venerable petitioning began. As the moments passed, filled with the rhythmic recital, despite the ship's continual violent pitching, despite muffled retching, the tendrils of mounting panic receded.

God, Father of Heaven...
Have mercy on us!
God, the Son, Redeemer of the World...
Have mercy on us!
God, the Holy Ghost...
Have mercy on us!

More women joined the litany at each repetition. Mother Bonifacia prayed in her Lombardia tongue, others from Italy spoke in their own home dialects. There were Slovak women as well, and Ukrainians, Poles, Finns from the northlands. But they too knew Holy Maria, and easily fell into repeating the refrain. Even the Jews and Rhinelander Protestants intently murmured along.

The volume as more voices responded with *Pray for us!* to Mother Bonifacia's acclamations of Maria's divine glory.

Maria Inviolate...
Star of the Morning...
Virgin Most Amiable...
Mystical Rose...
Mother of Good Counsel...
Light of the Despairing...

The deck beneath their knees shook angrily, as if the hull was being wrenched by an aroused demon of the deep. The women grasped each other to steady themselves. Their voices exclaimed the ancient paean to the Mother of the World, the power and mystery of womanhood's enduring resilience through ages of nurturing and lamentation, violence and calm, exhilarant joy, of unendurable heartbreaks endured.

Mirror of Justice...
Mother Most Merciful...
Virgin Most Powerful...
Seat of All Wisdom...
Maria, Star of the Sea!

The overhead electric lights, the one reliable amenity they had encountered aboard ship, went suddenly dark. The praying continued in near ink-blackness, Bonifacia relying now on her memory to conclude.

"Grant, we beseech thee, O Blessed Maria, that through your glorious intercession you deliver us from our tribulations!"

The ship bucked, heaved hard to starboard, swung upright again. The lights blinked, blanked, blinkered.

* * *

29 October 1912: New York Harbor

The ship sighted the spires of New York City on day ten. Angelina and the nuns crammed themselves onto the ladderway to the open deck. Once on the fantail, they joined hundreds of passengers craning to see, but only those pressed against the rail had a good view. What remained for the rest were overheard exclamations of excited marvel, more than enough to fire the communal imagination.

After a few minutes, Mother Bonifacia told her little group, "Now is a good time for us to ready our things for departure. Few are in the compartment, we will be able to move freely." The faces around her fell. Arrival in New York Harbor was the greatest anticipation of the voyage. And the great statue, Lady *Libertà* herself, a wonder of the modern world—surely, she would soon loom above the railings for all to see!

Bonificia noted the crestfallen young faces, remembered she had been young once, albeit a thousand years before. Her charges had met every challenge without complaint; even the shoemaker's daughter had managed to make herself useful.

"But first," Mother Superior decided, "I believe a prayer of gratitude is in order. With that intent, each of us will say two rosaries, slowly and privately. Only when everyone's prayers are complete, including mine, will we leave the deck." She lightly smiled.

The novices all but clapped in joy. Two slow rosaries on deck? They rattled happily for their beads.

When *Auvergne* docked the next morning, the ship's lighters ferried steerage passengers to Ellis Island, where they spent the day undergoing identification proceedings, medical inspections, and lengthy questioning that covered everything from final destinations to prior participation in anarchist activity.

Each step of the numbing process required waiting in queues. The jumble of overwhelming new impressions and the tension of wondering if, by fate's cruel intervention, immigration officers would deny entry, kept Angelina on edge. Forty-one steerage passengers failed the medical inspection. Regardless of age, these went into quarantine and were marked for immediate transport back to Europe. The pleading of divided families was heart-rending but ignored.

Entry rules required that everyone from steerage take gang showers, thirty at a time, to wash off parasites and the accumulated stink of the voyage. Some considered the process demeaning. Not Angelina. Feeling the clammy filth rinse from her skin made her want to go through the process twice. The thin lather from the raw block of lye soap smelled like perfume.

She collected her single leather suitcase from the luggage brought over from the ship's hold. In the large common room reserved for women, she changed into a clean black dress for the first time in two weeks. She tied a piece of black ribbon on one arm and adjusted her modest bonnet. Traveling alone as a widow might elicit pity, such was Angelina's hope. I have become a widow before a wife, she thought ruefully.

She faced two final lines. The first was to exchange her Italian lire for United States dollars. The other led to a customs agent who validated her papers with a loud thump of his stamp, pointed at the door that led outside, and looking past her head to the line behind, shouted, "Next!"

Angelina Scrivatti had arrived in America.

She ate dinner and spent the night at the Sisters of Charity convent. In the morning Angelina embraced her friends farewell. Then, at Reverend Mother's insistence and the convent's expense, Angelina took a motor-taxi ride to New York's cavernous Grand Central Station.

Fighting her panic, she stepped into the din of the huge terminal. Massive scaffolds and loud shouts of workers within various roped-off areas under reconstruction magnified her confusion. She repeatedly stood in lines at the wrong ticket windows, then was sent to a different one by harried agents. Unable to say anything that anybody understood, she had only an envelope with Francesco Como's return address on it.

Finally, one clerk took a longer moment with her, squinting at the small handwriting on the envelope. "Detroit, Michigan?" the man deciphered.

Angelina nodded, "*Si, il treno.*"

The clerk produced two tickets, stamped them with the date, and said, "Track eleven." He wrote the information on a slip of paper with a pencil. "One, one," he said, pointing at each number as he spoke, then in the direction of the rows of waiting trains aligned at the far end of the terminal.

Not satisfied that the foreign woman yet understood, the agent pulled out a long schedule sheet from a stack. He drew an oblong around an entire column and underlined the city, "Buffalo." He held up one finger. "First," he said. "Take 'el trane-oh' to Buffalo." He gave her one of the tickets. "Buffalo," he repeated. "Understand?"

"Detroit," Angelina answered.

"Yes, but first..." He noted the somber black dress that she wore, the black ribbon tied to her arm. The lengthening line behind her. Never mind, he sighed. This is your good deed for the day, Charles, he told himself.

He sketched quickly on a blank note sheet. "This," he pointed to the ticket he had given her. "New York to Buffalo." His finger traced the line he had drawn between the two cities on his diagram. "This," he pointed to a second line. "Buffalo to Detroit." The agent handed her the second ticket, pointing to the word "Detroit" printed on it, pointed back to the map.

The agent noted Angelina's furrowed-brow effort to follow his words and turned the map over and printed:

Mr. Conductor, please help me. I speak no English. I am a widow going alone to a funeral. I travel from New York to Buffalo, then Buffalo to Detroit. Please see my tickets.

Then he scrawled in his own handwriting, *Thanks, friend. Chas. Abernathy, Senior Ticket Agent, NYC.* "For conductor," he told her. "On 'trane-oh'."

Chapter 29

Detroit, Michigan

"Frankie, *la gallina!*" Gemella Como shouted as she stopped plucking the feathers from the carcass in front of her. Exasperated, she wiped her brow with the back of her bare forearm. Franco was already in pursuit of the hen he had just slaughtered. The severed head lay on the butcher block, dispassionately staring at the abandoned cleaver, while its body ran spastically onto the store's main floor, neck flailing in all directions like a dropped water hose.

"I've got it, I've got it," the boy cried, smacking the dancing feathered corpse with a broom. The headless bird flopped at his feet, jerked two quick kicks, and lay still in a spreading red puddle.

"I hate when they do that," said Franco. "I thought I was holding it tight enough, Nonna."

"No matter now, you clean the floor," replied his grandmother in heavily accented English. "Give me him," she said. "Only three now, then *finito.*" The trio of live chickens in the small cage behind her fluttered, clucked, watched her movements.

"We return!" said a sudden loud voice in Italian at the market door, jangling the brass entry bell. It was Gemella's oldest son, Paolo, shaking off the rain falling in torrents. He put down the leather case in his hand and stepped to the side. A young woman dressed in dark clothing followed him inside.

"*Madonn'!*" Paolo cried as he saw the catastrophe on the floorboards. He looked at his son Frankie still holding the broom, gestured for him to continue. "So, clean it up. Get more sawdust down." The boy nodded but looked at the new woman.

Angelina took another step forward into the grocery. "I am Angelina Scrivatti," she said boldly, extending her hand.

The boy froze, but Gemella had already come from behind the counter, speaking Italian.

"Angelina, Angelina, welcome! What a journey for you!" She wiped her hands on her apron. "Here is Franco, we call him Frankie, my grandson, Paolo's boy." Gemella looked accusingly at Paolo. "Frankie is such a help to his nonna, such a good boy. You do not shout at him, Paolo!"

The ten-year-old went crimson. "*Ciao*, Angelina," he said. He grabbed the dead fowl by its splayed legs and retreated for the sawdust bucket and pushbroom.

"Watch what you are doing, the blood is dripping, Frankie!" Paolo turned to Angelina. "This is my mother, Gemella," he said, by way of belated introduction.

"*Ciao*, Signora Como, I am pleased to meet you," said Angelina. The two women embraced, touched cheeks with each other. "Thank you for this warm shawl you sent with your son," she added, unwrapping the sopping brown garment from her shoulders.

"November here is not like Castrubello," said Gemella, smiling.

"My wife Marianna is in the house behind the store. We just go through there." Paolo indicated a door behind the counter. "As I said on the way, Pa built this place with help from the neighbors. Where is Pa, Mamma?" he asked, watching Franco clean up the dark stain and feather-fluffs.

"At the new house with your brother Luca," his mother answered. "The man with the water pipes, he changed his price. Your father needed to talk to him." She looked at Angelina and smiled. "Everyone is so greedy sometimes, isn't that true, Angelina? Same in Castrubello, same here."

"When they get back, you will meet him," Paolo said. There was a momentary silence. He expanded both arms. "As you can see, here we are at the market of Francesco Como & Sons!"

"So much," Angelina said and meant it. The sheer number of products on the shelves behind the counter and the two aisles of canned goods was overwhelming. In the storefront window, crates of local produce were open to display. A glass case with meat and fish on ice was next to the main counter, enticing salamis and sausages hung above.

Gemella went to work on the recently renegade chicken Frankie had plopped on her table. "I must finish, Angelina, excuse me. Paolo! Take Angelina to meet Marianna." Paolo picked up the suitcase. "We are so happy you are with us, Angelina," she said, smiling and plucking.

That evening, the family sat at a long table covered with a linen tablecloth embroidered with yellow flowers. Francesco, the father, presided over the large Como brood. There was Luca, his mother Gemella, Paolo and his wife Marianna, who helped set the food, with their boy Franco and three younger daughters. Paolo and Luca's newly married sister Claudia and her husband, Rodrigo, the suspect Cremoan, sat at the opposite end.

Angelina relaxed as the meal unfolded. Dinner was ample and delicious. *Il secondo*, the main course, was *cassoeula*, a Lombardia favorite when pork was available. The rich stew started with a boiled pig's trotter cut lengthwise, sautéed with chopped onion, garlic. Gemella had added the animal's ears along with pork rind and scraps. And in this American rendition, Angelina also saw chicken parts—the headless dancer, no doubt. Carrots, celery, tomatoes, and Savoia cabbage, fresh from the Como garden, filled the rest of the pot. Instead of polenta, there was freshly baked bread for sopping up the rich juice.

"Angelina! I knew your people," Zio Francesco said, after everyone served themselves. "Shoemakers, no? And good shoes, I remember." He shut his eyes. "Yes, the shop was always a pleasure to visit. How good that leather smelled. It took me a while to afford my first pair of *stivaletti*, the ones with soles made of oak!" he added, laughing.

Francesco was a more wrinkled copy of his brother Carlo, Angelina thought. He was three years older than his sibling, as she recalled, which made him about fifty-seven. His hair was thinner than Carlo's but the identical dark brown. Like his brother, he was quite tall among his peers, nearly 5'10". He is happy here, she thought, observing her host as he described the new rental house he was building. Is this the life Renzo is seeking? If so, why is he not here?

Luca, younger than Paolo, sitting across, helped himself to the stew. Breaking off a piece of the bread and placing it on the tablecloth next to his plate, he said, "What a voyage to make alone, Angelina. I am impressed."

She laughed. "I hid among nuns. My mother told me, 'An ocean lies between what is said and what is done.' But I said I will come to America to marry Renzo, and now I am here. The ocean, I have crossed it, and *fortuna* has smiled. There is still farther to go, I know. But I am meant to be with Renzo, so I will be."

Luca plunked a bread crust in the juice on his plate. "Yes, a good saying, that one of your mother's."

The family had many questions for their visitor, not only about Renzo but also of Gianni's death, what did she know about that? She told them the little she knew, then described her work in the rice fields. They talked of the end of the Ottoman war three weeks before and the kingdom's new colony of Italian North Africa. The conversation veered into wistful remembrances, laughing stories, and nosy inquiries about daily life in Castrubello. They sat at the table for hours, punning and teasing her and each other.

When that long first day in Detroit finally ended, Angelina, safe in the bosom in what she now felt was family, slept her deepest in weeks.

Over the next several days, Angelina fell into the rhythm of the family's workdays. She insisted she help at the store, although she could do little more than dust cans and stock shelves. But it gave her the chance to meet some of the Castrubellese families and their children who made up the neighborhood. There were Diamontes and Grigios and Pasquallis and Boschis. They remembered her father and family, and on Sunday, after Mass with the Comos, she stayed for an hour on the church steps, catching up with well-wishers.

The Como's neighborhood was roughly eight square blocks containing the houses of some sixty-five families, all from Castrubello and a few other Lombardia towns. Physically separated by several miles from the better-known "Little Italy" of the city, where mainly immigrants from the south had settled, the area was bordered on the east by the big Polish enclave of Hamtramck and by a cluster of German blocks to the west.

Southward, the neighborhood butted against the streets comprising Detroit's vast Eastern Market. The wholesale district provided the city's numerous corner groceries and most of its restaurants with bushels of fresh produce, sides of beef, pork, live or butchered poultry. The fish were fresh daily, large live ones flashing silver in big glass-sided tanks, taken straight from the Detroit River and nearby Lake St. Claire. Mounds of canned and boxed goods awaited pickup in front of bustling, clamorous warehouse entries. From morning until night, the great open-air market throbbed with energetic commerce.

To the north of the neighborhood, the city thinned out into flat broad fields heavy with low brush where Francesco and his boys sometimes hunted wild pheasant and dove.

On Monday, Francesco took Angelina aside before leaving for his building site. "I want you to meet the man who last saw

Renzo," he told her. "He served as a sailor on a freighter with him. I will bring him to the store at lunchtime."

When Francesco arrived with his companion, Angelina was behind the counter, using the store's wood-handled extension grabber to stock the higher shelves. The man, Giaco Colombo, was 5'4", somewhere in his forties. His weatherbeaten features spoke of a lifetime out-of-doors. He wore a knitted cap and blue-black pea coat against the persistent rain. Francesco made the introductions.

"You have seen my Renzo?" Angelina asked.

"As I told Francesco," Colombo said, "I worked with a Lorenzo Como on a steamship run I made this summer. He came on in Buffalo, said he had been working the docks on Lake Erie awhile. He told me, 'I just go by Como'. Right away he reminded me of his zio here, how he looked and talked. That is why I mentioned it." He nodded at Francesco. "He and I were not truly friends, I cannot say that we were. He had no real friends. Not much happiness in him, I think."

Angelina flared. "What was he like, then, for you to say that?"

The sailor saw the concern creased in her face. Ah, might as well say it, he thought.

"Always with a bottle. I should say not always, never on the job. He was a good worker as far as that went. But when he had time off, he drank. Whiskey in his coffee every night, I know that. None of us told the officers, why would we, as long as he did his share of work?" He shrugged. "I will say when we had shore leave, he usually had to be carried back to the ship. Sometimes by the *polizia*." He tried to soften his words. "I mean, signorina, he was not the only one who drank on that crew. Not me, of course." He snorted at his own joke, grinned brown teeth, winked at Francesco.

"How do you know where he went?"

"He told me when we got to Escanaba Bay. It was not like Como never talked. He had heard about the mining jobs in Terrouge. I told him it was out in the wilderness, two hundred miles north of Escanaba! He did not care. 'I will hop a freight,' was what he said, like he had done it before." Colombo shrugged. "So. That is all I know, signorina. He drew his pay, left the ship, no farewells."

Angelina digested this news. She knew the name 'Terrouge' before she had set out, but Colombo's account made it a real place. *"Grazie mille,* Signor Colombo, for taking the time to speak to me," she told him.

"I wish you success. And if you must travel, do it soon! You do not want to sail the lakes in winter! Take it from someone who knows!" He gave his cap a slight tug and went out the door, jangling the customer bell.

Francesco watched to see her reaction to the stark news.

"Zio, thank you for having him speak to me. Thank you for allowing me to stay here with you. But now I must pack."

At midafternoon the next day, Angelina found herself again on the covered outdoor platform at Detroit's Michigan Central Railroad Depot. The imposing stone and brick building with its turrets and massive four-sided clock tower reminded her of an Italian castle and cathedral combined.

In her hand was the ticket for what she hoped would be the final leg of her journey. From New York to Detroit via Buffalo had been over six hundred miles. Detroit to Terrouge was another six hundred. But the second journey would be far slower with a great many stops. And at the Straits of Mackinac, a ferry was involved. The schedule said she still had over three days to travel.

Francesco stood beside her, waiting for her train's arrival. Angelina could tell he fretted.

"Zio Francesco, thank you so much," she said. "You and the signora have made me feel I am already one of the family."

"I would come with you if I could," Francesco replied. "To see you go alone, I do not like it. Do you have enough money to get back? I mean to return here, to us in this city?" he asked, knowing she did. The envelope he had given her contained exactly enough.

"Do not worry, Zio Francesco. I have come this far, nothing can stop me!" She smiled with a confidence she forced herself to feel. "I will write to you and Zia when I arrive and tell you what I learn about Renzo. I know he is there. He is meant to be there after this long journey of mine!"

The arriving train announced itself with a loud, shrill *hoot!* that momentarily deafened bystanders. The black locomotive came to a squealing halt in a cloud of steam.

Angelina embraced Francesco, who patted her kindly on the back. He looked into her face. "When you find that boy, Angelina," he said, "tell Renzo I said that you are truly an angel! Come back together, stay with us. This is where you both should be, with your *famiglia*. There is plenty of work for Renzo right here."

Angelina gave him a peck on both cheeks, brushed back grateful tears, and boarded.

* * *

The train chugged past the late autumn landscape, first heading inland from Detroit, then arcing north. Once out of the big city, civilization gradually gave over to open countryside, regularly interrupted by scattered hamlets and towns separated by farmland. Tall copses of trees stood as windbreaks that sometimes extended right up to the tracks. The last remnants of bright colored leaves fluttered from nearly bare branches next to the clacking line of passenger cars. When they reached the Straits of Mackinac, a specially fitted ferry transported the complete string of railcars across in one passage.

The train to Terrouge was a local line and did not warrant a dining car. Instead, it stopped once each day at mealtime. Passengers debarked, grabbed a quick dinner in a station cafeteria and reboarded, all within twenty minutes. The fare was poor—shoe leather meat, flavorless mushed beans, cold bitter coffee. The meal break was also a chance to relieve oneself in one of the station's outhouses around the back. Inside the car, the single toilet in its stifling enclosure stayed generally occupied.

This late in the year, night fell with surprising suddenness. Lamplights of isolated farmhouses pierced the pitch dark, pictures of lonely emptiness. No stars, no moon broke the blank expanse of the night sky.

The third-class passengers slept sitting up in their seats. Always uncomfortable, Angelina napped, woke up, napped again. Another day passed. Conversation was slight; most of those in her car were foreign workers hailing from different lands. At the midday stop, she bought bread, cheese, and a hard-boiled egg that she wrapped in one of her extra handkerchiefs. She snacked as the interminable journey continued, barely holding her hunger at bay. The aged porter kept two pots of coffee hot on the stove. They passed through more towns as they turned north at Escanada. Again, darkness fell early, shortly after 4:30. Again the gaslights were dimmed, and extra wool blankets distributed. Angelina ate the last of her meager provisions and slept fitfully.

* * *

10 November 1912: Terrouge, Michigan

The Terrouge station was brick-clad with a sharply slanted roof. Its outdoor clock read 11:30 pm when the train's wheels finally squealed to a stop. A station agent inside watched the arrival through a window and pulled on his parka and gloves to go unload the luggage, but he was not eager about it. The station thermometer read nineteen degrees. The locomotive chugged in place, releasing steam, its long journey that night by no means complete.

A sharp wind whipped at the passengers as they debarked. Not everyone got off, some were going to mining camps farther west. A few wagons and an automobile stood waiting nearby.

After the overheated railcar, the cold was shattering. Angelina's breath was a cloud as she quickly blew on her bare hands. She gathered her suitcase from the growing stack of luggage on the platform. Electric streetlights illuminated the nearby streets, where two hotels were within view of the station. Fluttering red awnings adorned the nearest, brightly lit with ornate lanterns. The nightshift doorman in a double-breasted coat and a fur cap with earflaps stood waiting to assist. The hotel further down the avenue was clapboard-sided, two stories, no doorman. She chose it. Several other passengers made the same decision and followed along.

The name on the sign read, 'Terrouge House'. When she walked into the lobby, behind the desk was a young man with red hair and a face troubled with pimples. He pulled himself out of his bored lean. The clerk looked her over, saw more dark-haired others arriving behind her. He said, "You a dago? A wop?" Impatient with her incomprehension, he called out, "Simona!"

From around the corner of an adjacent hallway came a middle-aged woman in an apron and cap. "Have you come from *la patria*, signorina?" she asked in Tuscanized Italian. When Angelina nodded, she smiled. "I bid you welcome, signorina, welcome to Terrouge!"

Her first night at Terrouge House passed so quickly Angelina later hardly remembered it. A blur of trudging down a long hallway, sleeping like the dead, waking, washing.

When she went to leave her room, she found a note slipped under her door. Before the end of her shift, Simona had helpfully provided the name and address of a local woman who boarded single females. There was also a flyer with information printed in Italian, featuring a sketch of Garibaldi Hall, where the local Italian Assistance League was located. After a simple breakfast of hot oatmeal in the hotel café, Angelina checked out.

Widow Trengroat, who ran the boarding house, was of Cornish descent. Cornishmen had immigrated to Terrouge's rich copper mines in the mid-1800s. Like other descendants of "The Originals", the widow viewed the recent influx of Italians, Finns, Czechs, Poles, and the rest warily. But at the end of the day, they were customers. The small room she provided Angelina was clean, snug, and tidy, and for the young woman afforded a level of privacy she had never known in her life. When she showed Mrs. Trengroat the flyer, the landlady nodded her head. "Yes, yes, you 'eye-talians' have your own place." She took her to the doorstep and pointed. "On Pigeon Street. Go down there," she said loudly, then louder. "Straight down. Straight down!"

Seven years earlier, the first Italian mine workers founded their Mutual Assistance League. Pooling resources over time, they put a down payment on a rambling downtown building. As more Italians arrived throughout the township, the organization had evolved into a vibrant social center. There, the League's business took place on the second story. Along with the League membership's monthly dues, the ground floor paid the mortgage, rented out to a Scot named Wally Wallace whose Pigeon Street Tavern did an especially brisk business on League meeting nights.

Angelina found the building with little trouble. After climbing a steep flight of stairs to the second floor, she spoke to an old man playing an animated game of *scopa* with three of his cronies. *Si, si,* he told her. He had met a Lorenzo Como two months ago right here at the Hall.

"No talker, I remember that," rasped the card player in a Trentino dialect. Balding and thick-bellied, plump warts peppered Alfonso's wide forehead. "He asked about work. I told him that Phipps & Horton was always looking for trammers." Alfonso twisted in his chair, looked up at Angelina, raised his hands chest high, palms out. "I cannot say if he took my advice or not. I would be careful, signorina, between you and me. He was rough. Stank of drink. If you cannot find him at the mine, look to the saloons. They are all up and down Main Street. 'Whiskey John', 'Billy B's', 'Logan's', 'Great Lakes', all of those."

A fellow wizened and white-haired card player slapped his hand hard on the table, rattling the wine glasses. "*Managgia*, Alfonso! For God's sake, send this woman away. Are we here to play cards or gossip?"

Alfonso shrugged. "Eh, 'Stanza, how crude you are. Forgive this unmannerly old goat, signorina. He finds himself stirred by you standing so near, but for the life of him cannot recall why!" The four men burst into laughter at this enormous witticism. Angelina, having become invisible to them, descended the stairs. Now to this Phipps & Horton Mine, she thought.

Chapter 30

Sciara Sciatt stands derelict, street littered with papers, scraps of clothing, a child's sandal; a corpse lies stiff by a grinning dead dog, dead, but slowly turning its head...

Renzo sat bolt upright, shouting his terror. His fellow boarders, their roar of buzz-saw snoring interrupted, wearily pelted him with whatever they could seize next to their beds, laced with exasperated profanity.

A handbell violently clanged at the foot of the stairs. Time for the workday to begin.

Renzo and four other men boarded together at the house of another miner. The cramped attic space that served as their dormitory held several metal bunk beds with wall hooks for clothes. His day started sharp at 4:30 a.m. Like many others who took in boarders for extra income, the miner's wife did all the cooking, laundered the bedsheets, kept the place reasonably clean, and, like today, clanged them awake every morning.

Renzo gathered himself, splashed the night-sweat off his face with the cold water of the washbasin the men shared. He withstood the rough comments and surly looks of the others, and, as always, offered no apologies.

Once dressed and fed, the three Italians and two Finns took the lunch pails the housewife packed and trekked the half-mile to Main Street. There they caught one of the horse-drawn trolleys provided by Phipps & Horton Mining to haul its workers to the company's seven great copper shafts on the edge of town.

This day saw the true start of snowfall in the region; overnight, a crisp whiteness had covered the town's roofs and streets. Icicles trimmed the eaves of most buildings. It would be warm enough once in the deep mineshaft, Renzo knew, where temperatures hovered near sixty degrees, year-round.

Phipps & Horton was the biggest and oldest of the numerous mine operations in Michigan's copper-rich Upper Peninsula. The massive company boasted five thousand workers producing sixty thousand tons of copper a year. The core of its workforce was descended from the sturdy immigrants from Cornwall whose local copper mines had largely played out by the mid-1800s. The Cornishmen brought an intense professional pride to their work in their new homeland. The second and third generations took over jobs forged by their forebearers; Cornishmen now held the best positions and made the most money. Underground, they were usually the drillers. They worked in teams of three, a Cornwall tradition, most often members of the same family. They bore the holes for the dynamite that tore open thick veins of copper, then gouged the walls to follow the reddish gold-green of the metal wherever it led.

Despite new machinery and sources of power, the mines still needed many less skilled laborers to do work that required only brute force. A typical job was tramming, the hand-loading and hauling of individual ore cars. After the drillers drove directly into the veins with their pneumatic chisel-hammer drills, trammers stepped in with their shovels, their 'muck-sticks', to scoop the broken ore into tramcars. They pushed the iron cars by hand on tracks and dumped the mined ore into the skip. When the container was full, a cable extending from the shaft house hauled the load above ground, then dumped it into waiting rail cars alongside the building.

Tramming took no brains, only stamina and a strong back. The task was so simple that the mine did not even need these laborers to talk, in fact, preferred that they didn't. Trammers came from a mixed bag of immigrants who happily worked for a minimal wage. Italians were among those who flocked to the opportunity.

The Cornish disdained these opportunistic outsiders with no past affinity with the mining craft. So many were swarthy pope-lovers with their strange habits, talk, and unpronounceable names! Few of them spoke American or even seemed to want to. Their only saving grace, besides strong backs, was that they kept to themselves.

But the mine owners hired the foreigners without reservation. Smarter than typical beasts of burden, immigrants could be trained to reliably perform a series of repetitive tasks. And the bosses particularly appreciated their inability to voice intelligible complaints.

Along with all the other mines throughout the region, Phipps & Horton worked to maintain a stable labor force, one that stayed content enough to remain reliably loyal to the company over the long term. Not waiting for raw Terrouge Township to provide community services, Phipps & Horton provided its workers with company stores, a lending library, a police station, and even a clean and beautiful communal bathhouse. Most importantly, it provided sturdy houses for their miners and other skilled workers with families, who tended to be American citizens. Common laborers—the trammers, ore-sorters, timber haulers, sweepers, blacksmith boys and the like—they too received housing, if available, but there were no guarantees.

In exchange, the company expected its beneficiaries to do as they were told. Disorderly behavior, excessive drinking, chronic immorality—all led to dismissal. Management's goal was to create a perfect, self-perpetuating circle, a law-abiding community of workers joined at the hip to the best interests of the company, cradle to grave.

But to the company's enormous displeasure, organized labor had recently made inroads in Terrouge. Issues of one-man drills, sliding pay scales, ten-hour workdays, and child labor abuse drew large numbers of workers to meetings of the National Union of Mine Workers.

For months, the N.U.M.W. had been holding weekly meetings, using speakers of multiple languages to directly address the diverse workforce. There was talk of a list of worker demands, even of a potential walkout. In response, management recruited a small army of company-deputized, swaggering toughs from the streets of Detroit and Windsor. As the union's activity grew, these semi-official security men were making themselves increasingly visible around town. Some brandished ax-handles, twirling them like batons. Others had revolvers jammed in their belts. All wore white and red buttons on their lapels with the words, "Peace-Keeper."

Such doings meant nothing to Renzo. Between burying himself in work during the day, and concussing himself with alcohol at night, he had found a measure of grimly functional stability.

He squeezed his eyes tight against the rotgut headache hammering between his ears. Arriving at the great mine works, he joined a line of workers at Shaft Five starting their shifts. He spoke to no one, finding his ignorance of the language a blessing. He had been at the mine for two months without making the acquaintance of anyone.

The line of men advanced to the doorway of the shaft where the thirty-seat mancar waited. The open metal box held ten slanted benches and angled steeply downward on an iron track. A thick cable lowered the vehicle into the depths of the mine, nearly a vertical mile. Renzo sat alongside two others on one of the narrow benches.

He kept his hands in his lap and stayed very still during his ride as did his fellow workers. As they slid down the track, the rock walls were incredibly close to the railings on the car's sides. It took only a small movement to strike the wall with a knee, foot, or elbow. The car had no emergency stop. At least twice a year someone had his foot ground to a stump after catching it in the gap between the sliding car and the tight, craggy walls.

The deeper the mancar descended within its snug shaft, the crisper became the metallic tang of the rich copper ore infusing the earth. The mancar jolted as it made numerous stops at the various levels, each marked by a wooden sign. Renzo finally saw his twenty-seventh level coming up next. He pulled his felt cap on tighter and when the rig stopped next to the platform, he smoothly got off. He stopped to light the carbide lamp attached to the front of his cap, then followed the guttering lanterns mounted on the tunnel walls until he arrived at his stope, his workstation.

Renzo's stope was essentially a cave, a side tunnel extending three-quarters of a mile into the heart of the earth. Drillers had chased the vein to a wide deposit that now lay exposed. Digging out the ore had been underway for the past two weeks, aided by small, controlled dynamite blasts that ripped the stubborn copper loose of the earth's grip. As he entered the tunnel today, Renzo heard the drillers already creating a pile of ore. Removing and loading the pile was the job of the trammers.

The mine did not use electricity. While the copper it produced was in heavy demand by new power companies stringing electric lines throughout the country, Phipps & Horton found the technology too expensive to employ in its own operations. Consequently, steam powered the mancar and skip, carbide or paraffin candles fueled the underground lighting, compressed air ran the drills, and raw human sinew drove the rest.

For the past month, Renzo had been half of a two-man trammer team, himself and Gratia, a stumpy, brawny Sicilian, brand new to Terrouge. The southerner had tried to strike up a conversation their first day together, animatedly telling of his wife joining him from Messina with their young child. Renzo ignored these guttural pleasantries in complete silence. It took no time for Gratia to realize the slight. He wanted to unleash a profanity and rude gesture at the northern jackass but had seen the suffering the man carried in his face. "*Meschineddu*," he muttered, then returned to his work. He and the pathetic one had labored in silence ever since, unsmiling nods and brusque motions serving as their only communication.

Renzo took up a wide, flat shovel and began mucking loose ore into the tram. The raw rock's reddish gold, tinged with strands of green, caught the light of his cap-lamp.

Today, Gratia arrived a few moments after Renzo. He picked up his shovel from where he had left it leaning against a wall, approached the same pile of ore as Renzo. Without greeting each other beyond brief eye contact and curt nods, both men bent to their tasks.

When the ore tram was full, the men unlocked its rear brakes, dug their boots into the gravel of the narrow gauge track, and heaved. The cast-iron wheels squealed in protest and started rolling. The gradual decline of the track added gravity's assistance to their progress.

Flickering wall lamps on hooks periodically broke the tunnel's darkness. Neither man wore gloves, their heavily calloused hands were well beyond superficial damage. Both breathed hard, their overdeveloped shoulder and calf muscles strained at the weight of the steel car. They fell into matching steps.

At the end of the track, the tram jolted onto a wooden cradle parallel to an open shaft. At its bottom, twenty feet down, an empty skip container awaited filling.

Matthews, their stope captain, stepped up to check the two men's first ore delivery of the shift. The mines paid trammers by the rock tonnage they unloaded during their ten-hour shift. Renzo was averaging over $2.00 per shift, had once even hit $3.10. The company didn't use scales to weigh the trams, just the estimating eye of its captains. Matthews surveyed the trams' contents, looked at the two men, wrote figures into a black book. "Check," he said.

Using a pair of mechanical levers, Renzo and Gratia gave the cradle a sustained heave. The car tipped sideways, its unlocked side swinging open at the motion. With a noisy *whoosh!* the ore battered its way down the shaft and into the square metal skip below.

They trundled the empty car back along the same tracks, the return trip now slightly uphill. The mound of broken ore at the stope was bigger by the time they returned. The two men locked the tram's brakes in place, picked up their muck-sticks, and after each took a swig of water from a flask, resumed shoveling.

As the unchanging routine continued, Renzo fixed himself into his usual dull trance. The sledgehammering of ore chunks into a manageable size, the loading, hauling, and unloading of the tram was mindless hard labor, fit for a prisoner. Perfect, he thought. In the work's numbing monotony Renzo found a modicum of peace, his mental stupefaction punctured only by intermittent flashes of his familiar, crashing hangover.

His goal since leaving Tripoli had been oblivious anonymity, to escape all reminders of whom he once thought he was. He often remembered something his Zio Ettore had once told him, that in every person's life there are moments of truth that reveal a man's essence with stark clarity. A lesson taught to him, Ettore had said, by a mentor, long dead. When he first heard his uncle, Renzo nodded, as if he understood. After Tripoli, he actually did.

His personal moment of truth had proved him a failure: as brother-protector, as a son to his parents, as a good man, one of honor. He had proven himself the opposite: an impotent guardian and a murderer of the innocent. Images of carnage, of ragged, slaughtered civilians and the corpses of soldiers terribly butchered, and, always, Gianni—these were his nocturnal companions. He was a fugitive hunted by demons: burying his guilt underground by day, drowning it every night. And always, in sleep, his terrible sins awaited.

Renzo suddenly found himself with his face in his hands, quickly turned it into the act of wiping away sweat. If Gratia noticed, he showed no sign. The day pressed inexorably on.

As the end of the shift finally approached, they spent the last half-hour mounding up drilled ore to have a starting supply the following day. They could hear a loaded ore skip ascending as its screeching steel cable wound onto the giant reel far above.

The distant blast of level twenty-seven's quitting horn sounded. Gratia said, "*Grazie Dio.*"

Renzo answered, "Eh," with the barest glance. The two men hiked silently behind the drillers to the mancar platform to await their hoist to the surface.

After exchanging his grimy jacket and coveralls for a clean set to wear home and back to work the next day, Renzo emerged from the shaft's dry house into the late afternoon. A stiff wind sheeted fat snow into his face. He brought out the flask from under his overcoat pocket, pulled up his collar, and with a quick check for supervisors, took his first burning whiskey pull of the day. Tucking his bottle back inside his coat, tin lunch bucket under his arm, he joined the herd of workers beginning to exit the gates. The sky whipped wet white flakes against his head and coat.

* * *

Angelina stood near the gates and watched the change of shifts through the wood-slatted fence. She huddled with a few other women waiting for their husbands. For fifty cents she had bought a heavy wool shawl left by some traveler at the hotel where she'd found work as a scullery maid. The wool was coarse against her face but warm against the appalling cold. So bitter were these northern winters that many of the women from Mediterranean climes had descended into hopeless depression. Angelina hated the cold as much as the others. But she would not let it defeat her purpose.

She had trekked to the Phipps & Horton Mining works for five days in a row now, waiting outside the gate of a different mining shaft each time. Today was Shaft Five, and if she did not spot him here, she would be at number six shaft tomorrow.

She heard the mighty whistle blast and saw bundled workmen bobbing from the mine buildings en masse. The cold didn't make recognizing faces any easier, many of them obscured by bearded chins tucked into coat-tops or mouths wrapped with scarves, heads covered by a variety of workmen caps.

But not all. Amid the pack, she spotted one hatless, scarf-less, familiar-shaped face, thick with dark stubble. But the man was much older than Renzo in posture and demeanor, with gray streaks in his hair. But, no, it was undeniably him, the one she had come to marry. She swallowed her reaction. Whatever it was that changed him this way, she would mend. As he passed a mere twenty feet away, she cried, "Renzo!"

Walking heavily within the mob, he raised his head. *Renzo?* What woman here even knows my name, he wondered. That whore at Logan's Saloon? He turned to the sound and saw, who? Angelina?

Of course, not really her, could not be, she was a world and a lifetime away. It was just another somber-shawled woman braving the cold, calling her husband. But when Angelina's eyes met his, an electric jolt shot from the base of his skull to his feet. His enormous guilt sprang anew.

She fought her way past other men to warmly embrace the end of her journey. Renzo stepped to her instead, grabbed her shoulders with locked arms to stay apart. "Angelina," he said. "Why are you here?"

Her shocked impulse was to gouge out his eyes with her fingernails at such words. Instead, she cried, "Renzo! That is no greeting!" They flowed along with the thinning crowd. "I am here because we are meant to be man and wife! You told me that once, and I will meet you here every day until you say it again. And each day after you do."

Renzo wanted to hurt her with words to drive her away. But he was too exhausted to muster deliberate cruelty. Exhausted from the day's work, exhausted far more by the burden he carried with him every hour and day and month since Sciara Sciatt.

"We will take the trolley back to town," he told her.

They slushed through the sloppy snow without speaking until they reached the trolley stop. A group of the mine owners' black-cloaked security men wearing Peace-Keeper badges warmed their hands over an open fire in a large metal drum. They talked and laughed loudly, eyes roving over the line, living up to their role of being menacingly obvious.

Renzo paid the conductor two nickels. He squeezed his way down the middle aisle. Angelina followed. The trolley was already full of Finns, Slavs, other Italians. There were no empty seats, so they stood crowded among the others. Angelina pressed close to Renzo in the cramped compartment. As it jerked and jolted along the tracks, pausing for cross traffic or making stops, the two of them bounced against each other. He felt her warmth, the random physical contact waking his blood.

"I have enough money for you to go back," he said. He felt her sudden tenseness, saw her face and eyes set hard. He began again before she could speak. "Go back, Angelina. Marry another. The war has ruined me. I cannot change what has happened or who I have become."

The roar of noise on the trolley increased in volume. So did Angelina's response, close to his ear.

"Stop your self-pity, Renzo, you always mocked it in others. You talk of ruin? Think of me instead of yourself for once. It has been bad enough waiting, Renzo, no word from you, disappearing as you did. Do you hate me so much, that you would now have me return alone to Castrubello, the pathetic spinster who made herself a fool, desperately chasing after her man? And who is it exactly I am to marry, if not you? No one will have me after this. Will I marry someone in America? Who knows me here? I am only in this terrible place because of you!"

The car jolted again as it made a midpoint stop, others came aboard, there was no space between them. They were face to face, she at the base of his chin looking up.

He leaned away as much as he could. "Go back, Angelina," he said. "I get off here." With that, he forced himself through the other passengers and off the tram. Angelina watched him trudge to the sidewalk and a saloon on the corner.

The bar was hot and loud under a haze of tobacco smoke. Renzo ordered a bottle and a glass, found a table for himself, belted a shot. As he started to pour another, Angelina sat down across from him. "*Dio mio*, Angelina," he said.

She looked him in the eye. "In Castrubello you told me of your love, you promised we would marry."

Renzo squeezed his face tightly shut, opened it. She was still there. Her words bit.

"What you see is all I am, Angelina. I drink every day. I do not know if I can stop, or if I want to. My nights are terrors." He drew a long breath. "In Tripoli, I..." he stopped.

"Tell me, Renzo, tell me. In Tripoli, what? What is it that drove you away? I do not judge you, Renzo. Nothing you say can change my heart."

She waited. Renzo finished his second shot, swallowed another. He heaved a great sigh. "I hope that is true," he said.

He began his disjointed account at the ending. His medical discharge. Two months in the field hospital where he had arrived in a feverish delirium. He rolled up his sleeve to show the terrible scars of the infected burn on his arm and the slash by the sword. He described Gianni's burial in an unmarked mass grave, the vacant-eyed priest mumbling prayers about burnt bones. The terrible day after Maqba when General Caneva ordered Italian troops to attack those civilians who had betrayed them. But which ones were they? They all looked alike; all became targets. Streams of captured men, women, and children yoked together. Gianni's canteen, the screaming woman and child; a rooftop execution where he emptied his magazine into a line of helpless prisoners—including the Ottoman major who at the last moment fell to his knees and bowed his forehead to the ground. The roaming, officer-less squads looking to avenge their mutilated comrades. The long night. The day before.

Three heads, in a row.

Angelina reached across to touch Renzo's perspiring head, his face in his hands on the tabletop.

He leaned back away, roughly wiping his eyes with both palms, smearing wet grime. "Ah, *merda*! Now you see me as I am, Angelina, this weakling, this whimperer. No man acts in this way."

Angelina spoke. "I grieve for Gianni, I do. I grieve for your terrible wound. You have guilt for your brother's death, for those terrible things you did. Every man is guilty in war, Renzo, even I, a woman, know this. But Gianni was no child. Honor him for his brave sacrifice. You did what you could, for him you risked your life. And in the end, you found him, saw him blessed and buried. You must make amends for your sins, Renzo, but you still being alive is not one of them!"

She put her hands on each side of his face, made him see her. "Renzo, do not doubt this. I have come all this way to take you as you are."

Chapter 31

19 November 1912: Terrouge, Michigan

They were married by the Terrouge County Justice of the Peace who prompted them when to say 'Yes' to the vows he read them in English. Their uncomprehending witnesses were two Finns waiting to go next. A wedding at the town's one Catholic parish of Santa Giuliana Falconieri must wait until the spring. With winter on the way, they needed to find a place to live together. In Terrouge, that took a marriage license.

Angelina spoke to her employers at the Terrouge House. A small extension attached to the larger building included an apartment; she had seen it as she went about her work. Used only briefly as a domicile, it had refilled with dismantled lighting fixtures, extra chairs, stacks of mattresses and the like. The hotel agreed to rent it to the newlyweds at twenty dollars a month. Sorted out, thoroughly scrubbed, its old stove put back into working condition, with a borrowed table and a few chairs as furnishings, the two-room unit sufficed.

"Will we stay in Terrouge?" Angelina asked Renzo a few nights after they had settled in. He sat finishing his gin.

"Some of the miners want a walkout soon. A workers' vote is scheduled for early January."

Angelina scraped off his dish into the garbage pail. "What will that mean for us?"

"It means do nothing all day until the owners say yes to what the union demands. But they won't. Do you think they hired those guards for decoration? They are for when the owners bring in outside workers at lower wages. The union says it will pay strikers for going off the job. But the miners are richer than the organizers. They will sit tight, wait it out, stretch the matter until union money is gone." He finished his gin, broke his resolve it was his last, poured another, somewhat less full. "They assume when the strikers start starving, we will take whatever crumbs the owners offer."

Angelina deliberately clattered his dried plate into the cupboard. How stupid men are, she thought. "So, will you join the strike when it happens?"

255

"Anyone who doesn't is in for a tough time. While others are striking, those who cross their picket lines will suffer. The mines may pay in dollars, but the strikers will pay them in bruises and split lips."

His wife whirled to face him. "So, I have come all this way, to this so-called promised land, to watch fools starve and fight?"

He shrugged. "Not me. No violence from me. But for now, I stay with the union. If it wins, I will work to advance myself in the mine. If the union fails, we go."

"Go where, Renzo?"

"Not back. We find something else here. There are clay mines in a city called San Louis in the west. Castrubellese neighborhoods are there."

Angelina had seen several small changes in Renzo in the two weeks of their marriage. Drinking still, but less. At least he was no longer dosing her minestrone with grappa like at first. Nightmares still, but her presence seemed to calm him. Their lovemaking was basic. She had seen rams mounted on ewes hump the same mindless way. *Non importa.* It would be enough to get her pregnant soon, another means to bind Renzo to her.

But mostly the change in Renzo was along the lines of what she just heard, an awareness of what might lie beyond today. That was what gave Angelina her greatest hope. She knew nothing about this San Louis that Renzo spoke of. She favored Detroit and her husband's family there. She knew that his shame kept him from facing his uncle and aunt, but she would wait to make her case. Wherever they went, it would be away from this wasteland! She found herself hoping the strike would fail.

"Since we speak of the miners' union," Angelina said, changing subjects, "my friend Simona at the hotel is married to a sweeper at one of the mine shafts. She said the union has rented Garibaldi Hall for a holiday party on Christmas Eve. It is to be for everyone, for all the miners' families."

"What of it?"

"If there is to be a strike, she says, it will be the last celebration before everyone must tighten their belts. Simona and some of the women are decorating the hall and will assist with gifts and food that afternoon. She asked me to help, and I told her I would."

Renzo felt her waiting for his response. This marriage, he thought, was that of two strangers, she living with a shadow, and he, with what? Some *strega* who crossed half the earth to interrupt his exile? And alone! What normal woman did that? Arriving from thin air, forcing him to push aside his terrors, insisting always on the here and now? Yet if his resentment was so great, why did the thought of her make his long days less despairing?

"I see you want to go." Renzo paused, surprised how her growing smile warmed him. "So, we will go! Our first Christmas Eve in this Promised Land!"

* * *

The red bricks of Garibaldi Hall had come from the Welsh-style kiln in nearby New Truro. Large square windows marked the tavern on street level, its street-corner doorway was set at an angle. On the opposite end of the building, an imposing granite archway framed large double doors. This marked the entrance to the Assistance League ballroom and facilities on the second floor. Italians in the area were still largely inarticulate in the speech of their new land, but the building and its entrance spoke loud and clear: Our destiny has brought us here to stay.

Besides hosting Italian League functions, Garibaldi Hall also was available for wedding receptions and celebrations of every type. Of them all, the Christmas festivities always brought a crowd. While Anglo-Americans primly avoided alien events, the Christmas party was the calendar's social highlight for families of Italian and the other ethnicities.

This year promised to be one of the best attended. With the miner's union footing the bill, the only cost of admission was attending one union meeting in the previous six months. By mid-December, the ticket count was high, though no one had thought to keep a written record. But the hall had accommodated large events before; it would certainly suffice.

Angelina and Simona worked with two other women from the League making decorations for the coming party. They met on two Sunday afternoons in one of the women's homes. Angelina was no seamstress, but she knew her way around a pair of scissors well enough to cut cloth for the red, white, and green bunting for dressing the hall's windows. Decorations would also adorn three freshly chopped fir trees, and for those, she helped cut stars from sheets of foil. There were bows made of ribbon, preserved bird nests with handmade crepe starlings, even a few glass ornaments from the fantastical Sears Catalog.

On stage would be one of the trees, flanked by a large chair. Upon it, generous Santa Claus, in a nod to this new culture they found themselves in and played by none other than old, card-playing Alfonso, would hand out small gifts to the children.

Having a role in such planning was new to Angelina. For the first time since she left Castrubello, other than finding Renzo, she felt joyful anticipation.

* * *

Renzo tried to ignore all talk of union and strikes but could not escape it. On the mancar, at their stopes, in the dry room at shift's end, the workers spoke of little else.

Most of the drillers were dead set against striking, but not all. On a recent morning, as they rode the car down, while Renzo could only follow part of what he heard, it was clear the drillers were of two minds.

"Why should we give up our work at all? So that the eye-ties and pollacks get more pay? One union for all makes no sense. We need to settle with the owners ourselves; let the monkeys have their strike."

"That is what I say, Mike. We cut a separate deal, no union. We've done it before."

A man named James Roland spoke up. "Ah, you two forget the owners want to go to the one-man drill. No more teams of three like we've always had and our fathers before us. That means a two-thirds layoff."

"Let them go to the one-man, Jim," Mike responded. "The owners are smart. They will just open more levels and then we all get a drill. The ones who don't will take over the tramming, force the outsiders to move on."

Roland answered, "Supply and demand, Mikey, supply and demand. The mines produce what the market can bear. More men with more drills mean a glut of ore. Prices go down and there are layoffs, pure and simple. And think about this. We know that drilling in three-man crews is dangerous enough! What happens when you're drilling alone, and you get into trouble? Sixty miners have died this year here in the north."

The three debaters left the mancar at level twenty-one, to Renzo's relief.

Such debates were not common at all among the Italian trammers and others less skilled, and not only because of language differences. This group was solid in its desire for something better. Solid and silent, that was Renzo's approach. Still, he sought out Pinello, a lead carpenter who built tunnel supports. He was openly pro-union with a back pocket full of Christmas party tickets.

Pinello told Renzo, "I heard your wife is helping," pulling out two yellow tickets and handing them over. "At least one of you is committed to the Movement."

"My wife is committed to not being homesick on Christmas Eve, Pinello. But *grazie* for these, we will honor the holiday."

"And support the strike in the spring?"

"I will support my best interests. Right now, that means I wait and see."

The mine owners continued to build their security forces. Presently a deterrent, perhaps later head-breakers, the Peace-Keeper brigade grew daily. The owners had men meet the new outside recruits with welcome signs at every train's arrival. Phipps & Horton procured an abandoned National Guard barracks for their accommodations.

The company's thugs appeared out in force now, loose squads of a half-dozen or more. All carried weapons. They stalked the streets of Terrouge, loud and wolfish. A few nights before Renzo procured his tickets, residents had discovered a trammer from Abruzzo laid out in an alley, his skull cracked and bleeding. The rumor was he ran afoul of a Peace-Keeper during a saloon poker game.

The police stayed out of such matters. The mine owners controlled the city council, comprised in part by the grandsons of earlier miners. In turn, the city council hired the police, who understood their employers' expectations.

After work the Friday before the Christmas Gala, Renzo headed for the Pigeon Street Tavern. It was not his usual haunt, but Angelina told him that morning she would be at Garibaldi Hall decorating after her shift. He intended to surprise her, even lend a hand. Provided he refreshed himself first.

The sidewalks were alive with pedestrians, the street with several motorcars but mostly horse-drawn traffic. Electric lights, new to the district, courtesy of Phipps & Horton Mining, glowed softly over the snowbanks along the roadway. The temperature was near zero.

At the door of the saloon, Renzo passed a man in a red cloak and tasseled stocking cap standing next to a tripod bearing a metal pot marked *La lega di assistenza italiana*. He clanged a handbell, offering a hearty *Buon Natale!* to passersby. Renzo ignored him, entered the tobacco-smoke cloud within the tavern. He shouldered his way to the long bar where two bartenders wearing green sleeve garters stayed busy filling glasses. A player-piano pounded a loud ditty into the din. Renzo ordered a whiskey straight up and threw it back with a gulp. "Another," he said. "A double."

Glass in hand, he took a free pickle from the jar at his elbow, turned his back to the counter, and surveyed the lively, loud room. The Pigeon had an eclectic mix of regulars. Most were Italians, arguing and laughing. But there were Finns at one table, Czechs at another. A cluster of Germans toasted something with gusto as they drank at the far end of the bar. The place was a babble of tongues. All were unskilled laborers, unified for the moment by wanting to boisterously socialize before going home to their roles as fathers and husbands.

He sipped at his double, crunching off sharp bites of the large, briny pickle. The comfortable warmth of the whiskey soothed him, his mind unclenching just enough for a moment of peace, despite the jovial uproar.

Not everyone was festive, however. On Renzo's left, two men had their heads down, talking low into their drinks. They wore workmen caps and mining overalls under overcoats. Renzo knew one of them, had seen him before on the mancar. One of the ore-sorters from Abruzzi, he thought. Just then the man nudged his partner. They both twisted off their stools and abruptly left.

Renzo finished his drink, paid what he owed, went to the tavern door. He walked down the sidewalk through the icy night to the opposite end of the building, then through the archway to the staircase. He trudged up the steep wooden steps that led to the hall doorway.

"Renzo!" Angelina called as he entered, in her coat.

"I came to help. But you look like you're done."

Angelina hid her surprise. She put both hands on the sleeve of his unscarred arm. She smelled the heavy whiskey breath. His eyes were red-rimmed. Her elation at seeing him subsided. "Thank you, Renzo. Come, we walk home. There is leftover trout from the hotel kitchen for dinner tonight. That and fresh bread." The cold night ought to sober him up, she thought.

"A good plan," Renzo responded. "I could eat fish." With the whiskey, and now Angelina's arm in his, he felt rare, tentative contentment.

He held the stair rail with one hand as they descended. Exiting the door, they quickly took a step back as two policemen ran past toward a commotion down the street. Renzo saw blue uniforms swinging nightsticks at a dozen men pummeling each other with fists and bats.

Several officers broke off from the melee to face the gathering bystanders. "Get out of here, you nosy pricks!" shouted one with gold bars on his overcoat shoulders. "Beat it, or I will run all of you in for inciting civil disorder!" He whacked the end of his billy club on the wooden plank walkway, making the nearest pedestrians jump back. Most of those watching knew enough English to understand his threat, and everyone had seen what an enthused clubbing could do. The crowd instantly retreated out of range of his swing, then resumed watching from a safer distance.

Renzo gathered Angelina to him under his arm, still in the doorway. The drinking crowd inside the tavern peered out of the windows, some emerging onto the sidewalk for a better view. Far enough away to avoid the law's annoyed wrath, they fortified themselves against the elements with gulps from their tankards and bottles and glasses, dourly offering running commentary.

Angelina spoke into Renzo's ear, "L'America." Renzo grunted. "Eh. Stupidity has no nationality."

"Those are ore men, certainly," Renzo heard the red-capped bell ringer declare. "They jumped two of the mine security men, probably revenge for their man, the one that the bastards waylaid the other night. My cousin's friend works with some of those Abruzzi ore sorters, knows a bit of their dialect. He says they've been talking of a reprisal all day."

"Not much of a reprisal, from what I see," said a Piedmontese workman standing close by. "Look at them. The police are not stopping it, they are reinforcing the Peace-Keepers the Italians attacked. They were stupid to be so open about it, and now they take it up the ass. Excuse my rude expression, signorina, I beg you," he added gallantly, suddenly aware of Angelina's presence.

Renzo declared, "It is nothing to us. Time to eat." He guided Angelina in the direction of their apartment, five blocks away, against the flow of more pedestrians drawn to the violence. A gas-powered police paddy wagon rumbled by, its blue-uniformed driver, face close to the windshield, leaning angrily on the horn.

Chapter 32

24 December 1912: Garibaldi Hall

The children began arriving as soon as the doors opened at 1:30 p.m. They came in packs with mothers and neighbors and sometimes with fathers lucky enough to be off shift. Pine wreaths tied with large red bows festooned every wall; green, white, and red bunting framed the long front windows. Tall Christmas trees, glittering with ornaments, popcorn strings, and festive bows of ribbon, lent their green woodsy smell to the room. Onstage, Big Noreen, a former Duluth dancehall girl turned union entertainer, crashed the keys of a battered upright piano in a jaunty rendition of *Angels We Have Heard on High*.

Every ethnicity of the unskilled mine workforce seemed present, blending their own languages with rough pidgin English. The adults who walked through the door shared a common resolve. If this was to be the last holiday before the privations that a strike would bring, then they would make certain it was one to remember for their young daughters and sons.

The crèche on the floor by the stage was a center of attention. Several children lay small gifts near the scene, drawings and cards they had worked on at school. There were lumpy clay sheep and a four-legged figurine that could be a cow or a camel or both. The straw manger was naturally empty, the arrival of the Christ child not due until the next day. But Mary and Joseph, three kings, assorted angels on foot, and shepherds stood solemnly frozen awaiting the great miracle.

From the back of the stage, Angelina saw the hall was rapidly filling. People kept arriving at the top of the stairs where ticket-takers passed them rapidly through. Those already seated, shouted and waved hands to greet newcomers. Laughter and talk resounded, chair legs scraped as people forced themselves and their broods through the aisles. At the back of the hall men in the crowd pulled out extra chairs to form more rows until they were gone. By half past two the room was full, with more families still arriving.

Big Noreen's upright piano blasted a fanfare, and to the delight of the audience, Saint Nicolas appeared from off-stage in his full regalia. He carried a large sack on his back bulging with promise. Alfonso looked out to the audience, patted his padded belly, stroked his pasted white beard. By way of a welcome, he leaned back on his heels and emitted a startling, high-pitched, *"Buon Natale a tutti!"* With that, he proceeded to the highbacked chair to his right, plunked himself down along with his sack, and offered a wide, yellow-toothed smile.

The amazed children squealed and applauded, turning to their parents who assured them that it was indeed who they thought.

A woman was accompanying Big Noreen. She knew a range of languages. Without further ado, she took center stage and spoke in English followed by translations.

"We will begin this afternoon by singing together hymns and carols of the season. They will be songs from all our countries. If you do not know the words, hum, whistle, or clap along. Or listen, and think of our Savior, the Christ child!"

Noreen raised her hands high dramatically then brought them down softly on the keyboard.

* * *

Pigeon Street Tavern was a busy place. Renzo looked through the windows as he walked by, saw the crowd three-deep at the bar, paused. No, getting a drink would take too long. The program upstairs was starting, he could hear singing even from outside. He took a last slug from his flask, draining it, and tightened its cap back on with a hard twist. Maybe he could slip out once things got going.

He went down to the archway entrance and joined the stream still heading up a full half-hour after festivities had started.

At the top of the stairs, Renzo moved past the doorway but did not get far. Only standing room remained in the packed hall. Swearing softly, he pressed himself along the wall with other latecomers. Some were men whose people were back somewhere in inaccessible seats, but most were families. Fathers held their small children on their shoulders or necks to let them see. With easily six hundred bodies wedged into every nook and cranny, the room was uncomfortably hot and noisy.

Renzo saw Angelina up on stage, over by a fat, bearded man in a chair. Probably that *santa* somebody she had told him about, the American elf. I thought elves were supposed to be small, Renzo mused, just look at this one! Give me *La Befana* any day. He raised a hand at Angelina to catch her attention; after all, she was the reason he was in here packed in like an anchovy and not at the Pigeon. But his wife was helping with a bag next to the Santa and did not look up. On stage, a piano was playing as a woman led the room in a Polish rendition of *Good King Wenceslaus*. Renzo folded his arms. Once Angelina sees me, I can leave for a while, he thought, thirsty.

Across the street from the Hall, two men leaned against a corner pharmacy, closed for the day. They looked at the activity around the arched entryway.

"Christ, how many of those wops and hunkies and Finnish fucks can they pack in that place? There must be a thousand up there," said one, pulling on a bottle.

"Think what it's like in there with them, hot, all that sweat. Try to move around, you would be slipping in grease," sniggered the other. He accepted the proffered bottle. Like his partner, he wore a long, black coat but also a woolen stocking cap. They both had round white-and-red buttons pinned on their lapels. "I call it, 'guinea-slick'. That's how they manage to squeeze past each other in that mob."

They both guffawed at that one. "What apes. Going on strike, but happy as jaybirds. Ready to knock one of us down on a Friday, no worries in the world by Tuesday," said the first. "How many times do the lamebrains need schooling?"

Stocking Cap did not answer right away. It was years since he'd helped lynch those five dagoes in Tallulah, down south. He had seen and been part of much violence since, but nothing quite as exhilarating as on that night.

He watched the silhouettes bobbing at the arched windows of the second floor. Laughter and song drifted in the mid-afternoon air. Those arrogant shits. His bosses paid him to deliver messages to those people. Right now, one seemed in order.

"Here, Bill," he said, handing his partner the club he kept slung under his coat in a harness. He started in the direction of Garibaldi Hall.

"Where are you going?" Bill asked. "Do you need me to come too?

"Wait here, don't go anywhere. I'll be back in a minute," he answered. "These assholes like fun? Watch this."

* * *

The program had moved on to giving the children their gifts. The youngsters were filing up the short stairs to the platform with some trepidation. Parents accompanied most of them. When they spoke to the Santa in their various tongues, he nodded and ho-hoed. If they just stood there in terror, he patted their heads. As each one walked past to go back on the floor, Angelina took a plainly wrapped parcel—a small bag of candy or some trinket—out of the big sack and handed it to the child.

Renzo stood pressed against the wall. He regretted not having gone to the tavern earlier when he had the chance. Perhaps there was still time.

A man in a woolen stocking cap entered the doorway from the stairs. He pushed directly in front of Renzo. As he did, Renzo clearly saw the Peace-Keeper badge on his coat. The man pivoted right and left as if surveying the room, cupped his hands to his mouth, and bellowed at the top of his lungs, "FIRE! FIRE!"

When he cried it out again, the crowded room erupted. The man in the cap spun back to the doorway and forced his way down the staircase. "Fuoco! Fuoco!" someone started shouting. Others repeated the same cry in their own tongues. Then the tidal wave struck.

A roar of panic engulfed the hall. Voices rose in a hysterical repetition of "Fire! Fire!" The slat folding chairs tangled, collapsed, flipped over, as the aisles disintegrated. Everyone in the hall was on their feet, clamoring for the exits.

There were two. One was a narrow iron fire escape on the side of the hall near the stage. Getting to it meant traversing a vestibule through a closed doorway. Hardly anyone knew it was there; the few that did, and who were close, fought in its direction.

The other exit everyone knew. It was the front door they had all entered when they'd arrived. Instinctively, the great mass turned and crashed through the chairs, over the chairs, past each other, over each other, children in hand, carrying children, driven by the sheer animal terror of the looming, nonexistent, inferno.

Onstage, Angelina saw the holiday audience transform itself into a panicked beast. Alfonso pulled off his beard, headed down the stage steps, and helplessly disappeared into the crowd's momentum as if caught in an ocean's undercurrent.

"I see no fire, no smoke," she said to Big Noreen, who was on her feet screaming for calm. The woman stopped, stared at Angelina, sat back at the piano. She began playing *Silent Night*.

Angelina looked for Renzo. The crowd was frantically packing itself into the main stairway, hundreds desperately trying to simultaneously flee into a sloping tunnel barely six feet wide. Was that Renzo? The figure disappeared into the maelstrom.

All she knew was that the stage was the safest place to be for now. Some among the audience came to the same conclusion, and now the stage had dozens of people on it, more scrambling to join them. Others were lifting their children from their place on the floor to ready hands waiting to pull them up. The deafening tumult of panic-charged shouts, shrieks, screams, only grew louder.

At the first cry of fire, Renzo knew it was a hoax but had no way to grab the man who had called out. Instead, he instinctively stepped a few feet off the wall and immediately found himself caught in the swirl of the crowd rushing the stairs.

On the Pirino River, there was a short series of churning rapids. As boys, he and his brothers had sometimes dared each other to ride through them, a foolish game that could have ended badly. The technique was to head downstream feet-first, keeping one's toes high above the froth, arms working hard in a backstroke. Most times, Renzo finished it prematurely, angling to the bank before passing all the way through. He knew his brother Pietro was always determined to outdo him. By pulling up short, he allowed Pietro to succeed without thinking he had to take stupid chances. One time, however, Renzo determined he would ride out the full stretch. With the trickiest part behind him, he had taken his eyes off the river and looked to a spot near the grassy bank his father had once told him about. His feet struck a rock, whirling him around, and he became totally at the mercy of the unpredictable current until fighting his way ashore.

Only sheer luck had permitted him to survive. Now he felt the same helplessness, as the wave of stampeding humans caught him in its flow. The steep stairway sucked him down as if into a dark drain.

He found himself forced against one wall, the handrail biting into his thigh. Gravity and blind herd frenzy propelled him and everyone downward step by rapid step. Some tried to turn, to struggle against the tide, only to be swept along backward. Of course, someone had shut the big outside doors against the cold. The maddened pack was descending very quickly, too quickly.

Somebody at the bottom fell.

The entire body of people on the stairs took a mighty jolt forward as those ahead tripped over the one who lost balance, hitting the backs of others, driving them onto the steps face first, falling sideways, twisted, screaming. The ones behind them fell on top, those next in back also lost their balance, grabbing wildly at each other until the first dozen steps of hapless victims began stacking like cordwood, two deep, then four, then nearly to the top of the slanted staircase ceiling. Slamming against the closed doors below, burying the doorknobs beyond grasping, they created a barrier of human flesh and bone that the rest of the throng, over a hundred souls, could not burst past. Instead, every person on the staircase tilted into the pile at an angle relative to where they were on the steps, like a fallen squeeze-box arching with one end on the floor, the other still on the musician's lap. In a matter of minutes, all were locked flailing in place, those underneath buried immobile in wild despair.

Renzo, trapped leaning forward but still standing, barely could draw a breath. Many of those around him were children, some alone, some with parents. The little ones stood only half as tall as the adults or less, muffled screams marking their terror in the sightless, motionless dark that engulfed them.

From behind, the pressure of the hundreds still in the big hall kept bearing down. Unaware of the disaster on the steps, the terrified mob reflexively redoubled its effort to break the unknown impasse impeding escape. But their constant surging, pushing, prodding, heaving forward, only mortally condensed the space and the air of everyone in the stairwell.

Someone outside the building opened the double doors below. The fading daylight barely penetrated inside. The foundering mash of people in the staircase did not, could not, budge. Those at the bottom of the stairs lay crushed flat. Piled above them, strata by strata, were tangled, wriggling bodies that could not extricate themselves from the weight suffocating them. The more anyone moved, the more lethal the damage to heads, lungs, and limbs. Many had stopped moving at all. Determined firemen already on the scene tried but could not pull anyone out; inside, the compacted bodies were stacked higher than the doorway. The thwarted rescuers ran to gain entry upstairs from the mostly unused fire escape at the building's side.

Renzo lifted his face to breathe. He was far enough back to be still on his feet, though pressed downward at a steep angle. Pinned against the wall on one side and against his neighbors on every other, only the surrounding human mass kept him halfway upright. The wailing and screaming, the hopeless cries for help, the sound of bones snapping, the awareness of unstoppable, gasping suffocation made the staircase a horror. The electric wall sconces projected the hellish shadows of the doomed in a gesticulating pantomime against the low ceiling.

I am dying, Renzo thought. The sights and sounds of Sciara Sciatt flooded to mind: the cemetery, the objects with ragged hair unthinkably projecting from the dirt. The woman and child cringing, bleeding, dying, begging, trapped under his terrible wrath.

"Help me, help me with him," said the man directly in front. At first, it was just another desperate voice from the morass. But looking down Renzo saw, turning mindlessly from side to side, the face of his fellow trammer, Gratia.

The short man, packed against other writhing bodies, couldn't even tell who he was talking to. He was calling to any neighbor within earshot, he was calling to God, to Maria, to *fortuna*, to *mazzamuredda* from the world of spirits, all of them at once.

Renzo said from behind in two breathless gasps. "Help. Who?"

Gratia tried to turn to see, could not, spoke louder, gulping after every several words. "My son. My wife is at my feet, my son stands on her. My boy, he cannot breathe. Help me, help me free him from this pit, I beg you, man."

Renzo's arms were pressed to his sides. With a mighty effort, he pulled them free. To some extent, they had been protecting his ribs. Now he felt the full crush of tilted bodies jammed like a wedge against his spine, his ribs, felt a crack, then a second.

He reached over the shorter man who now pulled as hard as he could on the hands of his toddler. Renzo's hands grasped above Gratia's and together, inch by inch, they hoisted the child upward. It is a wonder the boy's arms do not pull out of his shoulders, Renzo thought. Little by little his small, dark-haired head emerged. His nose bled from the crush. Gratia raised his elbows as high as he could, fully extending the boy's arms.

Renzo felt his slanted weight driving Gratia further down, could not do anything to relieve the suffocating pressure, felt it himself from those behind him. Gratia let go, expelling a cry of air, knees buckling, wordlessly sagging down and away like a man being sucked into quicksand.

Renzo heaved at the boy, still trapped, tried to pull him free, could not do it, his arms tiring, feeling his own feet being lifted clear off the steps by the relentless squeeze of bodies, the little boy sinking like his father back into the abyss, toward his parents' corpses, but then, a sudden surge, somebody helping, Gratia's son rising again, as if from the earth, to Renzo's chest, then free of the turmoil to above his head, to where Renzo lifted him straight up, one hand grasping the boy's shirt, the other his legs, hoisting him aloft, to the meager air, an offering to *fortuna*, nearly touching the ceiling!

Around them, the staircase was growing more still, the struggle slowing, life reluctantly surrendering to its timeless enemy. Long low moans, like exhaled organ notes, gradually replaced sharp cries. Renzo was a statue, hardly able to breathe, still holding the boy who looked down upon him, moving his arms but remarkably calm, his nose dripping red onto Renzo's face. Renzo had no breath now, was clammy with sweat, the light dimming, air thick around him, enclosed tight by damp bodies. He shut his eyes and suddenly, shockingly opened them to the face of Gianni next to his, not the face at the cemetery but the Gianni he knew, smiling, his arms supporting his own, keeping them rigid, holding the boy free; Gianni, serious now, forehead to forehead, comforting now, loving, whispering, *"I knew you would save me, Brother."*

* * *

5 January 1913: Straits of Mackinac

The bow propeller of the ferry *Chief Wawatam* churned at the solid sheet of ice covering the channel. Crossing the straits in any January was a special challenge; this winter of 1912-13 was one of the severest on record.

Angelina Como stood watching the icebreaker force its way south from St. Ignace to Mackinac Harbor at the tip of Michigan's lower peninsula. The low winter sun slanted the dark shadow of the ferry and its billow of smoke over silvery ice and across a stone-white sky.

She wore a dress of black crepe and a veil, her false widowhood come true. After the fire brigade finally cleared the stairway at Garibaldi Hall, the full dimension of the tragedy staggered the community. Of the hundred and five trapped in the stairwell, seventy-three persons died, including fifty-nine children. Some families lost all of their little daughters and sons that brutal day.

Witnesses attested they had heard a man wearing a Peace-Keeper button cry, "Fire!", that he fled one step ahead of the crowd he had deliberately panicked into a lethal stampede. Others claimed that someone had locked the hall doors against those trying to escape. The authorities took adamant exception to every allegation. The court agreed.

Throughout that terrible night, a stream of wagons and other vehicles transported the scores of deceased to the Terrouge Theatre, the only place nearby with room enough to serve as a morgue. Identification was difficult, some of the victims were new to the community, hardly known, or not known at all. A newspaper photographer took a picture of the rows of dead children lying on slabs. Only their faces and bare legs and feet showed under the long white sheets that covered the rest. In the photograph, they looked like cherubs calmly sleeping, faces smooth and perfect, wisps of hair on foreheads, as if about to awaken and sing forth their joyous innocence.

The photograph appeared in newspapers above the caption, *Christmas Eve at the Morgue.*

Two days later came the funerals and burials. Local churches of all denominations coordinated their services to end at the same time, the congregations with their coffins leaving their doors and merging in a common procession extending two miles. A long, open grave-trench lay on each side of Cemetery Road, one side for Protestants, the other for Catholics. The white pine coffins, some full-size but most much smaller, were solemnly laid side by side. The identification of individual caskets proved difficult. Plain white crosses marked each grave.

Angelina had found Renzo's body in the morgue. In death, Angelina thought, he looked younger, tranquil. Her heart raged with grief, for him, for the struggle for happiness together she had been certain they would win.

One of the morticians said Renzo was a hero, he had saved their son's life. Dead himself, Renzo was found somehow still holding the one-year-old boy up to the air pocket near the ceiling. Not knowing who the youngster was, no one claiming him in the confusion, the firemen drew their own conclusion. They took the red horn pendant from the dead man's neck and put it on the boy's before sending him on to the hospital. The mortician wrote a note for Angelina to give to the nurse on station. "Your son is safe," he kindly told her, "and waiting for you."

From the enclosed upper deck, she heard the ice slabs cracking as the *Chief* sliced ahead, could just make out the distant line of Mackinaw City's low buildings and docks on the southern peninsula. Angelina bent to the carriage, lifted the little Sicilian boy up into her arms and smiled. "We are journeying home to our family, my little Lorenzo," she said. "To Detroit."

BOOK THREE
DEATH TO THE WOLF

As wave is driven by wave
and each, pursued, pursues the wave ahead,
so time flies on and follows, flies, and follows,
always, forever, and new.

—Ovid, Metamorphoses

Part I: The Don
1942

Chapter 33

13 May 1942: Castrubello

"Come, Papà," said Regina, hurrying through the doorway and into her adoptive father's dressing room. "Guests are arriving, you are the host!"

Ettore Vacci turned from the elaborately carved wooden-framed mirror where he had been struggling to properly attach his *Cavaliere dell'Ordine della Corona* medallion. The badge representing Ettore's knighthood was an impressive, white-enameled cross emblazoned with the Iron Crown of Lombardia. It currently hung askew from a short red and white ribbon on his left chest.

"The crown is crooked," Ettore fussed. "And I tell you, I will not wear that preposterous red sash. It makes me look like a doorman."

Regina Collina Vacci went to her father and with a few deft adjustments straightened the badge, adjusted his black bow tie, tweaked the winged collar at the top of his starched shirt, then held up the ceremonial sash presented to Ettore by the town in honor of his knighthood.

"We are celebrating your eightieth birthday, Papà. It is no day for informalities. The house is filling with guests come to pay their respects to one of Italia's great modern builders, and now a new Knight of the Crown! What a pleasure it will be for each to be seen with you! Do not deny them their moment to bask in your glory," she said playfully. "You must at least look the part, or they will leave with such dashed expectations!"

"What a game," Ettore sighed. He stood fidgeting while the young woman arrayed the sash from his right shoulder down to his waist on the left. She turned him around, stood next to him in front of the full-length mirror.

"*Ecco*," she said. "Here you are, just as you like it. Poised to be the unrivaled center of attention!" She smiled, eyes shining.

Ettore snorted derisively. "So, you must not have invited il Duce, eh?" He looked himself over, black tuxedo, white shirt, black tie. The badge, symbol of his knighthood. The damnable sash. His old-fashioned, bushy white mustache matched the color of the thin, unruly shock of hair on his head. He dabbed his rheumy eyes with his handkerchief, looked up again. At least they remain gray-blue, he thought. He noted the sag of skin at his neck, his sun-mottled face permanently darkened after his decades of work outdoors. The coat jacket hung loosely from his thin shoulders, its sleeves a trifle too long. His manicured nails looked strangely civilized on his large, rugged hands, nicked and scarred from so many early years of manual labor.

"That *pozzo nero*," he muttered. A memory of hand-shoveling a reeking cesspit with Muto crossed his mind. Had it really been a lifetime ago?

"What is that you say, Papà?" Regina asked from behind him. She smoothed the shoulders of his jacket with her hands. "How long have you had this tuxedo, Papà?"

"Forever," he answered absently. "I last wore it to Pietro Como's wedding, I think."

Regina sized up Ettore with a critical eye, gradually concluding he was presentable. "You look like a bridegroom yourself today, Papà."

She checked her long, yellow gown in the mirror, pulled the front up a bit. Her face was framed by dark curly hair tied in a ribbon. A fine-looking young woman of elegant bearing, thought Ettore. At twenty-four, a real catch for a fortunate someone. Much better-looking than Maurizio, her grandfather, Ettore thought. Even Pezzoli, vain as he was, would have had to admit it. How he still grieved for his old friend.

"Stay here for now, Papà," Regina said. "I will reconnoiter the room, see who has arrived, then come back to get you. For your grand entrance!"

As she exited, Regina inwardly beamed. How good was this day! She was happy she'd insisted on making an occasion of it. Anyone's eightieth birthday deserved special note. And Ettore's recent knighthood had preceded the date by only two months. Why not take this moment to celebrate? Her unassuming father deserved every accolade he received, a worthy man receiving his due. He would always be the most important, most admirable man in her life, more papà than zio to her. When she had once tried to tell him words to that effect, Ettore had thanked her but said, "Never forget your true parents."

Her natural father had been Andrea Collina, a former clerk of Ettore's who had run into difficulty while working at Naviglio Quarry. In Turin, he received a new start with Maurizio Pezzoli, Ettore's late brother-in-law and former partner. Collina eventually married Anna Pezzoli, Maurizio's daughter. Regina was their child, grandniece to Ettore and his wife Marietta. One terrible night in 1924, Regina's parents both died in an auto accident on a rainy country road.

With Maurizio's blessing, Ettore and Marietta, childless, adopted the six-year-old despite being in their sixties themselves. The young girl became Regina Vacci and had lived with them since. After her adoptive mother's death in 1939, she assumed managing the household and, as Ettore had aged, increasingly attended to his needs.

Not that the old gentleman needs excessive care, she admitted. Ettore Vacci had been a force to reckon with among Italia's major businessmen since the late nineteenth century. Throughout his seventies he had remained a formidable entrepreneur, though slowing these days. His company, Vacci Costruzioni d'Italia, VCI, had loomed large on the Italian industrial scene for decades. Though still in the business of roadbuilding, it now specialized in concrete projects of all types. Business was brisk.

The Kingdom of Italy's bloody role in the Great War from 1915 to 1918 had yielded human tragedy and infrastructure disaster for the nation. But the conflagration proved a boon for construction, and the company engaged in massive reconstruction projects. Later, when the Fascists took control, determined to transform Italy into an industrial power, VCI won contracts for work at grandiose projects like the vast *Esposizione Universale* and the great monument to the Bersaglieri at Porta Pia in Rome. Now, since the kingdom's entry into the war on the side of the Axis, defense contracts of all types had further multiplied.

Ettore sat in one of the stiff French Empire chairs that Marietta had chosen for the villa's living quarters. This party too shall pass, he sighed to himself. The light from a soupy gray sky filtered past heavy drapes, partially opened.

It will be good to see some of my old acquaintances, he thought, although it was usually their offspring he dealt with these days. And the place was sure to be full of political types from the government. His ambitious nephew Pietro would have seen to that. Ettore sighed. The truth was, he had no idea who he would be greeting down there. With any luck, he thought, even some of my fellow Castrubellese might get through the door.

Where had Regina gone to? He stood and looked again into the mirror. An old, wizened man stared hard back at him. How in God's name has this happened, he wondered? Wasn't it just yesterday I was a strapping crew chief laying down rails in Milan? He felt the same now as he did then, plenty of sap flowing, same brain, same eyes on the horizon. Much less strapping these days, that I must admit, he thought. And yet, I feel as if I am ready for another eighty years! He hacked a loud cough, noted his rueful expression in the glass. Ah, well. It is enough to concentrate on today.

Ettore understood that one key to a successful life was timing. He had seen stubborn friends try to control their companies long past their prime. When decline came, it came quickly and irrevocably. He knew of former towers of respect reduced to befuddled has-beens in saggy suits, shitting themselves without knowing. The truth was, he felt a fatigue far deeper than ever before. In his heart of hearts, he knew. The time was nigh for him to pass his company, his life's work, over to younger hands.

He planned a simple succession. He would give Regina forty percent of VCI, his grandnephew Donato Como forty percent, and split the remainder between Pietro Como and Rina Ameretti, faithful Vito's widow. Pietro was already well-off. Ettore had sold his half of the quarry to Carlo Como some years earlier; Pietro inherited it all after his father's death. And he knew Rina, now sixty-nine, would be content with a minor stake. All were family members, and it was important the company remained in family hands. Within the month, Ettore thought, I will put my plan into action

Of course, Pietro Como was unhappy when Ettore had floated the matter with him earlier in the week. Nothing was ever enough for that man, Ettore reflected. If his brothers Gianni and Renzo were yet alive, Pietro would have had no more than a third of Naviglio Quarry & Concrete, at best. The quarry had made Pietro Como one of the richest men in the district. But something that Ettore did not understand drove his nephew to be ever the grasper, the manipulator.

And perhaps worse. I have my royal badge that I proudly wear on special occasions like today, he thought. Pietro has his membership pin of the *Partito Nazionale Fascista*. Ever since his nephew had opportunistically hitched himself to Benito Mussolini's rising star, Ettore had seen that Fascist symbol proudly affixed to Pietro's lapel.

With a knock at the door, Regina poked her head inside. "Papà, everyone awaits!" Ettore walked over, took her hands.

"You are so beautiful, *cara mia*. I am hardly worthy to have you on my arm. Come now, lead me to my fate!"

The reception was underway in the villa's great octagon ballroom, its polished parquet floor glistening. Stately columns supported the surrounding mezzanine where the string quartet played. Servants in black jackets bore silver trays offering small plates of savories to chattering guests. Others circulated with prosecco and mixed drinks from the well-tended bar.

The villa, built thirty years before, had exceeded the highest expectations of Ettore and Marietta. Built in the *Rinascimento* style, its interior was open and spacious, full of natural light. The ceiling was a masterpiece, a splendidly frescoed rendition of Victor Emanuel II meeting Giuseppe Garibaldi at Teano in 1861. The work's heroic subject and brightly robust colors cast a gravitas softened by airy elegance. The villa's numerous rooms were impeccably furnished; Marietta's unerring taste had seen to that. Tall, gilded-framed windows held panes of leaded glass wrought in elaborate geometric designs.

* * *

Near the foot of the staircase, Pietro Como plucked a piece of fuzz from his jacket. "No thank you. Again," he said pointedly to a waiter offering him a cocktail. The fifty-four-year-old had found alcohol to be the Achilles' heel of many of his business associates. Ever alert to gaining advantage, he had made a teetotaler of himself.

Shorter than both of his late brothers, he had a high forehead, indented hairline, no sideburns. His thin dark hair, neatly trimmed, combed back, was showing flecks of gray. There was a slight hint of the Como jawline, but the nose was his mother's, long with a bump. His eyes were dark and piercing. Whenever he spoke, Pietro lifted his chin, consciously some claimed, and literally looked down his nose at his listener.

Pietro had always been sharp with numbers and enjoyed reducing complexities to black and white equations. If of the three brothers Renzo had been the dutiful son, and Gianni the one possessed of a zest for life and people, Pietro was the family abacus, reducing each day to a series of systematic calculations in an unending battle for gain.

He had made certain Regina invited a collection of useful people to his uncle's octogenarian soiree. Without his suggestions, he would have faced only cane-tapping fossils from

Ettore's past life. What his uncle failed to realize, Pietro reflected, was that the Italia of today was awash with opportunity. It was no time to stay tied to old operating methods. Competition within a socialist fascist state meant sharp-elbowed battle not only with other businessmen but with the ganglia of bureaucrats who controlled regulations and made allotment decisions. Always staying one step ahead was crucial. Pietro touched his party pin, patted his hair, resumed perusing each entering personage.

The assembled guests numbered over a hundred. Family members, of course, like his Zia Rina and her son, Berto Ameretti. Donato Como was somewhere, he knew. Business acquaintances abounded; the current Vacci family solicitor, Fiori, and their banker, Abramo Basillea, were among them.

Pietro stood alone. His wife had died giving birth to their one child over twenty years earlier. He didn't miss her. A pity my mother is not here to share her brother's triumph, he thought. Like his own dead brothers, both his parents were gone. On a rare fishing excursion, Carlo's battello had flipped one Sunday in 1929 on the Pirino; his foot became trapped between submerged rocks. His wife Tonia, who had worn black every day since November of 1911, joined him in death within only a few weeks, falling asleep one night to never awaken.

Pietro's eyes went to his son, Captain Carlo Arturo Como, wearing the blue-gray wool tunic of the *Regia Aeronautica*. Pietro could not fathom young Carlo Arturo's willingness to strap himself into a G-50 fighter and go risk his life in the clouds. Each day he awoke with a crushing fear for his boy's life, though he never shared such misgivings. Being fawned over never made anyone stronger. And to be perfectly frank, Carlo Arturo's patriotism was a politically useful reflection on his father.

Notably absent was the public servant Carlo Brambilla, home dying in bed. Free elections were a thing of the past. Instead, provincial Fascist prefects now appointed each town's mayor, called by the medieval title *podestà*, who ruled by decree. With Brambilla's demise expected daily, the pending leadership vacancy was of considerable local interest.

Pietro was particularly gratified to note the presence of formidable Eduardo Degligatti, a Mussolini confidant and the Minister of Corporations & State Transport. An ardent Fascist, Degligatti was known to be close friends with Heinrich Himmler, the German SS chief. Pietro knew the official well;

many quarry contracts went across his desk. The two had struck up several mutually beneficial collaborations. With Degligatti was a German SS officer whom Pietro had not yet met.

The quartet on the mezzanine abruptly broke off its rendering of Wolf's *Serenata Italiana*. The sudden musical blankness stilled the crowd.

Regina Vacci, radiant in dress and demeanor, stood at the top of the curved stairway. She waited until the room settled attentively.

"Honored guests," she began in a clear voice. "We are so pleased you have joined us to honor the eightieth birthday of your colleague and friend, my dear papà, Ettore Vacci, Cavaliere of the Crown!"

Ettore stepped into view. *Madonn'*, he thought, what a production! What happens when I turn one hundred?

The guests below broke into spontaneous applause. Honesty, accountability, love of fellow man—all stood personified at the top of the staircase. What began among some as polite repayment for free alcohol and tasty hors d'oeuvres evolved into a sustained crescendo, including cries of *"Bravo, Ettore! Bravo!"*

He carefully descended, step by step. Regina hovered but knew not to embarrass her adoptive father with physical support. Ettore smiled warmly at his reception, holding up one hand in acknowledgment. The other firmly gripped the handrail. He halted a few steps from the bottom, from where he could still see the entire room, sturdily balanced himself, tamped both arms downward several times.

"Thank you, my friends. I am so pleased you are here." Even at eighty, his voice retained a measure of the timbre that had made it so audible at his worksites for years.

"Thank you, and as always, welcome to Villa Vacci! We have a great quantity of beverages and food to consume, so please, partake! Regina tells me the *torta compleanno* is a culinary masterpiece. Please, do not leave any, or I will certainly become even fatter!

"Daughter, I thank you for this." Ettore nodded to Regina. "I have only one other thing to say." He paused, smiled, caught his breath. "I see friends and colleagues from our years of doing wonderful things together. We went out into the world many times to build roads across majestic countrysides and through great cities. But it was only those times when the road brought me home to our Castrubello that I ever said to myself, 'My heart is full.' Today my heart is full indeed. *Grazie, grazie* to all."

Ettore took his final steps down to the ballroom floor. Well-wishers greeted him warmly with a barrage of, "*Auguri*, Signor Vacci!" "*Cent'anni*, Ettore!" And from Lanzi, his barber of forty years, "Mah, Etto, eighty years is nothing. An old man asleep knows more than a young one awake!"

A quartet of servants entered, bearing immense trays laden with large, round *torte montavane*, Ettore's favorite. To a smatter of applause, the servants set the pastries on the long serving table. The party resumed.

Suddenly, a short, white-haired man brushed past the servants, took a position in front of the dessert table, and hastily handkerchiefed perspiration from his face.

"Apologies to all present!" the man announced, clinking a knife on an empty prosecco glass. "My apologies!" he repeated with a louder shout, stopping the restarted music and the room's conversations. Setting the glass and knife aside, he bowed nervously toward the faces before him.

"Please allow me to humbly say I am Giuseppe Prego, the watchmaker, like you a friend of our esteemed host." He bowed at the waist toward Ettore. "While no official person, and I do not speak now as if I were, I have been asked, on behalf of Castrubello's craftsmen and merchants, to express these thoughts to Don Ettore, in honor of this day and his recent knighthood." His Adam's apple bobbed as he swallowed. "May I proceed?"

The audience nodded, murmuring assent. Prego again dabbed his forehead. He took a sheet of paper from his coat pocket, unfolded it carefully, adjusted his spectacles, swallowed once more, and began to read.

"To our own dear knight, Cavaliere Ettore, friend and benefactor of our town and its people, Castrubello has always followed you with a loving eye." Swallow. "We share great pride to see the Knight's Cross on your chest shining with splendor in the Lombardian sun. The bright sash you wear is as the coursing red blood of our hearts, bursting with joy!" He paused. Almost at the end, he thought. Just a few moments more.

A sudden heavy drop of face-sweat *thwacked* onto his paper, running the ink. Prego lost his place, floundered. He restarted by repeating his comment about blood, of hearts bursting, stopped again, befuddled. A bemused female listener whispered, "All that blood! Does he need a bandage?" Stifled sniggering ensued.

Prego blanched, stared unseeing at his paper, felt the roomful of eyes. Hot panic-lava rose in his throat. I cannot proceed, he thought. Flee, you buffoon, his mind shouted. He felt a light touch on his arm.

Ettore said quietly, "Please, Giuseppe, continue. I am moved by your words and more by your courage." Ettore's eyes crinkled his encouragement. The merchant rallied, found his place.

"Over many decades you have brought our people employment, Don Ettore," he continued with a slight bow to his host without taking his eyes off the page. "Because of you, we have seen the world and sustained our families; because of you, we have never forgotten we are Castrubellese!" He took a final deep breath.

"Thus, in this eightieth year of your notable life, please know Castrubello will forever hold you up to its sons and daughters as someone who realized his dreams through persistence, intelligence, and enterprise, while never losing his modesty or his goodness of heart!"

The little merchant folded the paper in his damp hands.

Much applause followed, the crowd highly relieved their host had deftly spared them the embarrassment of Prego's public unraveling.

"*Bravo*, Signor Prego, well done!" exclaimed Ettore, patting his back. "*Grazie*, my friend." They shook hands, embraced. Conversation resumed, glasses clinked, enthusiastic clustering began in earnest around the table of cakes. The quartet returned to its score.

"I understand that other congratulations are in order."

Pietro Como turned to the voice. Minister Degligatti smiled benevolently, snapped shut his gold-plated lighter. He pushed his empty bourbon glass onto the tray of a passing waiter. "The same," he said.

With Degligatti was the German officer Pietro had noted earlier. "Ah," said Degligatti, tracking Como's eyes. "Signor Pietro Como, please allow me to introduce a friend and colleague. May I present Standartenführer Manfred von Gottlieb, of the famed Schutzstaffel!"

The SS colonel snapped to attention, extended his right arm. "Heil Hitler! Signor Como, permit me to offer congratulations on the occasion of your uncle's birthday. And for his recent royal honor."

Pietro returned the pro forma salute. "Thank you, Standartenführer, exceedingly kind of you. Yes, we are proud of our Zio Ettore. A life of consistent achievement." He noted the cut of the officer's earth-gray tunic, the crisp lightning-bolt insignia on its right collar. "A very fine uniform, Colonel."

"Thank you, sir," von Gottlieb said. "Hugo Boss Fashion House, Berlin. Tailors to the SS."

"Ah." Pietro did not know the firm. "Quality, indeed. Do forgive my curiosity. We Italians habitually take note of good style. But tell me, Standartenführer, are you stationed in Milan?"

Degligatti dragged on his cigarette. "The colonel is en route from France to his new assignment in Rome. His expertise is in the area of, how did you name it, Manfred?"

"Anti-partisan operations, Minister."

Pietro expressed his surprise. "Anti-partisan, Colonel? I take the term to mean saboteurs, assassins? But, no, can there be such traitors here, in Italia? The people love the regime and their Duce. Does such business keep you busy, dealing with these men?"

"Men and also women," von Gottlieb clarified. "You are correct, in Italia there have been only a few scattered incidents, mainly in the south. But I come from Paris where, yes, I am sorry to say, disloyal criminals, largely Jews and Communists as you'd expect, are bent on creating social instability." He sipped at his drink. "They are somewhat less active now."

Degligatti interrupted. "Enough shoptalk, gentlemen, please. This is hardly the time for such boredom. Allow me to congratulate you on a different matter, Pietro. I understand you are high on the list to become Castrubello's new podestà!" He lifted his refilled glass slightly.

Pietro hid his surprise. Who else knew he had put himself into contention? "Thank you, Signor Minister. I am but one candidate among several. The final decision is yet to be made."

Degligatti flicked his cigarette ash on the parquet floor. "I have spoken with the prefetto. He soon will give Rome his recommendation. You are very much under consideration, that is all I will say. Your generous loyalty to the Party is well known." He knew Como's type, what he craved. "Becoming podestà would be quite a feather in your cap, no?"

Pietro blushed despite his efforts. "You exaggerate, signore. The appointment, in the off chance I receive it, would hardly make me a *condottiere*. One only needs to recall the unfortunate Belloni, an object lesson for us all." Everyone still remembered how a dozen years earlier, police had ignominiously hauled the podestà of Milan straight from his office into a prison cell, ostensibly for financial irregularities.

Degligatti laughed, tipped his face, expelled smoke at the fresco. "Belloni? Belloni was a fool. You are not. Do not play modest with me, Como. We have done business before. I know you are always thinking, thinking, thinking." He allowed Como to bask slightly in the assumption the comment was a compliment. "Your concrete operation on the canal, Como. It thrives?"

"Thrives and more," Pietro responded. He sensed an opening. "But, if certain pieces fall into place, I foresee an even greater opportunity, and not only for myself. "

"Eh, see there, Manfred, what did I say? A chess player, this one."

The officer laughed, shook his head. "You Italians. Everyone a Machiavelli! Simple soldiering is my bailiwick. But if you will kindly excuse me, gentlemen, I see a colleague from the Royal Army. A true pleasure, signori." Bowing, clacking his heels together, he left the small circle.

"Speaks passable Italian, wouldn't you say?" Degligatti noted. "But tell me, Pietro, what scheme are you cooking up now? Might it possibly serve, shall we say, the mutual interests of both the State and its loyal sons?"

This is as good a time as any, Pietro thought. Ever since his uncle had told him of his inane succession plan for VCI, Pietro had been fuming. The company would disintegrate if those two naïfs were given the reins. And one a woman! Meanwhile, he, Pietro, possessed a wealth of experience as an owner and manager. It only made sense that control of the company should pass to himself.

But for any such outcome, he must get Zio to postpone his decision to sign shares of the company over to Donato and Regina. The old man still had enough wits to manage things himself for a while longer. Time enough for Pietro to get the doddering dinosaur to permanently change his mind.

"Vacci Costruzioni d'Italia faces a change soon," he began carefully. "I believe my uncle will soon be naming a successor, a family member."

"Ah," Degligatti said. He pulled smoke through the Turkish Sulima, his favorite brand. "Yourself, perhaps?"

"He is still thinking it through," Pietro answered. "Naturally, I am under consideration. But my uncle is so loyal to the memory of my late brother, Gianni. What to do with Gianni's son, Donato, poses a dilemma for him.

"Now, should it happen I do receive the company, I have a suggestion for you in mind. One that I believe would do both VCI and," he paused, "the Italian nation, much good. And as Minister of Corporations and Transport, I consider it critical that you be directly involved. Both as a government servant and a private citizen, I mean."

He noted Degligatti's pursed lips. Now his ears have perked up, thought Pietro. "I suggest a silent partnership for yourself in VCI of ten percent. With you directing government contracts on the scale that you do, your decisions regarding the country's need for roadways, airfields, defense work, with Vacci Costruzioni d'Italia kept in mind..." He paused. "You do see the potential."

Degligatti put down his drink and faux-pondered for a moment, chin in hand. "I believe I do. I am certain that I do if I heard you clearly. You say twenty-five percent?"

Pietro sighed through his nose, tight-lipped. The greedy prick, he thought. But the man's avarice could prove useful. With Degligatti's enthusiastic buy-in, social doors might suddenly open and Pietro vaulted into the regime's elite.

He answered, smiling. "Signor Minister, as always, your hearing is excellent. But what I actually said was that should the office of podestà come my way, then, yes, I would absolutely need a more invested, engaged partner. One with a hefty twenty percent."

Degligatti listened without expression but inwardly smiled. Twenty percent of a major Italian company without lifting a finger? He inclined his face toward Como's. "Did I mention I happen to be lunching with the prefetto this coming week? The day before his decision is expected?" He leaned back. "Tsk, tsk. Business succession. Such a crucial decision for your dear uncle. Tell me, Como, can I be of any direct assistance in the matter, perhaps?"

Ah, thought Pietro. "It is interesting you should ask. Without boring you with details, Minister, let me say this. And it may seem unrelated to the topic, but I assure you, it is not. I have heard our army needs all the good officers it can get. Is this true?"

Degligatti looked at Pietro, hiding his surprise, trying to see where this was going. Did Como want a commission? He shrugged. "Yes, naturally, Italia needs all of its best men. Between you and me, there has been talk that our Duce is considering a significant new troop commitment to the Fuhrer. Headed eastward." The men exchanged knowing looks.

"Then I have an excellent candidate for consideration," Pietro answered. "As a young man, he served in the Alpini Division in the early thirties. A junior officer, largely garrison duty at Aosta, but from all reports, commendable at his job."

Well, obviously it is not Como who seeks a posting, thought Degligatti. Who then?

"Since his discharge, he has had ten years of important civilian responsibility; I can attest to his competence. Seasoned, capable, reliable. He has been well-schooled in engineering matters by none other than his granduncle, Cavaliere Vacci. He is more than qualified to lead men into action. On any front," he added.

Degligatti raised his hands in mock awe. "I must warn Manfred to look out for his job! Your man sounds like another Rommel!" He became serious. "What you ask is not impossible. So, tell me, who is this paragon, Como? I will not ask how the matter fits with our other arrangement but only trust you that it does. I can start the paperwork within the week!"

Pietro dropped his voice. "I refer to my nephew, Donato Como." He sidled closer. "And, perhaps, Signor Degligatti, the paperwork can start tomorrow?"

* * *

With his back to a window, thirty-year-old Donato Como watched Zio Ettore and Regina as they circulated among guests.

He smiled at his grand-uncle's badge of knighthood. The monarchy had always been central to Ettore's notion of Italian nationhood, the villa's ceiling fresco alone was proof of that! The current Fascist regime was neither to Ettore's nor Donato's liking, but after the tumult of post-war Italia—the political street violence, crippling labor strikes, economic havoc—the country had at least stabilized. But they both understood that stability sustained by a strongman came with a cost.

Both considered the Duce's continual talk of a new Roman Empire unrealistic, at the least. Thus far, the new empire consisted mainly of problematic backwaters. Even some of those conquests had taken German intervention for Italian arms to prevail. But despite costly setbacks, there had been no epic military catastrophe. This, Rome declared, proved that il Duce's Italia was on the march to its glorious destiny!

Donato and his uncle also agreed that Mussolini's German alliance was a mistake. The rigid, goose-stepping Nazis seemed a radically different species than Italians, but the Third Reich nonetheless infatuated many in the dictator's circle. Still, Italian Fascism had not yet fully embraced every Nazi policy. For one thing, the Savoia monarchy still reigned, led by popular, diminutive, Victor Emmanuel III, affectionately nicknamed *Sciaboletta*, "Little Saber." And unlike the German model, the physical oppression of Italian Jews had thus far been relatively muted.

"Eh, 'Nato, daydreaming in the middle of a party, an act of social suicide."

Donato smiled to see Regina approaching with two glasses of prosecco from a waiter's tray. "Here, have one of these," she said. "It will bring you back to earth!"

"My cousin, the perfect hostess," Donato laughed, taking one of the effervescent flutes. He clinked her glass. "To Don Ettore's birthday celebration, all because of you!"

Not for the first time, Donato found his pulse quickening in Regina's presence. Previously, he had enjoyed an older-brother sort of rapport with her. But in the years after she returned from university, Regina had blossomed. More and more, Donato was seeing her in a different light.

His mother, Bianca, had remarried two years after his father Gianni's death at Tripoli and began producing infants like clockwork. It soon became clear that his stepfather, the carpenter Fumagalli, considered Donato more a nonpaying boarder than a son. And with each new babe, his mother had increasingly followed suit.

E' cosa di niente. Donato had made his peace with the situation long ago. He left Casa Como for a set of rooms at Vacci headquarters in the old Torrquadro, long stripped of its silk mill machinery and refitted yet again as the local seat of VCI. As far as women went, the roving nature of his work provided all the opportunities that a bachelor could ask for.

Then again, he thought, smelling Regina's fragrance, no man should live alone forever. And she was only a cousin on paper. Her blood was Pezzoli and Collina, not Como or Vacci.

They strolled the edge of the room. Regina took Donato's arm. "Have you seen the orchids from the Naples project you brought us? They love the greenhouse here at the villa. What new exotic plants will you show up with next?"

"How do you like obnoxious weeds? We have plenty of tall ones at our staging yards in Pavia, alive with thistles. I can bring you all you need!"

She laughed. "No, no thistles if you please!" She enjoyed his easy way. Donato is quite handsome, she thought, noting his good jaw, cleanly shaven, his sturdy build. The gray-blue eyes, a trace of his Vacci grandmother.

"What new plans do you have these days, Signor Donatello?" she asked lightly.

"Whatever Zio Ettore wants. There's talk of more naval docks at Genoa. That means new access roads and foundations. I have not heard anything definite yet. But this war," he stopped walking, glanced around, then at Regina. "This war, 'Gina, I hope Italia comes through it all right. I have seen the damage already from enemy bombings. It has been just a taste so far, some ports, the raid on Milan. But we best end this thing quickly. I do not want our only work to be repairing the country's destruction."

The quartet struck up its first dance number just then, a lively *mazurche*. As couples came onto the dance floor, Donato took one of Regina's gloved hands. "So, enough of that, 'Gina. There are no bombs right now, right here, today. It's time you and I danced!"

Chapter 34

2 June 1942: Rome

The glossy black Lancia Artena limousine pulled to a stop at the main entrance of stately Palazzo Venezia overlooking the great piazza. Minister of Corporations and Transport Eduardo Degligatti glanced up the building's classical stone facade as he exited the vehicle. Directly above the massive doorway, an Italian flag hung lengthwise from a balcony's balustrade. The world knew this balcony from the countless newsreels the regime had filmed since il Duce's first speeches from the dramatic site in the mid-1930s. The dictator's jutting jaw, his trim, impeccably tailored field marshal's uniform, his emphatic gestures, his arms folded while nodding, as thousands of adulating Italian supporters saluted him from the square—all were images burnt indelibly into the minds of moviegoers from Rome to Berlin to London to New York City. What a *maestro* the Leader is, Degligatti marveled.

Inside, he hurried up the stairway that took him to the anteroom of Benito Mussolini's office suite. A military aide consulted his appointment book and immediately stood. He moved to a side door. "Please, Signor Minister. Il Duce is expecting you to join him as soon as you arrive."

Degligatti adjusted his necktie, flattened his double-breasted suit coat, and nodded. The aide opened the door.

The Italian dictator had commandeered the palace's famous Sala del Mappamondo for his office space. The room was vast. Smooth marble pillars set flush to the walls vaulted the frescoed ceiling fifty feet above. Degligatti's heels clacked as he trod down the gleaming black and white marble floor past a row of massive, deeply set square windows. At the far end, the Leader's desk, larger than most banquet tables, angled out from a corner and centered on a fine, rectangular Persian carpet that easily covered two hundred square feet. On the sleek marble wall behind was a fireplace so large a tall man could walk into its hearth without bowing his head. An enormous, intricately embellished, wrought-iron grate prevented any such unlikely occurrence.

Mussolini saw Degligatti approach—from the anteroom door to the edge of the carpet was easily sixty paces. Drawn up to his full five-foot, six inches, he stood behind his desk addressing a military officer seated before him. The Leader wore his customary black military shirt and tie and gray pantaloons tucked into high black leather boots. His shaven head glistened in the warmth of the room, despite the balcony door being half ajar.

Degligatti knew the seated officer, had met him once at a reception in the capital. General Messe was in Rome on a week's leave from his sixty-thousand-man CSIR expeditionary corps fighting in Russia alongside the Nazis. Mussolini had ordered the force to quickly join Germany's invasion of the Soviet Union the previous year, a signal of solidarity with Germany's attack on the Communist regime. And, Degligatti knew, the Leader's way of putting his poker chips on the table in anticipation of inevitable German victory.

Mussolini waved his trusted advisor into the room. "Degligatti, at last. As you see we did not wait. General Messe, I believe you know Minister Degligatti. His portfolio is Corporations and Transport, but I find his insight most useful on all types of state matters. I have asked him to join us, simply to provide me an additional pair of ears." The dictator's voice boomed loudly off the walls although he spoke in a normal voice.

The general stood. He and Degligatti exchanged polite greetings after their crisp salutes.

"So, Messe, you were saying," Mussolini resumed. "Sit, sit." He waved both men into their empty chairs, then sat in his own.

"Excuse me, my Duce, if I am too blunt. But I strongly recommend that we do not send any more men, let alone an entire new army, against the Soviets. I am convinced that an Italian expedition of the size you are contemplating will face immense challenges, perhaps insurmountable ones, if deployed on the Russian front without proper preparation."

Degligatti had heard of this new army, although he was not formally a military insider. But informally, Mussolini had sounded him out about the idea of Italy dramatically increasing its commitment to the current invasion, including a formal declaration of war against Stalin. Degligatti heartily supported such a move. As a good Fascist and an admirer of the German Fuhrer, he fervently agreed that exterminating Communism was central to the Axis Powers' mission of properly re-ordering human civilization. A real Italian army on the Russian front, two hundred thousand men or more—not just a smattering of divisions like CSIR—would gain Italy its new empire in a single, masterful stroke.

Mussolini answered Messe, "I am surprised by your, I will not say pessimism, but your lukewarm enthusiasm, General. What reasons can you have for saying this? Are you doubtful of the spirit of the Italian fighting man? Our troops have thus far given a solid accounting of themselves."

"You are correct, sir, they have done so. My doubts are not about our spirit. But my experience this past year is this. The army, and specifically our supply system, are not ready for an enterprise of this size. It is one thing to send a corps to fight in Ethiopia, in Egypt, the Baltic states, or Greece. Supply lines are much closer, the troops are much easier to support and reinforce. Even there, in those places, you know we have struggled at times; it was only with German assistance that Greece fell, for example."

Mussolini frowned and for a moment his piercing eyes flashed. Reminders of military excursions that had not paid off as expected was not the topic here.

Despite noting il Duce's hardening countenance, Messe stubbornly pressed on. "Our armaments are antiquated, sir. We are using rifles designed in 1896! There is an absolute lack of suitable armored vehicles. The steppes are made for tanks, my Duce, and the Russian T-34s are monsters—each of them weighs twenty-nine tons! Even German panzers struggle against them. Our own seven-ton L6/40s are mere popguns, tankettes, in comparison. Our transport system has proven woeful, without enough trucks, not enough fuel, constantly dependent on German supplies. All made more difficult by the Germans' attitude, I must say. They have repeatedly shown unyielding selfishness in all their interactions. Their high command does not communicate smoothly with our own leadership. Because they are mechanized and we are not, German units blaze forward while we can only march in their dust. Then we hear nothing but complaints about Italian dawdling, while they guzzle the fuel that we need for the trucks we do have!"

The man will have a stroke at this rate, Degligatti thought. Nothing like the military for complaining. What does he expect? It is called 'war'. How dare he whine this way! Eduardo cleared his throat, wanted to apply a saying of his nonna's, "Either eat the soup in front of you or go jump out the window!' But he held his tongue.

Mussolini responded in a conciliatory tone. "My dear General Messe, I see that you seek the ideal for your men—you would not be a good commander if you did not! But your training is of a very practical, of-this-moment nature. You have the mind of a tactician, and an excellent one, as the success of your force has shown, I hasten to add! But here is an analogy. You are like a person who walks into a room gazing at the floor, to assure his movement is efficient, with no false steps. I, on the other hand, think in terms of grand strategy. I stride into the same room and my gaze goes immediately to the window, past the glass, to the far horizon!

"The truth is this regarding Russia. I must be fully at the Fuhrer's side in this war. Italy's future is irrevocably tied to that of Germany's. It is true, not every military expedition of ours has gone as smoothly as planned. But the Soviet Union is a far greater prize than all of them combined. The oil fields of the Caucasus alone will power our industries for generations! And since we joined in Barbarossa, look at the progress we have made, both German forces and our Italian Expeditionary Corps. The Russians flee, disorganized, in the face of the assault! Whole Red armies have been surrounded, gobbled up, crushed, vast tracts of land have fallen under our control. With a renewed push now, reinforced by our brave new Italian Eighth Army, the key cities, the great population centers, await plucking like ripe fruit. And with that, Stalin will be finished!"

Mussolini rose again, signaled for the two men to stay seated, paced behind his desk, right to left, left to right.

"The Germans want us by their side, despite what you say about their attitude in the field, Messe. They are calling for troops from our other allies as well, the Romanians and Hungarians. Yes, they are arrogant, but the arrogance of superiority is exactly the ingredient needed for conquest, an ingredient that we Italians must learn to possess. They are conquerors. And they have signed specific contracts for our addition to their force, contracts covering all the essentials that you have articulated."

Messe was not cowed by Mussolini; he had heard plenty of patriotic bombast from the man before. "My Duce," he persisted, "we already have signed agreements and the Germans ignore them. It is a continuous effort to get them to do for us what they agreed in writing to do, from food to transport, to ammunition, to air cover for our operations. Frankly, sir, given all of that, we are lucky our sixty thousand men have not been ground to dust out there on the steppes, either by the giant we face or the one alongside us!"

Mussolini came from behind his desk. He put a hand on his general's shoulder as the officer stood rapidly to attention. The dictator brought his face close to the general's nose. "Dear Messe, when all is over, when the Soviet foe is slain and that madman Stalin is hauled through Rome in chains, as I sit beside the Fuhrer, I guarantee you this. In terms of splitting the spoils, my risking the lives of two hundred thousand Italian soldiers will far outweigh risking just sixty!"

The general looked down at his boots, back to his commander, fought any involuntary facial reaction. He had heard of the dictator's penchant for eating salads made only of sliced raw garlic and olive oil. It was clearly no idle rumor. He coughed slightly into his fist. "I understand, my Duce." He took a breath. He had made his argument, done his best, the rest was in the hands of *fortuna*. "I would fail you as commander if I did not express such practical concerns. What you propose is daring and dangerous. But your army does not shrink from such tests, just the opposite. It rises to greatness!"

Mussolini replied with a slap on the desk, "Exactly, Messe!" He smiled, nodded, indicating the meeting was done. The general took one step back, saluted, acknowledged Degligatti with a mechanically polite bow, and left the room.

The dictator leaned back from his desk, took out a cigarette from its silver case by the blotter. He lit it with a monogrammed lighter, also silver. "So, what do you think?"

"Masterful as always, my Duce. The general can be a thorn at times, always angling for more of this, more of that. But Messe is well-respected. And with experience against the Russians, I assume you will want him out there. But perhaps it would be wise to keep him with the corps he has, not give him command of the entire new army. You do not need grumbling from the top."

"No, no, I agree. The Eighth goes to Italo Gariboldi, he is due for a big assignment. And nothing is bigger than this one, Degligatti. I have already decided we shall go forward! Italy declares war against Russia next week, on June 10!"

Degligatti remembered his promise in Castrubello the prior weekend. "As I have heard you say often, my Leader, 'War is to a man as motherhood is to a woman!' We will succeed, there is no doubt. And," he added, as if by afterthought, "if I may receive a list of the divisions being assigned to Eighth Army, my office will assure their smooth rail transport to the front!"

* * *

4 June 1942: Castrubello

A uniformed army private arrived at the VCI offices on a bicycle. He personally delivered a letter to Donato at his desk in the open-spaced main floor company office. Mission accomplished, the private briskly nodded his head, clicked his heels, remounted his bicycle, and pedaled off.

Donato, wondering what all that was about, tore open the envelope and read:

Pursuant to this missive, dated 2 June 1942, Donato Luigi Como is herewith called to active duty in the Royal Army of the Kingdom of Italy with the rank of Primo-Tenente of Engineers. He is ordered to report to duty on the date of 9 June 1942 and will proceed at his own expense to Alessandria, Lombardia, reporting on the aforementioned date to the Commanding Officer, 3rd Infantry Division 'Ravenna', for unit assignment.
By Order of the Undersecretary of the Minister of War.
Antonio Scuero

Donato snorted in disbelief. An obvious mistake, so typical. While many of his acquaintances had been called to the colors since 1940, most of those in their thirties had volunteered. As a reserve officer, Donato understood his duty to respond. But only the year before, a letter had notified him—signed by this very same Scuero!—that his work in a war-related industry was essential for the good of the state, and he was therefore exempt from further service!

What a waste of time, Donato thought. He went to his uncle's office down the hall, told him he had to leave on an errand, and promptly drove a company car to the Royal Army recruiting station, a former barbershop, in Piazza Santo Giorgio. He confronted the sub-lieutenant in a braided dress uniform who was manning the counter.

"I need you to clear something up," Donato said perfunctorily. "This telegram, a mistake, no?"

The sergeant took the proffered paper, read it carefully. "One moment, sir," he said, then went to his work desk facing the back wall, picked up a black candlestick style telephone, and spoke into the transmitter while holding the receiver to his ear.

Donato could not hear what the man was saying. The young officer nodded, nodded again, hung up, returned to the counter. He came to attention.

"Sir, I have the honor of confirming that you have been commissioned first-lieutenant of engineers in the Royal Army of Italia. Congratulations on your posting, Tenente. Long live il Duce!" He snapped a straight-armed salute.

Donato suppressed his shock. After ten years of inactive duty, he was to rejoin the colors! Of course, the country needed officers, and of course, there was no question that he would report. He had barely one week to organize his affairs, purchase a uniform, and pull the rest of his kit together, not to mention travel to Alessandria, a day's journey by train.

On his return to Torrquadro, he contemplated what this turn of events meant. He found himself, with the surprise of the message wearing off, anticipating the challenge ahead. Donato had liked his previous active military duty and appreciated his promotion. He was thankful he could pick up and go without having excessive emotional regrets. His half-siblings meant little to him. For one thing, he was six years older than the oldest of them. Fumagalli was no father he would miss. His mother, that may be more difficult. But even she was preoccupied with more immediate matters than the departure of the grown son she hardly knew anymore.

A brief image of Regina suddenly came to mind. Her eyes and quick-witted laughter. Her shapely figure. He had been vaguely musing they may have a future, though he had yet to act on the thought. Donato decided he would see her before he left. Perhaps they would write.

The first thing he did upon returning to Torrquadro was to tell Ettore the news, who only shook his head.

"Eh, what, are they thinking, if at all? When they take people away from work that moves troops and supplies from one place to another, don't they see? They will have their big army but without the means to keep it in the field!"

"I doubt they see me as an essential cog in the state machine, Zio Ettore," Donato replied. "The urgency of this summons is what's unusual. As far as I know, the 3rd has been sitting idle in

Alessandria for months. It makes me think that perhaps it now has a sudden new role in the big picture."

Ettore answered, "If there is a big picture. We seem to lurch from one battlefield to another without rhyme or reason. Difficult places that despise the idea of our ruling them. Even in Russia, with the Germans. Why there? We are too much with the Germans, I think. Why should more Italian blood spill just to make those *crucchi* masters of the world?"

Donato patted his uncle's hand. "You must take care who you tell such thoughts to. Nosy OVRA agents from Rome have their ears everywhere. We do not want to see you bundled off some night in one of their panel trucks!"

* * *

The two men sat over glasses of fresh *limonata* on the loggia. Pietro's villetta near the Pirino, one of several properties he had recently acquired, enjoyed a pleasant view of the streaming river. Good timing here, a good business tip there—Pietro was finding the art of party politics rewarding. Now to apply some of that art to the old man.

"Zio, what terrible news regarding Donato. I talked to my contacts in Rome, but to no avail. The bureaucracy, you know, such a frustrating thicket!"

Ettore detested dissembling in any form and detested it now in his nephew. He had heard the rumors of Pietro's pending appointment as the next podestà of Castrubello, of his growing clout. He shrugged. "Donato wrote from Alessandria. His division will ship out soon. He did not say where."

"May God be with him," said Pietro, piously. "And such awkward timing. With you about to announce your decision regarding the future of VCI."

Ettore put his half-full glass down, waved off Pietro's offer of a refill. "Yes, bad timing. But I will wait. I have no problem doing what I have done for sixty years. I will make the changes when Donato returns."

This was the answer Pietro had expected. "Have you thought about conducting business from your villa, Zio? Certainly, there is plenty of room. Now with Donato gone, the old Torrquadro is largely empty. Consider its upkeep alone. Use Villa Vacci. It would save you the effort of going back and forth."

The suggestion caught Ettore by surprise. "I know you think I am old, Pietro, and I am. But I am no invalid. The villa is my retreat from the troubles of work. Why would I make it anything different?"

Because I need the building, Pietro thought. "The truth is, Zio Ettore, someone approached me about leasing Torrquadro. I told him, 'It is not mine to lease! Cavaliere Vacci is your man!' Still, he persisted. I promised to bring the matter to you, on his behalf."

Ettore considered. He had bought the building for a song after the silk industry collapsed; VCI had never occupied more than a small part of the expansive structure. And it was true, the Torrquadro had now become rather superfluous to daily operations. Construction projects largely ran themselves from staging areas throughout the north and elsewhere. Financial decisions came out of company offices in Milan where the banks were. At this point, Ettore's role was primarily saying yea or nay to various company matters by long distance. The nation's telephone system was not perfect, but reliable enough.

"Who wants the lease?" he asked.

"You know the gentleman. He was present on your eightieth birthday. I speak of Minister Eduardo Degligatti. Not him personally, of course, the government. The kingdom."

"Degligatti? Yes. What does the kingdom need that building for?"

"I did not ask. Probably a field office of Degligatti's ministry. He makes a straightforward offer of ten thousand lire a year, paid in advance. Generous by any stretch."

Ettore squinted. It was generous indeed, a big-city rate. Pietro sensed his uncle wavering. "If you like, I can inquire if the minister is willing to go higher. In these uncertain times an additional income stream for our company, I speak as a board member now, would be desirable, no?"

Ettore sighed. Once, he had found deal-making exciting, energizing, back when he and Maurizio were still building the company. Now he just felt tired.

"Very well, talk to him. And since it is for the kingdom, do not quibble. Firm up his number but do not gouge. Create a time frame, write the lease. If it looks good, I will sign."

Pietro smiled to himself. Another chit with Degligatti. As for why the man wanted Torrquadro, he neither knew nor cared.

Chapter 35

17 June — 10 July 1942

The Italian Eighth Army totaled over two hundred twenty thousand men. Its 35th Corps, under Messe, composed of the CSIR divisions sent the previous year, was already alongside the Germans. The three divisions of 2nd Corps, including 3rd Ravenna, were scheduled to ship out this day, June 17th, on a collection of trains leaving from various mobilization centers. The Alpine Corps, consisting of the Tridentina, Julia, and Cuneense mountain divisions, would set out near the end of the month.

Donato viewed his contingent's departure from Alessandria through the window of an officers' car. A colorful military band pumped out patriotic airs as raw recruits joined the veterans boarding. Stoic fathers embraced their uniformed sons. Blackshirt militia stood at attention under patriotic bunting, chanting in unison, "Long live il Duce! Long live sacrifice! Long live war!" Lovers embraced with tears and promises, sobbing mammas clutched at their boys' hands through open railcar windows. As troopers passed by, a Fascist women's club distributed holy medals with the Blessed Virgin's image on one side, Benito Mussolini's on the other.

When the train blasted its whistle to depart, group *agita* heightened. Waving frantically or clasping hands over faces, snapping salutes or sagging to knees, at Alessandria and each of 2nd Corps' debarkation stations, Italia bade farewell to her sons.

"An allegory in need of painting," offered the captain next to Como, as he peered at the station scene through the coach window. "But never a Botticelli around when you need one." Older than Donato, with a full head of wiry gray hair, he wore the uniform of a medical doctor. "I am Antonio Parma, by the way. 495th Field Hospital. It seems we are to share this bench for some days."

Parma told Donato he had served on the Russian steppes with Messe's expeditionary corps the previous summer. Home on extended leave because of a family death, he now had new orders to report to the 495th and was hitching a ride with the Ravenna.

The two officers soon became friends. It was a month's journey for the troop train to wend its way to where the division would unload at Voroshilovgrad in Ukraine. Parma spoke several languages; with the help of a phrasebook and the doctor's coaching Donato worked on improving his German vocabulary. He also found Parma's previous experience on the Eastern front a primer on what to expect once they got there.

"Our men are willing to battle, there is no lack of courage," Parma told Donato one day as they rattled along. Outside the window, the Brenner Pass had given way to tidy Austrian farms and villages tucked in green valleys. "But the men I was with received too little training before being sent out to fight. In this army, the mantra is always, 'Learn on the job'. And the obsolete junk they give them to fight with! *Porco dio!*

"We talk as if victory is all but certain. Without being a defeatist, I am not so convinced. I know a bit of Russian; last year I practiced by talking with peasants. Stalin does not pamper these people, by any means. Yet every one of them told me Russia will ultimately defeat our invasion. There was no doubt at all. They hate the Germans with a visceral passion. They judge us less harshly. I think our simple Italian boys remind them of their own."

A week later, signs of fighting from the previous summer began appearing. Flattened buildings, an overturned locomotive, charred fuselages of crashed aircraft, and similar debris littered stretches of landscape.

The troop train stopped outside the modest town of Bratislava to allow higher-priority traffic to pass by. It waited on a siding, baking in the heat. Crews of Russian prisoners under heavy guard worked to clean up refuse and make repairs on the rail line. Starving civilians, desperate for scraps, gleaned the tracks for discarded food tins from passing troop cars. Their sunken, dark eyes stared back at Donato from time to time.

The railcars were stifling hot, the air breathlessly still. The men had every window open. A futile effort; they only admitted more mid-afternoon heat.

On an adjacent track, a string of flatcars loaded with German panzers slowly glided past. Young German tankers, most shirtless to the waist, lounged on their machines enjoying the sun and the breeze. The panzers were massive and factory-new, each emblazoned with the Wehrmacht's black and white *balkenkreuz* cross. The German train blasted a high-pitched shriek.

The sudden whistle woke everybody from their stupor. Immediately a loud racket arose. At the rear of Ravenna's train, ten cattle cars carried the division's pack mules. Already stressed, the sudden sound spooked the fly-tortured, miserable beasts. The animals worked themselves into a frenzy, stomping the floors and kicking out the slatted wood sides of their cars, then sticking their toothy, wide-mouthed muzzles through the gaps, braying at the top of their lungs. Several pounded their hoofs right through the floorboards, fracturing their legs. Donato became aware of a rising stench as panicked animals released their bowels in pain and terror. Plaintive beast-screams added their unearthly chorus to the hellish cacophony.

The passing Germans at first looked perplexed by the noise. Then, recognizing the commotion for what it was, the young soldiers started to point, then to hoot and slap their thighs. Some held their noses as they mockingly waved *auf wiedersehen, makkaroni!* It took ten minutes for the trainload of armor to move past.

Donato, alongside Parma, endured the humiliation with the rest of their comrades. "And thus, my friend, here is your snapshot of two far different armies," commented the doctor.

As the train pushed east, it made other stops. Whenever it did, Donato could not understand the brutality the Nazis displayed to the local conquered populations. The first time it hit home was at a nameless wayside station as their locomotive's boiler took on water. The troops had time to stretch their legs after sitting twelve hours inertly.

Near the tracks where he and Parma smoked cigarettes, Donato watched twenty civilians walk single file. A Nazi *Einsatzgruppen* squad, in belted, field-gray tunics and jaunty garrison caps, strolled casually alongside the group, brandishing rifles. Donato thought to offer a cigarette to one youngish woman as she passed, but Dottore Parma held him back by his elbow.

"A mistake, Como. Do not be seen aiding enemies of the Reich."

"What are you saying?" Donato asked. "They appear harmless enough; those two oldsters there, they could be our nonnas. What could be their offense? Besides, that redhead is pretty."

"Most likely Jews. If not Jews, then the associates of Jews. In any event, if a death squad has them, they have been judged guilty of something. Look where I'm pointing." Donato followed his arm and saw at a distance a small dirt pile on a flat stretch of ground. The line of prisoners moved slowly toward it.

"They are being marched out to a slit trench, probably there, by that dirt, where they will be treated to a bullet in the back of the head, one by one. Your friendly cigarette would end up between the lips of one of the execution squad. That redhead you like? She walks but is already dead, Como."

Donato tried to cover his shock. Death squad? War is war, and he was a realist. But it was one thing to know he would soon be fighting alongside soldiers proficient at killing. Proficient killing was a soldier's job, in any case. But it was something else to be the comrade of executioners. He knew of the Nazis' hatred of Jews. But before today, the hatred had been abstract. Now Donato saw the reality: an obscure mass grave in the middle of nowhere.

* * *

11 July 1942: Voroshilovgrad, Ukraine

The men of the Ravenna gradually assembled themselves as various trains unloaded the division's 38th and 37th infantry regiments, artillery battalions, support units, vehicles, weapons, animals, field guns, and supplies. The tent encampment covered acres of Ukrainian farmland, already stripped bare by the retreating Russians. The land around Voroshilovgrad sloped very gently toward the yet unseen River Don, two hundred fifty miles east. Of the Ravenna's brother divisions, the 2nd Sforzesca, fresh from Greece, had already seen action and was closing in on the Don. The other, 5th Cosseria, was still somewhere south; it and the Ravenna would link at Donetsk and finish their final leg together.

Ravenna's 118th Engineer Battalion consisted of two companies. The 5th maintained communications and the generators necessary for providing electricity to the division. 6th Company's duties ranged much wider. They included planning the division's strongpoint system, stringing barbed wire, clearing enemy minefields, and laying their own. The company also was expected to take the fight to the enemy by planting demolition charges against fixed defenses. During battles, the unit served as regular infantry. Besides their weapons and vehicles, equipment included TNT, Bakelite-encased antitank mines, reels of barbed wire, Lanciafiammi flamethrowers, Breda M35 grenades, and more. Donato commanded one of the company's forty-man platoons.

After the engineers settled in, battalion commander Major Raimondo called an officers' meeting. Leaning over outdated field maps, they reviewed the march ahead. The battalion's two company captains then met with their separate staffs. Finally, platoon lieutenants had the chance to talk to their men.

Swatting at mosquitoes, the soldiers sat on the dry grass just beyond the tent line. Donato fanned himself with his helmet until all eyes were on him.

"I am Lieutenant Como. If you don't know me, I am not surprised. We barely had a week together before leaving. During the journey, I talked to some of you. The ones I did not, I promise to get to know you.

"You may have heard I've served before. What I learned was to never assume you have learned enough. About anything. Our platoon will be doing many different tasks, we must be able to back each other up. So, we will all learn how to do that. How to plant mines. How to build defensive structures. How to use a flamethrower."

"Just ask Fellini," called out a voice, eliciting general laughter.

Donato's sergeant-major, Massimo Biella, spoke up sharply. "It is one thing to entertain your mates by flatulating into a lit match, Fellini. It takes expertise to use it as a weapon!" A burst of laughter again.

Donato laughed with them. "Yes, even I know of Private Fellini's talent, despite traveling in a separate train car." More guffaws, playful punches to Fellini's shoulder. "But," Como loudly continued, before the buffoonery got out of hand, "I guarantee you, there will come a time when knowing how to use a machine gun, ignite a charge, or map a minefield will save your comrades' lives.

"One last thing," he added, "and I will talk more to the sergeants about this. All of us miss our families. Our farewells were not easy." He saw many men's eyes go down among those seated before him, hands plucking dry grass. "So here is what we will do. Our platoon has forty men at full strength. I want you sergeants," Donato made eye contact with each noncom, "to break your squads into 'families' of five or six men. I expect each family to quarter together, eat together, take care of each other, trust in each other. Whoever is the oldest within each group, I hold you responsible for your younger brothers. As the eldest, your job is to play the nag, to make certain everyone's weapons are kept clean, oiled, ready to use, and to see that important matters like wearing dry socks, keeping shoes repaired—the housekeeping details—are taken care of. Turn to each other when you need help, like families do. When the fighting comes, yes, we will fight for *la Patria*, for Savoia. But we will fight for each other more."

"Good speech," said Donato's master sergeant Biella afterward, as the group broke up. "Haven't heard that one before."

"My captain organized our company like that when I served in '32," Donato answered. "Mainly it worked. Most of these boys, it is the first time in their life away from mamma, from papà, the first time out of the sound of their parish bell. Everything is unfamiliar to them—trains and trucks, villages full of foreigners. Most of them are already scared out of their wits, what happens when the bullets start flying? But they all understand *famiglia*. The idea is something to grab hold of. It can only help, I think, if they see the older men in their groups as somebody to look up to, go to. They won't come to me with their questions and fears, I am too distant, all we officers are. And you sergeants, you scare even us!"

Biella laughed. He liked what he had seen of this Como so far. No stuffed shirt, no pompous-ass, born-to-the-manor, aristocratic cocksucker. Too many officers like that in this army for his liking.

"Makes sense." The noncom corrected himself. "Makes sense, sir."

* * *

5 August 1942: Ukraine

2nd Corp's long march to the Don proceeded over recently contested ground. Increased signs of earlier fighting surrounded their passage: turretless tanks, upended lorries, long lines of beleaguered Soviet prisoners snaking to the rear. The Ivans had slowly given way, but not in a panic, blowing bridges and buildings, stripping the land of anything the invaders might use themselves. Russian tractors had plowed the roads with deep zig-zag ruts, slowing Italian vehicles and troops to half their regular pace. Only German tracked armor could still move with some alacrity.

At the rear of his platoon, Donato heard engines roaring up from over his shoulder. German tanks had been overtaking the corps all day, continually forcing the Italians off the side of the road and into the fields. As always, the German formations passed without slowing. Once the armor roared through, churning billows of dust, the Italian columns reformed their double files and resumed plodding east.

The Ravenna strung out for two miles as it marched, its transports and supply vehicles intermixed with the infantry. Mule teams pulled an assortment of small field guns; old Pavesi tractors towed the larger artillery. All the Italian vehicles shared the same problem: reliance on German fuel, both gasoline and diesel. Refueling tankers met the column at sporadic checkpoints, invariably late. The replacement fuel they pumped often ran out before the Italians' numerous dry gas tanks did. A third of 2nd Corps' motorized equipment sat stranded every day, waiting for service, miles behind the army's advance.

Though the day was sweltering, it ended with a brief, fierce thunderstorm. Black clouds blew in from nowhere, and the skies poured blinding rain, punctuated by lightning strikes and thunderous booms that rattled helmets and teeth. Vehicles sank to their axles in the instant mud, men slipped and slopped trying to extricate themselves from quagmires.

The pack animals suffered immensely, terrified by the jagged lightning, thoroughly drenched, and struggling in mud they could not escape. Some stopped in their tracks completely overwhelmed, ignoring the teamsters' efforts to beat them into motion. Others, wide-eyed, bucked wildly, forcing the packs on their backs to slip under their bellies or career into the muck. Some of the beasts slipped and fell, breaking their legs, and required putting down.

At daybreak, the roads started firming again, by ten they were brick. By noon, dust rose again in a white talcum mist above the Italians' resigned, tramping columns.

* * *

13 August 1942: Ukraine

"Como, what are you doing?" demanded Parma. The lieutenant continued trotting away from the doctor toward the shouting.

The weatherworn village consisted of an onion-towered clapboard church, a collection of peasants' log cabins, called *izbas*, and assorted wooden, unpainted shacks and animal pens sprawled across a crossroads. A company of German signalmen had moved in a day before. It planned to use the hamlet as a staging area while stringing telegraph wire along that stretch of road.

Italian troops continued to trudge dustily past. Donato's platoon had taken itself out of the column to wait for the rest of the straggling 118th to catch up. Dottore Parma waited with them. He had learned his field hospital was now in the Stalingrad sector, diverted there to help tend the growing number of casualties. A motorized regiment of PanzerGrenadiers was due the next morning; he had orders to travel with them.

Ignoring Parma's shouts, directly ahead Donato saw animated villagers to one side, a dozen German troops on the other, with a loud confrontation taking place center ring. A German corporal had his Gewehr rifle to the head of an old Russian man who half-crouched by a log wall. A young woman, dressed in a ragged blouse and dress—the granddaughter?—tugged to be free of another trooper, all the while screaming vitriolic protest. In his boney arms, the old man hugged a rough door made of splintery boards.

"What is this?" Donato demanded in rudimentary German as he arrived on the scene. The German corporal glanced his way then back down his gun barrel. He motioned with his weapon for the old man to drop the door. *"Leg es jetzt runter!"*

The old man stuck his chin up defiantly, shook his head. *"Nyet!"* he spat.

The Ukrainian woman began shrilly exclaiming anew, still trying to twist from the grasp of the German behind her, who laughed.

"She says they need the door for their shelter," translated Doctor Parma, who'd followed Donato toward the melee.

A white-bearded villager stepped forth. He wore the black cassock and pectoral cross of an Orthodox priest, with a cylindrical *klimavkion* on his head. At his voice, the townspeople calmed. He then addressed Como and Parma in Russian.

The doctor told Donato, "Whitebeard here is their *stariyshyna*, their elder and pastor. He says the Germans took the izba of this woman and her grandfather and booted them out. The two of them then built a lean-to from scraps but needed a door. They took it from their izba's outhouse. The Germans want it back."

"*Che cazzo*,'" muttered Donato. He looked at the German with the rifle. He knew enough about Germans to never project doubt in their presence. He came to attention facing the corporal. "*Soldat! Heil Hitler!*" he said loudly. His arm flashed the Nazi salute.

The soldier stayed in place for a moment, then came to attention and loudly returned the salute. Donato saw with amazement that every German within range did likewise.

"*Wer ist il offizier, der tuo capitano, soldato?*" Donato said, hoping the spell cast by Hitler's name would cover for his slaughtered attempt at German.

"I am here, Lieutenant," called a voice speaking impeccable Italian. "You may stand down."

The Wehrmacht signals officer strode alongside Dottore Parma. Thank God, thought Donato, acknowledging Parma's initiative by arching his eyebrows. He straightened in the presence of superior rank.

The captain conversed with the corporal and, upon learning the issue, laughed out loud. He jovially dispersed his men. With long strides, he approached the old man and woman, clicked his heels, touched the brim of his hat, and about-faced. The *stariyshyna* waved his arms, shooed his villagers back to work. The old man and his granddaughter scuttled off to their makeshift hovel, sharing the burden of the splintery door.

"It is not every day I see an Italian giving orders to the Wehrmacht," said the captain, facing Donato. "What is your country's expression? '*Che palle!*' The officer scoffed drily. "Your intervention, I am guessing it was an impulse of the moment." The silver wreath above his cap's visor flashed in the sunlight.

Not sure how to respond, Donato chose, "Thank you, sir."

"Naturally, disorderliness can never be tolerated. Discipline is what sets us apart from the beasts, after all. Your instincts are good, for a non-professional. May I ask from what part of Italia you hail?"

"Lombardia, sir."

"Ah, Lombardia! I should have suspected! Once such a fine Austrian province!" He faintly smirked, as if sharing an inside joke with a confidant. "But, Lieutenant, these Slavic drudges," he gestured toward the village. His tone hardened. "My experience is they learn only insolence if allowed the upper hand. As, I fear, your interference today allowed." He flexed his fingers within leather gloves. "Something to remember next time, perhaps." His iron eyes bore into Donato's. After a deadlocked moment, the captain smiled thinly. *"Auf Wiedersehen, Herr Leutnant."* He waited for and returned the Italian officer's salute.

At reveille the next morning, Donato emerged from his tent and stretched toward the rising sun. Parma was also afoot, his packed duffel at his feet.

"Dottore," Donato acknowledged, rubbing sleep-crud from his eyes with his fingers. His eyesight focused toward where the doctor stared. From the last telegraph pole set at the crossroads hung the old man and the granddaughter. Black tongues distended, eyes open wide, they creaked in their nooses, ragged clothes fluttering in the breeze like ribbons.

On the chests of both bodies were pinned signs that read: 'Filthy Saboteur!'

From across the road, the village pastor also peered up at the bodies. He approached the two officers. As he spoke, he brought their attention to the crucifix around his neck with its carved image of the dying Savior.

Parma interpreted. "He says thank you for trying. But never forget—not Christ himself could escape Fate."

From a distance came the roar of an approaching PanzerGrenadier unit, Parma's ride to the war, slowing down.

Chapter 36

September 1942: Castrubello

"The Torrquadro, if you please, Tommaso," said Pietro Como to the man behind the wheel. Of all the advantages of being Castrubello's new podestà, none pleased him more than the chauffeured 1938 Lancia sedan that came with the job. He valued its chauffeur just as much. A burly, unexpressive man of thirty-seven, Tommaso Contadino not only took care of driving chores but added gravitas to Pietro's presence anywhere.

Como had assumed the gold chain and medallion of office the month previous. His appointment surprised the village, Pietro not being known in Castrubello as a public figure. But the townspeople, old acquaintances of life's vagaries, accepted the situation with typical detachment, keeping their thoughts to themselves while striving, the way survivors do, to hedge their bets.

Thus, Pietro ascended to chief magistrate of his hometown with little fuss. He quickly moved into offices at the town's *municipio*, its center of government, located in a wing of the former d'Ambrosso manorhouse. Not the main building, empty since the dairy had gone bankrupt after the Great War, but the old west wing, refitted with the commune's Carabinieri headquarters, offices for civil servants, and the post office. Pietro had his own large office on the second floor in what had been the villa's library. Bookshelves once lined with the marchese's collection of first editions now bulged with shabby binders of documents related to commune affairs. Behind Pietro's desk hung a photograph of il Duce wearing his First Marshal of the Empire uniform, staring resolutely into the middle distance, cross-armed.

The black four-door sedan pulled away from the walkway with a spatter of Naviglio Quarry gravel from under its wheels. The ride to Torrquadro was quick. Pietro could see the towers of the fortress-turned-silk factory-turned-VCI headquarters. Now what had it become? Degligatti hadn't said why he wanted the building, and the matter actually had stayed secret—no small accomplishment in a rumor mill like Castrubello, Pietro mused.

Then yesterday came an invitation from Degligatti for Pietro to see the renovated building for himself, the move-in apparently complete.

The sedan approached the Torrquadro entrance through heavy iron gates. On a flagpole snapped the Tricolore of the Italian kingdom, the same Savoia arms centered on green, white, red bands of color as always. However, a great coat of arms hung over the doorway. With a jolt, Pietro recognized the symbol of the Organization for Vigilance and the Repression of Anti-Fascism, Mussolini's secret police, OVRA.

An officer in silver and black opened Pietro's door. As he debarked, he smoothed his suit jacket with both hands. Two guardsmen flanking the entrance saluted briskly. They stopped Contadino from following his chief inside, to Pietro's annoyance. Before he could protest, an Italian captain hastened across the lobby.

"Welcome, Podestà Como, welcome!" Pietro's greeter was a man his same height with a horizontal hairline across his forehead. "I am Captain Costello. Please follow me to the office of the comandante!"

They made their way across the foyer toward a door in the back. Pietro knew the place well. The orderly ushered him into what had once been Ettore Vacci's own office, now starkly undecorated. An Italian officer stood behind a plain wooden desk, gave the Fascist salute.

"I am Major Gabinno, in command," he said. "I am pleased you came. Sit, signore, please. An espresso, perhaps?"

Pietro noted Degligatti's absence. "The minister...?"

"Sends his deepest regrets. Urgent business, I'm afraid. But please do sit, Signor Podestà."

Suppressing his chagrin, Pietro sank into a soft chair opposite Gabinno, who took a caffè service off a sidebar and placed it between them on the desk. He poured caffè into two demitasses, indicated the bowl of sugar cubes, and sat back in his own taller armchair. Pietro found himself forced to look slightly upward.

Non importa, he thought, and lifted his cup in a gesture of sociability. "Major, to say I am surprised is to understate. To see OVRA installed here, it is the last thing I expected."

Gabinno offered a tight-lipped smile. "We *are* called the 'secret' police, signore."

They shared a brief chuckle.

"I am sure you know our mission, Signor Podestà, I wanted to meet you, of course, and to assure you we are not here to interfere with your duties as magistrate in any way.

"We find Castrubello to be a superb location from which to carry out our work. That work, among other things, consists heavily of information gathering. You may know this already. Perhaps you also know that besides serving our Duce in a civilian capacity, Signor Degligatti holds the rank of Luogotenente Generale in OVRA. Ah, I see from your face you were not aware. In any event, at his initiative we have established this new regional intelligence center."

Degligatti was OVRA? Pietro knew he held a military rank of some type but assumed it was something honorific.

"So here, in Castrubello?"

"Here in Castrubello we will collect our information alongside the pleasant Naviglio, serenaded by birdsong. We will do our work discreetly, compiling information on every potential subversive in this region. Only by knowing the minute details of each suspect's life, his friends, family, education, public behavior, personal predilections, moral turpitude and the like, can we guarantee the perpetual preservation of the homeland!"

He touched the frame of his dark-rimmed glasses. "Another caffè?"

Pietro shook his head, held up one hand, cleared his throat. "No thank you, Major Gabinno. Regarding location, I do see the advantages of our commune. But such a large building, what will you do with all the space?"

"Yes, room to grow, it is true. We will use all of it in time, I assure you. We continue to make modifications. Our surveillance teams require darkrooms for developing film, adequate storage space for our extensive files. Larger areas will be divided into secure compartments for questioning suspects." The commandant poured himself a second demitasse, slightly lifted the pot with eyebrows raised at Pietro, who again politely demurred. "And, regretfully, our work requires we interrogate certain persons of interest over prolonged periods. The Torrquadro offers ample space for such, shall I say, 'open-ended' incarcerations." He shrugged. "You would be surprised at the stubbornness of guilty men, Signor Como. And women, for that matter." He barked a short laugh. Pietro smiled wanly. "Rest assured, we like this building for its practical potential in all regards. We are here to stay."

Pietro was annoyed. Had he known the Torrquadro was to be on the front lines against subversives, he would have certainly asked for a more lucrative lease arrangement. Eh, Degligatti, he thought, with begrudging admiration.

The major leaned back and pressed a button under the lip of his desktop. An orderly entered, cleared away the tray and the silver service, and shut the door again.

The commandant folded his arms across his chest. "Minister Degligatti, as I said, spoke highly of you. And he encouraged me to broach this next subject. You, Signor Podestà, are in a perfect position to regularly provide OVRA with information. The circles you move in—government officials, entrepreneurs, tradesmen, commoners—place you at a veritable crossroads of potential anti-regime comments, compromising data, questionable communications. We are certain that you will be patriotically eager to inform OVRA of anything anti-fascist in fact or intent. On a regular basis. Are we correct to assume this?"

"Signore, I am a loyal Italian, loyal to His Majesty, to our Duce, and to the Party," replied Pietro, heat rising on his neck. "As such, I will always defend the regime. But, sir, I am no *boccatone*, to report every misjudged word I hear. I leave that to those who care nothing of *onore*."

The major leaned forward, elbows on desk. To Pietro's dismay, he openly scoffed at him. "Ah, yes, 'honor'. May I ask the esteemed podestà, with what unit did you serve when you fulfilled your military requirement? During the Ottoman war, no?"

Pietro had answered the question enough times over the years to not lose his aplomb. "Unfortunately, Major, I drew a high number and missed active service." He raised his chin yet higher. "I proudly served with the provincial militia. Since then, I have never spared a moment to build our Italia through my business."

"Yes," said the major, drily. "At some profit, naturally." He took a folder from a drawer, perused it. "In school, signore, I believe you studied under a teacher named De Stefano?"

De Stefano! Pietro stared at the back of the folder in the officer's hands.

"I only ask," Gabinno continued, "because he also appears to have served on the draft board your induction year. As it turns out, the man was a raving sodomite, a detestable moral subversive! Did you know this?"

Como willed his suddenly thumping heart to slow. His sexual congress at age sixteen with his male schoolteacher was a difficult memory. The man's grunting violation of Pietro in the cloakroom after school, though fairly exchanged for a better final exam score, had been extraordinarily humiliating. Yet it had proved a smart move in the long run. Besides yielding Pietro the highest grade in the class, the act provided unexpected leverage when he later became eligible for conscription. "Make certain you record my draft number as a high one," he told De Stefano, who served on the district's draft council. "No matter what number I actually pick from that metal drum. Or shall I tell the Carabinieri how you assaulted the nephew of Ettore Vacci?" A risky bluff, but the terrified De Stefano had meekly complied. Pietro was assigned to the militia, a convenient, home-based, part-time commitment.

"I know nothing of this. Excuse me, Major Gabinno, but what bearing does such gossipy prattle have on anything?"

"Only this." He held up several sheets of paper from the file. "From the late professor's diary. It goes into disgusting detail about his various sexual encounters, including," he looked at Pietro's eyes widening, voice raising, "a certain 'lover' from among his male students. To hear him tell it, a quite satisfactory, and, as he tells it, consensual tryst. Quite explicit. De Stefano even provides the name." He peered across his desk with steady eyes. "We acquired the diary after the old *culattone* committed suicide."

Pietro quailed. Homosexuality was anathema; offenders were publicly disgraced, even jailed for 'unnatural indecency'. Public disclosure would ruin him. An unacceptable outcome, he determined. Better to cut his losses. "And so, then?" he asked.

An extended silence ensued. Pietro counted twenty ticks of the pendulum clock on the wall. He tried to hold the major's eyes. Submit, he thought, it is what this is all about. When he dropped his gaze, Gabinno finally spoke.

"And so, nothing, Signor Podestà. I do want to thank you for your willingness to serve Italia as another loyal set of its eyes and ears." He replaced the damning paper, closed the file. "Here are the terms. Two names by the last day of each month. Hardly taxing." The commandant watched the podestà's face blanch. He leaned forward across the desk, hard-eyed. He jabbed his right thumb up, then his forefinger as he counted. "*Uno! Due!* You start this month. This," Gabinno leaned back, knuckled the dossier. "This then goes back to sleep.

"Now, I must not further detain you, Como, an important man like yourself with many duties of much importance. But before you depart, I am to give you this." The officer passed over a sealed note.

Pietro took the message, excused himself. Contadino, cooling his heels in the portico, joined him as he hurriedly strode to the parked auto, looking neither right nor left. Once underway, controlled breathing restored, Pietro opened the sealed note. He read:

Regarding the business matter we earlier discussed, of which I have since heard nothing, I remind you of two things. First, the law states that should a business owner be guilty of treasonous opinions, he shall forfeit his holdings. Second, do not expect my patience to hang in the wind forever.

D.

Chapter 37

September 1942: The River Don

Advance formations of 2nd Corps had first arrived at the west bank of the Don by mid-August. As the divisions inserted themselves into existing defensive lines, replacing battered German and Hungarian units, Soviet forces began hard, probing attacks from across the river. These subsided by early September, allowing both sides to consolidate their positions.

The great river divided the enemy forces, Axis west, Soviets east, with one exception. On the west bank of the Don, opposite the village of Verchnij Mamon, the Russians held a heavily wooded salient, measuring roughly six miles by eight. The Soviets had thrown up a heavy pontoon bridge connecting the crescent to the Don's east bank, from where, the Italians knew, Russian armor gathered. Half of 3rd Ravenna's fifteen-mile front lay opposite this dangerous bulge in the lines.

The Wehrmacht's 318th Infantry Regiment was wedged against Ravenna's left flank and the 5th Cosseria Division. On Ravenna's right were the German 298th Grenadiers.

Nazi high command was committed to an extremely forward defense that staked everything on stopping the enemy at the river's edge, relying on swift armor reserves to plug breakthroughs. But now, the best reserves were moving to support the attack on Stalingrad southward. Quick-response forces behind the Italian front were diminishing weekly.

Eighth Army turned to a strategy the Italian generals had long espoused: a network of interlocked strongpoints somewhat back from the river, garrisoned by platoons armed with mortars, antitank weapons, and heavy machine guns. The rudimentary defenses they had inherited on the Don were devoid of such preparations.

There was no time to waste. Once the ground froze, only bombs would be able to dent it. While riflemen crouched behind trees on the existing forwardmost line, the rest of the division started building emplacements that would double as winter shelters.

6th Company was immediately engaged. With brute assistance from Ravenna's infantrymen, the engineers strung barbed wire across the sector's length. Behind the thin rifle line at the river edge, they dug antitank ditches sixteen feet wide by four feet deep. Newly laid minefields came next, Ravenna's main anti-armor deterrent. The Pignone antitank mines could be temperamental; in the cold, fingers easily fumbled. More than one man died or was maimed in a sudden blast.

The engineers laid out the strongpoints to provide interlocking fields of fire and linked them together with trenches. Men excavated large squares, shored them with logs surrounded with earthworks. Within the depressions soldiers built bunkers roofed with two layers of logs, covered with dirt. Heavy machine gun crews installed their weapons within sandbagged embrasures to cover every direction, backed up by 45mm Brixia mortar batteries.

Pack mules hauled logs to the work sites. And not only mules. Every day, men from the best-led companies strapped harnesses to their own backs and dragged chopped trees to wherever needed. Most of the conscripts knew their way around common tools. Hammering and sawing resounded from dawn to dusk. Others fired clay bricks for indoor stoves and ovens.

Construction quality depended on the zeal of supervising officers. For those who insisted on thoroughness, the results were sturdy structures, deep trenches, and stout barriers. Others were more casual with their standards, considering the digging of holes a slight to their rank. Such indifference was palpable, which affected their sergeants, then the men, making some work parties more eager to return to their tents and warm campfires than to throw up strong defenses. And beyond the attitude of individual officers, an incomprehensible shortage of basic entrenching tools hindered even the most zealous efforts.

As a result, despite the crisp, precise markings on the engineers' maps, Ravenna's defenses were inconsistent, strong in some places while dangerously crude in others.

Strafing runs by Russian LaGG-3-2 fighters increasingly harassed Eighth Army's positions. The Ravenna's meager antiaircraft batteries always spiritedly popped away in response, but Donato never saw any hits. Most often, Luftwaffe fighters not otherwise engaged temporarily chased off the menace. Yet there always seemed to be red-starred warplanes in the sky. One day, a light aircraft dropped leaflets over the engineers' work details.

"Look at this, Lieutenant," said an illiterate infantryman who had picked up one of the sheets. "What does it say? Does Ivan want peace?" A few men gathered. Donato silently read the leaflet, written in Italian under a hammer and sickle bannerhead. "Not exactly," he said, then read aloud:

"Woe to all warm-blooded Italians! Russia's greatest Comrade soon reports for duty! Hail and Welcome Field Marshal Winter!"

* * *

10 October 1942: The River Don

A scattering of gunshots to the immediate north told Donato the Soviets had spotted Biella. His own team had penetrated Russian lines a thousand yards, covered by darkness. Ivan's sentries must have detected the other six-man squad as it also tried to advance. He heard the return fire fade; the sergeant's unit must be pulling back into the woods. Donato and his men were on their own.

Recently, Soviet small unit excursions across the lines had become a debilitating annoyance. The Russians were ambushing outgunned Italian patrols on a regular basis. Battalion ordered 6th Company sappers to inflict retribution.

German intelligence had discovered that although the enemy's main arsenal consisted of fearsome T-34s, they had deployed less formidable models for reconnaissance closer to the front. Volunteers from 1st Platoon formed two tank killer squads with Donato and Sergeant Biella each leading six men. The night raid was directed at the Russian foothold on the west bank of the Don, eliminating the complication of crossing the river.

Donato's men had squirmed their way under a thin string of Russian barbed wire, then through a deep copse of trees, worming themselves forward on their bellies for the last hundred yards toward the camp of a Soviet scout squadron. Six armored vehicles—four light T-26s and two American-built mediums, called 'Stuarts'—were lined ten feet apart, muzzles pointed west. None were currently manned. A lone, nervous sentry watched how his encamped comrades would react to the continuing gunfire, his back to the woods.

Tents formed a line behind the vehicles, three hundred feet away, where the Russian tankmen had been singing sad peasant songs around a blazing bonfire and passing a bottle. They stopped at the sound of Biella's gunfight.

The sabotage mission was simple and dangerous. Two bombers per squad carried satchels of TNT. Their task was to pack the satchels under a tank and light the twenty-second fuse. Meanwhile, the remaining four men and their Breda submachine guns were to lay down covering fire. After detonation, the squad would escape in the confusion. To be on the safe side, the teams assumed they would be facing T-34s. Consequently, the canvas satchels bulged.

For his squad, Donato carried one satchel, private Fellini the other. The shooters went first, one of them clubbing the distracted sentry into a coma. All four dropped to a knee at the tanks, aimed at the enemy tents, and held their fire.

The squad's bombers came next. Donato went beneath a Stuart headfirst, twisted onto his back. Awkwardly contorting his neck, he saw the Russians strapping on gear and moving toward their vehicles. An officer fired a flare gun. The nearby landscape lit up in stark white light.

As the flare's illuminance reached ground level, Donato looked straight above him at the underbelly of the chassis. Stenciled in gray letters he read, 'GENERAL MOTORS, DETROIT, MICH. USA'.

Russian crews began scrambling toward their line of tanks. Italian submachine guns opened fire. The four Bredas could not hold the Soviets at bay for long. The raid had been intended to be a covert hit-and-run, not a blazing gun battle. Donato wedged his explosives against the fuel tank and set the quick fuse. Above him, boots clambered onto the metal behemoth. He squirmed out from under the front of the tank as its heavy engine thrummed to life.

He ran in the darkness toward the woods. Another flare. More gunfire banged away from within the woods, covering Donato and his fleeing men. Biella must have circled over this way to lend his support, he realized. The flare's stark pure light lit the landscape like a frozen lightning strike. Bullets zinged past his ears. A shell roared close overhead, struck near the Italians' gunfire. A warm hand pushed him down face-first, as from behind his exploding satchel blasted a horizontal hailstorm of metal scraps, bolts, cylinders, and stones over and past him. A helmeted German head thumped a few feet away and bounded into the bushes. Orange flames backlit the terrain.

Who had pushed him? An angel? Stupid, he thought. No one, of course, a shock wave. As he looked back over his shoulder, the wheels of the second tank blew out sideways, metal tracks whipping like flat snakes across the weeds. The turret hatch popped open; only a cloud of oily smoke emerged.

The remaining Russian armor pivoted in confusion. Unsure of the threat, they blindly unleashed their shells into the trees. The swiveling machine guns of the tanks raked in all directions, periodically ricocheting rounds off each other in their frenzy. The crescendo sounded like a full-scale armored engagement.

Donato ran for his life. Parallel to himself, not twenty feet away, his fellow bomber, Private Fellini, sprinted. The rest of his squad was ahead except for one who inexplicably paused and now looked Donato's way, unsure. Donato waved him out of there. *Vai!* At the same moment, young Fellini twisted to the ground in a red spray. Muzzle flashes strobed erratic light over the landscape. The tanks started grinding toward the tree line.

Donato scrambled to the fallen soldier's side. Machine gun rounds had torn through his lower body, splaying his intestines on the ground. Gurgling black blood, he somehow still lived, writhing on his back, his arms weakly flailing. He screamed from the agony of his evisceration. "Oh my, Papà!" the boy cried. "I am killed, Papà!"

Donato grabbed Fellini's jacket with both hands and tried to lift, but the dying man shrieked as his body further unraveled from the movement. Donato lay him back in his bloody puddle. There was no time. "Go with God, Fellini," he said. He unsheathed his field knife, covered the eyes of the boy with one hand, and ended his torment with a quick slash.

Then he ran. The ragged landscape of stones and bushes, fallen trunks and ripped branches hindered his speed. Then, miraculously, friendly artillery started dropping a few rounds near the tank encampment.

Approaching the Italian barbed wire, Donato slowed down, looking for landmarks. *Go with God, Fellini, Go with God.* The words hammered through his head. Keep your fucking wits, you fool, he told himself.

Before setting forth, the squads had received the current challenge and countersign. Today's was an idiom for good luck. Near a bone-white tree, a sentry called out: "Into the mouth of the wolf!"

"Death to the wolf!" Donato answered, completing the expression, his voice and his hands, red to the wrists, shaking.

Chapter 38

Regina Vacci was the best-educated woman in Castrubello. Most women in the town seldom advanced beyond eighth grade, if that. The daughters of prominent local families typically attended finishing school in Milan or Turin, concentrating on the social graces, French, perhaps a touch of light literature.

But from the day six-year-old Regina came into their home, Ettore and Marietta decided the girl's intellectual formation was a priority. As a Pezzoli, Marietta herself had benefited from good schooling. She was convinced of the power a thinking woman could exert in a male-centric society that expected just the opposite.

Ettore, too, wanted a proper education for Regina, seeing no reason she could not eventually assume a dominant role in his business. With her adoptive parents like-minded about her potential, Regina attended every grade of the local school, advancing with honors. In 1935 she was off to Switzerland for two years at the University of Zurich, a turn of events that dumbfounded Castrubello wags for months. She returned with the confidence to refuse being condescended to by anyone.

As Pietro is doing right now, she thought. They sat on a bench facing the cherubic stone fountain outside the Municipio. "You are a smart girl, Regina, you know how the game is played," Pietro was saying, in an apologetic voice. He tried to pat her hand, she slid it away. "As podestà, I find myself in these difficult situations. Please, help me help my uncle." He eyed Regina carefully. Difficult to read, he observed. But this conversation must go his way.

Pietro had visited Ettore the week prior, ostensibly to present the old man with a novel he wanted to read, *Il Deserto dei Tartari* by Buzzati. But, truth be told, he was there to press business. He'd arrived at an opportune time. He found Ettore ill with one of his bouts of malaria. The old man was reclining in his robe on a sitting room divan, using a fan to keep air breezing his hot face.

Patiently, Pietro laid out his argument. Yes, he understood Ettore still intended to give Donato forty percent of Vacci Costruzioni d'Italia. And it would happen! But Donato was God knew where? How it anguished Pietro to see his poor zio's health destroyed by the burden of managing the company. There was but one solution. He, Pietro, would step in to take up the mantle for the family. Never mind the sacrifice, he would do it, gladly. If Ettore would but sign over Donato's forty percent to him—temporarily, of course, temporarily!—Pietro could then lift the terrible anvil from Ettore's back. When Donato returned—God willing, the reports were troubling—Pietro would happily relinquish the shares back to the war hero. This Pietro swore on the memory of his dear late brothers.

"And as to Regina, this means no change for her?" queried Ettore, gesturing at a water glass that Pietro helped into his hand.

How ancient he looks, thought Pietro. "No, no, nothing changes there. If you still wish to assign her so much responsibility, and she is willing to take on the burden, so be it." He shrugged. "In these times can anything be certain? But no, she receives forty percent, as you desire. I have the papers with me, Zio, why delay for a second your journey back to good health?"

Despite misgivings—he always had misgivings about his nephew's actions these days—Ettore had signed. He knew his own increasing limitations. And for all his faults, Pietro was Carlo's boy. Carlo, to whom Ettore was still and forever indebted.

That was a week ago. Pietro had immediately set this meeting with Regina.

Regina said, "When you asked that we talk, you spoke of my father's enemies. What enemies, Pietro? Everyone knows how respected he is. Suddenly his countless 'enemies' are preparing to denounce him to OVRA?"

Pietro sighed patiently. How naive she was. "It is not complicated, Regina. There are those in government who want to seize VCI for themselves. They see an elderly, sick man at the helm. These people care nothing for any respect he commands, they see only vulnerability. We both know what his opinions are about the current regime, so do many others. A single charge of treason and they will pounce!"

"He makes a joke about that man in Rome from time to time. Everyone does. How can anyone think he is a threat?"

"His enemies do not need the truth, they are more powerful than that. Truth is whatever they say it is. I tell you, we must act quickly, or they will take away Ettore and his enterprise both! The only way is if I take majority control of VCI. As I say, that is the juicy plum that they all want. But I am a member of the Party and the commune's podestà. With me as the owner—on paper only, Regina—Vacci Costruzioni d'Italia is safe. If Zio no longer has a legal claim to the business, no one gains by denouncing him. He also will be safe! Ettore sees this and is why he has awarded me Donato's forty percent. But that is not enough, Regina. I need full control of VCI to fight those corrupt scoundrels! I need the forty percent he promised you. Temporarily, as I say, an emergency measure. After the crisis, I will return your shares. In the meantime, you will receive regular dividends! I know, this business is complicated, even for us men. Will you tell Ettore to release your shares to me? For his sake, will you trust me, Regina?"

Regina did not trust him. Ettore had always found ways to harness his nephew's energy to the benefit of the family's business interests. But now, she thought sadly, Papà is weary. Pietro seeks to gain the upper hand. That he lusts for VCI is abundantly clear. And she knew that Pietro was perfectly capable of denouncing the old padrone himself, uncle or not, if that was what it took. Ettore understood the same. They had talked for an hour after Pietro's visit last week and arrived at a strategy.

"So, you ask, will I ask Papà to give you my shares?" She waited, dangled the image of Pietro's prize before his imagination.

"Only for the time being, as I say," Pietro interjected.

"No, I will not."

Pietro jerked his chin up. "What—?"

"A counteroffer for you instead. I propose a complete trade. Your Naviglio Quarry & Concrete for my part of VCI, permanently." She saw Pietro's shock. "Think before you speak. It is a fair trade, Pietro. More than fair. Your concrete plant is productive but barely a sixth of VCI. Yet it will be enough for me. I will accept the loss to protect my Papà and to keep both companies secure."

"Impossible," Pietro sputtered, his mind working fast. "That quarry was my dear father's; it will go to Carlo Arturo one day! No, if you do not do as I suggest, Regina, I guarantee you, the government will sweep in like a hawk, destroy Ettore, and fly off with VCI!"

"If that should happen, I guarantee you in return, all Castrubello will know Ettore Vacci was betrayed by his own flesh and blood, Pietro Como!"

"But no! Why would that be? I am forever a faithful, loyal—"

Regina interrupted. If Pietro had reacted with anger, she would have reconsidered. But his defensive whimpering proved she had struck close to home. Pietro was complicit in the scheme, somehow. "Everyone knows your status within the Party, Pietro, of your slavish devotion to your beloved *Fascisti*. Yet, with all your prestige, and in your vaunted position, you are unable to stop the defamation of your beloved uncle or to halt his arrest? In Castrubello's eyes, you will be the impotent poseur who failed to protect—or worse, the ingrate who chose not to protect—the village's great benefactor, its famed Cavaliere of the Crown, and your own flesh and blood to boot! And how suspicious it would be, were you to then arise as the new majority owner of VCI as a result! A word here, a nod there, is all it will take, Pietro. We both know how such things work in this commune. I personally guarantee it will happen!"

Suppressing indignant rage and also anger at himself for not suspecting this side of Regina, Pietro felt her cool eyes daring him to call her bluff. She did not know anything about his arrangement with Degligatti, how could she? She guessed? Ettore guessed?

Non importa. Above all, Pietro was a good businessman. Her threats aside, he had to admit she offered a painful but interesting proposal.

Certainly, his gain would far outweigh the loss. He would control VCI, Degligatti would get his piece, and Vacci Costruzioni d'Italia would climb to new heights. Ettore would be pleased his Regina held property entirely her own, arranged at her request! And who knew what the future held? Regina was bold and, this time, lucky. But still, a woman. What did she know of rocks and concrete? Her failure at the quarry was all but certain. And he, Pietro, would be waiting.

He stood. "You so disappoint me, Regina, with your mercenary attitude. Why must everything be about money? The protection of Ettore Vacci is my sole concern. If that means your greed must take precedence for me to save him, then so be it. I accept your proposal!"

Chapter 39

6 November 1942: The River Don

The Engineer Battalion's officers were generally pleased with the progress made building up Ravenna's defenses. But of equal concern was the dismal state of the Italian supply chain. Essential materials had been glacially slow to arrive from the big depots in the rear. In six weeks of fighting the division had spent a great amount of ammunition and lost equipment of all types, much, as of yet, unreplaced. The food supply was an issue, as always, and fuel.

Worse, even as snow swirled from grim skies, many soldiers still wore the now tattered, light wool uniforms issued back in Ravenna. Their laughably shabby boots hardened like wood from the wet and cold. Hobnails popped loose and trailed from their soles as they marched. Many men overlaid them with rubber cut from the tires of destroyed Russian trucks.

Moreover, the troops lacked enough winter coats. The Ravenna needed fifteen thousand; less than half had arrived. None had gone to the engineers.

The daily ration of two hardtack galettes, turned into tooth-cracking concrete by the cold, and their single tin of meat stamped "M.A." for "Military Administration" but nicknamed "Mussolini's Ass" for its vile color and smell, barely provided the calories to keep a man functional. Italian pickets spent as much time searching abandoned root cellars for scraps as they did standing sentry. Donato wondered how much worse things would be if Italian mothers and wives had not responded to their soldiers' pleas for nuts and baked bread from home. Though stale upon arrival, the men savored the loaves like fine pastry.

Donato's growing concern for the welfare of his men, now garrisoned at one of the strongpoints, echoed that of 6th Company's other two platoon lieutenants, Palerma and Tulliu. One night, what began as a grousing, informal blowing-off-steam session, fueled by two bottles of very rough clear alcohol, led the three officers to vow, by God, they would take the matter to Captain Frati himself! At one point in their ranting discourse, Donato sat heavily down and took the group's slurred dictation as they drafted a joint letter of concern. They had blearily left it with the captain's orderly that very evening.

At daybreak, abruptly summoned to 6th Company HQ, the three officers stood at green-gilled, tilting attention.

Captain Frati was a former civil engineer and a practical man. From behind his camp desk, he waved their message at them from the previous night.

"You fools. I now clearly see my platoon leaders are imbeciles! This whining," he held the letter above his head, "is the act of schoolgirls, only actual schoolgirls would have written complete sentences. If you have a thought, express it directly to me, like a grown man. A fatuous midnight missive such as this, barely legible, written by a committee of craven drunks, does no one credit. Here is some advice, signori. Do not ever put anything into writing when under the influence! Your pathetic petition is grounds for court martial!"

Still holding the letter, Frati walked around to stand in front of his officers. At least they show concern for their men, he gave them credit for that.

"Having said that, our current supply crisis does not disappear. This suggestion of yours, to go outside the supply chain, to acquire goods from," he looked down at the badly sloped lines of lettering on the sheet, "from 'patriotic entrepreneurs' offering 'military surplus'. I take this to be your clumsy recommendation that we start buying from the local *economia sommersa?*"

All three answered faintly in bedraggled unison, "Yes, sir."

"Need I remind you, signori, that engaging in the 'hidden economy' is illegal?" the captain asked. He paused, changed his tone. "If one is caught, that is. Tell me, have any of you ever approached one of these 'patriotic entrepreneurs'?"

Donato said slowly, concentrating on his words, "I am willing to so attempt such." He slightly swayed. "Sir."

The officer snorted. "Oh, good. Well said, Tenente. Nonetheless, I do have the name of a man in Kantemirovka. My cousin gave it to me. He says this person is somebody important in the black market." The three officers allowed no surprise. "So, sober up fast, Como, and pick a few men. I will arrange for a truck."

He went to his chair, dabbed his old-fashioned ink pen in its well, scribbled on a sheet of paper. "His name is on the top, where to find him. I added a brief introduction." He made a show of tearing their own petition letter into the wastepaper pail. "Gentlemen, in the future, discretion. Understood?"

They nodded, eager to escape. Donato scanned the captain's note, then read it slower.

"Sir, permission to speak?"

Frati arched his eyebrows. "Well?"

"This name, sir. I believe my family and his are acquainted!"

* * *

9 November 1942: Kantemirovka, Ukraine

The gears of the snout-nosed Alfa Romeo 500 squealed in agony as the driver, Roberto Fasone, a sallow nineteen-year-old out of Trieste, did his best to navigate the rutted backroad. According to the Hungarian troops they had replaced on the Don, this less-traveled route to the supply dump was a time-saver.

"It would be good to avoid snapping an axle with only a mile to go," Donato said testily, as the three-ton truck bucked, changing gears. The rig had averaged twenty miles an hour, Donato reckoned. He looked at his watch; almost ten in the morning. They had set out at seven. The outbuildings of the huge base at Kantemirovka began heaving into view. .

As they approached, the number of army trucks and wagons headed for the railhead multiplied. Snow had arrived on the steppes; the road into the depot was a mash of mud and gray slush, torn up by heavy use.

"Steer for those two brick warehouses by the tracks," Donato told the driver. "That nearest one there."

The Alfa Romeo screeched to a stop near a busy siding. Russian prisoners were unloading boxcars crammed with crates of all sizes, under the close supervision of a platoon of Italian soldiers. Each trooper wore new winter overcoats, boots, gloves, and fur caps.

Biella, squeezed in between Donato and the driver, exclaimed. "What the hell? Look at these *bellimbusti*, dressed for a ball! So, these criminals in the rear get the first pickings?"

Donato and his sergeant major climbed from the cab and stretched. "Do not wander far, soldier," he ordered the driver. "Run the engine for heat, if you have to."

He told the name of their contact to the guard posted at the door, who waved them through.

Inside, at the far end of the warehouse, the seated private eyed the approaching two men with expectation and wariness. Those traits and a cunning ruthlessness, tied to an iron code, kept his crime clan, his *casca*, alive and thriving in Naples' treacherous underworld.

He was quite old for his nominal rank, early fifties, solid, big-bellied, ape-armed, and the acknowledged ruler of this military district's extensive black market.

The river of war materials flowing to the front was such prime inventory that the Neapolitan crime families had quickly monopolized its underground sales potential. A tight network of soldier-thieves and civilians systematically looted arriving deliveries. Not everything naturally, but a respectable ten percent. Much of it was repacked in unmarked parcels and trucked to the Sea of Azov. Nondescript fishing boats loaded the cargo and sailed it across the Black Sea to occupied Greece, then across the Adriatic to Bari and points west. Anything not shipped went for sale near the very depots they came from.

As local capo, the private enjoyed enormous deference. Not only did he spread around the wealth—scores of men fed at his trough—but he was sure to make severe examples of any who dared intervene, whether rivals or military meddlers who hadn't gotten the word.

"Yes?" he said, as his visitors came closer. When he folded his arms, his half-rolled sleeves revealed a large tattooed "X" on one forearm, a "Y" on the other.

"If you are the man to see, I'm here to do business," Donato said. He handed over the captain's message.

The capo read the note. A good judge of imposters, he sized up the two men. "I am Vino Penna," he finally replied. He glanced at the note. "Como?"

"I am Lieutenant Como, here is Sergeant Biella," said Donato. He took a chance. "My Zio Ettore Vacci once did business with a man named Penna. Many years ago, near Monte Terminio. He built a road down there. You are of that *famiglia*?"

"Ettore Vacci." Penna held his chin in his right hand, stared at Donato. "Ettore Vacci? I know of Ettore Vacci, him and his partner, what was his name, Pizzaro, Piazzo?"

"Pezzoli. Maurizio Pezzoli."

"Pezzoli! *Sì!* Vacci and Pezzoli! The ones who built Vaccivia across our mountain. Back when my father Fulvio was starting his thing."

"Vaccivia?"

"That road of theirs, of course. We call it that. Its real name is Umberto-something-something. Rome eventually found the stretch through the mountains too expensive to keep up, too remote. Ten, twelve years ago, they sold it to the highest bidder. It is now our family's private toll road, lucrative at that, and very handy for moving goods. So, Ettore Vacci. I will be damned. You are his grandson then?"

"His nephew, his grandnephew. Zio is still alive, still running his company."

"*Dio mio*. How old is he now, a thousand? I know that my father Fulvio," Penna crossed himself, "my father respected Vacci. 'That man understands secrets,' my father told me. I saw your uncle once, you know, years after the road. He was building that stretch through the Pontine swamps. My father had a meeting with him in Naples. Some right-of-way issue. Again, one hand washing the other. I was young, there to learn." He stood up. "So. Good. A relationship that has worked in the past, always a basis for trust. To business, then."

Donato passed Penna a list of items, held up a silver lira. "We will pay for it with these."

Penna grunted favorably at the coin, read the list briefly, then handed it back. "You find me in the process of liquidating my stock. Much is already gone. Not all. The easiest thing is to go through the storeroom, find whatever you can use. Come with me."

In an adjacent warehouse, workers were moving goods onto unmarked trucks. "All headed west," Penna said. "While we still can." He winked at Donato. "Take your time, I will see you before you go." He waved over one of the workers calling, "Filio! Show these boys anything."

Two hours later, Donato counted out the final coins. When done, the leather pouch was nearly empty. Vino watched his clerk handle the last of the transaction.

"Good business, Como," he said. "You bargain but are not obnoxious. My father said your uncle was that way. I see why our relatives found common ground."

In lightly falling snow, men continued to load the canvas-covered truck with boxes of gloves, woolen scarves, brown twill balaclavas. Already aboard were barrels of hardtack, ammunition, rolls of wire, and a few Breda M37 machine guns with boxes of their twenty-round feed-strips, along with a random accumulation of other weapons. A crate of long-barreled, Wzór-35 antitank rifles, captured by the Germans from Poland, was a late addition. Their high-velocity rounds could pierce one inch of armor, creating a ricocheting shrapnel hell inside a tank. A T-34's skin was double that thickness. "Better than nothing," shrugged Biella.

Filio, their guide, critiqued everything for them as they had worked through their list: Breda "Red Devil" M35 grenades—"I hope you won't miss your throwing hand!"; Carcano rifles—"Rugged, tough, six-round clips. But Ivan's Papàshas! There is a gun! Seventy-one round magazines!"; shells for Brixia 45mm mortars—"Too light, but perfect for rabbit hunting." "An outstanding weapon," he did grudgingly admit when Donato seized a case of Beretta 38 submachine guns, typically issued to Blackshirt units.

With none of the practical felt boots they really needed on hand, they settled for four boxes of inadequate ones like those they already had. There also was no supply of the warm, padded coats issued to Germans. "Oh, those. Long gone," Filio grinned, snaggle-toothed. Instead, nine dozen knee-length woolen versions went into the truck.

Donato added several dozen 'comfort packages': ration boxes containing chocolate, sugar, candy, and cognac. For lice-ridden men surrounded by a hellscape of violence, such small amenities could help make the difference between hope and despair. But to date, the packages had mostly wound up in rear echelon officer clubs or salons of bigwigs in Rome.

When the truck loading finished, four warehousemen hitched a Russian 76mm antitank gun to the Alfa Romeo's rear. They packed a single crate of shells into the truck bed.

"A nice fieldpiece, captured from Ivan and somehow ending up here. My gift," said Penna. "In honor of my father and your zio and the very old days!"

Donato appreciated the largesse. "Generous of you. *Grazie.*"

"Generous, but, eh," he motioned to the weapon. "Only four rounds. Not enough for anyone to want it, a pain in the ass to store, taking up space. But enjoy. Kill some Ivans with their own damn cannon."

He motioned Donato out of earshot of the rest. "Here is something much better. My advice. As a man of business, I must think ahead. To do that, I have people on both sides of the Don." He bent closer. "They tell me the Russians will hold at Stalingrad. Reinforcements are arriving. Ivan is planning to bag the whole German army, and your Italian one, very, very soon!"

Penna raised a hand. "A word of warning, that is all. As I say, I am moving my goods west. Then I return to Naples, where the victorious Americans are stockpiling unbelievable mountains of everything. My brothers and I are eager to meet our new friends!

"But, of course, you heroes must stay and do battle. For Savoia!" Penna shook his head. "That sawdust Caesar of ours, so heroically prepared to fight to the last Italian. Such courage! But listen. After you make your noble gesture and you suddenly find yourself fighting just to survive, head south to the Sea of Azov, to the fishing village of Sjedove. Look for a trawler in the harbor with a black hull and mast. Give its captain this." He handed Donato a playing card from a *briscola* deck, a *due dei denari*, with an 'X' in black ink drawn across one side, a 'Y' on the other.

Donato shrugged, "This is what?"

"A message without words, Como," said Penna. "It says to my people that I find you a man worthy of trust!"

Chapter 40

16 December 1942: The River Don

The eastern horizon flickered with yellow-white flames as the Katyusha barrage entered its second hour. Not only were the fearsome Russian rocket batteries at full throttle; numberless Soviet artillery pieces added to the hell raining down onto 2nd Corps' lines.

"*Porca puttana!*" cried a terrified private, as a thunderous explosion unleashed a deluge of debris. The men in the dugout, coated in grime, pulled their heads into their coats, curled into balls, clung to each other, anything to escape flying dirt, rocks, and splintered shards torn loose from ceiling timbers.

A whining shell struck thirty yards from where, outside on the rampart, Donato tried to see through the murk. He ducked as shrapnel spattered the face of the strongpoint's sandbagged rampart, then raised his field glasses again.

"The boys in Lupo just took a hit," called out a soldier from his observation post on the opposite corner. "Still people moving, though."

Ravenna's strongpoints called themselves by the names of wild beasts. 'Lupo' was on the right with Lieutenant Palerma's platoon; to their left 'Tigre' with Lieutenant Tulliu's men, while farther to the rear Captain Frati and the HQ complement, supported by several machine gun and mortar teams, manned 'Orso.' Donato's platoon named their own fortress 'Cinghiale' and not only because boars were fierce. Sick of rancid cans of M.A., they'd all agreed that living to eat wild boar sausage again one day was a goal worth fighting for.

"The fog is still thick," Donato told the men in the bunker, ducking inside. "For now, Ivan is blind." His breath was a frozen cloud.

The temperature outside was minus-twenty degrees. Inside, it was warmer but not warm. At their firing slits, machine gun crews had filled their helmets with hot coals and slid them under their Breda 37s to keep the lubricating oil thawed. Others did the same with rifles and submachine guns; some kept their weapons close by the bunker's potbellied stove.

The week before, another immense shelling had raked the division's entire front, followed by sharp infantry probes, only narrowly beaten back. Today's encore meant Ivan knew the defensive lines in the sector were thin and shallow. If Russian armor punched through here, they would encircle the Italian Eighth Army like they already had the Germans' Sixth.

With ripping screeches, a pair of rockets struck near the bunker. The blast knocked Donato to the floor. Ammunition boxes flew off tables; bunks and stools bounced and broke. The iron stove overturned; the disconnected stovepipe spewed acrid ash. Men struggled to pull their weapons away from the open heat, others doused the fire with blankets. Donato, bruised but unwounded, wrapped a scarf around his face and, helped by his sergeant, got men back to their posts.

On their left, Tigre strongpoint's cached ammunition furiously exploded. Orange flames stabbed skyward as its remaining garrison scrambled out for their lives.

"Try again," Donato ordered his radioman, Lamberti, a farm boy from Lucca. He probably lied about his age to join this great adventure, Donato thought. "Well?" he pressed.

The soldier cranked the device, turned dials, tried speaking. His answer was static. "Nothing, sir."

Donato cursed. Their obsolete field phones were true shit, dependent on vulnerable wire strung through now-blasted trenches. He called to Biella. "Get volunteers to chase the wire, fix the breaks." Biella paused, stared back. They both knew how futile—and deadly—the order was likely to be. "Now," Donato said.

Entrenched on the other side of Lupo, under 2nd Corps command, was the partial-strength German 298th Grenadiers. Corps HQ had lost radio contact with the 298th and told Cinghiale to pass along its order that the Germans were to reinforce Ravenna as needed. Lamberti had been trying for two hours, with no reply.

Donato exited the bunker. Despite his balaclava, gloves, and long wool coat, the cold hit him with a piercing shock. He quickly hoisted himself up on the foot ledge his men had chopped into the frozen embankment wall and lifted his eyes just over the edge. Fog still hung at ground level. Tigre strongpoint was a smoldering hole, its bunker still afire. A handful of survivors and a makeshift rifle squad were taking positions along its adjoining trenches, Lieutenant Tulliu not among them. On Cinghiale's immediate right, a thin line of smoke rose from Lupo where there was murky human activity and no flames.

He was relieved to see that the wires connected to their remote-controlled explosives still stretched forward from the strongpoint's rim. They had planted the TNT box-mines on forward ground that attacking armor might find tempting. As a tank reached the small red pennants marking each mine's location, Donato would order its remote detonation. Provided the wires stayed intact, that is.

Heavy gunfire began rattling and quickly spread. Italian 47/32 field guns, interspersed among the bunkers, began blasting blindly into the fog.

"Ivans! Ivans!" a spotter shouted. Soldiers scrambled to firing positions, machine guns rattled to life. Numerous figures were emerging from the gloom. "Hold your damned fire!" someone called out. "We are Italians!"

Gray-green clad troopers from Ravenna's 37th Regiment, some with rifles, others unarmed, ran wild-eyed past the Cinghiale perimeter. Gear jangling, they jumped the narrow communication trenches and kept going. Many looked neither right nor left, officers included. The strongpoint's defenders yelled at them to stop, but they scrambled past like grouse flushed from the brush.

A lieutenant leapt over the barrier and landed in a sprawl at Donato's boots.

"The front trench is overwhelmed! We did what we could but there are a million of those bastards," he gasped, short of breath. "No armor yet, all riflemen. We made them pay a heavy price, I assure you of that!"

Anti-personnel mines were exploding at a heavy rate. The officer, his face hidden by his balaclava except for dark eyes and icicle eyebrows, shook his head in distress "My poor men. Those are my own men! I have the map, I told them to follow me, I know the way. Why did they not listen?"

You were running too fast for them to keep up, most likely, was Donato's first cynical thought. "Help me stop them now," he said. He stood at the sandbags, half his body exposed, cupped his hands. "Rally here, Ravenna, rally here!"

The new officer did one better, took out his assault whistle and blasted three times, paused, then three again. A few of the retreating men recognized the sound and scrabbled over the broken terrain and into the enclosure.

335

Automatic fire from pursuing Soviet infantry peppered the compound. Bullets struck the sandbags and chunked up frozen ground. The newly arrived lieutenant took a ricochet in the throat and slammed against the embankment before pitching face-first to the earth. The Italians answered with a solid volley, then reloaded and fired independently. Some simply stuck their Carcanos one-armed over the top and pulled the trigger.

Breda machine guns traversed right and left, sawing at the enemy's ranks. A handful of lighter Modello 30s added their clatter despite sporadic jamming. The disorganized Russians, arriving piecemeal, could not advance against the storm of lead, no matter how their relentless political commissars harangued. At every rush forward, white parkas bloomed blood-red carnations.

Nearby, Palerma's strongpoint was overrun. But instead of succumbing to the panic around them, the survivors, led by Palerma himself, made a break for Cinghiale.

"It's getting warm," said Donato, reloading his Beretta. *"Minchia!"* cursed Palerma, landing hard from his jump past the sandbags. "Those assholes!" He stuffed another seven-round magazine into his own outdated Glisenti pistol.

With the addition of twenty more men, along with the gaggle of earlier strays, Donato estimated he had eighty or more defenders at his position. The mortar squad, commanded by Lieutenant Uccello, was hard at work; shells *phunked!* hot and heavy from tube barrels. Cinghiale was proving to be a nasty nut for Ivan to crack. From the deafening gunfire throughout the battle zone, it sounded as if other strongpoints were holding their own. Italian field guns, moved up to trench corners and the edges of minefields, provided crucial support. Infantry officers had rallied a portion of their troops; Italian return fire increased. Numerous mortar teams kept arcing shells out into the foggy void.

The Soviets inflicted casualties on the Italians, but the overlapping defenses thwarted concerted attacks. Soviet soldiers entangled themselves in snagging barbed wire or stumbled from minefields into merciless crossfires.

"Maybe not what Ivan was expecting, eh, sir?" Biella reloaded his Beretta, patted its smoking barrel. "I like this weapon," he said.

"We are drawing blood, there is no doubt." Donato rose slightly, fired a burst, crouched again. "What about us?"

"Heavy. Little chance to tend to the ones who have been hit."

"I have a signal from Division, sir!" cried Lamberti at the battered Marconi set up beside the field phone. The radioman's breath billowed in the cold. "A call to all units."

The steady *tac-tac-tac* from the heavy Bredas made Como wonder how the radioman heard anything, earphones or not.

"It's a repeated message, sir, no code, in the clear. A counterattack, that's all I can tell. Somebody is counterattacking somewhere." He took off the earphones. "I tried the 298th again, sir, but nothing."

Donato found Biella, handed him a folded message. "Get this to the Germans on our right. They're the orders we've been trying to send from Division. Do it yourself, Sergeant. Those fucking *tedeschi* need to get off their asses and give us some help."

A new noise. Russian armor. An uneven line of tanks, forty yards apart, approached in support of their pinned-down infantry. Sharp, bright daggers of yellow-orange blazed from their cannons. But even as they did, antitank minefields started playing their parts. Up and down the tank line, to where it disappeared in the persistent fog, the armored vehicles were triggering blasts. Still, most of them kept grinding ahead. Their machine guns and cannon swept Italian positions.

Time for the box-mines? Visible from the strongpoint, six of the red markers still fluttered. No tanks were yet near, although if several kept plowing straight ahead they'd soon be within range.

No, Donato decided, looking at the armor screen lumbering ahead. No Russian T-34s were involved in this assault, this armor was more like what they had encountered on their raid. Their big boys have not yet entered the fight, he realized. We'll save the fireworks for them.

Before he could gather a grenade squad together, he saw a team of Blackshirts zig-zag past the strongpoint toward the nearest tank. Three men opened fire with their submachine guns as two others threw incendiary grenades. Flames burst on the armor plating, doing little damage but sticking like glue. One of the Blackshirts threw a TNT satchel into the blaze, then the team broke and ran, like high-spirited boys stealing figs from some nobleman's tree. The explosion shuddered the tank to a standstill, its cannon barrel flopping down on the chassis with a bang. The turret lid flew open. As the Russian crew escaped, backlit by fire, Cinghiale riflemen unloaded their weapons at them.

A clamor of iron came from the rear, as a mixed collection of German mechanized tank destroyers, just over a dozen, rumbled through the snow over the broken ground.

"This is the counterattack?" called out Lieutenant Palerma. "I thought we would be seeing an entire division!"

Though the tank destroyers could not match a tank in speed or maneuverability, their weapons were deadly effective. Donato knew this unit, recently created from pieces of others. Its commander was an Oberstleutnant named Rolf Maempel, known for his overweening self-confidence and outstanding soldiering.

The unexpected attack by the Panzerkamfgruppe wreaked havoc on the Soviets. Russian infantrymen fumbled back into the anti-personnel minefields. Maempel's guns methodically blasted the lighter enemy armor into twisted rubbish. Without losing a vehicle, the armor group pivoted north. Russian infantry pulled back toward the river.

"Ivan has faltered," Donato commented, scanning the ground in front of the strongpoint. Rifle fire sporadically continued, but Soviet mortar bursts slowed. Though bullet-riddled and blasted, Cinghiale had held out.

"Faltered, true," Palerma agreed. "But those bastards feed men into the fight like kindling, and they have a lot of kindling. The Russians intend to bleed us out."

The garrison removed their dead to outside the bunker, thirty-three already stiff corpses stacked like wood. Inside, Corporal Lugano, the unit's single medic, tended a floorful of moaning wounded. A lack of most essentials rendered him more caretaker than healer.

In less than an hour, Biella returned. "I got to the Germans," he reported, stamping his icy boots. "Their communications officer said they will no longer talk to us. 'We answer only to German orders now' he told me." The sergeant's gloved hands hissed as he pressed them directly onto the re-rigged stove.

Donato seethed. "*Che cazzo!* And Maempel's group won't be back any time soon. We must stand, regardless."

Thirty functional defenders crowded inside the bunker, by Donato's best estimate. Outside, another two dozen or so manned the ramparts, trading off with shifts from the bunker every half-hour. The ones who were able tried to eat.

After warming himself, Donato pulled his balaclava back over his head. He laced up his boots, which he hadn't dared to take off. Frozen stiff, the leather was iron. He tugged on his gloves, thawed just enough to bend his fingers into. He pushed open the log door and stepped out.

The fog had lifted, and he looked up to see stars. The sky was clear except for the distant southeast quadrant. There, eerie flashes and the delayed thump of artillery marked where the German Sixth Army was strangling to death in Ivan's noose. Tracer fire laced the heavens like rosary beads.

"Stay alert," he demanded loudly. "They may wait for light, or we may be at this nonstop. Have heart. The longer we hold, the closer our reinforcements get." He doubted that was true. "We must be strong for each other!"

He had no idea if his little pep talk helped. The men stayed exactly as they were. His brain felt like it was shrinking from the cold. He stamped his feet, flapped his arms, felt the start of a tingle. He went to the west of the compound. There, two trucks sat rumbling, the garrison's entire mobile capacity. One was the Alfa Romeo 500 diesel he had taken to Kantemirovka. A pair of mechanics had a small fire going under the truck's differential. The only fuel they had was already in the truck's tank.

The second truck was a gas-engined Fiat 626. The strongpoint did hold some petrol reserves. Garrison mechanics assured Donato the transport would start on its first try, but he still ordered its engine idled ten minutes every hour.

The garrison's three 45mm Brixia mortars sat apart at the rear of the compound. Their crews huddled over a fire in an empty oil drum.

"You did good work today, boys," Donato told them. By way of acknowledgment, they stiffly twisted their shivering torsos to him without moving their hands from over the flames. "How long do we stay here, sir?" a man asked through a scarf mummied around his head and under his helmet.

"The long answer is, we wait for German reinforcements to come up, but HQ has no idea when." He had to say something.

"And the short answer, sir?"

Lieutenant Uccello, standing at the fire, got Donato off the hook.

"The short answer is, Eugenio, what do you care? Your wife and her boyfriend are praying you stay right here!"

Chapter 41

17 December: Cinghiale strongpoint, morning

A great roar of *"Ura!"* erupted from the Russian lines. Biella had heard the war cry numerous times over the preceding twenty-four hours. The Italians' scattered response of *"Savoia!"* hardly matched the enemy's volume. But from what the sergeant could see from his observation post, there was a far larger problem.

Past the barbed wire and minefields, above the bare branches of the river trees, rose a vast cloud of engine exhaust.

"Lieutenant!" he called out. "Ivan's big stuff!"

Donato joined his noncom on the rampart. There was no doubt. For weeks, scouts and deserters told of heavy armor formations amassing across the Don. In the last twenty-four hours, the Soviets had sent five rifle divisions to clear away Ravenna's line, the armor waiting to blow through the gap and cut off retreat. But dented islands of the Italian defenses still resisted. Now it appeared the Soviet commander could no longer wait. He was sending his tanks to kick open the door themselves.

Russian infantry crashed ahead, pausing at times to lay down heavy fire. The hoarded T-34s roared forward. Squadrons fanned north and south, but the bulk of the enemy corps plowed straight at the Italian center, exactly where the 118th Battalion engineers had excavated tank traps and sown antitank mines. The ground rocked with explosions. Italian 47/32 gun batteries lit into the struggling first vehicles. Shells battered the monstrous tanks, many glanced off the slanted plating. But some struck turret seams and wheelbases and sent hot metal chunks into the sky. Tanks that escaped the traps gunned their engines, only to charge into murderous minefields.

Russian infantry began wiping out Ravenna's artillery crews, and not every tank struggled into the mines. Taking time to swivel and aim, their 76-millimeter cannons zeroed in on the closest Italian 47/32, which was no match at all. As one bothersome Italian gun after another was destroyed or abandoned, more of the T-34s lumbered forward, led by companies of Russian pioneers forging a path.

Yet not quite a breakthrough. Of the tanks that lucked their way past mines, many rammed snout-down into tank traps. Most made it out with enough frantic gear-stripping, but some were fully stymied and forced to wait for tractor-tows under lethal Italian shelling.

The Cinghiale garrison faced increasingly stiff fire. The wood embrasures of the pillbox disintegrated into splinters after the Russians half-dragged their two-wheeled Maxims into position and raked the structure's face. The grind of Soviet tanks moving ahead grew even louder. Superior Russian firepower began to tell.

"Get somebody over to the German 298th again," Donato yelled at Gornati, Palerma's platoon sergeant. "We need those heavy antitank guns of theirs. Tell them who cares who they report to? If we go down, so will they. It's now or never."

Donato leaned back into the cold sandbagged parapet outside the bunker, firing his Beretta in bursts, reloading. Along the same wall, his men manned compact German army GIHz explosion igniters numbered one to six, matching each of the mines. The soldiers hunched below the barrier waiting to hear the lieutenant call out their numbers.

The roar of individual tanks had climbed to a deafening crescendo as Soviet armor units pressed relentlessly ahead. Donato watched more and more of the humped metal beasts shoulder their way out of the woods, cannons blazing. The Russian pioneers had steadily opened gaps in the barbed wire, staked paths past the tank traps, and cleared the way through minefields. The tanks accelerated through the openings.

Donato kept his eyes on the string of small flapping pennants that marked where his platoon had set their mines. He watched as one T-34 lumbered within feet of a buried box of TNT.

"Three! Fire three!" he loudly ordered.

With a thunderous roar, the tank flipped like a giant's toy. When metal debris and rocks stopped showering down, Donato saw the tank upside down, its cannon buckled, one row of wheels missing. After a moment, an escape hatch clanged opened in the tank's exposed bottom, as four crewmen awkwardly exited. Two went down to the strongpoint's Bredas. The other pair scrambled into a nearby mound of greasy snow, bullets clipping at their heels.

"To Satan's hell with you, red scum!" cried the man who'd blown the charge. The tanks kept coming.

"Number Four!" shouted Donato, then, "Now, one! One!"

The first explosion convulsed the ground close to their position. The T-34, centered directly over the TNT bundle, launched ten feet, crashed down on its tracks, and disappeared in a yellow fireball, its smoke and heat billowing toward the strongpoint.

The other charge failed, despite the operator re-twisting the igniter knob. The tank pivoted hard toward the Cinghiale position. Behind it was another.

"Two!" shouted Donato, but this was desperation. The explosion blasted a deep crater, but the intended target shook off a downpour of rocks, kept trundling ahead.

Both tanks fired. One round landed short, the other whistled hot and close just past their heads. The tanks' twin machine guns sprayed the Italian ramparts; defenders ducked and dived, some too late. With the T-34s only forty feet away, Lieutenant Uccello's crews desperately struggled to depress their mortar angles nearly parallel. The turret on the forward tank swiveled.

The captured Russian 76mm antitank gun, Penna's last-minute gift to Donato, suddenly roared from its sandbagged position next to the compound. Its crew had saved its four rounds as if they were gold, under orders to fire only if they could not miss. It fired now.

The shell flew over the tank into the torn ground beyond. *"Sangue dei santi!'* cried Biella, nearby. *"Favanculo porco cane!"* The first T-34 returned fire point-blank. Half the bunker roof vaporized in a cloud of jagged shards. The Italians' 76 hit home with its second shot. Steel tracks whip-cracked across the battlefield at decapitation-level. Immobilized but still alive, the big tank re-aimed at the 76mm gun.

The Italian crew fired first. The round catapulted the T-34's turret into the minefield, triggering two explosions, the second one shredding a Soviet infantry platoon with hissing shrapnel.

The remaining tank ignored the cannon and charged the Cinghiale perimeter at full speed and crashed through the thin belt of barbed wire surrounding the base. Its twin Degtyaryov machine guns began pumping two thousand rounds a minute into the enclosure. The onslaught chewed the rear mortar crews and weapons to bits, catching Lieutenant Uccello madly trying to load a final round.

Donato shouted, "Hand grenades! The machine guns!" Men, fixed to the ground, did their best to respond and heaved the red-cased grenades blind.

Most fell short. A few struck the tank without doing much damage. But the racket forced the Russian machine gunners to instinctively pause, and the Italian antitank cannon fired its last round. It tore a jagged hole in the plating that exposed the deafened cannoneer and top-seated gunner. A second volley of grenades hit the mark. Furious flames and thick, stinking smoke billowed out.

The bunker was ablaze. Through the smoke, the sound of more armor on the move. "No time to rest!" shouted Donato. "To your positions!" Men stumbled back to where they could sight the enemy. The fierce cold, momentarily pushed back by adrenalin and the heat of the infernos in front and behind, blasted the troopers' senses again. A stinging wind lifted the battle-haze.

The battlefield had changed drastically during Cinghiale's private war. Hundreds of Russian tanks poured through and past the remaining Italian positions in a race to the Italians' rear, to the command posts and supply depots that gave life to Eighth Army.

Sergeant Gornati appeared at Donato's side. "The courier has returned from the Germans. They're pulling the hell out!" Donato shook his head, said nothing. The front was fragmenting. Would the extra antitank guns have made the difference? No time for this, he thought. "Tell the men nothing," he instructed.

Fresh Russian infantry was following the tanks to clean out remaining defenders. After thirty-six hours of fighting, not only Ravenna but the entire 2nd Corps was on the verge of collapse. Troops everywhere were pulling themselves out of overrun compounds, mostly on foot, a few kicking the flanks of terrified, spavined mules, others commandeering any vehicle they could find. Artillerymen were driving off in gun tractors, the intact detached guns left behind. Soldiers clung to overloaded trucks that bounced west from the river. Panic was taking hold.

"I have orders, Lieutenant!" The unexpected voice was that of the radioman, Lamberti. Donato thought the private was dead. "One long transmission then silence." He handed over the hastily scrawled note, stuck his freezing hands back under his armpits.

"We are ordered to retreat to 2nd Corps HQ at Taly," Donato shouted to Palerma, over the din of gunfire. The Ukrainian town lay thirty miles southwest. The officer looked from Donato to the Russians on three sides. "How?"

"Gather the remaining TNT against the front wall. We'll blow it when we go. Pull every other man off. Tell Biella to load them onto one truck, get things started. We will keep the heavy machine guns firing until the last minute. Then, after a grenade into the TNT, I bring up the rear with the other half of the men. Gather whatever supplies we can, and no one drops his weapon. Those beet-suckers catch us in the open, they won't accept surrender."

Palerma waved he understood.

Donato ran into the burning log structure. From under a cot, he pulled the leather pouch containing his maps, slung it across his chest. Other men arrived and grabbed what they could. It was not much; the blaze was out of control.

Outside again, Donato appreciated that there was no wild-eyed hysteria among the troops. We're all too exhausted for that, he thought. He joined the remaining troopers firing at the attackers. The fight was desperate, though not yet hand-to-hand. He lost track of time in the melee.

"Lieutenant Palerma says, done, sir!" a private announced. Donato saw the TNT, piled at the wall of the compound opposite the flaming bunker. He shouted to the remaining men, "Pull back. Stay in order!"

The remaining heavy machine gun kept sawing away throughout the preparations until Donato sent a runner to pull those men as well and blow the gun with a grenade.

When the Soviet infantry realized they were no longer under fire, they crashed over the embankment in a rush. They met a volley from the rearguard.

"Go! Now!" Donato ordered. The garrison's last men ran, scaled the back of the Fiat, hung onto the tailgate, climbed on top of the cab and hood. The truck, in low gear, started up the ramp.

Donato pitched one of his M35s toward the heap of TNT, then another. Bullets whizzed past him, one tore through his coat sleeve. He turned and ran hard after the truck. Behind him, with an unearthly roar and an upheaval of earth, Cinghiale strongpoint volcanoed.

Chapter 42

17 December: West of the Don

The garrison convoy gathered itself after pushing a rugged two miles west. The two forlorn trucks rested in the shadow of an annihilated artillery emplacement, next to a wall of leaky sandbags. Ravenna survivors streamed past. The fireball that once was Cinghiale had blended into the glowing cauldron of the entire 2nd Corps front.

Firing continued ahead, behind, on both flanks from Russian infantry following up on the armored breakthrough. Mortar shells crumped, machine guns rattled, artillery shells screamed on their long arcs west. Soviet tanks by the score roared past, ignoring the withdrawing enemy all around them, intent instead on ravaging the Axis line of retreat.

Palerma told Donato, "Our count is thirty-nine healthy, eight wounded. Three of those can still shoot a rifle. Lugano says the others are touch and go." Both men flapped their arms across their chests, paced in place. The wounded were problematic, space-wise, food-wise. "You and me, Sergeant Major Biella, Sergeant Gornati from my platoon, that's what remains of command."

"What of the trucks? Our weapons?"

"Both trucks are running, but the Alfa is low on diesel, half a tank at best. The Fiat is all right and has forty gallons of petrol in reserve. We brought some food, not much, including three crates of galettes, frozen solid. The men saved the extra blankets we had in the shed. Other odds and ends, weapons, lanterns, a few clothes besides what's in the duffels we managed to grab. We will not be staying this pretty." He paused as both he and Donato looked to their shabby, whiskered men. Donato snorted. "The least of our worries."

"As far as weapons go," Palerma continued, "everybody is armed. Adequate ammunition in their pouches, more in the trucks. We are not lacking in that regard. The men carry maybe a grenade apiece, but there are three boxes of them in the back of the Fiat. No TNT, no machine guns, nothing like that. No radios."

Donato pressed his eyes. "All right. Here's what I think. Taly's no good, that one road can't handle all the troops pulling back. By the time they finally get there, HQ will already be gone, I guarantee. We are smarter to try to beat Ivan to Kantemirovka where we know there are supplies." He unrolled the map from his leather case. Palerma took off a glove, snapped a match with his thumb to make light in the late afternoon gloom.

"Here is Kantemirovka." Donato stabbed with his free hand. "Us, we are here. We take the Hungarian shortcut like last time. That's this line. We arrive and find what we find." He paused, looked at Palerma, decided to hold back any talk of a trawler on the Azov. "From there we see where others are headed."

Palerma nodded. It was freezing standing there. He did not care where they went. "All right, Lieutenant. Just give me my orders."

Donato patted Palerma's shoulder. "I order you to help me not make mistakes."

The officers hiked to the two trucks. Donato climbed into the Fiat 626.

"Kantemirovka. The back way," he told the driver.

"I remember, sir," said Private Fasone.

* * *

A bleak sunrise lifted night's black shroud, exposing the completeness of 2nd Corps' collapse. Frigid winds blasted snow across miles of abandoned equipment. Roadside corpses, mouths frozen agape, rigidly guarded the withdrawal. An assortment of disconnected, ragtag columns had spontaneously formed as units fled the battlefield. No one seemed to know exactly where to go except west. The bulk of the retreating corps moved down the wide road to Taly, but formal command had evaporated. Junior officers managed whatever men they had with them; generals were absent. Radio communication did not exist. Men simply followed men in front of them, and while some formations struggled to keep a military semblance, with officers shouting them into lines, many gave up on such pretense.

For the past twenty hours, the Cinghiale garrison had bounced along the ice-covered back trail toward Kantemirovka in a line of other retreating survivors. So much for secret Hungarian shortcuts, Donato glumly thought. Pillars of smoke to the west, north, and behind marked the range of the Russian armor's rapid advance. Donato prayed to God that Kantemirovka with its railhead was still intact.

The trucks followed behind a tattered Blackshirt contingent trying to keep pace with the PanzerGrenadier company in the lead. The Germans, in their bulky, white winter outfits and felt-padded boots, used their motley collection of halftracks, trucks, and mule-drawn sleds to alternate men marching or riding. They never paused or looked back, except to fend off any Italians who tried to hitch rides. The *tedeschi* are happy to keep us at their rear, Donato thought, between them and relentless, bloody-minded Ivan. Only the need to conserve their limited fuel kept the Wehrmacht vehicles from racing beyond sight.

The rest of the column was a shambling herd formed from pieces of a dozen units. They trudged hollow-eyed, blankets shawled over shoulders and heads, many without weapons. Altogether, from the Germans plowing ahead to the handful of teamsters riding bareback on their unharnessed mules at the rear, the force, if force it was, numbered close to seven hundred men.

The undulating landscape was stark, vast, and solid white. Temperatures approached twenty-five below. After a time, Biella, hanging to the cab roof as he stood on the Fiat's running board, rapped on the side window. He jerked a thumb to the snowy field they were passing. Beyond him, Donato watched a German *Feldgendarmerie* captain execute prisoners as a tracked carrier idled nearby. The officer methodically snapped Luger rounds into the napes of dark forms already lying on the ground face-first. The rest of the unit waited at ease. The German field police were known as the *kettenhundos*, 'chain dogs', for the large steel crescents they wore on chains around their necks. The unit had the authority to shoot deserters on sight. Donato ran a gloved hand across his stubbled chin. With thousands of men on the wander, the Nazis were still chasing deserters?

Biella pressed his mouth to his cupped hands against the window glass. "Those were Italian boys!" he shouted.

Two hours later, Donato awoke from a fitful nap to his driver's voice. "The second truck is stopping, it is signaling." Donato looked to the wing mirror, saw the Alfa Romeo's lights flashing. "Pull over," he said.

As the retreating column kept shuffling by, both trucks squealed to a halt. The men aboard peeled out, flexed their arms, stamped their feet in place. Others were off to snowbanks to release their bladders and bowels.

"No more diesel," Lieutenant Palerma said, walking up from the Alfa Romeo. "And, sir, check your men. If you are like us, there may be dead."

Gornati approached. "Robustelli makes it three, Lieutenant," he said. "Corporal Lugano here says exposure."

Biella went back to his truck to see how things stood. He shook his head at Donato's unspoken inquiry. "All right for now," he reported.

They carried away the dead men with their frozen, purple-skinned faces, rigid in their seated postures, and left them in a roadside snowbank.

"The men must start walking, sirs," Lugano told the officers. "Frostbite is a danger. They must get their blood circulating, or soon I will be chopping off noses and toes."

"I will march with half, you ride with the rest," Donato told Palerma. "We trade groups off every half-hour." Reloaded, reorganized, the remaining truck and the men forced their way back into the slogging mob.

* * *

19 December 1942

A haggard army courier on a spectral gray horse exhaling dense steam plodded the length of the column and announced the dire news: Taly had fallen. Far worse, Kantemirovka was under heavy attack by two Soviet armored brigades; part of the depot was already burning. Beleaguered Italian generals had escaped in a handful of vehicles. No new orders were forthcoming.

For the first time since the march began, the four PanzerGrenadier officers, led by a major, and a smattering of captains and lieutenants from among the Italians, met to discuss how to proceed. They decided to keep pushing southwest to the German defenses at Luhansk, about a hundred miles. Certainly, the Russians could not have reached that far!

After three hours, with early darkness approaching, they arrived at a sizeable village. The column stopped in its tracks, numb with fatigue. Most men sat straight down in the snow. After a brief reconnoiter, two of the German halftracks approached the village down the main road, trailed by a platoon in two lines.

Donato and Biella hiked across a snow-crusted rise for a better view. The town appeared dead.

"The Vicenza, I think," said the sergeant, handing the field glasses back. Comprised of older conscripts, poorly equipped, the 156th Vicenza Division was sent to Russia to keep civilian order behind the front lines. But after the Germans had diverted their reserves to Stalingrad, the Vicenza received orders to advance into combat. Without motorized transport, the division arrived late to the fight and piecemeal at that. This is what happened to one of the pieces, Donato thought.

"Russian armor caught them. Looks like they stayed to fight," he said.

Biella grunted. "Old men can't run."

The town was a typical collection of wooden buildings clustered around a square. Gray tendrils of smoke still rose from a few half-burnt structures, their walls tattooed by bullets. A truck had embedded itself in a brick garden wall. Open-hatched, an obsolete Italian tankette sat wheelless in the snow, looking like a half-sunk boat. Encrusted in the falling sleet, prone figures dressed in gray rags littered walkways and streets. An Italian antitank gun sat alone in the small piazza. There were no destroyed Russian tanks or dead.

The PanzerGrenadier vehicles clanked directly down the main street, not bothering with the nicety of avoiding corpses. Nazi troopers fanned out, efficient as always, kicking at doors, securing intact buildings. To their surprise, seventy or eighty Eighth Army troops emerged from a few of the buildings, a random fragment of early refugees from the debacle on the Don.

The Blackshirts shook themselves into a skirmish line and advanced. With a keening squeal of abused gearboxes, the handful of Italian trucks in the column jolted, then moved. Behind them, the shabby crowd of numb men stirred.

"A few Italian platoons beat us here," Donato told Palerma upon his return. "The Germans are taking over, moving into the best buildings. It will be a scramble for the rest of us to find enough roofs for everybody. If anything of food or supplies remains in the village, the *tudri* will surely hoard it."

Around them, a swirling wind whipped the snow into spirals.

"*Merda*, Lieutenant, we must find ourselves cover, someplace to sleep." Palerma pulled at his woolen coat collar as if he could stretch it over his head. "And food. The men have not eaten in a day and a half."

Donato cleared his balaclava of ice with a swipe of his gloved hand. "No, you're right. But here we are at the ass-end of things, among the last to go in." He pointed off to his left. "I will take a squad, circle around that hill and enter from the south. We'll look for a farm building we can use, something just outside of town. You and the boys come in on the main road through the village. I will meet you as you arrive."

It took Donato and nine men a long sixty minutes through thickening snowdrifts to skirt the town. Two-thirds of a mile from the first of the hamlet's buildings, next to a burnt-out dwelling, they came to a barn. It was a ramshackle wreck with a hole in the roof. Inside was empty, only bales of straw remained. But within no time, Donato's squad had a fire going in the middle of the dirt floor, using worm-eaten planks torn from stalls as kindling. Although most of the smoke found its way out the opening in the roof, the air inside soon grayed. But it didn't matter to the men clustered at the saving heat.

Donato met Palerma's truck at the village's north end. They struggled through the mass of desperate men seeking shelter. When they arrived at the barn, serene in its relative remoteness, they drove the truck directly inside. It filled a quarter of the space, but the fire's warmth would keep the vehicle's transmission operational.

Men cracked off their stiff coats, frozen solid, and stood them along the walls to thaw. Frostbite had set in among some soldiers. As Corporal Lugano helped one pull off his sock, a swollen black toe came with it, the foot too frozen for the soldier to feel pain. The medic treated the grotesque wound with a mix of cognac and melted snow.

Within an hour, Biella and Gornati returned from a bartering foray into town, cursing at the mounting blizzard. They had left the barn with fifteen gallons of the Alfa Romeo's gasoline reserves. They entered carrying four large buckets of potatoes, with more stuffed in their coat pockets.

"The artillerymen on that gun tractor were ready to trade," said Gornati. The two men held their buckets up.

Donato handled some of the potatoes, scrubby but mostly not rotten. "Soup, I think," he said. "Use them all. Throw in hardtack to thicken it. One cup per man, we save what's left. It should be enough to last for a few days. Sergeants, good work."

Biella spoke up. "Something else, sir. Major Raimondo is here in the village." The sergeant paused as the news sank in. None of them had heard from the 118th Engineer Battalion's commander in over a week. "He commands some of the men who got here first, from 5th Company and our 6th, others from Battalion HQ. Less than fifty in all and no officers except him. They arrived yesterday, holed up in an izba, bigger than this. They have two trucks, a few mules, sleds. Lieutenant," Biella added, "he orders us to join him."

"What of Captain Frati?" asked Palerma before Donato could respond.

"The captain was killed, sir. The major is the last officer in the battalion besides yourselves. He is now the highest-ranked Italian in the village."

Donato considered the information, set it aside for the moment. "Who here wants to play chef? It will mean an extra bowl."

Thirty minutes later, the Cinghiales were fed. The officers and their noncoms sat to the side, sucking hot broth from tin mugs. Palerma asked Donato, "What about those orders?"

Donato sipped, trying to make the meager ration last. "We will comply, of course. But the men are exhausted, tonight we stay here. We couldn't get them to move if we promised naked women were waiting." Palerma smiled. Donato went on. "So, tonight we digest this feast of ours, get some rest, tomorrow morning we join forces. It will be good to have Raimondo in command. The major has always been level-headed."

* * *

THUMP! THUMP! THUMP! The barred barn door was a sudden drumhead of pounding.

"*Fica d'una puttana!*" Biella rolled from his bedroll. They had kept lanterns lit so they wouldn't stumble into their shit buckets in the dark. He approached the continuous racket. Ready to tangle with the late-night intruder, he removed the bar.

The doors blew open with a storm-blast of wind, along with a platoon of white-clad *Feldgendarmerie*, led by the same Nazi captain from that afternoon in the field. He was holding the same Luger. Behind them, Biella could see the shape of their troop carrier, engine running.

"Get out!" the captain shouted in harshly-accented Italian. He was a big man made bigger by the bulk of his winter gear. "Here is now our shelter!"

351

Donato was awake and on his feet. This unit was straight from hunting down deserters in a snowstorm, ready to eat and sleep. But he'd be damned if this *pezzo di merda* thought he could order his men out into the cold.

"Capitan," he said, willing himself to remain tactful. "There is room for all." He kept his German words simple. "The fire, join us," he added, gesturing.

The German officer sized up the limited space.

"Out!" he repeated and signaled to his lieutenant, who gave a guttural command. The Germans spread out, unslung their MP 38 *maschinenpistoles*, and pointed them at the room. When Gornati made a move toward his rifle, the lieutenant aimed his weapon upward and fired a deafening burst into the rafters. The Italians froze.

"Out! Out!" the commander repeated. "Out, *makkaroni!*

Donato stood hands on hips. "We give you half, but we stay!"

The captain struck him in the face with the stock of the Luger.

Donato fell backward, his broken nose gushed gore like a fountain. The room erupted with shouts. A German fired, men dove for cover, an exchange of gunshots ripped the room. Officers on both sides shouted to regain control. Someone, Lugano, yelled, "Stop! Stop!" as he crouched by a figure on the floor. The inane firefight ended as abruptly as it had begun.

Donato, his nose slopping blood, saw that the man down was the radio operator, Lamberti. The boy stared at the medic, on his face an unspoken question.

"Gone," Lugano said.

Hot rage filled Donato. He fought his urge to lunge at the Nazi captain, to strangle the man to death with his bare hands. But the Germans would simply kill them all, name them deserters. He looked around, saw no other casualties on either side.

The captain ignored the dead man, loudly addressed Donato instead. "Your fault. Now, OUT!"

His men disarmed the Italians and drove them coatless, some bootless, into the subfreezing night. Gornati and Biella carried out their dead man. The Germans went through the Italian truck, removed its cans of reserve petrol. At his captain's command, a sergeant started the battered vehicle and backed it out the double doors into the blizzard. The Germans replaced it with their armored troop carrier. The door closed momentarily then flew open again. Grenadiers disgustedly tossed out armfuls of coats and bags and other rags and gear the Italians had left behind. The door banged closed again. The lock-bar slammed into place.

The men grabbed garments and blankets to keep themselves warm, huddled near the truck against each other, too immediately cold, too needy, to register a reaction at events.

The searing pain in Donato's face and head provided him an intense focus. He scraped the fast-freezing blood and snot from his face.

"Lieutenant Palerma will take you to Major Raimondi. He is here in this village and will lead you now. I will stay. I want all our weapons back. When the Germans calm down, I will talk to them again."

The soldiers quickly acquiesced. Self-preservation was all that mattered, and the storm was worsening. They gathered up the rest of the jetsam the Germans had thrown out. Donato found his bedroll and precious map case in the heap. He bid Palerma and sergeants farewell.

"If I do not see you again, thank you," he told them. "Get these men there fast and be certain Raimondi marks the time you arrive. There may be questions later."

"Yes, sir," Palerma nodded, astute enough to leave things at that. Donato watched as he, Gornati, and Biella tramped the little troop into town.

Heavy sleet and the sub-zero winds had already frozen shut the truck door. Donato dragged Lamberti's body from the truck bed, then stood on the running board and urinated on the door handle to thaw it open. He propped the corpse in the passenger seat, sat next to it behind the wheel and waited. The cold had stopped his nose from bleeding. He checked the Fiat's fuel gauge. One-quarter full.

After forty minutes, more than enough time for the Cinghiale contingent to have reached Raimondi's doorstep, Donato exited the cab. As he did, a figure suddenly loomed from the dark, cutting through the curtain of swirling snow. He carried two knapsacks and two rifles.

"Here to assist, sir," Sergeant Biella said.

Donato jerked a curt nod. He had not expected this.

They tore a strip of canvas from the tarp arching over the truck bed and fed it into the gas tank, leaving one end to hang out as a fuse.

With a gaspy sputter, the truck started up. Donato backed it off twenty feet, aimed it at the door of the barn. He took off his lieutenant's coat, traded it with Lamberti's, then strapped his officer's holster around the boy's waist. He slid the soldier into the driver's seat. Wedging a half-box of the frozen hardtack onto the gas pedal, the truck idled in neutral.

Awkwardly squeezing himself over Lamberti's lap, Donato put the rig into first gear. He hit the ground hard, rolled to the side. At the same time, Biella lit the fuse on the moving truck. It crashed through the barn door and, after a long moment, exploded. Cries sounded from inside.

The two men jogged to where they had left their gear in a dark stand of trees, then kept moving. They heard the rumble of the German halftrack. With a crash, the flaming vehicle blasted out of the barn, pushed back the mangled Fiat, and blew apart. Desperate figures, some afire, fled the building. Heavy white smoke poured into the sky, quickly lost in the dense snowfall of the rapidly thickening, howling tempest. Further down the road, from the town, no reaction.

"The boy is avenged," Biella said, as they slowed to a steady trudge. The blizzard erased their footprints. "Where now?"

"Shelter fast or die. I studied our map. It shows a collective farm that lies not far south. We find someplace there, sleep a few hours, get going before dawn, set out for the Sea of Azov. Two hundred miles."

"Huh. Sea of Azov." He looked at Donato, realizing the officer had been harboring a plan since the start. "A good stroll. What then?" The unrelenting wind whipped from behind, adding a boost to their steps.

Donato patted his breast pocket where he kept the marked *due dei denari* card from Penna. "Then, Biella, we play our hand."

Part II: The Piazza

1944

Chapter 43

November 1944: Above the Gothic Line

The throaty roar of forty B-24 Liberator bombers reverberated over the Tuscan landscape, spooking underfed swine in their pens and rattling cookware on shelves in dozens of villages below.

First Lieutenant Lawrence Salski concentrated on maintaining his aircraft's place in formation. The squadron flew in four 'boxes' of ten bombers each, staggered at varying altitudes. His bomber's position was at the left edge of three planes flying nearly wingtip to wingtip in V formation. Salski's squadron leader expected every aircraft to stay snug to each other, convinced it meant more concentrated firepower against enemy fighters. The squadron leader had no problem calling out pilots whose aircraft could not keep close formation.

Salski and his crew had flown together with the U.S. 15th Air Force, based at Foggia, since late February. Their Liberator, its fuselage emblazoned with the words *Motor City Minx* and the laviscious image of a semi-clad, buxom flirt, had been factory-new when they began. Now, after multiple missions, crew and aircraft were both hitting their stride, the bugs long since shaken out, the fit between men and machine seamless.

"We're at forty-two hundred feet, Skip," reported Jimmy O'Brien, the copilot.

"Check," answered Salski. He cast a glance past O'Brien's nose where Tom Shaw's Liberator held position ahead and to their right. "The old man can't bitch about us not being snug enough today," he told his co-pilot. "Any closer and we'll be sitting in Tommy's lap."

They were coming up on the city of Florence. He held the bomber steady on course, both hands on the control yoke.

From the start of the Italian campaign, the Germans had made the Allied offensive pay for every mile it gained, retreating in good order to one strong defensive line after another, yielding ground grudgingly. They called their latest defensive position the Gothic Line, a massive redoubt that extended from Spezia on the west coast past Ravenna on the east—two hundred miles of bunkers, trenches, machine gun nests, mortar and howitzer emplacements.

American, British, Canadian, Polish, Indian, French, and Brazilian troops had been hammering at the stubborn fortifications since August. With the intense effort of fifteen thousand slave laborers building and repairing defenses around the clock, aided by the impending winter, the Germans had succeeded in stopping the Allied offensive in its tracks.

Today's bombing mission was only one in a series of attempts to pound the battlements into rubble. Salski hoped this time it would lead to a breakthrough on the ground; none had succeeded before. If anything illustrated the enemy's absolute determination to continue fighting, it was how the Germans and the Italian troops still loyal to Mussolini stubbornly refused to yield.

The formation thundered on. Below, a forest of tiny church spires and towers crowded Florence's ancient skyline, crowned by the famous cathedral with Brunelleschi's great brick dome, orange-red in the morning light. Barely within Allied lines, the city had escaped total devastation, though battles had raged nearby. Below, like a sparkling blue jewel, Lago di Biancina glittered. In the near distance lay the snowy mountaintops of the Apennines.

The pilot noted the foliage below turning from olive groves and cypress to evergreen forestation. Of obscure Italian heritage himself, he felt an affinity for the land he flew above and had been so efficiently blasting to pulp on previous missions. Despite the tension of impending combat, he said aloud, "What a spectacular day for flying!"

It was certainly a long way from those airmail routes he'd started with back in the Midwest, Salski reflected. In 1940, he'd graduated from the government's Civilian Pilot Training Program, designed to provide pilots for America's burgeoning airline industry. The tuition was free but came with the requirement that graduates must enlist in the Army Air Corps in the event of war.

After graduation, his first job as a pilot had been flying a Stinson Reliant making nonstop airmail pickups and deliveries. The remarkable system was the brainstorm of postal officials looking to provide service to locations without standard mail links. All-American Airways stepped up to meet the challenge. The pilots of its fleet of durable, single-engine aircraft perfected the art of mail pickup and delivery with wheels never touching the ground.

Swooping an aircraft so low the flight officer could snag mail canisters with a grappling hook then flying off again gave Salski all the confidence he needed to volunteer for bomber service after Pearl Harbor. He did not regret that decision in the least; never did he feel more alive than when flying *Minx* on missions like this one.

Over his headpiece he heard, "Skipper, we're fifteen minutes out."

"Roger that, Lieutenant," the pilot answered his navigator. "Everything good so far."

The Allies had achieved air superiority over the battlefield long before. The once vaunted Luftwaffe, so terrifying in the early years of the war, was only a shell of its former self, decimated not only by swarms of Allied fighters but by the fleets of bombers pummeling the Reich's aircraft manufacturing centers day and night.

Ahead were the fortified defenses of the enemy, and as the armada closed on its target, German antiaircraft batteries began throwing up increasingly heavy flak. Above, the bombers' escort of P-38 Mustangs scoured the clear skies for Messerschmidt interference. There was none.

The B-24 shuddered as a blast detonated thirty feet away. Salski said over his intercom, "Damned *krauts* have to do better than that!"

"Approaching target," came the report from the navigator, sitting backward and below in the nose compartment.

"We're ordered to begin our run," announced Sergeant Gephardt.

"Your plane, Eugene," Salski said, turning control of the aircraft over to his bombardier. "Let's make it count!"

Already the embedded concrete German positions lining the mountain ridge below were blossoming with hits from the Liberators in front. Soon the *Minx* added its eight-thousand-pound drop to the mushrooming conflagration.

"Back to you, Skipper," said the bombardier.

"Suds are on me, fellas," Salski declared, resuming control. "Now let's get old Minxy home!"

* * *

November 1944: Salò, Italian Social Republic

Hot tears streaked both of Minister Degligatti's cheeks as he sat, transfixed. The ardent lyrics from the magnificent aria had always affected him deeply, especially its climax, and he fought now to not lose total control. He was unashamed of his emotion—what heart could not be moved? But he knew sobbing out loud in front of Nazis was terribly bad form.

Tenor Giovanni Monte-Volta, alone on the stage, concluded his dynamic performance of *Nessun Dorma* by altering slightly the masterpiece's closing words, drawing the audience into his passion:

We shall win!
We shall win!
At dawn, we shall win!

The maestro stood defiant, his tears now streaming, clenched fist held high, chin raised in heroic resolve. The select audience was on its feet even before the orchestra's final notes faded. Cries of *"Bravo! Bravissimo!"* filled the room, Degligatti enthusiastically leading the ovation, no longer restraining himself, his cheeks glistening. After such an intensely emotional experience, he found standing, clapping, and shouting to be an enormous cathartic release.

"Here, my friend, allow me to assist."

Degligatti smiled, accepted the proffered handkerchief with its discreet black swastika neatly embroidered in one corner. He dabbed at his eyes.

Heinrich Himmler, Reichsführer of Germany's Schutzstaffel forces, looked upon his companion with tolerant amusement. "You hotblooded Latins, hearts always on your sleeve. Both your people's charm and great weakness, I fear."

Degligatti smiled slightly, answered in heavily accented German. "Thank you, Herr Reichsführer, for your handkerchief and your compliment. Yes, I admit, we are an intensely heartfelt people."

They were in a sitting room of a large villa in Salò, capital of the new Italian Social Republic. The caprices of fate that led him to this place, Degligatti thought, will make a fine memoir one day. What a whirlwind!

Following the utter destruction of the Italian army in Russia the previous year, King Victor Emmanuel III ordered

Mussolini's arrest. The new government soon abandoned its German alliance and aligned itself with the Allies invading from the south. Forewarned, German forces moved swiftly to take over all peninsular defenses. Lacking clear orders, the Italian military devolved into shambles. Some units, most notably the Blackshirt brigades, remained loyal to the Nazis and in time became the core of Mussolini's small new army. Other units, caught unawares by their government's realignment, were swiftly disarmed by the Germans and sent to prisoner stockades and labor camps. Thousands of soldiers simply took off their uniforms and melted into the hills, many of whom later re-emerged as anti-German partisans. The Savoia dynasty fled Rome for Brindisi, behind Allied lines.

The battles had been continuous since, the Wehrmacht under Field Marshal Kesselring forcing the British and American armies to pay a stiff price for each forward step. But the sheer mass of the Allied advance had steadily shoved the Germans north, mile by blood-soaked mile. Five months earlier, in June, Rome had fallen.

The same month, Allied armies successfully landed at Normandy and were now pushing hard from the west. Degligatti had only recently learned American forces were across the Moselle River near Metz. On the Eastern front, vengeful Soviet forces relentlessly reclaimed lost ground and much more.

Degligatti desperately wanted the closing words of the aria to be true. He was frustrated with his countrymen who bent to and fro with each breeze. To him, the unyielding willpower of the Nazis was the model to follow. Like all true believers, he was fully convinced that maintaining a steely resolve would turn the tide.

As for Benito Mussolini, German paratroopers had rescued the dictator within two months of his imprisonment. Backed by the Fuhrer, he declared a new Fascist state. The so-called Italian Social Republic consisted of northern provinces not yet taken by the Allies. Now, here in the commune of Salò, near magnificent Lago Garda, Mussolini was once more il Duce, though gaunt with stress and a relative political pygmy. But he, Eduardo Degligatti, was a Council Minister and vice commander-in-chief of the Republic's nascent National Guard.

A memoir indeed, he thought. Perhaps a movie script one day!

Tonight was a brief break from the uncertainty of it all. Luminaries included much German brass. Il Duce was not present. Officially, his stomach problems, persistent since his reinstatement, had flared up; other rumors claimed the shrill battles between his wife and mistress were making his domestic life a living hell.

"You are lost in thought, *Silenzioso*," Himmler said, using Degligatti's nickname. "Not a terrible trait, but silence with a friend? It borders on the rude." The Reichsführer smiled tightly. The light of the glittering chandeliers glinted off his round spectacle lenses, obscuring his eyes.

"My apologies, Reichsführer, of course," said Degligatti, momentarily embarrassed. "I am thinking, what a pity for the Duce to miss an evening of arias by Monte-Volta."

Degligatti had joined Mussolini several times at La Scala for such performances. Of course, no longer. The great Milan opera house lay a bomb-stripped ruin, along with the nearby Galleria.

No such memory troubled the German. "Ah, yes, 'che peccato', indeed. But of course, your Duce's health must always come first. He must preserve his strength for the final victory ahead. Our rockets are pummeling London, and the fastest aircraft in the world are rolling from German assembly lines. Moreover, the Fuhrer is convinced the Allies cannot maintain their unity, that soon their conflicting agendas will turn them against each other. Our ultimate victory is but a matter of time, Degligatti. Maintain an iron grip, now more than ever! It is essential."

Degligatti declined a champagne flute proffered by a passing waiter in an Alpini uniform.

"A cogent point, Herr Reichsführer. It suggests a topic I hope to broach with you tonight. Or perhaps tomorrow?"

"Now is fine. In the morning, I must leave for Berlin."

Degligatti cleared his throat. "As you know, partisan activity in the Social Republic continues to spread. Our National Guard is actively hunting the traitors down, as do the Black Brigades. OVRA remains active as well. Still, the threat grows, not lessens.

"Thus, I suggest an increased German SS presence in the countryside. I admire our Italian security forces; please, I beg, do not misunderstand. But OVRA is most effective when acting hand-in-glove with your SS."

"*Ach*, Degligatti. I think you want us to do all the hard work."

"Not at all! No, I only ask that you consider a limited increase of Schutzstaffel units stationed in certain critical communes. To coordinate the Republic's forces already engaged." He managed a mild jibe. "Of course, more active assistance would be of great benefit, but I do understand there is a call for your resources from multiple directions."

A touch of annoyance crept into Himmler's voice. "We are equal to whatever is asked of us, have no fear, Minister." The Italian's oblique reference to the steady drain on Germany's diminishing military stores was uncalled for.

The Italian nodded and smiled. "Of course, sir."

Himmler permitted himself to unstiffen slightly. Overreaction implied self-doubt. "The growing violence by your political malcontents concerns us as well. Moreover, we remain unimpressed by the lack of vigor with which Italian authorities are rooting out Jews. Weak stomachs have no place in the Third Reich, Minister Degligatti." He sniffed. "Or your Italian Social Republic. Sovereign though it be."

This last was meant to humble him, Degligatti knew. Both understood the Italian state was little more than a Nazi province. Still, it existed. Degligatti harbored hope that from humble beginnings a new Italia would arise of a far greater stature. For that, German goodwill was paramount.

"My country understands the Jewish question, Reichsführer," he replied. "And we are prepared to implement in full the Fuhrer's wise policies on the matter."

Himmler, expressionless, nodded curtly. "Very well, Herr Minister, the SS stands ready as always. I will authorize an augmentation of SS posts throughout the Social Republic. Regarding German officers of merit for the task, several names come to mind. You have but to identify the communes in question."

* * *

December 1944: Lombardia

"Tell me your story." The partisan chief sat, arms folded, on a tree stump at the edge of a woods. A few dozen paces away, his band of sixty men went about making camp for the night. Three armed fighters stood nearby.

They stared at a bearded man with hard eyes, filthy with the grime of a forest journey on foot. He is like the *Omm*

Selvadegh, the crazed forest wildman of Lombardian nightmares, thought the commander. The man's long shag of hair was thick with debris, his bare feet clustered with sores. He wore a rag of a uniform, buttonless and beltless, his trousers held up by two cords crisscrossed over his shoulders like braces.

"Como," the apparition said. "Lieutenant, 3rd Division, Ravenna. Eighth Army."

"You look the part," said the chief, known by his grim *nom de guerre,* 'Colonel Morte'. "We have some other hard-used Eighth Army men with us. But continue, Tenente."

"I left the Eastern front with a comrade, my sergeant, name of Biella. Germans entered our camp looking for shelter. They killed one of my men, and they paid for it." He described the event to his listeners' rapt attention.

"Afterward, the two of us struck out on our own. We headed south in a snowstorm, found refuge that same night down the road. We fashioned snowshoes out of pine boughs and set out, walking at night, sleeping by day, trying to stay ahead of the *kettenhunde.* We never saw them but always felt them close. Sometimes we slept in abandoned izbas or barns, sometimes in snow caves we dug with our helmets. We were always searching for food. At one farm there was a cellar with a pile of cabbages. We took them along, they lasted a while."

The commander pointed to Donato's left hand. "What of that?"

Donato held the bare hand up, flexed it. His thumb and first two fingers were intact. The other two were stubbed off at the second knuckles.

"The two that aren't there became frostbitten and turned black after two weeks. Unless I did something, gangrene would have set in. But neither of us had knives; I was about ready to ask Biella to shoot them off! As luck would have it, we came across a village where an old *babushka* saw my hand. She took pity on me, as many of those villagers did once they knew we were Italian. Her husband was the town blacksmith; she took us to his shop in the village. After he and she talked for a moment, he took out a bottle and gave me a drink. It tasted like raw gasoline going down! Then the blacksmith had Biella hold my hand flat on his anvil. His wife held my other arm at my side. He took a pair of iron tongs and snapped my dead fingers off at the joint. The woman sewed the skin to cover the bone, according to Biella. I was unconscious for that part. But those Russians saved my life. Another few days meant death."

Colonel Morte grunted. Quite a tale, he thought. It could even be true. "Keep talking."

"Our progress was slow, the weather sometimes too difficult to travel at all. It took us until March to get to Sjedove at the Sea of Azov. The area was still under German control, full of ruined Romanian and Hungarian units trying to regroup. But I had a particular plan." Donato told of Vino Penna and the playing card given to him as a token of the black marketeer's trust.

"Even so, I was surprised when I presented it to the trawler captain. He treated us like old friends. He told me his boss Penna had gotten off three weeks before! I was afraid the sea would be iced over, but the only ice was along the shoreline. We had little trouble with German patrol craft. Whether the Camorra paid off people or made other arrangements, I cannot say. All I know is that we flew a long black streamer from the trawler's black mast, and no one dared bother us.

"The first weeks were the most difficult. Freezing winds day and night, wild seas. Biella and I had a rough time of it, I tell you. I was born near the Pirino River and grew up around boats. But I was not ready for that boat ride. Biella far less so. A miserable passage.

"We only put into land when we needed refueling. The captain paid his way past the Istanbul port authorities, everyone very congenial. It all went smoothly, obviously old business for everyone.

"We made our way through the Aegean Sea and south around the Greek islands. It seemed to take forever, though the weather became far better. The captain had contacts to meet along the way and business to conduct. We took on various loads of contraband from small boats that sometimes met us in harbor, and we offloaded deliveries dockside elsewhere.

"Shipping was heavy in the main channels as we traveled. We saw British dive bombers attacking freighters, but our captain kept us well distant.

"In early May we arrived off Italy's coast. By this time Biella and I were old seadogs, earning our keep. The trawler wanted to put in near Pesara, south of Rimini. But over the ship's radio, the captain heard the British army was beginning to drive from the south. We steered north, but a German destroyer spotted us and fired a shot across our bow. Our captain did not know the ship, or if it came to help us or sink us. He tried to escape by sailing the trawler close to shore. We thought we had succeeded when we struck hidden rocks. The collision tore a hole in the hull.

"We were close enough to shore to take our chances in the surf. A few of us made it. Not Biella, I never saw him again." Donato took a deep breath, annoyed at his welling emotion, fought it away.

"The destroyer must have signaled our position because as we started to get off the beach, Germans called down from the dunes. Running was pointless.

"They were Todt Organization *Schutzkommandos*, herding a forced labor brigade north with them. They pressed the six of us into the column. It was full of Italian ex-soldiers captured after the monarchy sided with the Allies.

"Since that time, I have been building fortifications for the Nazis. Until three weeks ago, my job was to pour concrete walls on the Gothic Line. Finally, I felt ready to attempt an escape."

Colonel Morte held up his hand. "Wait. You have been strengthening German positions against the Allies?"

"What could I do? They had guns to our heads. But I will tell you this. I know construction, it is what I did before they called me up. As a prisoner, I worked in a team of a dozen, pouring concrete to make barriers. Every day, under the noses of those standing guard, we did what we could to weaken the defenses. We left out steel mesh, overwatered the concrete when we mixed it, used too much sand so the barriers would more easily crumble. Not easy to do; you know how diligent the Germans are. But we were persistent, and such activity was going on up and down the entire line."

He stopped, hacked a hard cough. Morte gestured for a man to offer a canteen. Como noted it had 'U.S.A.' stamped on its canvas cover, tapped his finger. "America?" he said.

"Yes, the Allies have found us. Both American OSS and the British SOE. They are especially keen to help republican partisans. I suspect they will want us to take on the Yugoslavian Marxists after Germany surrenders. My band is a division of *La Patria Sempre*, aligned with the Church and in favor of a democratic republic. The last thing we want is for godless Russians to end up as our masters. You do not sound like that is something you would want either." Donato had stopped gulping water. "Tell us the rest, Tenente."

Donato wiped his mouth with his maimed hand. "Getting away was not so difficult. Three weeks ago, a storm struck. The guard sat under a tarp to keep dry, hardly watching. It was dark,

I pulled a blanket over my head and walked right past him, twenty yards away, and kept going.

"Since then, I have been heading north to join the partisans, any partisans. A fellow laborer said he knew such bands were active in these parts. That is all I had to go by. Your men found me at random." Donato squinted at the commander. "I ask you, accept me into your ranks."

Colonel Morte shrugged, stroked his chin. "Perhaps, Como." His band was full of tough men like this with their own grueling histories. Still. He motioned again to Donato's damaged left hand.

"You can fight like that, shoot?"

"Yes, it healed well. With this hand as it is, I have sailed a sea, built concrete forts, and marched through a forest to get here." He pointed to his confiscated knife at the partisan's feet. "That was my only tool, made at the work camp forge. I do not need my left hand to pull a trigger." He balled his damaged hand into a three-knuckled fist. "And I carry my weight in any fight, Commander."

"Your politics. In what do you believe?"

"Killing Nazis is my politics. And their tail-wagging lapdogs."

The chief broke into a broad grin. "A religious man, then, like us!" His men laughed along. "If what you say is true, execute that pet dog of OVRA over there, that informer." He pointed to a small man tethered to a nearby elm, hands tied. "Use only your left hand."

The prisoner heard the exchange and started begging. "No, a mistake, I say. It is not me you want. I know the one, I will tell you!" Coils of rope strapped the standing man to the trunk. He cried out loud, "A moment, wait a moment, I beg of you! I am a loyal Italian, the same as you! *Viva La Patria Sempre!*"

Donato approached the wailing traitor. His left hand flashed hard into the man's Adam's apple and twisted, his three long, ragged fingernails a flesh-tearing claw. The choking prisoner writhed, his eyes wide in animal terror, gabbling for air, unable to shake off the death grip at his throat.

Donato felt a sudden, restraining hand hold him back. "Enough! Actually, we need him alive." Morte patted the prisoner's tear-streaked cheek. "Am I right, Matteo?" He turned to his men, a hand on Donato's shoulder. "Bid welcome to our new comrade! 'Tenente' is now one of us!"

Chapter 44

January 1945: Castrubello

Pietro swiveled the chair at his desk a methodical slight distance back and forth, back and forth. What a dilemma, he thought, fingers pressed to his temples. From outside came the sounds of the Waffen-SS infantry company going through its biweekly close-order drill.

This part of his job never came easily, Pietro thought, not even after two years. He lurched his mind from the distraction outside. The first time he submitted his names of potential anti-fascists, he had suffered a migraine that lasted two days. Every month since had brought a version of the same.

He had appreciated the short hiatus of a few months between Mussolini's fall and his restoration. But as the Nazis consolidated their hold in the north through their surrogate Italian Social Republic, all previous policies were back in force. That included Pietro again producing *uno, due* accused traitors a month to OVRA.

The actual names had come more easily than expected. But then, thought Pietro, he heard so many rumors in the course of his various duties that it had become mostly a case of which one to choose. Nobody he knew had any problem sharing the most salacious gossip at the slightest nudge. And Pietro had learned to listen and watch others carefully in every conversation. A surprising number of people compromised themselves with indiscreet comments that betrayed an animus toward the regime. He stockpiled the information, no matter how slight, in a thick notebook he kept locked in his wall safe.

Many of the names were perpetrators of about an equal level of thoughtless indiscretion. Pietro decided which to inform upon by using a simple criterion. Were any of his political or business adversaries implicated? His careful evaluations along that line had removed many a competitor—and sometimes freed up valuable properties for purchase! Otherwise, he sorted through the rumors and submitted those he thought would earn him OVRA's favor.

Were any of those he had turned in a bonafide enemy of the state apparatus? Pietro had his doubts. His experience was that often the bigger the talk, the lesser the deed. In any event, establishing guilt was not his task, that job fell to Major Gabinno and his agents. And now, OVRA had the added expertise of a new SS interrogation team at their side.

Pietro did appreciate that no matter whom he named, OVRA and the SS always acted. They pulled people in and questioned them relentlessly. Some prisoners since released had claimed they'd been tortured. Pietro had never seen it. Whatever their exact experience, he did know many prisoners were blackmailed into becoming informers themselves. In other cases, the accused disappeared off to the political prisoner camp near Trieste, *Risiera di San Sabba*, the one with the great smokestacks. All were welcome grist for the state security mill, one way or another, Pietro thought.

Still, whom exactly to inform upon took thought and diligence. It was nothing to be flippant about. His role in the apprehension of suspects certainly must never be known. It was an exhausting business, and despite trying to consider the task only another bureaucratic chore, Pietro found no relief from his bouts of a pounding head.

But now, at the instigation of the SS, OVRA was insisting on a different focus. Major Gabinno had last week demanded that in the future, Pietro's two monthly names must be those of Jews.

He had no trouble with the policy of wiping Jewdom off the map. The dilemma lay in finding such suspects. The nearest large grouping of Hebrews had lived in Milan, but many of those had fled into the countryside. The authorities wanted to root them out of their holes. I hardly need such pressure, thought Pietro, while realizing he had no recourse but to comply. But *fortuna* had provided him with a solution already at hand. There was no point in putting the matter off longer.

"Contadino, the sedan," he called to the anteroom. The burly chauffeur-protector poked his closely cropped head in the room. "As you wish, signore," he said.

Within a few minutes, Pietro was ensconced in the comfortable leather backseat of the Lancia Berlina that his man always kept at a high shine. The day was warm but not oppressively so, although from where he sat Pietro noted the sweat-stained tunics of the drilling SS troopers.

Pietro had been pleased when he learned that the local OVRA was being joined by a reinforced SS detachment. In particular, he viewed the arrival of commander Manfred von

Gottlieb as a known quantity skilled at his craft, as well as a boost to Pietro's status. Not that OVRA was not ruthlessly zealous. But no one knew its business like the *Sicherheitsdienst* intelligence people.

That he already knew von Gottlieb, now an SS-brigadeführer, was a bonus. When Pietro hosted a reception upon the officer's arrival, he found the German far grimmer than when they had first met at Ettore's birthday celebration. Small wonder! Through contacts, Pietro learned that von Gottlieb had participated in a reprisal execution of over three hundred Italian prisoners in Rome. Trucks hauled the doomed victims to caves where von Gottlieb and others had executed them with pistol shots to their heads. Afterward, bulldozers sealed the site. The brigadier and his officers were now comfortably ensconced in d'Ambrosso's old residence. Along with the SS agents sharing office space with OVRA at Torrquadro, the Waffen-SS company had also arrived. Those one hundred seventy-five men were now billeted in the refitted villa stables.

As the Berlina slowly rolled toward the gates, Pietro watched as most of the unit continued to drill in the old dairy cow pasture still called *cacacampo*. Their company captain, at a short distance, noted the podestà's vehicle and offered a pleasant, *"Heil!"* Pietro raised his arm at the elbow in response.

The auto took a quarter-hour to arrive at Luponotte on Castrubello's outskirts. It turned onto a gravel road that led to a stand of poplar trees. Though their branches were bare, the heavy thicket still obscured an isolated farmhouse made of rock and rough mortar. As the auto pulled up, a man adjusted his braces and peered from the door with double-bagged eyes, his cheeks scraggy with unshaved bristles.

Pietro was a bit shocked at the man's unkempt appearance. Abramo Basillea usually cut a much finer figure than this. Why, at Zio's eightieth, Pietro recalled, the man was wearing a Caraceni suit! He approached his former banker with a friendly tone.

"My, my, Basillea, look at you. The life of the gentleman farmer certainly suits! It is almost midday, and you look as if you have only now risen!" He extended his hand.

Basillea gave it a quick shake—what else could he do? Looking past his guest's shoulder at Contadino, arms akimbo, he said in a dry, sandpaper voice, "Please, please enter, Podestà Como!"

The smell of boiled beets permeated the interior. This place never did have much ventilation, Pietro recalled. After its previous tenant had died—the worker known best as 'il Muto'—it had taken a week for the small house to air out. Zio Ettore had bought it from his old comrade at an exorbitant price, then let the useless dumb and deaf ancient live there for free! Technically, the dwelling was still Ettore's property. But after Muto's death, Pietro asked his uncle if he could use the building as a rental property, and Ettore agreed.

Its current use was to house the banker and his wife and four children, at Pietro's largesse. All of them stopped what they were doing and stood when he entered.

The month prior Basillea had telephoned Pietro in a panic. That day he had witnessed a fellow Jewish businessman hustled out of a city restaurant by Gestapo officers. Such aggressive arrests had become more commonplace. He begged Pietro to hide him and his family, to help arrange new papers to allow them to emigrate. For this he, of course, would gladly pay his former client.

After consideration, Pietro decided that the banker was worth the risk. And smart to have such a wealthy colleague in his debt! Without delay, he arranged for the family to simply disappear. The stone house at Luponotte was at an obscure location, safe from prying eyes.

"May I offer you refreshment, signore?" asked Sara, the oldest daughter, just eighteen. She cast a quick glance at Pietro, blushed. Her younger brother Aarone hurried to assist.

A more perfect mistress Pietro could not imagine. Shortly after the family's sudden relocation from Milan to this hovel, he and the young woman had reached an accommodation. Among his various properties was a tidy villetta near the Naviglio a short distance north of the quarry. He advised Basillea that one evening a week, if he approved, of course, Sara could come there to assist with the podestà's ponderous official correspondence. As payment, the family would receive a portion of meat every week. This was no small thing in a war economy, Pietro reminded the banker. Basillea had no choice but to agree to his benefactor's kind offer, adding his daughter would prove a most reliable secretary.

As a matter of fact, no secretarial skills were required. Instead, every week Pietro and the girl copulated on the leather divan in the villetta's drawing-room. After the first few times, the girl stopped resisting. It pleased Pietro that she came to her senses. After all, his attentions were a considerable compliment! He sometimes gave the girl a small gift, usually a trinket from his dead wife's costume jewelry box. Pietro considered the arrangement more than fair. The Basilleas ate meat and the girl occasionally took home a scrolled tin broach—all for an energetic bout of straightforward humping!

"Yes, that would be ideal, Sara," he answered. He watched her hips as she turned.

Pietro was aware that Basillea was watching him watch his daughter. Noting the banker's florid face, he offered a pleasant, banal expression. Did he suspect? Pietro wondered. So what if he did? Everybody knew these people would sell their own mothers for a few extra shekels.

"It seems you have managed to make the best of a difficult situation," Pietro commented as he sat in a proffered chair. Signora Basillea nodded courteously. "Wonderful," she said. She gestured at the cramped space. "It is so exceedingly kind of you to allow us to live here, Don Como. Peace, blessings, and good to you, signore."

"Nothing that any man of good conscience would not have done, signora." Pietro accepted the demitasse of caffè from Sara, resisted the urge to signal his anticipation of her next visit. He chastised himself for the foolish impulse. Instead, he turned to the banker. "Perhaps, Signor Basillea, you and I can take a short constitutional." He gestured to the door. "The day is quite fine."

Basillea brushed his sparse hair back one more time, slipped on a worn black coat—certainly no Caraceni, Pietro noted. The two men went out onto the gravel entry road.

"This is not easy, Pietro," said Basillea, absently slipping into the informal address he had used for years with his client. "The fear is the worst. In Milan, I heard such terrible things happening." He stopped, sighed, drew out a wrinkled handkerchief, mopped at his brow. "For years, the government turned a blind eye to these absurd racial laws. We could be both Jews and loyal Italians serving the motherland. But now, with the Nazis running the show..."

Pietro exercised patience. "Yes, yes, how unfair it all is. But come, you are safe here, your wife and beautiful children. Your freedom is only a matter of paperwork now, as I have told you. My people say they are steadily proceeding with your new certificates of births, baptisms, marriage records, other documents. I take a great risk, but that is no matter. I knew what was involved when I accepted this responsibility. Be patient, Basillea. Soon you will be a good Christian like me!"

Pietro had certainly not launched any such effort to create a new identity for the banker. Did the financier believe he would risk everything for such quixotic folly? The gullibility of the banker staggered him! Pietro remembered Basillea's steady nerves during his years in business. Keen, experienced, unflappable. Now? Pietro cast a disdainful glance at the man. Just another nervous pants-pisser.

Basillea shambled along, waiting for what came next. He understood fully his reliance on Pietro, whom in business he had never fully trusted. Ettore Vacci? Salt of the earth. The banker and Ettore had made a good combination, becoming friends in the process. But after Pietro Como assumed control at VCI, the old relationship was soon lost. The mutual trust and respect he had built with Ettore, those were gone. With Pietro, everything began and ended with Podestà Como making it clear who held the power.

The banker noted a silence had fallen between them, as if Pietro were waiting. A painful thought blossomed. Had he missed his cue?

"Excuse me, signore, I find my mind wants to wander these days. Is there some way, Signor Como, some way I can repay you for the risks you have assumed because of myself and my family?"

Pietro let a brief moment pass as if thinking.

"Since you do ask, as a matter of fact, my friend, there is. As I have told you, the pressure on me is intense. These Nazis, they are like the *cani corsi*, bloodthirsty mastiffs, always on the hunt. If I hesitate for one moment," he grabbed Basillea's arm hard at the elbow.

The older man made a startled yelp.

"They will bite, Basillea!" Pietro continued, letting loose his grip with a parting shake. "And if I am devoured, who remains to protect you all?"

"What is it they want?" asked Basillea, fighting to slow his breathing.

"As you say, you Jews obsess them. I have never seen such a fixation. But still, who can deny them? They want names from me. The names of Jews for questioning, and where they might be found." He shook his head as if in perplexity, touched both hands to his chest. "Abramo, I know of no Jews."

Abramo stared at Pietro in dawning horror. "Are you asking me to give you the names of men that I know? Jewish families with whom I have socialized, with whom I worshipped at synagogue? How can you say this, it is a monstrous thing to ask!"

Pietro suddenly stopped in midstride, drew himself up. Enough of this handholding. "Remember. It is not I who asks this. I am not monstrous. I am but a lowly functionary." He brought his face close to the banker's, put one hand on his shoulder, leaned in, spoke slowly, with emphasis. "They... want...names. Two Jew names a month." He saw Basillea shake his head and try to draw back, but Pietro's grip tightened. "Listen to me, I have myself and my son to consider. I brought you to Castrubello in the dead of night, an hour ahead of the police knock on your door! I provide you a place to hide, to live. I provide you with food, I provide your daughter work. If I had not intervened, you would all be long gone to San Sabba in a cattle car!

"But forget your duty to be grateful to me, Basillea. You people have always been ingrates. Think only about the situation you are in. It is quite simple. Make me a list of Jews in the city or hereabouts. I need to report only two every month, that is the quota expected from me. So, a list of two dozen names, to cover an entire year. In twelve months, who knows, perhaps the policy will be different."

He saw Basillea's expression of utter distress.

"Let me clear with you, Signor 'Morta-Cristo'. If the end of the month comes and I am without names, I will turn in two of the Jews I do know. I only know six. You, your signora, your boy, Sara, and your twins. You, I will save for last, so you can watch them all disappear, two by two."

The financier felt the threat like a physical blow. Of course, it had always been hanging between them, unspoken. But to Abramo, unspoken words implied hope, no matter how thin. But now he knew how perilously close his family was to the abyss. The podestà's naked bigotry heightened its immediacy. He wrung his hands, eyes downcast. Momentarily, a stunned hopelessness gripped him. Then, strangely, a fresh resolve sparked within.

Pietro bullied the weak, he thought, it was the only way the man knew how to operate. But I am not without power in this tragedy. Power enough to protect those whom I love. I will not play the victim here.

"Of course, signore, of course." Basillea began, masking his bitterness. "Forgive my reaction. How selfish of me. There are so many complications during these difficult times. But one must adapt. At day's end, my family's survival is all. I will provide the names." He looked at Pietro, measured his odds, went ahead. "Here are my terms. I will give you your names but not a full list all at once. With a year in your pocket, my family and I become expendable to you." He noted Pietro's frown. Was Como insulted by such effrontery or merely chagrined at being bargained down? Press on, Basillea, he told himself, do not falter.

"You will get your names. Two every month, starting tomorrow, until our departure papers are finalized. Then the rest. I would ask you to remember our long status in business, but I am clear eyed. You can tell OVRA or the SS of me and mine at any time. But doing so cuts off your supply of...criminals." The banker quickly raised his open hands. "But have no doubt. I will tell you what I know, over time. And I do know a great deal."

Pietro paused. This turn of events was a surprise. Apparently, the banker's *coglioni* had not completely withered to dust. How to play this brazenness? An hour at Torrquadro would have the old man singing every name he ever knew and all the 'begats' in the Torah to boot! But then what? Gabinno would demand he still come up with monthly Jews—but without Basillea as his source. Smarter to keep the man alive, make monthly withdrawals. Much like, what else? A bank.

"I will see you tomorrow, Basillea. Two names."

Basillea bowed his head. "Yes. Agreed." In silence, the men crunched their way back over the gravel to where the Lancia waited. The stolid chauffeur opened the rear passenger door.

"Oh, yes, and Basillea," Pietro added, one foot in the car. "Tell your Sara. I have a tall stack of documents that need her attention tonight. My man Contadino returns for her in three hours."

Chapter 45

March 1945: Castrubello

"No! No! Not there!" Regina shaded her eyes from the glare of the late winter sun. A dozen workmen on the scaffold and atop the concrete factory stopped, stared, awkwardly holding the bulky loose netting in place.

A crew chief stood on the flat roof of the structure covering the four silos, over thirty feet above the ground. A large rectangle of camouflage netting stretched halfway across; the rest hung in tangled disarray onto the scaffolding, held up by other members of the crew.

The man called down. "Padrona, I am sorry. I confess, I do not understand. You said to cover the building."

The plant owner, dressed in a gray sweater, brown skirt, and an overlarge pair of work boots, slammed shut the passenger door of the truck. She cupped her hands and shouted.

"Yes, but there is not enough netting for the sides. Cover the rooftop only."

The worker threw his arms up. "Now she tells me this," he exclaimed to the man beside him, who offered a sympathetic shrug.

Regina was still learning the art of managing males. Papà Ettore had helped during her first weeks in charge of Naviglio Quarry & Concrete, showing the workers he had faith in his daughter. He also privately had spoken with some of the key men. And Regina had watched Ettore operate for years, how he balanced a personal appreciation for the men with his unyielding standards of quality. Above all, she strove to emulate his decisiveness, right or wrong. For the most part, it was working. The men liked their jobs at the quarry, understood that she was the one who paid them now, and were willing to accept the padrone's decision. After the first month, Ettore stayed home.

It helped that concrete was in high demand. Relentless Allied bombing had brought the northern cities to their knees. Clearing wreckage and rebuilding never stopped. Roads streamed with trucks and wagons laden with concrete and building materials.

Farther south was another huge market where the Wehrmacht continued to consolidate its Gothic Line. The Allies bombarded the positions by day; the Germans rebuilt by night. The cycle required a constant flow of concrete, reinforcing bars, gravel, sand, mixers, and grading equipment into the mountains.

Consequently, a staggering amount of the Social Republic's lire flowed into Regina's accounts. The paper notes were valuable enough within the Fascist regime—to the extent any goods were available for purchase—but except for Germany and its vassal states, they were worthless. It was plain to Regina that the only lasting wealth she had were the buildings and equipment and the property they sat on.

The risk was increasing. A chain of small industries lined miles of the Naviglio, including other quarry operations. The previous week, American bombers attacked the parachute factory at Cascinetta. It was the first such raid in the area, and no local mill owner was under the illusion it would be the last.

Some level of protection was needed. A brisk north-south black market trade flourished across the front lines. Naviglio Quarry & Concrete often ran convoys that rendezvoused with smugglers out of Naples. Hard gold and silver bought construction supplies purloined from the vast Allied depots. On the most recent run, with help from her foreman, Eunizio Caderre, she'd acquired the truckload of the camouflage netting her work crew now struggled to install.

Caderre was among the oldest in a workforce of middling-old men. Cantankerous, opinionated, a lifelong Vacci loyalist, Eunizio was the first man Ettore had convinced to accept Regina as boss. The valuable foreman was a large reason Regina had accepted the challenge of Naviglio Quarry & Concrete.

Unlike many of his generation, the foreman felt no qualms about a woman as boss. Regina was a Vacci, adopted or not, that was enough. Still, he understood his workers. To them, appearances were critical, maintaining God's natural order paramount. Yes, she was the owner, *la padrona*, beyond dispute. But, as foreman, Eunizio could not appear to his men to be the pawn of a woman, whatever her status. If they thought such was the case, he would lose his authority. Fair, unfair, it was the simple truth of the matter.

Eunizio cupped his hands and called to the men on the roof, "Wait, wait, what are you doing?" He climbed to the top of the scaffold while everyone waited.

Regina watched, arms folded. Silhouetted against the sky, Eunizio made a show of surveying the American netting, hefted part of it up and down, looked carefully at the interwoven burlap strips of dark green, light green, field drab brown. He grunted his approval. "Yes, this is to cover the roof! Not the sides!" he announced loudly. "Let it only drape down slightly at the edges. But also, men, gather bricks and pieces of timber to thoroughly weigh it down once it's spread out. Fancy supplies are all well and good, but worthless if they blow away in the wind!" He looked around at the faces, cocked his head slightly toward where Regina stood below while lifting his eyebrows, implying he had caught a significant detail the well-meaning woman had missed.

The men, satisfied, returned to their tasks.

"Such a wise man," Regina said to the foreman upon his descent. "I assumed weighting the net was obvious."

Eunizio ran a hand over his grizzled gray chin. "Ah," he smiled. "You know us old men. We crave order, the predictable. If anyone doubts who is the boss, confusion follows."

Regina returned a small smile of her own. The two had gone through this galling dance before. "As long as you, Signor Caderre, have no doubts. Because any confusion of that importance would end quickly."

Eunizio laughed slightly, out of the workers' earshot now. He touched the brim of his flat cap. "*Si, si, padrona mia,*" he said with good humor. "I thank you from deep in my heart for allowing me to be so good at my job." With another touch of his cap, he returned to his tasks.

Regina watched the work a few more moments, then turned back across the yard with a certain eagerness. She could manage the rough culture of the big operation well enough, but it was paperwork—contracts and invoices and inventory—that consumed most of each day.

As she strode to the old priory building, Regina was surprised by a cowled figure in the shadows of its exterior stairs.

A young woman in a long skirt clutched at her shawl. Regina recognized the girl from somewhere, took a moment to place her. Ah, the daughter of their former banker, Basillea, who had abruptly dropped out of the public eye with all his family. Rumors had it his disappearance was because of an embezzlement scandal; others swore they had seen the entire family yoked behind a Wehrmacht *Kübelwagen* near the Borsa

Italiana in Milan. Regina, like Ettore, assumed they had fled north to neutral Switzerland.

The girl stepped forward and pushed back her shawl, revealing dark eyes, high cheekbones, and an aquiline nose. Her black hair was pinned in a bun at the nape of her neck.

This was the oldest one, Regina thought. Sara, was it?

"Signorina Basillea?" smiled Regina. "How good to see you after so long a time. How have you been, and your family?"

How have you been? Sara shuddered involuntarily at the query, recovered, focused on what mattered. She had decided on this course of action the last time Signor Como and she had liaisoned at the villetta. She had been enduring the man's crude exploitation of her body for her family's sake. But now, for her family's sake, a far more drastic step was needed.

"Signorina Vacci, please, excuse my impertinence," she said. As the daughter of a formerly respected Milanese financier, she had little experience at groveling. Yet the last few months had taught her how smoothly desperation propelled one's descent into ignominy. She stifled a sob.

"My dear, what can be the problem?" asked Regina, lightly embracing the girl. "Come, come. My office is just at the top of the stairs. Let us go up, tell me what is wrong."

Settled in a chair with a cup of tea, Sara unburdened herself. She told Regina of the family's desperate situation. Regina reacted with silent dismay as she heard of Pietro's involvement.

"My father went to Signor Como as the banker who had served the Vaccis and Comos faithfully and honestly for twenty years. Signor Como took full advantage. He would hide us, he said, and even help us escape, but at a cost. In exchange for food and a roof over our heads, father gave him his fine collection of Bartolozzi prints and all our mother's silver."

When she tearfully told Regina of her role as Pietro's mistress, the older woman stayed silent. It was not unusual for a successful man to have an *amante* besides a wife and home. But as the girl described the mercenary way Pietro used her, Regina's anger flared. She took Sara's hands. "You are doing what must be done to protect your own. But it is not right, none of it."

Sara sat up straighter, took a breath. "Nothing of what I have told you brings me here. It is the newest arrangement my father has promised the podestà. He claims to my mother he can manage it. But already I see the toll it takes on him. I know my father, in time he will collapse under guilt and remorse." She told Regina of the bargain Abramo had struck with Pietro.

"He acts out of love for us, but this will be his undoing. The names he gives are those of people he has known since boyhood. To continue to betray them, month after month, it will suck out his soul! He has given names to Signor Como for two months so far, and I see how he grieves."

Regina suddenly realized how dangerous Pietro was. Any attempt to corner him with this information could mean her own arrest. Pietro was far past the time when he would think twice before crushing a threat, even from family. "What do you ask of me?"

"Signorina Vacci, I beg you. Please, my family, we must flee. Despite my father's hopes, the podestà will never allow us to leave, especially now. We know no one who can navigate us over the mountains to Switzerland, so well-guarded and a difficult journey. I know your trucks travel south with concrete. I see them on the roads some evenings at the villetta. Is it within your heart to take our family close to American lines? It is the only chance for us. I appeal to you. Approach your father with my petition. All know that Signor Vacci is a good man. We lay our lives at his feet."

* * *

In the end, Ettore had nothing to do with it. The old man had slowed down greatly in the past few months. Arthritis in his feet, his back, his hands, made every day a weary ordeal; aching fatigue sent him to bed after dinner every day. Regina chose not to agitate him with the Basilleas' plight.

The route south that the company used for its black market traffic was fraught with peril. Such trading was punishable by death. Regina paid her drivers well for those trips; her foreman took great care to choose the right men.

The Germans' grim defenses marked the formidable divide between the Social Republic and the liberated south. But there were blind spots. The smugglers used tough, strong "shoulder boys" to haul huge packs of contraband strapped to their backs. The local guides they followed knew every gap in the defenses.

Regina met with Caderre to see if there was a way to help the Basilleas. Smuggling had largely stopped for the winter, but the trails would open again early spring. Using several go-betweens, her foreman made inquiries with the company's contacts in

Naples and reached an understanding. The fugitive family was to slip past the Germans on April 7th.

"We will do it in this way," the foreman said,. He, Regina, Sara, and Basillea himself stood together in the old Como fishing shed on the Pirino's east bank. The abandoned hut once stored tackle and small boats. An oil lamp hung from a roof crossbeam and cast a yellow halo on the floor.

"Please, allow me to speak," interrupted Basillea. "When my daughter came to me with this scheme, I said, no, absolutely not! Too dangerous for all concerned, not the least you, signorina," nodding to Regina. "But then I realized we have no choice. It is only a matter of time before my family becomes sticks thrown into the fire. So, I ask, what must we do?"

Caderre spoke. "Here is the plan. Get to the quarry the night of April 6th. Our convoy of dry concrete will depart early the following morning. One of the trucks will carry large wooden crates of disassembled concrete mixers." He gestured at Basillea. "You and your family will be hiding in two empty ones.

"We unload at a small village named La Rotta, within German lines but near the front. American positions are five miles south. In between is a ravine, difficult ground. The Wehrmacht considers it too rugged and too narrow for a major incursion. They did mine part of the area, and artillery spotters in the hills watch for infiltrators. Still, observation is difficult. The heavy woods provide plenty of good cover for a small band on the move.

"When we arrive at La Rotta, we unload everything, including your crates. Our empty trucks will leave, all but one. The Germans know that I and another man are staying to help assemble the mixers. At nightfall we open your crates and guide you into the woods. We will meet the smugglers at a small shrine to the Virgin on the trail. They take you from there to American lines."

"The mountains, they will be cold?" asked Basillea.

"Yes, of course. The snowmelt will have started, but the weather will be cold and wet. We will provide you coats, blankets, boots. Our friends will carry all of you out on their backs, in the harnesses they use for smuggled goods. Do not look so amazed, those boys can do it!" Eunizio glanced at Regina, back to the banker. "Bring the fee, in gold, to pay the smugglers. My advice? Give them more than agreed. This is a desperate act, signore, I will not lie. You are casting the dice. What numbers come up, only *fortuna* knows."

Chapter 46

6 April 1945: Castrubello

From the faces of the departing town council members, Tommaso Contadino knew the meeting had not gone well. Usually when the big doors of the conference room swung open, there were lighthearted remarks, cordial farewells. Today, the seven stern-faced *consiglieri* scurried out in a quick single file, glad to get away. Pietro still sat at the long table behind them.

Contadino stood silently outside the doorway, right hand grasping his left wrist at his waist.

Pietro fiddled with his ink pen. This nominal 'Consultative Council' of his had been more worthless today than usual. He had asked their views on a proposal to acquire a second water-tank truck for the town's street cleaning fleet. A banal enough question, surely. The response had been seven heads twitching like chickens hunting for spiders to peck from the wall, each member trying to fathom the minds of the others before committing himself. The hairy-tongued doubletalk that resulted was obtuse, even by this group's low standards.

Pietro missed the rough give-and-take sessions from back when his father was alive: emphatic foremen pushing the boss to meet their needs, Carlo insisting they justify every word out of their mouths. Meetings were long, loud, and messy, each one of them pure *opera buffa* minus the score. But, more times than not, they yielded smart decisions and, somehow, no permanently ruffled feathers. His son appreciated his father's knack for driving others in the direction he wanted, even as they believed they were getting their own way.

Abbastanza! Wasted daydreams from the dim long-ago, he thought. You handpicked these men for their incredible dullness so none could threaten your authority. Do not whimper now because you preside over turnips!

Pietro stood, adjusted his square, gold cufflinks, lightly smoothed his thin hair. His *agita* needed an outing. Only one thing seemed to suffice these days. He snapped open his pocket watch. At the same moment, a rap sounded at the open door.

A military messenger waited for acknowledgment. At Pietro's gesture, he gave Contadino a telegram who then brought it to the podestà. This day never ends, Pietro sighed. Yet another inane bureaucratic missive, likely regarding some misplaced triplicate. He dismissively opened the envelope, prepared to be impatiently bored.

Under the coat of arms of the Italian Social Republic he read:

It is my painful duty to convey the news that on the day of 2 April 1945 Carlo Arturo Como, captain, National Republican Air Force, son of Como, Pietro and of Grigio, Lucia, heroically lost his life defending the sacred homeland in an air battle over Turin.
Commander, 2nd Fighter Group,
Major Aldo Alessandrini

Pietro placed both hands on the table sitting stock-still. "Outside, please," he told Contadino. "Close the door." He slowly re-read the telegram.

His heart felt like exploding. He wanted to pick up the telephone and call somebody, but whom? Turin was the most bombed city in the country; he could hardly make a direct call to smoking ruins. He would require confirmation, of course, reports weren't infallible. Anything might have happened. Even as he stalled his emotions, he knew his only child was dead. The odds had been against him from the beginning. No, better to accept—for a moment he saw Carlo Arturo as a young boy, praying on his knees at his mother's grave. Convulsive sobs broke Pietro's chest. He smothered his nose and mouth with both hands, dropped his forehead to the table. His chest heaved, heaved again. He used all his strength to fight back the great hot tears that splashed his desk blotter. He gulped a deep breath, then another, wiped his sloppy eyes and nose, first with his hands, then his handkerchief. He rose, took another breath, unsteadily made his way to the door.

He told Contadino, "Take me to the villetta. Then drive to the stone house where the family dwells."

Pietro's sagged, raw face and hollow voice startled the driver. *Something worse than a council meeting has happened. The telegram?* He knew better than to ask.

"At the house, deliver a note I will give you to the Jew. Return to the villetta with his daughter."

Contadino nodded. He understood his boss was playing some deep game with the Hebrew banker, and part of it meant regularly defiling his daughter.

"Of course, signore," he replied.

A half-hour later, the grinding sound of the black Lancia's tires caught the Basillea household by surprise. Were they betrayed? This very night, within the hour, the convoy south was assembling at the quarry. Now, amid their final arrangements, the podestà himself was here?

But in fact, he was not. Sara looked through a slit in the sheet that covered one of the windows. As the car door slammed, she saw that the driver was alone.

"It is only Contadino," she told her parents, who had both frozen into statues.

Abramo Basillea answered the sharp rap.

His wife Rebecca had gathered their children to one side of the room and sat them at the dinner table as if waiting for food. Sara sat apart, closer to the door. She could only see the back of her father as he spoke with the podestà's man. After an inaudible exchange, Abramo shut the door. He held a note in his hand.

"This message is for you, from Como," he told Sara, handing her the slip of paper. "I will tell you right now, you will not do what he asks."

Sara scanned the words. She was to come to the villetta immediately. She raised her eyes.

Basillea's voice shook with anger and tension. "No. As head of this family, I tell you, no. If you do, who knows if you will join us in time? I will tell the driver you are feeling unwell."

Sara stood up, looked at her mother and younger siblings. The time for their rendezvous was imminent, all the arrangements locked in place. Nothing must raise suspicions. As soon as mother's eyes met daughter's, the only course of action became abundantly, painfully clear.

Rebecca spoke to her husband. "Abramo. The driver will only insist to see for himself. If he suspects something is amiss, all is lost. We cannot protect her from this. But by her going, we can protect our others."

Basillea turned to respond. As he did, Sara rose from her chair, took her shawl from its peg, and without a backward glance exited the door.

* * *

It was late at the villetta. Sara freshened herself in the basin of cold water, drying with a plush towel that draped the marble bar on the wall. She raked her fingers through her tangles. In the mirror, her careworn image stared back at her.

She had found Pietro unnervingly solicitous all night. He had talked far more than usual, of his childhood, his two brothers, his parents, and, incessantly, of his wonderful son, Carlo Arturo, the air force pilot stationed in Turin. Pietro had rushed through the sex even faster than usual; immediately afterward he had gone back to talking. As if his rambling reminisces about fishing with his boy meant anything to her, she thought. She hoped the Americans would blow up his plane!

The sedan was silent on the journey back. Sara prayed that her family had gotten out of the house safely. Once the Lancia left her at the house, she would run to the quarry, there was still time!

It was full dark now, few lights anywhere. The road up to the stone and mortar house was especially black. Sara immediately sensed its stark emptiness, wondered if the two men in the car had a similar inkling.

"All asleep," Pietro observed on their approach. "Contadino, keep things quiet." The driver cut the engines. As the Lancia glided to a stop, the headlights of the car shined full force at the blank front of the dwelling. "Here, Contadino," he said. He reached forward and gave the driver a tin of *mostaccioli* over his shoulder. "Give these cookies to Signora Basillea, for the family."

Sara's neck hair stood on end. She had planned to quickly slip in the door, close it behind her, and that would be that. But with the driver standing alongside, what chance did she have for a ruse?

"I will take your gift, sir," she told Pietro, reaching for the tin. "No need for..."

"Go up and present them to the signora, Contadino," Pietro repeated, louder.

The driver took the tin, strode to the door, prepared to knock. "I do not want to wake them," Sara whispered loudly, trailing behind. "Please, I have a key." The headlights cast giant shadows. She inserted the key, gave it a twist, tried to reach the door handle and slide past, but out of reflexive courtesy, Contadino swung it wide open.

The auto's harsh white headlights blasted the vacant room. Within two steps, Contadino knew that no one was present. The food shelves were empty, clothing pegs bare, nothing stirred. In civilized propriety, freshly laundered bedclothes lay neatly folded and stacked on the sleeping pallets.

Waiting in the sedan, Pietro saw Contadino step out of the doorway, grasping Sara's arm. With his free hand, he signaled Como to the house.

* * *

The three trucks were drawn up on the grounds of Naviglio Quarry & Concrete. The only light came from lanterns propped up on bumpers and fenders. Otherwise, the entire property was blacked out; Allied night bombing over Lombardia had increased of late.

"No, we must give her more time, I tell you," Abramo Basillea repeated. He paced distractedly. His family stood huddled next to one of the vehicles, their meager bundles of belongings at their feet. "What can be keeping her?" Two large empty crates that would carry himself and his family to freedom sat in the back of one of the three big Lancia Ro trucks waiting to go. Both crates remained open on one side, as two of the foreman's workers waited for their fugitive occupants.

"And I am saying there is no more time to wait, Signor Basillea," Caderre responded, with some agitation. The small convoy should have left south for the German positions an hour ago. Too much delay would prompt unwanted scrutiny upon their arrival at La Rotta. If discovered, Caderre knew full well, this night would be the last on earth for them all. The other two trucks already sat loaded; the remaining one still waited for the Jews to take their places. How selfish for this banker to place all of us at risk this way, the foreman fumed.

Rebecca Basillea took Abramo's arm. In her heart, she knew something had gone wrong. Sara's decision to go with the podestà's driver was one of courage. How could her family now abandon her to her fate? But when Rebecca looked at her son and the two younger girls, she pushed her fears away. May God be with Sara, she prayed. Perhaps they would one day see her again. But for now, she had her three other children to save.

"Abramo, my love," she told her husband. "We must go. We must trust that God will guide Sara's steps back to us. But we cannot throw her love and bravery away by ruining our escape."

Caderre spoke up. "I will leave one man here to wait for your daughter. When she comes, my wife and I will hide her in our own home. I give you my word on this."

The two Basilleas buried their faces in each other's shoulders, embraced, silently rocking. Abramo was first to lift his head. He wiped his sleeve across his eyes as his wife blew her nose. He approached his other children, drew them close. Seeing their parents weeping, they started weeping themselves.

"Come, come, children," Abramo said. "Enough tears. Sara will come to us soon. Meanwhile, we must find our way to our safe destination, so when she arrives, we will be waiting to welcome her with our joyful embraces."

Workers helped hoist each of the family onto the bed of the truck. Father and son went into one of the containers. Rebecca joined her two little daughters in the other, but not before she knew her husband and son Aarone had a blanket and a bit of bread and cheese wrapped in a handkerchief. They all sat with their knees drawn up as men hammered the final side of each box into place, enclosing the fugitives in darkness.

Caderre supervised the loading of the cement mixer crates, hiding those of the Basilleas from view. When the last one was in place, Caderre squeezed through the narrow path that remained and rapped his knuckles to signal to the family they were about to depart.

"Are you ready?" he called through the wooden slats.

"We are," returned Abramo's muffled voice. *"B'ezrat HaShem!"*

* * *

Since the arrival of the Germans, Torrquadro never slept. Three shifts of OVRA and SS agents kept the building manned around the clock.

Captain Bulow, the duty officer, returned from the holding pens in the adjacent west building. It being a Thursday, few criminals were currently in their hands. Wednesdays were when they hauled prisoners to the camps at San Sabba or Borgo San Dalmazzo. As the collecting point for all regional malcontents, the Torrquadro trucks were generally full. Both OVRA and the SS were diligent in chasing down undesirables, and the good-natured rivalry between the units added interest—and wagering!—to their relative yields. Nonetheless, a quiet night like this was always welcome. Enjoy, Bulow told himself.

The podestà's black sedan arrived just as the captain stepped outside to enjoy a cigarette. Bulow checked his wristwatch. Quite late for a visit.

The chauffeur, his name escaped the captain, got out from behind the wheel. He stepped next to the rear passenger door of the Lancia. "I am here at the behest of Podestà Como," Contadino said, opening the auto's door. "In his name, I deliver a prisoner. A partisan Jewess."

The captain returned his unlit cigarette to its silver case and peered into the back seat. He pulled back quickly.

"Your prisoner, is she alive?" Bulow asked. She did not look it.

"She was alive when we captured her," the driver said evenly. "She was in the podestà's temporary employ, a substitute housekeeper. He had never seen her before this night. Within moments of arriving, she tried to murder the podestà with a dagger, screaming in Yiddish. Signor Como defended himself. She fell down some stairs as she tried to flee." He took a cursory moment to view Sara slumped sideways in the auto. "At that point, she was breathing."

At Como's first outraged blow, Contadino had known Sara would never leave the small house alive. Realizing the Basilleas were gone, Pietro had snatched the cookie tin from Contadino and struck the woman full in the face. Once on the floor, his frenzied kicking had finished her quickly. Contadino finally pulled Pietro back, a weeping wreck. Contadino worked out this plan.

Serving in the SS intelligence service, Bulow had heard many strange stories. The truth of this tale? Ah, well, not impossible, he supposed. But, when an official as important as this one claimed it was so, Bulow understood his role as the solicitous middleman.

"How frightening for the signore," Captain Bulow said. "I trust he is unharmed." The chauffeur nodded.

The German called the nearby guards. One aimed his pocket lamp into the rear seat, squeezing its lever to generate light. There was no doubt that the pale woman, covered in bruises and with pulp for one eye, was dead. They wrapped the body in a canvas tarp, and with one man holding the shoulders and the other the feet, hauled the corpse around the side of the building toward the facility's morgue.

"Podestà Como will make a full report tomorrow," said Contadino. He slid back into the driver's seat. "He said to tell Major Gabinno to count her as one of his Jews for this month."

* * *

"You say this was the weapon?" Brigadeführer von Gottlieb held the blade by its handle. A basic carving knife, nothing special, the kind found in any kitchen.

Pietro Como emphatically nodded. "The woman attacked from behind, screaming gibberish. Luckily, I saw her reflection in the windowpane in front of me. When I struck her across the face, that dagger fell to the floor. She tried to run, but she stumbled on the stairs and struck her head." He looked down for a moment, startled to see a crimson-brown stain on his trousers' cuff. He slid his foot back. "The staircase is stone."

"A pity she came to us dead. It would have been better if we had the opportunity to question her." Von Gottlieb handed the knife to the OVRA commander. After a brief examination, Major Gabinno laid it on the round table where the three men sat.

Pietro felt the silence linger for too long, as if there may be doubts about his account. "I tell you, Brigadeführer, this murder attempt is irrefutable proof a nefarious network of Communist partisans is operating here in the area!"

The brigadier calmly considered Como. *The poor man has certainly worked himself into a froth, hasn't he? Of course, an attempt on one's life would agitate anyone. But this attack, out of the blue? Since his arrival in Castrubello, diligent SS and OVRA intelligence teams had reported no such local network, no conspiracies. Agitators and troublemakers, yes. An occasional partisan spy. But there had been no hint whatsoever of pending violence.*

Perhaps the matter was more personal than political, von Gottlieb thought. *Jewish mistresses were not unusual even among the Nazi elite. Was this the case, simply a domestic affair gone terribly awry? Far more probable than Como's story of a crazed, Yiddish-screaming assailant. He wondered what an investigation of Como's villetta might discover.*

Ach, stop conjecturing, the German told himself. *The truth was hardly important. The tale of the attempted murder was already in the wind and may well encourage others.* He turned to Gabinno.

"I see things this way, Major. Clearly, reprisals are in order. An assassination attempt by an Italian Jewess on an Italian official warrants that Italian security must act!"

"What number do you suggest, Brigadeführer?" Major Gabinno asked.

"For a failed attempt?" Von Gottlieb gave the matter a moment's thought. "Enough to sting. Eight, I think. Three days from today, in the town piazza."

Gabinno scribbled notes on a pad.

"Also," von Gottlieb added, "the eight must be staunch citizens, not nobodies swept from the jails. Men of good standing. The locals must think, 'If these ones are not safe from retribution, can anyone be?' No, no traitor is safe. That is our message." He presented Pietro an ingratiating smile. "As the offended party, Signor Podestà, we will defer to you as to whom Major Gabinno arrests."

Pietro registered no surprise. Why would he? He had gone through this scenario in his mind during the sleepless night before. Sara's death had been a reflexive action on his part, unintended, but when all was said and done, the slut deserved it. After baring his soul, talking so fondly of his boy as if he were still alive, she had played him for a buffoon. Now her insult was dead with her. As for the Basilleas, he assumed they were beyond anyone's reach, which suited him fine. No one to contradict his version of events or to reveal the fact that for months he had been harboring Jews!

He knew his fellow townsmen would blame him for the coming reprisals. It no longer mattered. He was the ranking civil official of Castrubello, in a regime his son had died for. Pietro absently touched the Fascist Party pin fastened to his lapel, straightened his shoulders. "So be it," he said.

Chapter 47

8 April 1945

Regina was on hand to meet the last quarry truck upon its return. Eunizio Caderre clambered from the cab, flexed his arms, stretched. Another man in the cab and two from the truck's covered bed did the same.

"Long haul," he said.

Once back in her office, a short glass of grappa in hand, Eunizio told her, "All went well. Timing is everything in such matters, you know this. Delays are the worry. But the smugglers were waiting when we arrived. The Basilleas were exhausted, cramped from the small space, to be expected. The smugglers were friendly enough, took them in tow, I saw the money change hands. I trust the band that met them, the usual crew." He rubbed his face.

"And you say the family was all right?"

He downed his drink with a noisy slurp. "The father and mother fretted greatly about their daughter. I assured them we would see what we could do. They had their other children to manage, it was dark, I could not see their every reaction.

"When we unloaded at our stop, they thanked us. The mother gave me this to give to you." He handed Regina a silver Star of David on a delicate chain. Regina held it to the light, placed it in the pocket of her smock.

"She said she wished she could have given you more. The father told me that once they were safe, they hoped to eventually go on to Palestine."

Regina refilled the small glass for Eunizio, poured one for herself.

"The last I saw of them, the wife and children were strapped onto the backs of four of the *spalloni*, their legs and feet hanging through holes in the big baskets. I had not ever seen anything like that. The father insisted on hiking with the men. Off they set out on their journey."

Regina sat. "Their journey has hardly begun if Palestine is their goal. As for the daughter, Sara, I sent Grillo to the house before dawn. The door was locked with no signs of her."

Eunizio made a noncommittal grunt. If the daughter were caught, she could implicate them all. He shrugged. It was out of their hands. What happens, happens.

"I heard another thing, from Reggio, the smugglers' chief. He knows this quarry once belonged to the Comos and said he heard news of a man named Como, an army engineer, a northerner."

Regina raised her head. "Not Donato!"

"It may be. Reggio's cousin crewed a smuggling trawler in the east. He said a Tenente Como came aboard in Russia a couple of months after the Italian lines were broken."

Regina carefully settled her glass on the table. "And now?"

"The boat foundered on the east coast. The Germans captured the survivors, marched them off in a work brigade. Reggio's cousin lay on his stomach in the breakers until they were gone."

Eunizio noted Regina's suppressed *agita*. "There is still room for hope. On the trawler, the tenente spoke of joining the partisans. Whether Signor Donato slaves for the Germans or has managed to escape, he is no weakling. If he survived Russia, he is capable of surviving this."

Regina stood and turned her back. "Thank you, Eunizio, the news will give Papà something to," she hesitated, "to cling to."

After a moment, Caderre awkwardly rose from his chair, clutched his cap. "It is time I am home, signorina. Returning this morning, I saw soldiers knocking on doors. Who knows why?"

* * *

10 April 1945: Castrubello

"Alzatevi!" At the barked command, the eight men rose to their feet in the back of the truck. Stefano Scrivatti lifted his face into the hard spring rain. OVRA had arrested him two days before along with Diamonte the baker, Brettone from the weaving mill, the watchmaker Prego, and four others pulled from workbenches and shops.

The guards marched the trussed men single file to the middle of Piazza San Giulio where perhaps a hundred soaked villagers had gathered. Earlier, an infantry platoon had gone door to door, haranguing them out of their dwellings. The spectacle must have witnesses if it was to serve as a deterrent.

Cold rain ran down Scrivatti's head and neck. He still wore his leather cobbler's apron. Only his feet were dry, protected by his shop's best boots.

In Castrubello's long history, there had never been a public execution in the church square. Tile-roofed shops and residential structures enclosed the space, except for the side that fronted San Giulio Church. There, a priest stood under a black umbrella held by a dripping altar boy.

As the guards lined him up with the others and forced him to his knees, Scrivatti prayed. He prayed to San Giulio, which was an easy inspiration, for they faced the saint's church. The padre came close, protected by the umbrella, his purple stole bright against his white surplice. He offered a blessing in Latin, gestured a cross over each one, stepped back again.

Major Gabinno took his place. His leather, knee-length overcoat glistened in the downpour. He spoke past their heads to the sullen gaggle of townspeople.

"Today we avenge the cowardly attack upon your podestà. You failed to stand vigilant against the assassin in your midst. These eight men perish to remind you all: in time of war, complacency is complicity!"

As the officer stepped behind the prisoners, he toggled his Luger with a crisp snap. Scrivatti's prayer froze at the first shot. *CRACK!* Prego, next to him, pitched face-first into the puddled cobblestones. Nearby, a metallic *Ping!* as the ejected brass casing struck the ground. Scrivatti's mind cleared. "Receive me, O..."

CRACK! ... Ping!

Major Gabinno continued down the short line.

* * *

17 April 1945: Approaching Castrubello

The partisan detachment had stopped for the night when the priest's message arrived. They were six miles north of Castrubello in the middle of an overgrown mulberry orchard. Tree cover offered some protection from a desultory drizzle, although occasional fat drops spattered down from the branches. Men unrolled their blankets on the ground, heads close to tree trunks, futilely seeking dryness. There were no cooking fires.

Donato told the reddish-haired courier, a boy from the village, to wait out of earshot of the camp. He took the folded note and brought it to the commander.

"The padre says the funeral remains set for ten a.m. tomorrow," Colonel Morte announced, after reading the note. "And he confirms Gabinno is one of the pallbearers. The priest will finish the ceremony at the cemetery at eleven o'clock sharp. He says our man will not attend the family's reception afterward, citing," he again looked at the note, "'official duties.' That means he will go directly back to Torrquadro."

Donato tried to remember his dead cousin, Carlo Arturo. With an eight year age difference, they had barely known each other. Zio Pietro must have moved heaven and earth to recover the body, he thought.

The partisans' assignment was straightforward: strike down the OVRA major, Gabinno, for his role in the reprisal executions. Donato was a logical addition to the fourteen-man strike team. He knew the area and had led men before. Effective in recent actions, the men had elected him their second-in-command for this mission.

Morte turned to him. "Tenente, run us through it all again."

Donato squatted on his haunches, cleared a spot in the wet dirt and used a stick to scrape a map. "Torrquadro, cemetery, the same road connecting both. The reception at the villa over here. The major travels by staff car, a Mercedes-Benz 320. His bodyguards sometimes stand on the running boards. A motorcycle precedes. He may forego it tomorrow, this being a funeral."

He drew a horizontal line touching the first. "A mile from the cemetery, a country road joins the main thoroughfare. Colonel Morte's squad blocks the main road here, forcing the sedan to veer down that road. After the car turns, they hit a second roadblock after two hundred feet." He looked up into the faces. "Squad two, your squad, Santo, you're on your bellies on the left." He stabbed a spot. "As soon as the sedan stops, roll your grenades underneath the chassis. Throw them if there's an open window, but do not overthrow or you'll blow the hell out of me and squad three here, across the way a bit forward. Once you toss the grenades, start shooting. My squad, we make sure Gabinno can't exit our side. Stay low everybody, bullets will be flying."

"Remember," Morte added. "We retrieve the major. Dead or alive, whole or in parts, he is to hang from a tree. After that, we scatter, rendezvous back here." He looked around the circle. "Questions? You already know all of this. Now then, check your weapons, keep them dry, no misfires tomorrow. We break camp early, so eat something, get as much sleep as you can. Squad one has first sentry duty." He told Donato, "Send the boy back. We have no reply."

Donato took a moment to jot a note of his own. He walked over and gave it to the waiting courier, a youth no more than fifteen. "Take this to Villa Vacci, you know the place?"

"*Certo*, signore, everyone does."

"Good. Put it into the hands of Signorina Vacci."

"I understand. But she may be at the concrete factory. She is the padrona there."

The news surprised Donato. Regina now owns the quarry? Yet, he did not doubt the information. The war had spawned an unpredictable version of the previous world. He clapped the boy on the shoulder. "Very well, then get her the message, wherever she is."

The boy nodded and hared off into the shadows.

That night, lying on his back on a damp blanket, Donato put aside his thoughts of Regina. He reviewed the coming mission within the blackness of the woolen cap pulled over his face.

They had wanted to kill the Nazi von Gottlieb and Gabinno together. But earlier news from the priest had canceled the possibility. The brigadeführer was off at a weeklong conference in Salò. For his part, Donato was glad of the news. To get them both, the attack would have been directly on the Como funeral procession.

Tomorrow, a killing blow was also to fall on Torrquadro. The partisans carried a ground-to-air radio transceiver, delivered the prior week by the American OSS, eager to maximize the day's chaos. After the assassination, they were to contact an American bomber stationed overhead. Its job was to drop bombs on Torrquadro then return to its base at Foggia. The local dwellings nearby? OSS agents assured them the bomb run would be precise.

A happy fantasy, in Donato's view. All the bombs he'd ever seen had fallen wherever they liked.

* * *

Donato stroked his whiskery chin and nodded to the colonel. The partisans shook themselves to their feet, secured their haversacks and hid them in trees or under debris. Each carried a Beretta M38 submachine gun, recent acquisitions from the great arms factory on Lago Como. A raid three weeks before had yielded a large supply of the prized firearms. And a bloodless raid to boot! While the great factory of Pietro Beretta and his sons produced arms for the Fascists, under duress, they simultaneously found ways to provide anti-fascist partisans with the same. The gun crates had been waiting, stacked on a loading dock. Donato had drawn the guards to one side of the factory with a diversion while fellow partisans loaded the boxes onto wagons at the other. Some of Beretta's workers had even helped. Asked about the arrangement, one worker answered Donato with a shrug. "What better way to handle *fortuna*, I ask you? Plant one foot firmly on each side of the stream, then piss in it!"

Donato hefted a munitions duffel, with its collection of twenty-round magazines and MK "pineapple" hand grenades on his back. Like the ground-to-air radio transceiver they packed with them, the explosives were the gift of the American OSS.

Donato flexed his mangled left hand. It still ached at times, but the surviving two fingers and thumb allowed him fair dexterity. He had long given up shooting a pistol with his left; he had never been very steady at it in any event. These days he far preferred the spray-power of his treasured twenty-round submachine gun.

* * *

This coffin is much lighter than I expected, thought Major Gabinno, as with the others he hefted the long box to his shoulder. He paid careful attention to the strides of his fellow pallbearers as they slowly paced to the marble mausoleum, engraved with "COMO" atop its metal doors. The octagon building was relatively new; its white marble walls gleamed unnaturally bright in Castrubello's ancient burial ground.

Gabinno did not want to think of what was inside the oaken box. The remains of the young aviator had taken two weeks to recover. His crashed fighter plane had been a heap of twisted steel buried nose-first in pulverized concrete.

After the interment, he shook hands with other attendees. He noticed old Ettore Vacci in his black suit, looking forlorn. Vacci's daughter guided him by the arm to their waiting auto.

"Time I am off," he said to Captain Costello. "You go on to the villa. Enjoy the gathering, if that's the correct sentiment." Costello saluted, snapped his fingers, gathering Gabinno's bodyguards to him. "You travel with the major," he said to one. "Ride inside. The motorcycle leads the way, as usual."

As his superior's vehicle pulled away, Costello felt a strange spasm of alarm. "You four," he said, pointing to nearby OVRA men. "Take my auto and follow the major. When he arrives safely, meet me at the reception." The detail hastened to organize itself.

Major Gabinno enjoyed the quaint country scenery as they drove. His right arm rested on the sill. One man sat next to him, silent, bracing his Mauser.

They traveled past a scrabble of old stone and masonry buildings. The structures thinned out, open country emerged.

The hum of the tires lulled the major. Nothing like traveling a good road for a rare chance to put one's head back, he thought. The straightaway allowed the driver to accelerate.

A sudden hard tattering sound—gunfire! The motorcyclist ahead crashed sideways in a spinning skid. As the car slowed, four men rolled a hay wagon directly across the roadway.

"Dio santo!" the driver cried. He yanked the wheel hard to the right, tires squealing. The auto bounced on the unpaved surface, throwing up mud. Gabinno heard more gunfire, now from behind. The driver braked hard, seeing the blockading ditch too late. The sedan fishtailed but plowed forward. With a crashing jolt, its front tires hit the camouflaged trench, wheels still spinning mud. His bodyguard pushed Gabinno to the floor. Three loud explosions in quick succession blew the sedan onto its right side.

Donato and his squad rose from beside the road. They peppered the Benz, their rounds relentlessly thunking through its roof. The man next to Donato screamed, threw up his arms, went down, his back laced with holes. Donato turned to where a second car had stopped up on the main road. Soldiers were firing from along its fenders and sides; a hail of rounds in his direction forced him to the ground.

They have the angle on us, he realized. The strada was slightly above the road that intersected it, presenting a perfect field of fire directed at his squad. He saw two of his five men splayed in the mud. He and the others turned from the wrecked auto to return fire on their attackers.

Gabinno pushed his dead bodyguard to the side, then dragged himself over his dead driver, and out through the shattered windshield. He crawled past the blocking ditch. His men were all dead or wounded from the attack. He would have been also if that second car hadn't arrived. A medal for Costello, Gabinno resolved.

He came to his feet, tried to unholster his sidearm but couldn't. Something was wrong with his right shoulder; he pulled out the weapon with his left hand. His right arm burnt as he moved. The open fields beckoned, his chance to escape! He scoffed at the idea. He had no chance. Besides, I have lived my life for my Duce, he thought. Today, I die for him. He turned back.

Donato heard a crack from behind and felt a sharp burn crease his scalp. Warm wetness trickled down the side of his head. He saw Gabinno staggering his way, aiming a pistol. The major slowly, deliberately, squeezed the trigger again. The bullet struck the mangled Mercedes. Gabinno's bloody arm dangled dead at his side. Donato tried to fire, but his Beretta was jammed with mud. Another round from Gabinno went high and left. The two men were a mere thirty feet apart. Donato drew his knife from its sheath, began a sloggy run forward. Gabinno stopped, raised his Luger one more time.

Before Donato took three strides, automatic fire stitched sudden holes across Gabinno's torso, compelling a spastic-armed jig. From his left, Donato saw the colonel and two others advancing. Riddled with bleeding holes, Gabinno sat straight down, twisted-legged, upright, chin on chest. No further sounds came from the field or the roadway.

Colonel Morte came up, kicked the body over. "My men and I will now hang him," he said. "You talk to our friend up there in heaven."

Chapter 48

The aircraft's radio squawked a series of static-broken words in Italian. Sergeant Gerhardt adjusted the volume down. The Joan-Eleanor ground-to-air system was quite new. Developed specifically for use by the OSS to allow its field agents to talk to air support, the SSTR-6 transceiver had been fitted into the *Minx* specifically for this mission. He'd been specially trained in the system's use only the week before.

Lou Gephardt didn't like it in the least. The forty-pound device took up just enough extra space to severely cramp the radioman in his already crowded, sideways-facing seat behind the pilots.

After further twisting dials to strengthen the signal, in his earphones he heard a tinny voice say, "*Garibaldi, okay. Ripeto. Garibaldi, okay.*"

"Skip," he said. "It's them. We're good to go."

At the controls, Salski was more than glad to hear it. The B-24 Liberator was nearing its second hour of circling at an altitude of five thousand feet. "Let them know we're five minutes away." He turned to O'Brien, his co-pilot. "Jimmy, I want to get out us of here before fuel is an issue. Here we go. I'm sliding us lower." As he pushed forward on the yoke with both hands, *Motor City Minx* banked gracefully downward.

Below, the silver Pirino River widened. Nearby was the canal that would guide them straight to their target. From this altitude, the world looked at peace. Salski loved the northern Italian countryside from the air, partly for its natural beauty but partly, he knew, because it was in his blood.

His widowed mother told him that she'd been born somewhere here in north Italy and that his father had died shortly after they emigrated to America. He always wanted to know more of that story, but his mother remained resolutely tight-lipped. She remarried a mechanic who serviced aircraft at Detroit Municipal Airport, the son of a Krakow-born butcher who provided meat for corner markets in the city. Both the Italian and Polish cultures heartily discouraged mixed marriages, but the woman was alone with a small child, and she accepted the first proposal she received.

His mother died of influenza when Lawrence, as he was called, was seven, and his stepfather, Jozef Salski, raised him in the city's robust Polish enclave of Hamtramck. With no wife at home, the mechanic brought the boy to work with him on his days off from school, including summers. It was there as an apprentice that young Lawrence fell in love with flying. The site of biplanes and single-wingers landing and taking off within sight of the repair hangar captivated him. By his teens he had his heart set on becoming a pilot.

No further stories of his mother's family were forthcoming, nor was contact with his Italian cousins in town maintained. The break was on both sides, a casualty of the unseemly remarriage.

He brought the aircraft to two thousand feet. This was low for a bomb run, but the target was small and precision a priority. As the bomber broke under the clouds, the compact castle lay dead ahead. "The approach looks good, Skip," said O'Brien. Neither officer was keen on this mission. Bomb Turin with the rest of the squadron, then hang around for hours, alone, to light up some dumpy fortress? Chalk up another dumbass OSS brainstorm, both men agreed.

The aircraft leveled. "No flak, no bogeys, we'll keep this run manual, Eugene, nice and simple," Salski said.

The bombardier, seated in the nose, worked to line the target up in his bombsite. The signal bell jangled as the bomb bay doors gaped open. Two five-hundred-pound eggs had been held back for this mission.

Minx closed quickly from the west. Just as the bombardier pulled the bomb release lever, the pilot shouted, "What the hell?" and lurched the plane hard to the left and up. The awkward jerk sent the bombs falling askew.

"Son of a bitch!" exclaimed O'Brien. "Where did that thing come from?" He squinted. "A Messerschmidt 262?" Profiles of the radical new weapon were posted in the base briefing room; nobody in the squadron had ever actually seen one. As the men in the cockpit watched the sweptwing jet fighter bank right, flashing a black swastika on its tail, the bomber shuddered from cannon rounds hammering its fuselage. A half-moment later, a second silver-skinned lightning bolt passed overhead with another ear-shattering screech, followed by the belated blasting of the *Minx's* top turret machine guns.

"Christ, they're doing four-fifty at least," said O'Brien, leaning into the cockpit's tempered glass windshield.

The intercom crackled in the pilot's ears. "Looks like just two of the bastards," reported *Minx's* top turret gunner. "They're circling back." Salski visually checked his four Pratt & Whitney engines. No signs of damage.

"Goddammit, Jimmy," Salski said to his co-pilot. "They told us there weren't going to be any of those things around here for months." Since late November, new German jets had begun making their appearance against Allied bomber formations over Germany. The enemy had been striving mightily to get their revolutionary aircraft produced and manned fast enough to make a difference in the war. But time was running out for their mass production, along with German pilots. Yet some were still trickling into action; somehow these two today had found their way to the Italian front.

Just our luck to be the first to face them, the pilot thought. He spoke into his mouthpiece. "Somebody get me a damage report, let's make sure nobody's hit. Sergeant, ring up Foggia, get them to scramble some P-38s to meet us on the way home. Gunners, remember to lead wide when you fire!" He kept his fingers crossed that the *Minx's* ten fifty-caliber Browning machine guns would throw up enough lead to at least ding their attackers. He hazarded a look at the tilted landscape. Rising smoke marked where the misguided bombs had randomly struck along the canal. He silently swore. The turreted castle stood intact.

The B-24 fled south, struggling to climb. Cloud cover was their only chance to elude their two tormentors, Salski knew. Brand new, these bombers only did two hundred ninety miles per hour; *Minx* was hardly new.

Another pass by both enemy aircraft peppered thirty-millimeter autocannon rounds into the Liberator's aluminum skin. From behind him, the pilot heard the cries of wounded men.

"Skipper," said O'Brien, jabbing a pointed finger past the pilot's nose. The outside left engine seeped a tendril of oil vapor; the propeller was feathering. Its cowling burst into flame. The inside engine began bleeding smoke, then fire engulfed it as well. The Liberator took a long lurch downward.

Both pilots fought to keep the nose up, to no avail. Their rate of descent increased by the second, too fast and steep for bailing out.

"Strap in!" Salski called to his crew. "Wheels down, Jimmy."

"Landing gear not engaging," O'Brien said in a tight voice.

"Screw it. Help me bring us down level." Below them was the wide Pirino, a flat sparkling ribbon in the sun. "I'm lining us up on the river. We're getting wet."

From where his squad hiked west, away from the ambush site, Donato saw the smoking B-24 dropping from the sky. Its burning left wing tilted precariously upward at the last moment. The bomber disappeared behind the Pirino's tree line, bounced high in a slow-motion cartwheel, then disappeared again in a deafening eruption of flame.

"Tenente?" asked the first man behind him tentatively, indicating the pluming black smoke from the crash.

"No time," Donato answered. "Keep moving."

High above, two silver dots banked north, white contrails streaking the sky.

Chapter 49

20 April 1945: Castrubello

Brigadeführer von Gottlieb had planned to return to Castrubello two days earlier, but stepped-up partisan attacks on Fascist forces, coordinated with factory strikes in the cities, were creating widespread havoc across the Social Republic. And yesterday, the anti-regime National Liberation Committee, speaking for all partisan units in the field, issued the most brazen of ultimatums. Its broadsheet read, in part:

> *Surrender or Perish! All members of the so-called armed forces of the Fascist government caught with weapons will face summary execution. Those who do not immediately surrender to the National Liberation Committee must prepare for extermination!*

The senior officer staff meeting in Salò had been beyond grim. Ultimatums aside, it was clear the Third Reich faced an existential crisis. Since the failure of Hitler's desperate winter offensive in the Ardennes forest, the regime's downward spiral had accelerated. The Gothic Line had finally cracked after a thousand Allied planes dropped twenty-five thousand bombs on German positions. Besides the enemy divisions now breaking into the Po Valley, Russian forces had closed within fifty miles of Berlin, while Allied armies, two hundred miles past the Rhine, relentlessly pursued Wehrmacht formations in full retreat.

The message at the meeting was clear. It was time for the military district to rally its remaining forces for the final stand. Von Gottlieb had returned to Castrubello to collect retreating troops and rendezvous at Lago Garda with elements of German Army Group C. The construction of yet another defensive redoubt was planned, this time across the Alps themselves.

But for von Gottlieb, meting out justice for Gabinno's assassination was the first order of business. The OVRA commander's slaughter was an unspeakable affront. The subsequent lynching of his bullet-flayed body compounded the atrocity. Moreover, a coinciding aerial attack, heroically thwarted by Luftwaffe pilots, spoke of sophisticated coordination with Allied forces. The partisans were flaunting an arrogance that demanded retribution.

Long ago, von Gottlieb had fully committed to his Fuhrer's ideals. He had acted with vigor against partisans in Rome, so would he now. There was no greater priority than a farewell assertion of Aryan superiority over these craven, ungrateful primitives.

* * *

22 April 1945: Castrubello

Ettore Vacci viewed the leaden sky. The landscape always seemed despairing these days, and yet it was spring, when the opposite should be true! The grayness outside was not only the refraction of light from an obscured sun, mused the old man. These days as much bleakness seemed to come from within as without.

But despair, like all things, ran in cycles, Ettore knew, and perhaps this cycle was nearing its end. His daughter had shared the latest jumble of rumors. The Americans were coming; no it was Yugoslav partisans. The British were in Austria; on the contrary, the British had all shipped to Greece. Mussolini was dead, but, on the other hand, seen alive and well in Buenos Aires. The stories were endless. Who knew what was true? The only certainty was uncertainty. All I know is today, Ettore thought. And today, all Castrubellese had received notice to gather in Piazza San Giulio by 11 a.m.

"Regina, why do you weep?" he asked, as he entered the morning room. She sat at the table, a handkerchief at her face. Ettore sat down. "Tell me, *cara mia*."

Regina looked up at her adoptive father, collecting herself. "I received a message, Papà." She handed Ettore the hurriedly scrawled note.

Regina. I am not far.

"It is Donato, Papà, who else could it be?" Regina said. "It is the first word from him in two years."

"Yes," Ettore said, refolding the note. "He will come back to you, Regina. That is the message. We must have faith in him.

Now, Regina, this must disappear." Ettore tore the note into shreds before she could react. "For the sake of everyone."

Their automobile ride to the piazza took only ten minutes. Leaving the villa, Ettore saw a German open-backed Horch armored car parked across the road, its crew lounging outside the vehicle, staring back at him.

"I have no idea why they are out there, signore," said his driver to Ettore's query. "Monitoring traffic? Taking a break? There are Germans all over the place this morning. Units are gathering at the bridge to move north as a convoy. SS men are knocking on doors to get people to the piazza. Something big is up, no doubt of that."

They parked near the square and took their places in the crowd. Regina had never seen the piazza so full. United by centuries of shared histories and family bloodlines, the Castrubellese were usually animated and social among each other. But today, voices stayed muted, movements restrained. In the church campanile above them, two German soldiers scanned the countryside, and occasionally the crowd, with field glasses.

Armored cars blocked the side streets. Across from the church, there were three more such vehicles with mounted machine guns, arrayed in an arc in front of the townspeople. A Waffen-SS platoon stood at attention, weapons slung on shoulders, to the side.

A black Lancia sedan swung into the square, followed by a covered troop transport. Ettore recognized the auto as Pietro's.

Podestà Como indeed did step out but then held the door for his fellow passenger.

Brigadeführer von Gottlieb wore his dress uniform. Two aides hastened forward to place a compact wooden platform, one tall step high, at von Gottlieb's feet. At the same time, additional troopers armed with submachine guns debarked from the truck and took positions facing the crowd.

"Papà," said Regina. "Let us slip away. This does not feel right."

"I know, my daughter," Ettore said, "but we stand with our townsmen. Stay behind me."

From his small stage, the brigadeführer surveyed his reluctant audience, nearly two thousand men, women, and children in all. At his glance, a sergeant used his signal whistle to make three long blasts. After repeating the shrill noise twice more, the piazza fell into complete silence.

The commander, reading from a paper he wrote the night before, in part to be certain his Italian was proper, spoke.

"People of Castrubello. When your government betrayed you, we Germans came to your defense. Because of us, the barbaric enemy has paid a bloody price for every footprint he dared place on Italian soil. We rescued your leader, Benito Mussolini, from ignominious captivity. Loyal Italian men have fought alongside us; together we have lost heroic lives in the name of honor and country.

"But instead of the gratitude we deserve, you have stabbed us in the back! You have harbored assassins, Communists, Jews, all manner of traitors! Even if you yourselves never raised a hand against the Reich, you are all guilty of a criminal indifference that directly led to the heinous murder of Major Gabinno. His death is on Castrubello, and upon Castrubello will retribution fall!"

He looked to the belltower where the two posted sentries were awaiting his signal. "Proceed!" he called out.

One man spoke into a radio phone. Within a moment, a nearby explosion boomed beyond the church, a cloud of smoke climbing past the rooftops. The crowd flinched. Some cried out. The armed guards held them back; the mounted machine guns swiveled in their direction.

"D'Ambrosso's," Ettore told Regina, as a light scattering of dust debris began falling. Children started to cry, parents trying to console them.

Several new explosions now, these at a greater distance. A second column of smoke rose from the south. Ettore froze.

"That shabby d'Ambrosso eyesore is now rubble," the Nazi commander called out. "As well as Castrubello's civic government offices. And, with the other detonation you heard, the pompous villa of your token knight has been also erased. Do not think," he continued, against a growing murmur, "do not think I forget that if not for the funeral reception at Villa Vacci, Major Gabinno would have traveled under full escort!"

He gave a wave of his arm. "Captain!"

Captain Steuben knew his orders. At his command, soldiers moved into the piazza. They pulled people randomly from the crowd and pushed them against a row of storefronts. The rest of the townspeople began to surge forward.

A short burst of warning gunfire stopped all movement. The three heavy machine guns swung their barrels toward the mass of the crowd itself. The villagers could only watch in anguish as the assemblage of manhandled prisoners grew to one hundred.

"This is the price of Gabinno's death," said von Gottlieb. Captain Steuben's men faced their captives and aimed their weapons at the cowering, weeping, begging, praying group. With a nod from his superior, Captain Steuben walked to the front of his waiting men and raised a hand.

"Stop this!"

The voice of command, one that had directed men in all sorts of tasks under all types of conditions, resonated in a way that even von Gottlieb's had not. It was the voice that every Castrubellese knew either directly as workers or by the legends told by their fathers and grandfathers.

Eschewing Regina's restraint, Ettore Vacci stepped forward from the crowd. The old man, using his cane for balance, held his head high and looked up into the eyes of the brigadeführer.

"Spare these men and women," he said. "Take me in their place."

"No!" cried Regina. "Papà!" Other cries rose up. Another deafening shatter of gunshots suppressed the dismayed reactions of the townspeople. If Castrubello ever had an iconic hero, it was this dogged entrepreneur who had kept families from starving despair by providing employment and purpose.

Von Gottlieb took only a moment to consider. *Something I should have thought of myself*, he thought. *The blood of a hundred insignificants as opposed to the revered paterfamilias of the village, of the entire region! What a blow to the commune, what perpetual guilt, for them to allow sainted Vacci to die before their eyes. Perfect. A lasting last gift.*

The Nazi stepped down, approached the old man, dignified in his pinstriped, three-piece suit. He noted the knighthood medallion on Ettore's coat.

"Ah, the cavaliere himself. I thought destroying your villa would be enough to debase you, Vacci," he said. "but your idea is better." Despite the danger, angry shouts rose from the crowd.

"You seek martyrdom? My pleasure." Von Gottlieb called over his shoulder, "Podestà!"

Pietro emerged from where he was watching the proceedings unfold. The chance to escape with the convoy had been enough to erase any last reservations about today's executions. "Brigadeführer?" he asked.

"Shoot this man!" von Gottlieb commanded, unholstering his sidearm, cocking and handing it to Pietro.

Vacci thinks he will die so nobly, the officer thought. But no. He will die knowing his family is irrevocably shamed.

Pietro took the weapon. His hand started to shake. Although he had hunted years ago with his father and brothers, he had never in his life fired a pistol. A hush fell over the piazza; all eyes were on him. The Nazi brigadier smirked lightly as he took a step back.

Pietro could barely lift his eyes to face his uncle, but Ettore put a hand on his shoulder and spoke kindly. "Do this, Nephew, as a gift. Apparently, I no longer have a house to go home to. I am old and will die soon in any event. An act of love, Pietro, for Castrubello. Let us save these lives together today."

Pietro raised the gun to Zio's chest. His own heart pounded furiously. Behind him, he heard the Lancia's engine start up, the sound of German jackboots moving back to the lorries. His eyes suddenly flooded with tears, and in the tears he saw a different Ettore, younger, a bag on his back, crossing Ponte Spagnolo over the Naviglio. His mother Tonia, crying in joy at the sight of her brother. How kindly, so kindly, his uncle greeted him. A gift, and a ride on the great stallion named *Zio Magnifico!* His hand trembled, the gun muzzle drooped.

"I cannot," he cried, blurting a sob. "Zio, I cannot, I cannot."

Ettore closed with his nephew, their faces inches apart. He fiercely pressed the barrel to his breast just next to his cavaliere badge, his hands around Pietro's. "Do this! For once, Pietro, behave with courage. Do you not see? It is how you and I save our townspeople!"

"Christi blut!" swore von Gottlieb impatiently. "These endless Latin operatics!" He turned to the rifleman at his side but had no time to give him an order.

Whether Pietro himself fired the shot or whether Ettore forced the trigger, the muffled report sent Ettore onto his back. Pietro stared first at his uncle, then his own hand. He dropped the Luger.

The crowd surged at the Germans. The mounted machine guns opened fire, aiming low. Townspeople scattered for cover, screaming.

Von Gottlieb boarded the Lancia as the other vehicles pulled ahead. Troops hastily loaded onto their idling trucks. Pietro shook himself into action, turned to his prized sedan, now pulling away. He hoisted himself on the running board, held onto the door handle, pounded on the side window for a moment, then hung on for dear life, as the big automobile squealed from the piazza.

* * *

Ettore Vacci lies on his back, colder each moment. He feels himself lifted, carried, hears lamentations, tumult. Regina's face is close to his, her tears fall on his cheeks. Do not die, Papà, do not die, he hears her voice call. Ah, Regina, he wants to tell her. This long life of mine, it has been well worth the dying. Ah, Regina, he wants to say.

Chapter 50

He arrived a dozen days later, provided a ride by an American 1st Armored Division halftrack loaded with partisans. The division was transporting the fighters, assembled in liberated Milan, back to their hometowns. The war was ending, Mussolini killed. A partisan band had captured the dictator trying to escape into Switzerland. They shot him to death along with his mistress and some of his henchmen, then hauled the bodies to Milan and dumped them in a piazza. Donato had watched as a mob enthusiastically mutilated the Duce's corpse, pale as a raw sausage, finally hanging it by its heels from the roof of a Standard Oil station. His battered mistress swayed alongside. Among the other broken-faced cadavers was that of Minister Eduardo Degligatti.

Castrubello was in turmoil when Donato dropped from the slow-rolling rig. Traffic through the town was heavy with military vehicles and refugee carts. American troops had swept through the countryside a few days before, busy securing the region's communes. The town was in woeful condition; the Germans had dynamited entire blocks of buildings to foil Allied pursuit, many streets remained clogged with rubble. The ancient stone pilings still supported Ponte Spagnolo; the Nazis' final demolition charge failed to explode. White-gloved MPs busily directed army traffic over the stone span; improvised ferries transported everything else.

Donato had hacked his beard off with a pair of dull scissors then dry-scraped the stubble with his knife. He wore a darkly dyed, unmarked, U.S. infantry uniform the OSS provided its partisan groups. The uniforms helped make the guerillas' widespread score-settling vendettas look more like official justice.

Donato only learned of Ettore's death that day. Throughout the village, posted notices of mourning for loved ones fluttered on the doors of dwellings. On hundreds of doors throughout the town, Donato saw the name written *Vacci, Ettore* and the words, *Caro padrone ed amico—*'Dear employer and friend'.

The cavaliere's body lay at rest in the Vacci crypt at the cemetery, next to his beloved Marietta. Flowers and small tokens left by villagers adorned the gravesite. Donato only stood at the tomb for a few minutes. Too many memories of his uncle flooded over him. "I will talk to you often, Zio," he said.

Donato walked through the villa's destruction. A few servants had burrowed makeshift shelters within the debris. Recognizing the padrone's nephew, they slowly emerged from their holes, offering blessings and news. Of Ettore's sacrifice, of the hated brigadeführer's escape, of finding the podestà's broken body among roadside weeds, cause of death uncertain. Of their starvation. Donato promised to approach the Americans for aid, but first, where was Regina? One aged servant scratched his cheek, shook his head, stared into space, then offered that old Rina Ameretti had taken her in at Casa Como.

* * *

At first, she thought the rap on the door was another homeless neighbor begging for bread. But it was not.

"You are here!" Regina cried. She threw her arms around his neck.

"For you, yes," Donato said.

* * *

It was late afternoon by the time they made their way along the Naviglio across from the quarry site.

"I never told Papà of the bombing by the American plane," Regina said as they stared at the scene. "You see what it did. One dropped in that field and did no harm, but the other struck by the Naviglio, here at the quarry, rupturing the breakwater. Look at what the blast did to our buildings; the whole property is a foot underwater. Eunizio Caderre told me it looked like the Americans were trying to hit Torrquadro. But instead, their bomb landed on us!"

Donato surveyed the wrecked structures, leaning cranes, upended vehicles. He did not tell her he had been the one who radioed the bomber to attack.

"Look at this," he told her. He took an object from his shirt pocket, held open his hand.

"What do you have there?" she asked, then, "Where did you get it?"

"After the bomber crashed, my commander, "Colonel Morte" was his battle-name, sent a squad to look for survivors. There were none.

"One thing the Americans wanted in return for their support was for we partisans to recover their dead if we could or at least collect their identifications. Morte's squad had no time to move the bodies, but when our squads reunited, he gave this to me."

The red ceramic cornicello in the rough palm of his hand was shiny with wear, its leather cord blackened.

"His men took it off an American officer, maybe the pilot, still strapped in his seat, sitting upright on the bank of the Pirino thirty yards from the crash. He wore this pendant around his neck, along with his identification medallions. Colonel Morte gave me one of those as well."

From another pocket he produced a small metal tag, stamped with the officer's name:

Como-Salski, Lorenzo

"I do not know him, or of him," Donato said, to Regina's quizzical expression. "I was told by my mother that I had a cousin in America called Lorenzo. Could this somehow have been that cousin? I have no idea of this other *polacco* name. Where did he get this pendant? Who knows where this horn has been? God knows those answers, no one else. In any event, I intend to keep it."

"Are you certain the pendant of a man killed in battle is a lucky thing to have around your neck, 'Nato?" Regina asked. "Perhaps it would be better to just throw it into the water."

Donato considered a moment. "Here is what I think, Regina. It is less important to live life with luck than it is to leave it with honor. Ettore thought this way, no? Whoever this Lorenzo was, he left life a brave man, one who stayed true to his duty." He scanned the random wreckage around them. "The outcome? Eh, outcomes lie in *fortuna's* hands, she deals those cards. But our own acts? It is we who choose those. I will wear this to remind me of that." He slipped the cord over his head.

Regina said nothing. She had heard talk of honor and duty all her life. So noble sounding, heroic, defiant. But so narrow, so incomplete. No, she thought. The truths of this life reside somewhere beyond the bold words of men.

The voice of the nearby church bell called Great Gabriele began tolling six, the hour of the *Angelus*. Regina silently seated herself on the wall edging the Naviglio. After a moment, Donato joined her. Together they viewed the wrecked family business. Half-sunken barges lined the water's edge. The jagged-edged, pane-less windows of the old *gesuiti* retreat house stared like square, vacuous eye sockets. All that remained of the shattered concrete factory were the shells of two silos, a few walls and a freestanding corner; shreds of khaki nets draped over the ruins. The flooded quarry glittered silver under the declining sun. Long-buried rocks from the canal bed, some speckled brown, some gray, several pure white, mingled with debris from the retaining wall and the collapsed gravel pile, partially obstructing the ravaged canal.

Donato had thought of Regina many times through the long months he had been gone. Of her beauty, of course, and of her appealing bearing and confidence. But now there was more. He could not name it. He only knew he wanted her. More than that.

He is a different man, thought Regina. How could he not be? Are any of us the same? She noted his features, though battered and scarred, seemed sharper, his eyes keener, all of him intensely alive. What children we might have, she found herself thinking.

Donato put his left arm around Regina's shoulder. She had been masking her shock at the condition of his damaged hand; its proximity now made her stiffen. Enough of such squeamishness, she thought. Childhood is ended. She twined his mangled fingers with her own.

The water, speckled with lengthening shadows, flowed serenely past the ruin of the concrete plant. He reached to her neck, gently drew her face to his. Their lips brushed, lingered, kissed deeply.

"What is next for us, Donato?" she asked, leaning into his shoulder.

He stared at the jumbled scene across the Naviglio. "Next, Regina?" He looked into her face, then back at the quarry. "Why, that much is clear. We start with the rocks!"

Author's Notes

BOOK ONE: GOD'S TEETH

The fear of cholera that drove the characters of *God's Teeth* was well known to the Italian population in the 19th century. The Fourth Cholera Pandemic that raged through Europe from 1863 to 1875 was followed within six years by a sequel lasting another fifteen. Experimental medicine was a matter of trial and error as desperate researchers applied the latest scientific discoveries, some barely tested, to affect a cure. The inadequate sewerage and waste management described in the story was a reality throughout Europe and beyond. Only after research proved the relationship between cholera and contaminated water was the disease finally put on the road to eradication.

Milan was a center of growth and construction in the late 1800s. Entrepreneurs teamed with Italian and foreign investors to vastly expand the country's rail and road systems. Upward mobility finally became possible for the bold and the enterprising, regardless of birth.

Banditry was rampant in the southern mountains throughout the 1860s and '70s. Although much suppressed by 1886, vestiges of lawlessness remained a lethal menace.

BOOK TWO: FATE'S RESTLESS FEET

Part I puts the main characters in the middle of the Kingdom of Italy's war with the Ottoman Empire and its invasion of Tripoli. Accounts of the Battle of Sciara Sciatt and its aftermath are varied; while journalists were on the scene shortly afterward, the "spin" of their accounts depends on the politics of their home countries. As author, I tried to strike a balance in my narrative; to this end, Stephenson's *A Box of Sand* was extremely helpful. The military units named were those actually deployed, and except for the name of the fateful cemetery, which I kept fictional to allow for narrative creativity, the locations included in the battle are real ones.

Historically, the role of the 8th Bersaglieri Regiment on October 23, 1911, was of prominent importance. My grandfather served at Tripoli during this time, and I have a hand-tinted photograph of him in his uniform and long-plumed vaira. He died before I was born, so I know little of his service, but I must surmise he was part of the 8th Bersaglieri. I do not know if he was with the regiment on October 23rd or deployed afterward. But for his sake and that of all the combatants on that harrowing day, I strived for accuracy of historical detail in my narrative.

Work in the rice fields of northern Italy was grueling but eagerly sought-after by the local populace. Emigration to the Americas was no walk in the park; my account of life in cross-Atlantic steamship steerage is typical of such passages. The tragedy described in the fictional town of Terrouge, Michigan, was inspired by true events that took place on December 24, 1913, in Calumet, Michigan. In his meticulously researched book, *Death's Door*, author Steven Lehto has written the definitive history of the heartbreaking calamity that occurred that night, later memorialized by Woody Guthrie's angry ballad, *The 1913 Massacre*.

BOOK THREE: DEATH TO THE WOLF

Death to the Wolf takes place during the last years of the Second World War amid the decline and fall of the Kingdom of Italy. The plight of troops fighting and retreating with the Italian 8th Army in Russia is well documented. In particular, the books by Eugenio Corti and Hope Hamilton provide many survivors' eyewitness accounts, some of which inspired various scenes in my novel. The retreat of Donato's fictional 118th Engineering Battalion does not describe the historical path of the bulk of the 3rd Ravenna Division in its effort to avoid encirclement.

Italian partisan attacks against Fascist forces became especially active in the later stages of the war; reprisals on both sides were brutal. Alessandro Portelli's book, *The Order Has Been Carried Out*, describes the reprisal massacre in Rome that I allude to in my novel.

Acknowledgements

This novel is as much my wife's work as my own. I thank her for her continual encouragement and patience, good humor and advice. When I told my children that I was writing this saga, their support and enthusiasm bolstered me then and every day thereafter.

My blood ties to Italy inspired me to create my story of the fictional Comos and Vaccis and their triumphs and travails. *Grazie, cugini miei.*

I am deeply grateful to Signor Leonard Nelson, my longtime colleague and close friend, for his time and generous assistance in carefully proofreading the early versions of the book.

I appreciate the fine work of Mariarosa Ramponi who very ably translated the trilogy into Italian for foreign publication. Her close reading of the manuscript helped to identify several key details that I improved at her suggestion.

The excellent website of the Museo Storico Civico Cuggionese (http://www.museocuggiono.it/) was a superb source of information throughout my research, offering a comprehensive virtual tour of its extensive archive of photos and artifacts.

My fictional story is set against the history of the Kingdom of Italy over its final sixty-three years, a time of enormous social, industrial, scientific, cultural, and military upheavals. Many writers chronicled those events, some as contemporary eyewitnesses, and I relied heavily on their publications for background material. I want to acknowledge the importance of the following writers, some of whom wrote as far back as the 1860s. They are in no particular order:

Carol Adams, Paula Bartley, Judy Lown, Cathy Loxton, Gary Ross Mormino, Rafaella Sarti, Craig Taylor, Giusy Lofrano, Jeanette Brown, G.K. Poole, MD., Marco Cascella, Giuseppe Leoni, Renato Giannetti, Margherita Velucchi, Elena Fani, Paola Scavizzi, William C. Moens, "Kepi", Giuseppe Bevione, Gaston Leroux, Vanda Wilcox, Sanjoy Mazumdar, Shampa Mazumdar, Francesco Signorile, Felice Piccioli, Richard Bosworth, Giuseppe Finaldi, Antonio de Martino, Russell M. Maghnaghi, Dr. Kris Belden-Adams, A.K. Ciongoli, Jay Parini, Georg F. Nafziger, Malcolm Tudor, Peter Tompkins, Italo G. Savella, Rick Atkinson, C. Peter Chen, Dr. Gian Franco Scotti, Rudolph M. Bell, Charles Stephenson, Bruce Vanderfort, Francis McCullagh, Steve Lehto, Hope Hamilton, and Eugenio Corti.

My final thank you is to you, Reader. If you enjoyed my effort to breathe life into an often overlooked piece of European history, I would appreciate you letting your friends and online followers know that, in your opinion, *The Last Italian: A Saga in Three Parts* is a story worth reading. Grazie mille!

Anthony Delstretto

Readers can offer their star rating of this book at: https://www.amazon.com/dp/B08N5MWBNX

* * *

About the Author

Anthony "Nino" Delstretto grew up in ethnic blue-collar Detroit in the 1950s, followed by a career in school administration. He holds dual Italian and American citizenship and lives with his wife in the western U.S.

The Last Italian: A Saga in Three Parts honors not only the heroic resiliency of the Italian people, past and present, but of diverse cultures everywhere that stubbornly defy the unpredictable turns of history and fate.

For a look at the chief research sources behind *The Last Italian: a Saga in Three Parts,* and for a link to the Italian language version of the trilogy, please visit:

https://anthonydelstretto.wixsite.com/mysite

Made in the USA
Columbia, SC
28 March 2023

14445329R00228